Praise for *New York Times* bestselling author
MICHELLE SAGARA
and The Chronicles of Elantra series

"No one provides an emotional payoff like Michelle Sagara.
Combine that with a fast-paced police procedural, deadly magics,
five very different races and a wickedly dry sense of humor—
well, it doesn't get any better than this."
—Bestselling author Tanya Huff on
The Chronicles of Elantra series

"Intense, fast-paced, intriguing, compelling
and hard to put down…unforgettable."
—*In the Library Reviews* on *Cast in Shadow*

"Readers will embrace this compelling,
strong-willed heroine with her often sarcastic voice."
—*Publishers Weekly* on *Cast in Courtlight*

"The impressively detailed setting and the book's spirited heroine
are sure to charm romance readers as well as fantasy fans
who like some mystery with their magic."
—*Publishers Weekly* on *Cast in Secret*

"Along with the exquisitely detailed worldbuilding, Sagara's character
development is mesmerizing. She expertly breathes life into a stubborn
yet evolving heroine. A true master of her craft!"
—*RT Book Reviews* (4 ½ stars) on *Cast in Fury*

"With prose that is elegantly descriptive,
Sagara answers some longstanding questions and
adds another layer of mystery. Each visit to this amazing world,
with its richness of place and character, is one to relish."
—*RT Book Reviews* (4 ½ stars) on *Cast in Silence*

"Another satisfying addition to
an already vivid and entertaining fantasy series."
—*Publishers Weekly* on *Cast in Chaos*

THE CHRONICLES OF ELANTRA
by *New York Times* bestselling author

MICHELLE SAGARA

CAST IN SHADOW
CAST IN COURTLIGHT
CAST IN SECRET
CAST IN FURY
CAST IN SILENCE
CAST IN CHAOS
CAST IN RUIN

And
"Cast in Moonlight"
found in
HARVEST MOON
an anthology with Mercedes Lackey
and Cameron Haley

MICHELLE SAGARA

CAST IN RUIN

LUNA™

LUNA™

Recycling programs
for this product may
not exist in your area.

CAST IN RUIN

ISBN-13: 978-0-373-80330-9

This edition published by arrangement with Harlequin Books S.A.

For questions and comments about the quality of this book
please contact us at Customer_eCare@Harlequin.ca.

® and TM are trademarks of Harlequin Books S.A., used under license.
Trademarks indicated with ® are registered in the United States Patent
and Trademark Office, the Canadian Trade Marks Office and in other
countries.

www.Harlequin.com

Printed in U.S.A.

I'd like to dedicate this book to the Harlequin/LUNA team.

Editorial—
Mary-Theresa Hussey, Elizabeth Mazer,
Margo Lipschultz and Tara Parsons;

Art—
Kathleen Oudit, Vanessa Karabegovic and Shane Rebenschied;

Marketing—
Marianna Ricciuto, Ashley Reid and Diana Wong;

and the Harlequin Sales Group

as well as all the others who touch the book behind the scenes.

CHAPTER 1

The worst thing about near-world-ending disasters according to Sergeant Marcus Kassan—at least the ones that had miraculously done very little damage—was the paperwork they generated. Two departments over, the Hawks required to man desks visible—and accessible—to the public would probably have disagreed. Vehemently. In Leontine.

In the day and a half since four very large Dragons, a small army, and every Sword on the roster had converged on Elani street, there'd been a steady stream of people coming to the office that bordered Missing Persons to make complaints, demand redress, or simply ask for some assurance that the world had not, in fact, ended. The numbers of civilian complaints had, in theory, peaked.

Theory, as usual, was invented by some bureaucrat in a high tower who didn't have to actually *deal* with said complaints. Private Neya, however, wasn't even Corporal, let alone lofty bureaucrat. She was part of the emergency shift of Hawks who'd been crammed into a workspace—already tight to begin with—in order to deal with the civilians. The Hawks who regularly manned these desks were generally older and certainly better suited to the task.

They appeared to appreciate the help about as much as the help appreciated being there.

"You're beat Hawks," her Sergeant had growled. For some of the officers who worked in the Halls of Law, growl would be figurative. In the case of Kaylin Neya, it was literal: her Sergeant was a Leontine. "You deal with the public every day."

"Right. We deal with the public accused of stealing, mugging, and murder." All in all, it didn't give the brightest window into the human condition. When Sergeant Kassan failed to even blink, she added, "You know them—they're the people I don't have to worry about offending?"

Marcus, however, had failed to be moved. Kaylin had not, which is why she currently occupied half a stranger's desk.

"You were assigned to Elani," he pointed out. "At the moment, Elani is still—"

"Under quarantine. Yes. I realize that."

"Since you can't do your job there for the next few days, you can make yourself useful in the front rooms, since we *are* still paying you."

Not surprisingly, many of the reports delivered by timid, angry, or deranged civilians involved descriptions of a giant Dragon roaming the streets. His color varied from report to report, as did his activities; he reportedly breathed fire, ate people—or at least large, stray dogs—and leveled buildings. He was alternately the usual Dragon size—which, to be fair, was not small—or giant; he was also deafening.

This last part was accurate. The rest, not so much. Kaylin, of course, knew the Dragon being described. Dragons were forbidden, by law, from assuming their native forms within the City of Elantra without express permission from the Eternal Emperor. Lord Tiamaris, however, had received that dispensation. He was, the last time she'd seen him, a shade that approached copper. He did have an impressive wingspan, but none of the eyewitnesses had claimed to see him fly.

Most of the witnesses, however, claimed that Tiamaris led a small army. The descriptions of this army varied almost as widely as descriptions of Tiamaris himself. The word *Barbarian* came up almost as often as *Savage,* but both ran a distant second and third to *Giant.* She particularly liked the two people—who had come in together and were shoving each other in between sentences—who claimed that they were an army of the shambling undead. Their size was, according to these civilian reports, all over the map; their numbers ranged from "lots" to "fifty thousand." Most accounts agreed, however, that the strangers were armed.

This last had the benefit of being accurate. The strangers—or refugees—themselves were, as far as anyone knew, newcomers to the world—the idea that this was *a* world, rather than the *only* world being almost as new to most of the authorities as the refugees themselves. According to the Palace, and more important, to Lord Sanabalis, the refugees numbered roughly three thousand strong. As their destination was the fief of Tiamaris, no formal census had been taken or even considered. They wouldn't technically be citizens of Elantra.

They weren't giants, a race that Kaylin privately thought entirely in the realm of children's stories, but they were about eight feet in height at the upper end; the children were taller than Kaylin. They didn't speak Elantran, which was Kaylin's mother tongue; they didn't speak Barrani, either, Barrani being the language in which the laws were written. But the Imperial linguists, with the aid of Ybelline Rabon'alani, had gone with Tiamaris. They'd been the only people who'd looked truly *excited* at the prospect of three thousand armed, hungry, and exhausted eight-foot-tall strangers. They were also, however, absent from the civilian reports, and therefore not her problem.

Kaylin had received some training in speaking with civilians, because some of her job did involve talking to possible witnesses in a way that didn't terrify them so much they denied seeing anything; putting it to use in the crowded office full of strangers was almost more than she could stomach. She did not, however, point out that they were blind or out of their minds; she transcribed most of what they said with unfailing attention.

This was, in part, because in the end Marcus would have to *read* most of these, or at least sign them. He loathed paperwork.

On the bright side? The unusual births, the rains of blood— and, in one area, frogs—and the unfortunate and inexplicable change in the City's geography, had ceased. Elani, however, now had a stream running along one side of the street, and the blood-red flowers that had popped up in the wake of the refugees were proving more hardy than tangleknot grass.

It would probably only be a matter of time before some enterprising fraud picked them, bottled them, and sold them as an elixir of youth; it *was* Elani street, after all.

Kaylin glanced at the small mirror at the end of the overwhelmed desk she was half behind. The Records of the Halls of Law, forbidden to the rank and file during the state of emergency, were now once again deemed safe to use, which meant the mirror added more external chatter to a loud and bustling office.

Kaylin tried to avoid listening to it; it only annoyed her. The Barrani Hawks were, of course, excused external desk duty. Something about tall, slender immortals put normal civilians off their stride; for some reason they felt the Barrani were arrogant and condescending. This was probably, in Kaylin's opinion, because they had working eyes and ears. The Aerian Hawks were excused the "emergency" shift work because the small size—and low ceilings—of the cramped room made having large wings a disadvantage. In theory.

Luckily, the force contained enough humans that the extra shifts decreed as necessary by some higher-up could be filled. If Kaylin knew who he—or she—was, there'd be a new picture on the dartboard in the office by the end of the week. Who knew a hand could cramp so damn badly when the only activity of the day was writing and trying to hide the fists that incredible stupidity normally caused?

Severn Handred, her Corporal partner, had fared better, in large part because he didn't *mind* the stupidity. He met her when she managed to edge her way out of the single door that led—from the inside of the Halls of Law—to the office itself. There was a door on the opposite wall, as well, but as it led *into* the people who were waiting to make their incredibly frustrating reports, Kaylin avoided that one.

"Well?" he asked. He was leaning against the wall, arms folded across his chest.

"I didn't kill anyone," she replied.

"That bad?"

"I think it was the conspiracy of evil chickens that did me in."

"Pardon?"

"You heard me. I honestly have no idea how more of the Hawks in that damn office aren't arraigned on assault charges."

"Bridget keeps them in line."

"Bridget?"

"Sergeant Keele."

Kaylin cringed. "I could see that." Sergeant Keele was one

of the staff regulars; this was her domain. She'd been entirely undelighted at the additional staff thrust upon her, in part because she felt it impugned her ability to handle the situation. She had, however, been brisk, if chilly, and she didn't mince words—or orders. If hazing was part of the unofficial schedule of the regular office workers, it wasn't something *she* had time for, so it had to be damn subtle.

"Can you top evil chickens?" she asked hopefully.

He thought about it for a minute. "Probably not."

"Dinner?"

He nodded slowly. "You didn't happen to check the mirror before you left?"

"I shut it off. Why?"

"Sergeant Kassan is expecting us."

"What? Why?"

"The important question is actually, 'When?'."

She swore.

Caitlin was still at her desk, but many of the regulars had already vacated theirs and headed home, something Kaylin had every hope of doing soon. The office den mother looked up as Kaylin entered. "Bad day, dear?" she asked.

Kaylin shrugged. "It could have been worse."

"Oh?"

"I could have been the one who had to listen to Mrs. Erickson."

Caitlin, used to seeing some of the paperwork that crossed between offices, grimaced. Mrs. Erickson was famous—or infamous—for the messages she carried; they were invariably from the dead. The nosy, busybody dead. They ranged in importance from left shoes—Kaylin had refused to believe this until the report was pulled and shoved under her nose—to Empire-spanning conspiracies against the Dragon Emperor.

Since Mrs. Erickson liked to bake, all her messages were conveyed alongside cookies or small cakes, none of which had ever caused even the slightest bit of indigestion.

"What was today's message?"

"I missed it—I was too busy dealing with the reports about the invading army and its Dragon. Whatever her dead messenger was concerned about, though, it was long. How were things here?"

"Well, Margot is threatening to join the Merchants' Guild and file a formal guild complaint if we don't lift the quarantine on Elani street soon. She's also seeking financial redress for economic losses taken because of the involuntary closure of her store."

Kaylin snorted. "Let her. I can't quite decide who'd be the loser in that transaction—Margot or the guild." Kaylin despised both with a frequently expressed and very colorful passion.

"I don't believe Lord Grammayre is looking for *more* official difficulty at the moment."

At that, Kaylin's expression flattened. "You've had word?"

"Not official word, no. But the investigation into the Exchequer is *not* going well. The Human Caste Court has closed ranks around him. The Emperor has not closed the investigation, but by all reports he is…not pleased." She paused, and then added, "Word was, however, sent from the Palace. For you."

Kaylin winced. "It's only been *two days*," she murmured.

"Two days, for Lord Diarmat, is long enough." Marcus's voice growled from behind her.

Marcus was at his desk, surrounded by the usual teetering piles of paper; Kaylin counted three. The gouges in the surface of said desk didn't appear to be deeper or more numerous, which probably meant his mood hadn't descended to foul, yet.

"You're late," he growled. Since his irises were a distinct gold, Kaylin said, "Not according to Sergeant Keele, sir." She walked over to his desk and took up position in front of it; Severn lingered behind.

Without preamble, he handed her a set of curved papers. She took them as if they were live cockroaches and began to read. The top letter—and it was a letter—was from Lord Sanabalis of the Dragon Court.

Sanabalis had extended the period of grace in which she was allowed to skip the magic class he was responsible for making certain she attended; the transitioning of three thousand refugees who required housing and food were of primary import for the next week. Or two. He wished her luck during the extra work that this type of emergency generated, by which she inferred he knew of her day's work in the outer office.

The second letter was from Diarmat, and it was not, by any reasonable definition, a letter; it was a set of orders. She read it once, and then glanced up over the top edge of the page to see Leontine eyes watching her carefully.

"He is," Marcus said drily, "the Commander of the Imperial Guard, a force that is almost entirely composed of humans."

"Have you had to interact with them?"

"On several occasions. I've survived."

"Have they?"

He raised a brow; his eyes, however, stayed the same mellow gold. She had a sneaking suspicion he was enjoying this.

Lord Diarmat—whose classes were to be conducted after-bloody-hours on her *own* time—considered three thousand refugees and a significant area of the city under quarantine unworthy of mention. She swore.

Caitlin coughed.

"He *reminds* me that the first of our lessons starts *tonight*."

"Then you'd best have something to eat, dear," Caitlin told

her. "I highly doubt that Lord Diarmat will be casual enough to offer to feed you."

Feed her? If she was lucky, he'd be civil enough not to eat her himself.

She looked at the window. "Time?" she asked it.

"Five hours and a half," the window replied. "Please check the duty roster on your way out."

Because she was feeling masochistic, she did. She was penciled in for yet another day on outsiders' desk duty.

Severn kept her company as she trudged down the street toward the baker's. He also handed her the coins she needed to pay Manners Forall, who happened to be manning his own stall. He smiled and said, "We don't usually see you this late in the month." It was true. This late in the month she was usually scrounging for less expensive food.

Severn said nothing, but he said it loudly, reminding her in silence of the budgeting discussion they'd failed to find the time for. It was the only silver lining on the thundercloud of Lord Diarmat and his so-called etiquette lessons. Severn didn't *remain* silent, however, and they wrangled over times for yet a different lesson in Kaylin's educational schedule while they made their way to the Palace.

The streets weren't noticeably less crowded than they had been; apparently the crazed fear of Dragons and their itinerant armies didn't stop most people from going about their daily business. Severn left her at the Palace gates, pausing only to check her wrist. There, the bracer that she wore by Imperial Decree caught the lights above. It was heavy enough to be the gold that it looked, and it was studded with what appeared to be three large gems: a diamond, a ruby, and a sapphire.

"I haven't taken it off since we got back from Evanton's," she told him. But she didn't resent his checking, much. Diarmat wasn't known for his flexibility. "I'll see you in the morning. If I'm still alive." Severn was also penciled in for crazy duty; he minded it less ferociously.

The very forbidding and starched man whose title she couldn't recall met her at the doors; he stood well inside them, and somewhat behind the Imperial Guards who gave her a quick once-over. It was cursory, however; the man stepped forward and said in his clipped High Barrani, "Lord Diarmat is expecting you, Private Neya. If you will follow me."

She did. She could now reliably make her way to the chambers in which Sanabalis frequently conducted his meetings, and she could—if she were feeling foolishly brave—find the Library unescorted. She had no idea what Diarmat called home—or office—in the Palace, and had she not been certain of finding him in it, she would have been genuinely curious.

But during the handful of times she'd met him, he'd failed to be anything remotely resembling friendly, and *tolerant* was a word that she suspected he'd failed to learn, although his High Barrani was otherwise flawless. Severn had said that his Elantran was also flawless—and completely free from colloquialisms. Kaylin had already decided it was best to stick with High Barrani; it was a lot harder to make verbal gaffes in that language.

The starched man paused in front of a set of double doors that looked suspiciously unlike any classroom doors she'd ever entered. There were no guards at the doors, which was good. The doors were warded, which was bad. Not only were they warded, but there appeared to be two damn wards, one on each door. She glanced at her guide and said without much hope, "I don't suppose those are just decorative?"

"No, they are not. You are required to touch both wards; you are not, however, required to touch them at the same time, should you find yourself, for reasons of injury, unable to do so."

Kaylin's natural aversion to magic was not quite as strong as her aversion to having her head bitten off by an angry Dragon Lord, but it was close. She stepped up to the doors, stood in arm's reach, and grimaced; the wards were higher than shoulder height. She guessed they'd been designed for the regular variety of Imperial Palace Guard; they had, among other things, fairly strict height requirements.

Grimacing, she placed her left palm on the left-door ward, and felt the strong bite of magic travel up her arm so forcefully her arm went numb. The ward, however, began to glow; it wasn't a comforting sight, given that the light was a sickly, pulsing green. Any hope that her guide had been wrong vanished; the door didn't budge. Aware of his presence, she kept her teeth shut firmly over the Leontine words that were trying to leap out, and lifted her hand again.

It was her left hand. She was right-handed, and with her luck, the first thing Diarmat would do was ask her to write some long Barranian test; she couldn't afford to have a numb, useless writing hand. It was awkward, but she lifted her left arm again—without cursing—and placed her palm more or less in the center of its damn ward.

The door ward began to glow a livid, pale purple. It hurt to touch, and given her arm was half-numb, this said something. Unfortunately, the door wards *also* said something—and from the sounds of the echo, it was in Dragon. She did curse, but then Leontine spoken with a human throat couldn't possibly be audible over the racket the ward had caused.

To make matters worse—as if the universe needed to remind her that they could be—the hall, which was long and high ceilinged, began to fill with Imperial Palace Guards. Her starched guide didn't blink or move as she turned to face them.

Give them this: they were impressive. They wore heavier armor than patrolling Hawks, they carried large swords, and they moved in frightening unison, as if this were some arcane drill and they'd be demoted if one foot was out of place.

She doubted she'd appreciate it more if their weapons had not, in fact, been pointing toward her. She didn't bother drawing her own; all she had at the moment were daggers, and one numb hand. Instead, she lifted her hands—slowly—and stood very still. The doors at her back rolled open.

"Thank you, gentlemen," a familiar voice said. "That will be all."

He received one very noisy salute—gauntlets did that in an otherwise silent hall—as she turned to face him. She could hear the guards form up and retreat, but didn't bother to watch them leave. Instead, she faced Lord Diarmat of the Dragon Court.

He was slightly taller than Tiamaris, and he had the broad—and, sadly, muscular—build of Dragons in human form; he also had Dragon eyes. His lower membranes muted their color, but in this light, they were gold, although the gold seemed tinted with orange. Then again, gold was a happy color, and she doubted that someone with an expression that consistently severe could *be* happy. He was not, however, dressed in natural Dragon armor; he wore robes with a distinct Imperial Crest blazoned across the chest.

"Lord Diarmat," she said, tendering as formal a bow as she could.

"I see that reports of your tardiness are exaggerated." He glanced at the doors. "And reports of your effect on some of the more formal wards are not."

She managed to say nothing.

"Nor, it appears, are reports about the need for some formal structure in your interactions with the Imperial Court." He looked past her to the man who had led her here. "Thank you," he said quietly. "Please send someone in two hours to escort Private Neya out; she is not, I believe, familiar with the Palace."

The man nodded briskly. "Lord Diarmat," he said, and then turned and walked off.

Diarmat now gestured toward the room behind the offending doors. "Please," he said. "Enter."

The room was, as the doors suggested, large. The ceilings were at least as high as the ones that characterized the public halls, and the walls were thirty feet away from the open doors on all sides. The whole of the office Kaylin generally called home would have comfortably fit in the space, although some of the furniture would have to be moved to accommodate it. There were two desks in the far corner, and an arrangement of chairs around one central table of medium height; there was a long table that seemed like a dining table, although no similar chairs were tucked beneath it.

Windows opened into a courtyard that had no view of the Halls of Law—and no view of the streets of the City, either; instead, there were stones that were arranged at various heights and distances, as if it were meant to be a garden. She saw doors leading out of the room to either side. This was as far from a typical classroom as a room could get. She glanced at Diarmat, waiting for his instructions.

He didn't bother with them. Instead, he crossed the room and headed toward his desk. It was unblemished, and no mounds of paperwork teetered precariously anywhere in sight; there was an inkstand, and three small bars of wax. Even paper was absent. He took the chair behind the desk, and then frowned at the doors behind Kaylin.

"Should I close them?"

He spoke a single curt word and the doors began to roll shut on their own, which was all of his reply. He then stared at her, unblinking, until she made her way to the front of the desk.

He took parchment out of a desk drawer, placed it—dead center—on its surface, and uncapped his ink. "You have been a student of Lord Sanabalis for some months now."

"Yes."

"You have, however, shown little progress in the classes he teaches."

It was a bit of a sore point, because little progress, to Kaylin's mind, meant waste of time. On the other hand, at least she was *paid* to attend Sanabalis's mandatory classes.

"Lord Sanabalis, under the auspices of the Imperial Order of Mages, has developed a level of tolerance for the lazy and the inexact that is almost unheard of among our kind. Mages are not generally considered either stable or biddable; were it not for the necessity of some of their services, and the existence of the Arcanum as a distinctly less welcome alternative, they would not be tolerated at all." His tone made clear that were it up to him, neither the Imperial Order nor the Arcanum would be long for this world.

Which was a pity, because Kaylin agreed with him, and this might be the *only* point on which there would be any common ground. Defending either organization was not, however, her job.

"I am not Lord Sanabalis. What he tolerates, I will not tolerate. I have perused some of your previous academic records, but not in any depth; I no longer consider them relevant. You were not raised in an environment with strong Barrani influences, and you will therefore have little understanding of the way in which those influences govern some parts of the Palace.

"They are not, however, your chief concern. I am told that

you have a strong grasp of High Barrani. When the Court is in session, the language of choice defaults to High Barrani in the presence of races that are not Dragon. Were you not required to interact with the Emperor, neither you, nor I, would be required to waste time in this endeavor." His tone made clear whose time he thought more valuable. "You will, however, be required to speak.

"Speech, were it the only requirement, you might be able to manage. Because you are considered *worthy* of such a privilege, however, correct form and behavior will be *assumed*. Any deviation from those forms will be seen as a breach, not of etiquette, but of respect. Disrespect of the Emperor is ill advised."

She nodded. This didn't make his expression any friendlier, and it didn't make her any happier; she bit back any words to that effect, and instead said, "What did I do wrong when you appeared at the doors?" She spoke as smoothly and neutrally as possible, but she couldn't quite stop her cheeks from reddening.

He raised a Dragon brow. "That," he told her, "is an almost perceptive question."

Not perceptive enough to answer? She waited. The problem with immortals was that, short of immediate emergencies, they *had* forever; what seemed a long time to a normal person was insignificant to them. Their arrogance seemed to stem from the fact that they'd seen and experienced so much more than a mortal could achieve in an entire lifetime, it negated mortal experience.

Kaylin didn't like being treated like a child in the best of circumstances—no one did—but Immortals *always* felt they were dealing with children when mortals were involved. Some were just way better at hiding it. Diarmat clearly couldn't be bothered. She waited, and he returned to the paper beneath his hands and began to write. She could actually read upside-down writing; it was one of the things she'd figured out when boredom had taken hold in her early classes and she was trying to be less obvious about it. But in this case, she had a suspicion he'd notice, and it seemed career limiting.

She was also no longer a bored student; she was here as a Hawk, not a mascot. She left her hands loosely by her sides, and stared at a point just past his left shoulder while she waited for some instruction—to sit, to stand, to go away, to answer questions. Anything.

What felt like half an hour later she was *still* standing in front of his damn desk, and he was *still* writing. He had told her nothing at all about the rules that governed the Imperial Court or its meetings. He hadn't spoken of any particular style of dress, hadn't given her any information about forms of address, hadn't demonstrated any of the salutes or bows with which one might open speech. Since she'd managed to eat something on the hurried walk over, her stomach didn't embarrass her by speaking when she wouldn't.

At the end of the page, he looked up. Folding the paper in three he reached for wax, and this, he melted by the simple expedient of breathing on it slightly. He then pressed a small seal into what had fallen on the seam. He reached across the desk and handed her the letter. "This," he said, "is for the perusal of Lord Grammayre on the morrow." He rose, and made his way out from behind his bastion of a desk; there, he exhaled. It was loud.

"Very well," he said, as if he was vaguely disappointed. "You have some ability to display patience. Your posture is not deplorable. Your ability to comport yourself does not directly affect the respect in which the Halls of Law are now held." He spoke in crisp, perfectly enunciated High Barrani.

He now opened a drawer, and a thick sheaf of papers appeared on the desk.

These, Kaylin thought, would be the various educational reports he had barely, in his own words, perused.

He handed them to her; she slid the letter to the Hawklord into her tunic, and took the offending pile, glancing briefly at what lay on top of it. Transcripts, yes. To her surprise, the first one was *not* a classroom diatribe from a frustrated or angry teacher.

"This is a case report," she said before she could stop herself.

"It is." He walked around to her side. "Do you recognize it?"

She nodded.

"You were working in concert with two Barrani Hawks."

"Teela and Tain," she said. She didn't flip through the report; she knew which case this was. All boredom or irritation fled, then.

"It was, I believe, the breaking of a child-prostitution ring."

"It was."

"Do you recall the chain of events that led to the deaths of some of the men involved?"

She nodded again, although it was almost untrue: she didn't remember the end clearly at all. She remembered her utter, unstoppable *rage*. And she remembered the deaths that rage—and her unbridled magic—had caused.

His silence could have meant many things, but since his face was as expressive as cold stone, she didn't bother to look at him.

"I would like you to peruse the rest of the documents," he finally said.

She did. It wasn't a small pile—although it wasn't Leontine in proportion—but there really weren't that many cases in which she'd lost control of her inexplicable magic to such devastating effect; she had literally skinned a man alive. She didn't regret it. Not in any real way. He would have died anyway, after his trial. But…the trial had been moot, and Marcus had *not* been happy.

The next report made her right hand tighten into a white-knuckled fist before she got halfway down the first page. It wasn't a case report. It wasn't a report that the Halls of Law would ever generate.

It was, instead, a report on the Guild of Midwives. She almost dropped the report on the desk. Instead, she forced her hand to relax—as much as it could—while she read. It detailed all the emergency call-ins she'd done—and it detailed, in some cases, the results. She lifted the top page. Her memory wasn't the best, but she thought, looking briefly at dates and commentary, none in a hand she recognized, that it was more complete than anything she could have written for him, had he asked.

Grim, she flipped through the pile, and was unsurprised to see that he also had a similar report for each visit she'd made to Evanton's shop on Elani street. This angered her less; she *knew* the Dragon Court spied on Evanton.

There was a brief report of her visits to the High Halls, again not much to fuss about; there was a report on every visit she had made in recent months to the fiefs—any fief crossing. There was a report that followed her movements to, and from, both the Leontine Quarter and the Tha'alani Quarter. Diarmat was silent as she read, as if waiting for a reaction she didn't want to give him the pleasure of seeing.

But the final report was of the Foundling Hall.

CHAPTER 2

It took all the self-control Kaylin had ever mastered not to crumple the document into a ball and throw it. She couldn't even read it, although her eyes grazed the words, recognizing dates and familiar names.

"So," Diarmat said in his cool, clipped voice. She forced herself to meet his gaze—or she tried. He wasn't looking at her face; he was staring, inner membranes fully extended, at her wrist. She glanced at it. The gems on the bracer she wore were flashing brightly enough that they could be clearly seen through layers of clothing.

The lights cut through her anger as if they were a cold, cold dagger.

Get a grip, she told herself. *It's a piece of paper. It's just another damn piece of paper.* It's not like all the *rest* of the reports didn't make clear that the Court had followed every damn move she'd made for years; why would she expect they'd somehow miss her visits to the Foundling Hall? She took a slow, deep breath—the type of breath she'd learned to take when she'd been injured and she was in pain.

The lights on the bracer began to dim, but they dimmed slowly.

Only when they were no longer visible did she turn to face Diarmat, the reports shaking in her tightened hands. Without a single word, she handed them back to him. He waited for a minute before nodding and retrieving them. "That will be all."

She turned and made her way toward the doors, but stopped before she touched them and turned back. "They're my hoard," she told him quietly. She didn't have to shout; Dragons, like Leontines, had a very acute sense of hearing.

His eyes were a pale shade of copper. "You are mortal," he replied with no hesitation whatsoever. "Mortals neither have, nor understand, the concept. The word *hoarding*," he added with genuine distaste, "is possibly as close as your inferior race can come."

She turned instantly on her heel and pushed the doors open; words were burning the insides of her mouth, and she couldn't let them out in his earshot. But when the doors were halfway open, he said, "Private."

Human hearing *was* inferior, and he hadn't raised his voice; he wasn't speaking his native tongue. She pretended not to hear him, and escaped into the hall.

She was halfway down that hall—her guide having failed to materialize—when she ran into Sanabalis. Sadly, head down, body tilted in that particular forward angle that was a fast walk threatening to break into an all-out run, it was literal. She bounced; he didn't budge. A half-formed apology slid out of her mouth as she righted herself and looked up.

"I see your first class ended early."

She nodded.

"Join me." It wasn't worded as a request, and he didn't actually wait to see if she was going to treat it as one; he turned and began to walk down the hall. Since this implied that he knew where he was going—and since she didn't—she fell in behind him. He led her from the unfamiliar halls to ones she'd walked through often enough that she could find her bearings.

He walked, not surprisingly, to his rooms, opening the door and holding it while she entered—as if he half suspected she'd turn and bolt for the exit if he wasn't watching. Since it happened to be true, she didn't begrudge him the suspicion. There was no food in the room, but the comforting set of impressive windows still looked out at the three towers of the Halls of Law, and even though it was now evening, they could be seen clearly in the moon's light, reminding her, at a remove, of why she was here at all.

She drew a deep breath, and the line of her shoulders sagged when she exhaled. But she faced the towers, not the Dragon Lord, as they did.

"The lesson?" Sanabalis asked quietly.

She shrugged. It was stiff, and she felt her shoulders bunching up around her neck again. "I survived."

"Did you walk out?"

"No. I was dismissed."

She heard Sanabalis exhale. "Lord Diarmat does not generally teach—when he is given to do so—in his personal quarters."

"No? Does he do it in an abattoir instead?"

She felt the brief heat of his snort, and turned. "The Palace Guard has several open yards, and a handful of enclosed rooms, for the purpose of training."

"He's not training me to be an Imperial Guard."

"No."

"What, exactly, is my relationship to Lord Diarmat in the Hierarchy, anyway?"

"What is your relationship to the Human Castelord?"

"Pardon?"

"I believe you heard the question."

She thought about it for a bit, and then said, "I don't have one. He presides over the Caste Court. He meets with the Emperor on matters of governance. I owe him nothing; he owes me nothing."

"Unless you choose to take refuge in the Caste Court."

It was never going to happen. "I don't understand the question."

"No. You don't. Lord Diarmat is part of the Dragon Court. In theory, you owe the Dragon Court itself no fealty; your oath of office is to the Emperor's Law, and not directly to the Emperor himself. The Emperor is, however, your Commander, in a strictly technical sense. The titles the Dragons are given are a sign of public respect, no more."

"You would not, however, sneer publicly at your caste lord."

"No." She would never, if Marcus or the Hawklord had anything to say about it, *meet* the human caste lord.

"In a like fashion, you tender Diarmat the respect that is his due as a councilor of the Emperor. He is not, however, your Commander; the line of command for the Halls of Law passes from the Emperor directly to the Lords of Law. You are not therefore required to offer him any of the narrow range of salutes or obeisances taught in the Halls. He is not, technically, your superior, where in this case, technically means legally."

"Which means?"

He smiled. His eyes were gold, and his lower membranes, unlike Diarmat's, were entirely lowered. "It means that legally you owe him no deference. Legally, you owe the Lord of the High Halls and his Consort no deference, either."

"I'm technically a Lord of the High Court."

"Believe that I am conversant with your history in the High Court. You are, however, not *required* by Imperial law to comport yourself according to the dictates of the High Court, outcaste exception laws notwithstanding."

"I'm not breaking any laws if I cease to breathe, either."

"Indeed. You see my point."

She could barely see his point, and begrudged the comprehension.

"The very deliberate and complicated social structure of the High Court evolved, in part, for what reason?"

"Sanabalis—"

"I have done you the courtesy of holding our classes in abeyance. If, however, it is necessary, I will rescind that courtesy."

"Those are *magic* lessons!"

"Indeed. But what one learns in one discipline can be applied to others in unpredictable ways; education is a process." He folded his arms across his chest, and waited.

Sanabalis's meeting room was littered with chairs; the walls contained shelves with glass doors, and a mirror lurked in one of them. Kaylin availed herself of a chair, sitting heavily as she did. Lowering her face into her hands, she forced herself to think about what she knew of the High Court; it didn't take all that long.

"The Barrani tend to kill each other as an idle pastime."

"So it's been rumored."

"Barrani crimes are *all* confined to the Barrani Caste Court. They don't reach the Imperial Court, ever."

"So the Barrani commit no interracial crimes?"

She snorted. "Of course they do. But if there's any chance we'll *catch* them and they'll be forced to trial in the Imperial Courts, the criminals wind up conveniently and messily dead.

And often on our doorstep, because gods know the Barrani have more important things to do than clean up their own mess."

Sanabalis actually chuckled at that. "An interesting digression. The rest of your answer?"

"There is no court of last resort among the Barrani. There are no Hawks or Swords that any *sane* Barrani will use. The Barrani are part of the City, but the only way they seem to really interact involves commerce. If I were Barrani, I would therefore have to live and act as if anyone—anyone at all— could be planning to assassinate me. Or if anyone could decide it was necessary if I somehow offended them.

"I could, if I felt powerful enough and secure enough, afford to offend the less powerful with impunity. I'm not sure I'd consider it wise. But…on the other hand, I suppose if I *did* behave that way, it would give people second thoughts about attempting to take *me* down."

"Does this sound familiar?"

"Yeah." She shrugged. "It sounds like any other sort of thug law. But it's got more money behind it."

"Good. The way in which it is clothed is crucial to its execution, but it is, in essence, something you do understand. It does not require your approval; survival has often been its own imperative."

"You're trying to tell me that the same is true of the Dragon Court."

"No. The Emperor *is* your Commander."

"Then what was your point?"

"Lord Diarmat is not. He is, however, dangerous in precisely the same way the Barrani are dangerous. He is not above the law—but if he chooses to break the law, the Emperor may grant him dispensation if he feels such extremes were merited."

"And total lack of respect—"

"For a Dragon of his stature? I leave you to draw your own conclusions."

"I'm sworn to uphold his laws. Saying that you killed someone because they annoyed you isn't codified as acceptable, by those laws, anywhere that I'm aware of."

"You are clearly not looking carefully enough." He let his arms drop to his sides. "How did the lesson go?"

"He didn't attempt to *teach* anything. I thought I'd get a list of things that were no-go around the Emperor. You know: don't burp, don't swear, don't scratch your armpit, don't wear green."

"Green?"

"Or whatever color he doesn't like. I thought he'd give me a list of acceptable ways to address the Emperor. With, you know, titles, and gestures—how to salute, how far down to kneel, whether or not you *ever* get to stand on your feet in his presence."

"And?"

"He made me stand in front of his desk for half an hour without saying a word while he wrote a letter to the Hawklord."

"I...see. And you did?"

"I work for Marcus. When Marcus is ticked, you stand in front of his desk at *attention* for as long as it damn well takes. I can do it for hours. I'm not *great* at it, and I don't *enjoy* it, but that's never mattered much."

Sanabalis said crisply, "Good." He smiled, but it was slender, and there was a trace of edge in the expression. "After the half hour?"

"He handed me a bunch of papers. I assumed they'd be the class transcripts from the Halls, which *every* prospective teacher seems to pore over. Even you."

"They were not."

"No. They were—" She sucked in air and almost pushed herself out of her chair. Or his chair. "Reports."

"Ah." He nodded. "They displeased you."

"No one's *pleased* to find out that every single thing they've ever done has been spied on, Sanabalis." She did push herself out of the chair then. "But the last report—or the last one I looked at—was the Foundling Hall report."

Sanabalis's inner membranes rose. "Your reaction?"

"I sat on my reaction," she told him, pacing around the chair. "But...the bracer started to light up."

The Dragon Lord lifted a hand. "You did not speak?"

"No."

"Bad," he told her grimly. "But it will have to do. The class was ended at that point?"

"More or less."

"I will attempt to augment your lessons with some of the material you expected to be handed. I am busy," he added more severely, "but I will take the time to compose a list. You will not, however, be short of work."

"I'm working on the outside desk at the moment. You've got a way to get me back in the streets?" It was the *only* possible bright spot in a day that had left her with the nausea that comes in the aftermath of fury.

"So to speak. I, too, have a letter which I wish you to deliver to Lord Grammayre. I guarantee that its contents will differ somewhat radically from those of Lord Diarmat's."

Kaylin went home in the dark. Not that it was ever completely dark in Elantra, and certainly not close to the Palace, where magic had been used the same way stones had: it made the streets passable. Kaylin was all for useful magic; she usually felt that there wasn't *enough* of it.

Severn wasn't waiting outside for her, which was a good

sign. It meant he trusted her to more or less survive a lesson with Diarmat intact. But she missed his company on the way home, because she was, in fact, still fighting fury, and it helped to have someone she could both shout at and not offend while she did. There were no muggings, and nothing that looked as though it demanded legal intervention. There were, on the other hand, a few people who'd already spent too much time or money in a tavern.

She could unlock the front door of the apartment building in her sleep; unlocking it in the dark wasn't much of an issue. Navigation in the dark only involved the narrow steps, and they were worn and warped enough that they creaked in a totally predictable way as she climbed them. It wasn't late, yet. She'd eaten, and if she was hungry, she wasn't starving. Hunger could wait until morning.

Her door was locked. It often was, but enough of her friends had keys that it wasn't a guarantee; if Teela or Tain were totally bored, they'd show up and hang around. Tain was a bit more circumspect than Teela, who would often lounge strewn across the narrow bed while she waited. Severn, if worried, would also show up, but like Tain, he generally waited in her one chair.

Unlike Tain, he often tidied while he waited.

But he wasn't waiting now, and the room was its usual mess. None of that mess generally caused her to trip and injure herself in the dark, as it was mostly clothing. There were, of course, magical lights that one could buy to alleviate the darkness—but those cost money, and Kaylin was chronically short of funding. She hesitated in the open door and glanced with trepidation at the mirror on the wall; she relaxed when she saw that it was, like the rest of the room, dark. No messages meant no emergencies.

No emergencies meant sleep.

Before she could sleep, she opened the shutters to her room and let the moonlight in. It wasn't bright enough to read by; it was bright enough for navigation. There was one thing she had to check before sleep was a possibility. Kneeling beside the bed—and shucking clothing into the rough and very spread-out pile she'd, in theory, wash any time now—she pulled a smallish box out from beneath its slats and removed the lid.

Nestled among scraps of cloth that were used mostly for cleaning in the midwives' hall, was an egg the size of two fists. Well, two of hers at any rate. It had been born during the inexplicable magical upheaval that had left the City with thousands of newcomers, and no place to house them before Tiamaris had volunteered his fief. Other children had been born during that time, and in the magical zone—but they'd been children with unusual features: extra arms, extra eyes, full speech. No one in the guildhall had any idea what was in the egg.

Nor did Kaylin. But when Marya had handed her the box—at the grieving and shocked father's insistence that the egg be disposed of—she had dutifully picked it up and carted it home. It didn't weigh much. She'd meant to mention it to someone who specialized in magical theory, such as it was, but she didn't really want to hand it over to the Dragon Court, the Imperial Mages, or the Arcanum. This left a much smaller pool—of one—and her desk duty had kept her off her current beat. Which was, sadly, where the single person she had in mind lived and worked.

The egg's shell had started out almost soft to the touch, but it had grown harder and stronger. She wasn't sure if this meant the egg actually had something living in it, because she wasn't sure if whatever it was could be sustained without magic. Which she didn't have. At least, not on purpose.

And thinking that, she carefully removed the bracer she

wore as a matter of course throughout most of her working days. Laying it to one side of the box, she lifted the egg out, set it on the bed, swaddled it in her own blankets, and curled around it protectively to keep it warm.

Morning happened, and judging from the fall of sunlight, she wasn't late, yet. Her sleep had, to her surprise, been untroubled, which did happen a handful of days each year. She had time to fish food out of the magical basket that Severn had given her. Of all the magic she'd seen, this one was the most quietly impressive: it preserved food. Even bread. She wasn't certain for how long, because food didn't generally last long in her apartment; she'd have to test it one day.

She then dressed, snapping the bracer back into place on her wrist and rooting through the clothing she'd thrown on the floor the night before to fish out the two letters she'd been handed by two entirely different Dragon Lords. The forlorn and unhatched egg went back into its box, and back under the bed.

The walk to work ended with Clint and Tanner at the doors. Clint nodded, and Tanner said, "You keep arriving at work on time and people are going to start worrying."

"Oh? Who?"

"The ones who are losing money." He laughed.

She grimaced. "They've started a different pool."

"I haven't heard about a new one."

"It's called the end-of-the-world pool, but if you don't like the odds, there's one about the next call from the midwives." They'd pulled her out of work during the day for the last three births; it meant she was on time for work, but still short hours.

Tanner chuckled and they stepped out of the way to let her pass. She ran a hand along Clint's wings as she cleared the door, and heard his friendly curse at her back.

★ ★ ★

Caitlin was at her desk. "You're early, dear. How did yesterday's lesson go?"

"I'm still alive."

"You don't sound particularly happy about it at the moment."

"Not at the moment, no. It only means I have to go back in three days."

"That bad?"

"Bad enough that I now consider any other teacher I've had to be friendly and put upon."

Caitlin raised a brow. "And that made you early?"

"No. Early," Kaylin replied, removing the two sealed letters from her side pouch, "was for these. I have hopes that one of them will get me out of desk duty."

"Kaylin…"

"And hopes that the other one won't be an immediate call for my execution. They're for the Hawklord."

"Were they urgent?"

"They were delivered by Dragons. One of them, at least, was written by Diarmat."

Caitlin winced. "Then at least one is urgent, for your sake."

"The Hawklord's busy?"

"Yes, dear. He and most of the Barrani Hawks are closeted in the Tower discussing the difficulties with the investigation into the Exchequer's suspected embezzlement."

Which meant he wasn't going to take any interruption well.

"Head up to his office and speak with his secretary. My guess is he'll interrupt the Hawklord, at least briefly."

Kaylin shrugged. "My job was to deliver the letters; it wasn't to stand over the Hawklord's shoulder making certain he reads them."

"Take them to his office, dear."

★ ★ ★

The Hawklord's office wasn't actually the Tower, although that's where he held most of his meetings; it was vastly more convenient for Aerians to reach, as the dome in the roof opened. He did, however, have an office, with a secretary whose function was similar to Caitlin's, albeit for a single man and not an entire office full of Hawks.

She liked the office better than the Tower for a variety of reasons. Chief among these was the fact that the Hawklord's office doors had no door wards. They barely had working hinges, on the other hand. Hanson sat behind his customary desk watching the door's progress. Magic wasn't needed for protection here; no one could sneak into this office through those doors.

"He's not here," Hanson said when she'd mostly managed to get the doors open.

"I know. He's in the Tower with the Barrani Hawks."

"Yes. And an expert who calls himself a Forensic Accountant." Hanson grimaced.

"A *what?*"

"Don't ask me. I just work here."

Kaylin, who also just worked here, nonetheless tried to wrap her thoughts around the title, and gave up. "I have two letters I was told to deliver to him in person."

"Do either of the sendees have any reason to want you dead or fired?"

"Not yet."

Hanson held out a hand. It was large, square, and belied the rather bookish clothing he generally wore for office work. Too many calluses, for one. "Let me have them."

She would normally have been more than happy to pass them off as his problem, but this time she was torn. She had hopes for the contents of Sanabalis's letter, and pure dread about the contents of Diarmat's. It didn't matter, though. Hanson lifted one gray brow and said, "I'm not opening either," in a flat tone of voice. "I recognize *both* seals. Were you told, in either case, to wait for a report?"

"No."

"And you are absolutely *certain* you did nothing to offend Diarmat?"

"Nothing besides breathing."

"Take a chair," Hanson said, rising as he made his decision. "Take any chair in my office *except* the one behind my desk."

Kaylin had been a bit of an explorer when she'd first been brought to the office. Hanson's chair wasn't entirely unfamiliar to her, even though she'd only sat in it a couple of times. Unfortunately, the last of those times had involved a rather irate citizen of great import to his Caste Court, an absent Hanson, *and* an absent Hawklord. It had *not* gone well.

She wasn't thirteen anymore in any case; she took a chair by the wall nearest the desk and waited. Hanson came in maybe a quarter of an hour later; the windows here weren't enchanted, so asking them for the time indicated a lower level of sanity or observation than the Hawks ideally liked in their employees.

"The Hawklord will see you. Now."

"Is he pissed off?"

"He was not entirely pleased by the interruption, no. I don't believe he holds it against you, on the other hand."

"How badly is the investigation going?"

"It is not going well, and the Emperor is not pleased."

Kaylin winced. "Thanks for the heads-up."

The Hawklord's Tower was empty when she arrived; she could see this because the doors were—thank the gods— already open. The landing in front of his Tower, on the other hand, was occupied. Teela was lounging against the height of the rails as Kaylin trudged up the stairs. She raised one dark brow in acknowledgment. "I saw Hanson. Two official letters, from actual Dragons, no less. Why were you at the Palace?"

"Etiquette lessons, if you must know."

Teela frowned for a second, and then nodded. The fact that she'd asked at all meant the investigation was going *very* badly; normally, she would have known exactly where Kaylin had been the previous day. Teela had taken to office betting pools like fish take to water.

"You didn't offend Diarmat, did you?"

"I believe my inferior existence is offense enough," Kaylin replied, sliding into very clipped and precise High Barrani.

Tain chuckled. "He's old school, Kaylin."

"Meaning?"

"You'll find out. Hawklord's waiting," he added. "And we're not allowed back in until you've finished."

Lord Grammayre's eyes were an unfortunate shade of blue; his wings were at full height, but at least they were only partially extended. He held what appeared to be two letters in one of his stiff hands, and he looked up when Kaylin entered. He didn't even tell her to close the doors; he gestured and they pretty much slammed shut at her back. Had she been Barrani, they would have closed on her hair. Or maybe not. Barrani hair never got in the way of anything.

"I have two completely conflicting requests, and I have very, *very* little time in which to reply. Are you aware of what either of these letters contain?"

"No, sir," she said truthfully. She did snap a salute, and she did stand pretty much at rigid attention.

Lord Grammayre looked peaked. Had she been Caitlin, she might have asked him if he'd been sleeping at all; as she wasn't, she didn't dare. "Since *neither* request has anything at all to do with the Human Caste Court or the Exchequer, I almost consider the interruption a favor. Sadly, it is not a favor I can indulge in for much longer.

"Lord Diarmat, after an hour of extracurricular lessons, has decided that things would work more smoothly with a cocurricular schedule."

Kaylin tried to make sense of this, and failed. "Cocurricular?"

"Yes. He would like your etiquette lessons—and his involvement in the same—to be more—" he glanced at the paper "—*comprehensive*. He feels that there is some danger you will take the lessons far too casually otherwise."

"I'm still stuck on cocurricular."

"Ah. The lesson schedule would become far more intensive, and the classes would be integrated into your duties to the Halls of Law. Your paycheck—and possible promotion, and yes, that's also on my desk—would depend on your success. He feels that separation of his lessons and your duties are not—" again he glanced at the paper "—*a strict advantage*."

Kaylin had drifted off the topic of cocurricular and Lord Diarmat, and latched onto the fact that a request for promotion—for her!—was on the Hawklord's desk.

He lifted a pale brow, and then his eyes narrowed; they were still blue. He'd seen Kaylin almost daily since she was thirteen years old, and if she wasn't that child anymore, he'd also become familiar with all the incremental changes time had made. He knew what she was thinking. "If," he said, pinching the bridge of his nose, "I might actually *have* your attention for the next five minutes?"

"Yes, sir!"

"Good. Lord Diarmat's vision of cocurricular would see you at the Imperial Palace for three days of each week, duty cycles notwithstanding. He specifically states some concern with your overall martial training and your deplorable self-indulgence; he wishes all trace of these deficiencies to be dealt with immediately."

Three days of *each* week? "What about my beat?"

"You would obviously not be patrolling for the duration."

"And the duration?"

"That was not specified, although I believe the implication is that his lessons will last until he is satisfied."

"Or I'm dead?"

"If you feel that's more likely."

Almost ashen, Kaylin grasped at straws. "And the—the other letter?"

"There is apparently some miscommunication among the members of the Dragon Court; given the relocation of the refugees and the absence of Lord Sanabalis from the Palace for much of each day, that is understandable." He glanced at the second letter. "Breathe," he said without looking up.

She tried.

"Lord Sanabalis apologizes for any inconvenience his request might cause the Hawks, but his request is, for Lord Sanabalis, quite urgently stated."

The Hawklord wasn't known for either his kindness or his cruelty. Kaylin was privately wondering about the latter. While it was true she'd interrupted a critical meeting at a very bad time, it was also true that the interruption wasn't her doing.

"He would like to see you seconded to the Imperial Court as an attaché."

"A what?"

"I believe he means a general aide of unspecified expertise. His request, however, would clash badly with Lord Diarmat's."

"Why?"

"He wants you as a full-time aide for an unspecified length of time. You would not report to Sergeant Kassan; you would report directly to Lord Sanabalis." The Hawklord lowered the hand that held the letters, and his irritation receded; the color of his eyes, however, was almost cobalt. "Your duties to the Court at this time would take you directly into the fiefs."

"The fiefs? But—"

"There have been some issues with the resettlement."

CHAPTER 3

"Issues?" Kaylin said, her voice sharpening. "What do you mean, issues?"

"I? I mean nothing. Lord Sanabalis has failed—entirely—to make explicit what those issues or concerns are. He has, however, stated unequivocally that the strangers, or at least one or two of them, would be comfortable, or perhaps comforted, by your presence. He acknowledges, of course, that the needs of the Halls of Law take precedence in this case, and that the jurisdiction is...hazy. He also feels, should we grant his request, Corporal Handred should accompany you." The Hawklord looked at Kaylin.

"While I feel it inadvisable to annoy Lord Diarmat, three thousand homeless strangers—none of whom speak Elantran or Barrani—seem, to me, to be the greater concern. While the fief of Tiamaris is *not* within the purview of the Halls of Law, if accommodations cannot be safely made, the strangers will no doubt become our problem, one way or the other.

"I will therefore accede to Lord Sanabalis's request, and I

will write my regrets to Lord Diarmat. I will not, however, attempt to get you out of his extracurricular lessons. Is that understood?"

Kaylin nodded.

"Therefore, if you must be late—or worse, miss one—have a reason with which even the most punctilious of people can find no fault."

"Such as being dead?"

"That would," was the wry reply, "be acceptable, but I think it goes a tad far." He exhaled. "Report to Lord Sanabalis directly upon leaving the Tower; he will have further instructions. Where it is possible, make your reports to Sergeant Kassan at the end of the day. He will no doubt have some issues with your placement, and this will mollify him somewhat. It is the only concession I can afford to make at this time."

Kaylin nodded and offered as perfect a salute as she could.

"I will mirror Sergeant Kassan to let him know of your reassignment." He placed one palm on the surface of his slender, tall mirror; the office—the one she usually called home when she wasn't dealing with nervous, angry, or insane people— swam into view. At the center of that office, in image, as in life, was the bristling golden fur of a Leontine. "Sergeant Kassan," the Hawklord said in brisk, clipped Elantran.

"What," Marcus said, catching the same glimpse of Kaylin that she'd caught of him, "has she done this time?"

"At the moment? She has apparently made herself all but necessary to the Dragon Court. Lord Sanabalis has seconded her for ancillary work in the fief of Tiamaris; I have granted the requested redeployment. Please have Corporal Handred report in; I believe he's in the outer office."

"I'm losing two Hawks for how long?"

"I'm certain that, after deliberations with Lord Sanabalis, Private Neya will be able to answer that question."

Marcus growled. His eyes shaded toward copper, and his fur began to stand up, increasing the size of his face. Kaylin, used to this, lifted her chin, exposing her throat. The Hawklord, however, was unmoved by this display of annoyance, and really, given Marcus, it was second-rate. He gestured briefly at the mirror, and Marcus's image dissolved in a sea of silvered waves.

The Hawklord then turned to Kaylin. "I have an interrupted meeting to resume. Please tell the Barrani Hawks to get back to work on your way out."

Severn wasn't waiting for her by the time she reached Marcus's desk; Marcus, however, was. He was also aware that the appearance of Kaylin's partner would end most conversation—although Marcus's idea of conversation suited most definitions of interrogation Kaylin had ever run across. "Caitlin said you had two letters."

Kaylin winced and nodded. "Yes, sir."

"The second letter was also from a Dragon Lord."

"Yes, sir."

Marcus growled.

"Lord Diarmat," she offered, aware that while this was what he wanted, it would in no way mollify him. She was right; he'd created three new runnels in the surface of a desk that already looked as if insane carpenters had gone on a drinking binge and then tried to have a carving contest.

"The letter's content?"

"I didn't read it; it was sent to Lord Grammayre."

"Is Lord Diarmat going to be annoyed at your new assignment?"

"Yes, sir. But with any luck he won't be annoyed at the Hawks."

"I'll speak with the Hawklord when he's done. Corporal

Handred is waiting." He growled before Kaylin turned. "*Try not to antagonize Lord Diarmat, Private. He's not known for his abundance of goodwill. He is also famous for his utter lack of anything that could remotely resemble a sense of humor."

With good damn reason. She managed not to say this out loud, but did turn to jog her way to where Severn was standing in order to leave an impression of good behavior intact.

Sanabalis was, of course, waiting for them in his usual rooms. Food was also—as it often was—waiting with him, albeit on small tables near the very heavy chairs that occupied the room. Sanabalis was, for a change, seated in one when they arrived.

"Corporal, Private," he said, gesturing toward the food. "There may not be a reasonable opportunity to eat later on in the day; I suggest you avail yourself of what's here."

Kaylin took a chair closest to the food. She often wondered how—or what—Dragons ate, because she'd never actually seen them do it. Today was not to be the exception, but as she was hungry, food at home being sparse because of the insanity of her schedule and the fact that the market was either closed when she managed to crawl out of the office, or sold out of anything that looked remotely edible, she ate.

Severn joined her, but ate less. "What," he said, while eating, "is the difficulty in Tiamaris? The borders of the fief have stabilized, haven't they?"

"Tiamaris is still hunting down Shadow remnants and infestations within the fief boundaries; the few that he has failed to destroy are subtle."

Very little destroyed the appetite of people who'd scrounged through fief garbage in their childhood, which is why Kaylin could continue to eat. Around a mouthful of something, she said, "Shadows aren't known for their subtlety."

He frowned. "You are well aware that that is not the case. Your experiences in the High Halls and in the Leontine Quarter are solid evidence that subtlety is not beyond their scope, nor planning."

She gave him the point. "Are the problems caused by the Shadows?"

"Not in their entirety. I know you're aware of the various building projects Tiamaris and his Tower have undertaken. What you are perhaps not entirely cognizant of is where the funds for that reconstruction have come from."

"Funds?"

"Funds. Money."

It was true. Until Sanabalis had, in fact, mentioned funding, she hadn't given it a thought. Her experience with fieflords had made clear that the *lords* of the fief were never strapped for cash; it was just anyone else who lived under them who had difficulty. Tiamaris had dismantled Barren's old tried-and-true method of bringing gold into the fiefs by strongly discouraging anyone who stepped foot across the Ablayne without a clear purpose. In only one of those cases had the discouragement caused friction with the Halls of Law, and in truth, not much.

Kaylin would have happily watched Tiamaris burn to ash anyone who'd made use of Barren's previous, very illegal services. She'd have brought marshmallows. "You're right. I have no idea at all where the money's coming from. If I had to guess, I'd say he's using Barren's money, or what was left of it."

"It would be a reasonable guess. It would not, however, be entirely accurate. He is using Barren's money, as you call it. He is utilizing the people of the fief, as well, and some of that money has gone to their pay. But the damage done to the fief during the breach of the barriers was extensive, and most of the border-side buildings were destroyed, either during the incursion, or afterward, depending on the contamination."

"Meaning Barren didn't have enough money."

"Meaning exactly that."

"But Tiamaris is still building."

"Yes. There have, however, been a few significant difficulties."

Kaylin started to eat again, but she did lift a hand before the Dragon could continue. "Please tell me that this has nothing to do with the Exchequer and his alleged embezzlement."

Sanabalis was notably silent. He was also, however, grimly pleased with the comment, in the way that teachers often are when a student says something unexpectedly clever. "You see the issue."

She did, and she bit down on the bread a little too hard. "The treasury doesn't have the money."

"The treasury is, by no means, approaching insolvency. But the funds are greatly reduced for projects of an unspecified nature. In emergencies, tax levies could be raised—"

"I know this one," was the grim reply. "I've done tax collector lookout before." This was the polite phrase for guarding the tax collectors, who had the dubious distinction of being the most despised men in the City, bar none. "The Emperor can't raise an unspecified levy without the Caste Courts bickering like starving dogs. He can't, in this case, raise a *specific* levy without causing idiots to cross the bridge in resentful fury with torches."

Severn, often quiet, said, "It would, on the other hand, rid us of dozens of idiots; the Swords would probably be grateful in the long term."

"I concede that the Emperor would not be distressed to see them go, either. Be that as it may, there has been a slowdown in the purchase of the materials required for the reconstruction. Tiamaris has, of course, his own funds, but these have been appropriated. The issue of food was initially problematic—but I forget myself. The food is entirely an internal matter."

"In theory, so is the reconstruction."

"Indeed. The investigation into the Exchequer is not going as well as the Emperor had hoped." He steepled his hands beneath his chin, teasing wisps of beard before he continued. "The funding is not the only problem, and frankly, were it, your presence would not be required."

"Got it. Shadows, then?" She watched his expression. "It's not just the Shadows."

"No. The strangers—who call themselves the People in their own tongue, which we may adopt as their formal racial designation in the archives—have their own customs and their own experiences in dealing with Shadow, and those customs are not in accordance with fief customs."

"Meaning?"

"They walk around more heavily armed than any previous fieflord's thugs, they are between seven and eight feet tall, they are silent and while they are not immediately violent, they are *not* friendly. They do not keep curfew, which, given their size and ability with their weapons, is not actually an issue—for them. It has led to some speculation on the part of the *humans* living in the fief that they are Shadows themselves, or in league with the Shadows."

Kaylin winced. "And since there *are* Shadows, of an unspecified and subtle nature, running around the fief—"

"Very good. You now understand most of the difficulties."

"I do."

"But?" He used the Elantran word for this.

"I don't understand why it requires *your* presence in the fief. The fief of Tiamaris demonstrably already *has* a Dragon

Lord of its own, and from all accounts he's a damn sight more effective at scouring the streets for Ferals and other nightmares than any of the previous fieflords before him."

Sanabalis nodded. "Your point is taken," he said, rising. "I have one meeting before I am free to leave the Palace. I will leave you both here, and return when I am able to depart."

"He didn't answer the damn question," she said—but only after the door had been closed for a good five minutes. Even Dragon hearing had its limits.

"You noticed." Severn was frowning, but it was a slight frown.

"What?"

"I don't think he thinks your presence in the fief of Tiamaris is necessary." Before she could speak, he held up one hand. "I think he wants you there. Why?"

She grimaced. "I'd like to think I was necessary or useful."

"But?"

"Diarmat also asked that I be seconded to the Palace. To him, directly, for more intensive lessons."

"This occurred at the same time?"

"If I had to guess, Sanabalis actually wrote out his request first. But...he probably had some idea of what Diarmat would demand. You don't know what he's like, Severn." ·

"I have a very good idea of what Lord Diarmat is like."

"Is he still alive only because he's a Dragon and they're so bloody hard to kill?"

"Probably. We're going to need to change," he added.

"Why?"

"Fiefs."

"They've got a Dragon for a fieflord. He's trying to institute reasonable laws—and install the people who'll enforce them. I don't think the Hawk is going to matter one way or the other."

He folded his arms across his chest, and Kaylin grimaced. "All right, I'll ditch the tabard, but I'm not ditching the armor until I have a better idea of what we're likely to be up against."

Severn rose and headed toward the window view that Kaylin liked so much. From the slight angle of the back of his head, Kaylin guessed that he was looking at the Halls of Law, or at the flags that stood atop each of its three towers. But after a minute, he turned.

"We haven't talked," he said after a long pause.

"About what?"

He didn't dignify the question with an answer, which was fair. Kaylin shifted in her chair in a way that was suspiciously like squirming. She hesitated, glad that there wasn't much in the way of food; the only time she had trouble eating was when she was nervous, and a life of near starvation hadn't managed to kill that response.

Severn said nothing, not with words. But he watched, gaze almost unblinking. It was hard to meet that gaze, and the floor suddenly became a whole lot more interesting.

"I don't—" She wasn't one of nature's natural liars, and Severn deserved better than that. Plus, he'd know. He always did. "I almost can't remember most of what happened when I was trapped in the…Other. No, that's not what I mean— I remember it, it just doesn't make sense. Here," she said, thumping the ground heavily with her foot, "things are solid. The wood is hard. The carpet is soft. There's wind and the noise of the street. Well, the halls, but you know what I mean. There's food. There are people.

"There are no elements wandering around. There are no true names floating in the air like signposts. It's normal—it's normal, but it's less—"

"Clean?"

"Maybe. Less simple. Everything there was absolute. To speak to any of it—elements, emptiness—I had to be as absolute as I could. I didn't have time to be afraid."

"You were afraid."

She grimaced. "Yes, but on most days I have a half-dozen *different* fears pulling me in different directions; I balance them."

"So, you're afraid?"

"No!" She paused and looked up at his face again. "...Maybe."

"Can you tell me what you're afraid of?"

"On the wrong day? My own shadow." It was a dodge, and he knew it. "...I'm not good at this. I suck at talking about anything really important."

"You asked me why I love you."

She nodded; she could hardly forget that.

"Can I ask you the same question?"

"Severn—"

"Why do you love me?"

She wanted to lie then. It was such a visceral reaction, her mouth was open and words were almost falling out. But she held them, offering different words in their stead. "Because you've always been there for me. Even, apparently, when I didn't know it. There's nothing you've got that you wouldn't give me if I asked for it. You *know* me. You understand me. You've seen me at my worst, and you're still here." She sucked in air. "You'll never ask me to do anything I *can't* do. You'd never ask me to do anything that would hurt me. You're stronger than I am, Severn. You always have been.

"I admire it. I...rely on it, even when I shouldn't."

"Kaylin, you think relying on anyone is proof that you're worthless."

"No—I don't. I don't anymore. I *did.* It's true. But…if we can't rely on each other some of the time, there'd be no point."

"No point?"

"No point in people existing at all. There'd be just one thing. If what I heard was true, that's all there was for a long time."

"Then I don't see the problem."

"No, you don't." She rose and began to pace. "And I—I'm *not good* at talking."

He waited, because he was good at waiting. "Are you afraid of losing me?"

"Yes. But not because you leave. Because you'll die." Gods, she hated this. She was squirming, he knew it. "I'm afraid," she finally said in as neutral a voice as she could manage, "that you want me."

"Want?"

"Want. Desire."

He stared at her. This was different from watchfulness. "You're not afraid of wanting me."

"…No."

"But you don't."

She walked to the window. Touched it with both her palms, framing the three Towers of Law that formed the triangular structure she called home. "It's not that I don't," she finally said. "But I'm not afraid of what I want. No—sometimes I am, but not in that way. I'm not afraid of what it will do to *me.*"

"And to me?"

She shook her head. "I don't have a lot of experience," she finally said. "But the experience I do have—it's all bad, Severn." Swallowing, throat becoming drier by the syllable, she made herself continue, because it was important. "If I had been prettier, if I had been more helpless, I would have been forced into one of Barren's brothels. If Morse hadn't found me, if someone else had found me first—

"I know that life. I understand what it means. I understand what sex is between the girls who weren't as lucky and the men who see them as something to buy. It's about power, it's about money, it's about—sex."

"Kaylin—"

"No, let me finish, because I don't know that I'll ever be able to say this again. For those girls, that's all it is. If they love anyone, if they can, they mostly love each other because men are just business, or far worse. There's no room in that for anything else.

"I didn't have to suffer that." She closed her eyes, blocking out the Halls of Law—and the temerity of her own transparent reflection. "I had Barren," she said in a much lower voice. "I don't—I can't—talk about that. Not directly. Not yet. But you understand what I mean, right?"

He was silent.

"I didn't want him. I never did. He was everything ugly to me, everything I feared. Everything I would have run from if I could. I can't think why I didn't. I would never be so afraid of him now. But—I wasn't me, then.

"I remember him so well. I have nightmares about him. But I did what he wanted me to do because he wanted me to do it. I killed people because he wanted it. I—" She wanted to choke. "I can still see his face. When I think of—when I—it's *his* face. It's his expression. I *don't know* if it was desire. I think it was. It was certainly about power. His, my lack. It was *always* about power." She opened her eyes again. She could see echoes of her face, of her distant, thirteen-year-old face, in the glass.

"…I'm afraid. Of seeing that. Of seeing that desire on anyone else's face. It's me I don't trust."

"Kaylin—"

"I tried," she continued, not looking at him. "When I was seventeen. I tried. We'd gone out together, we'd done a little drinking. I *was* attracted to him. I did want to be with him. He knew it; I knew it. We went back to his place—it was about the same size as mine.

"And he kissed me, and that was fine—it was awkward, but it was fine. But...there was more. I—I froze, and then I...I couldn't *stop myself*. I broke his jaw. Teela thought it was funny. I panicked, I—he didn't speak to me again for two months, and I don't blame him. It's just I—it's what I saw. It's what I saw in his expression. And he was a nice guy, Severn. He was a nice, decent guy. I knew he wasn't Barren. I wasn't thirteen. I wasn't helpless, and I had a choice.

"But knowing all that didn't matter. I couldn't look at him. I couldn't see that look on his face, that expression. I just—" She hit the glass hard. Nothing happened. "I don't want to see that in you." She turned then.

He was still standing, still watching her. "And Nightshade?"

It was *so* not the question she wanted to hear. She recoiled from it, as if it were a cockroach colony and she were food. But what she said was, "Ask me again later. I don't have an answer, and I don't want to find one right now."

Because he was Severn, he nodded. He didn't ask about their future; didn't ask if they even had one. He didn't ask her for empty words or for promises that she couldn't make or wouldn't keep.

Sanabalis took forty-five minutes to return, and if there had been any doubt about why he'd left, the distant, booming roar of Dragon "discussion" shook the floors. It was far enough away that Kaylin didn't try to cover her ears. She wondered if it was possible to learn the language without being deafened.

Sanabalis, however, returned in different clothing. It wasn't armor exactly—Dragons didn't wear any armor that wasn't natural. The wearing of their own armor in human form, however, made actual clothing difficult. He nodded his brief approval when he saw no obvious sign of the Hawk on their clothing. "A carriage will be waiting for us in the yard."

The carriage took them to the Ablayne, no farther. Given that it was an Imperial Carriage, Kaylin understood why. Dragons were touchy about their personal land. Even Tiamaris. She glanced at Sanabalis.

"I'm surprised," she finally said, when they stood at the foot of the bridge that led into the fief of Tiamaris.

"What surprises you?"

"You're coming with us." She glanced at Severn; Severn was content to leave the conversation in her hands for the moment.

"Oh?"

"You're a Dragon. He's a Dragon. It's his territory and you serve the Emperor, which would be, for his purposes, the wrong Dragon."

Sanabalis lifted a brow, and then a faint smile moved the corners of his lips. Not by much, though. "It is, as you surmise, tricky. I have been Lord Tiamaris's teacher, and I am definitely his senior; I am his superior in most areas of knowledge. He, however, has always possessed better information about the fiefs as they are now than any of the rest of the Dragon Court. I do not serve Lord Tiamaris.

"But Lord Tiamaris serves the Emperor as a member of the Dragon Court. Therefore accommodations can be requested."

"I'm surprised Diarmat allowed it."

"*Lord* Diarmat is not the Emperor. He is, as you've no doubt surmised, the most conservative member of the Court, and not without reason. Lord Tiamaris accepted the Emperor's request that I oversee some of the resettlement. The Emperor is concerned."

Kaylin nodded and led the way toward the Tower automatically. Sanabalis, however, shook his head. "Lord Tiamaris is not currently at the Tower; he is waiting near the interior border."

"Why?"

"There have been some difficulties. And no, before you ask, I will not elaborate. This *is* his domain, Kaylin; he will tell you what he wishes you to know. The etiquette that governs my presence here is of necessity more strict than any etiquette that governs yours."

The walk to the border took longer than the walk to the Tower. The streets weren't empty—but they were empty compared to the stretch of beat that Kaylin and Severn normally covered. Here and there, some obvious reconstruction was already under way, and in those locations, there were more people; they were busy enough that three strangers passing by didn't elicit panic, although it did elicit the usual suspicious looks that were at home on the face of fief citizens anywhere.

Sanabalis paused when Kaylin did, and resumed walking when Kaylin did; he didn't make any comment or otherwise attempt to interact with people. He did, however, pause in front of the small gardens that seemed to front most of the buildings along the streets.

"It's Tara's experiment," Kaylin told him. These gardens, unlike the usual streetside fare, were entirely practical, and given to the growing of food. "I think some of the more damaged areas now have no buildings; they have larger gardens—small farms, really."

"And the former occupants?"

"They lost a lot of people before Tiamaris took the Tower.

And even if they hadn't, no one would be stupid enough to complain to the fieflord about something as inconsequential as having a place to *live*." She didn't even attempt to keep the bitterness out of her voice, although she knew that particular fear was no longer warranted in *this* fief.

"You are wrong," Sanabalis said. It surprised her.

"People complain to Tiamaris about having no roof over their head?"

"Ah, no. They do, however, speak to the Lady."

"They have to get through Tiamaris first."

"No. Apparently, they don't. She hears them regardless."

Kaylin smiled. "She's nowhere near as terrifying as Tiamaris."

"No, and that is strange to me; Lord Tiamaris has the hearing that all our race are born with. He cannot hear the words the people speak if they are judicious about their location; the Avatar can. She can also see what she chooses to see, if she bends her will toward it, no matter where within the fief's boundaries it occurs. But she invokes a very strange awe in her people, and very little dread."

"Have you *met* Tara?"

"I have."

"And you don't understand why she doesn't terrify them?"

"No, I do not."

"Was she wearing her gardening clothing?"

"I fail to see what her clothing has to do with the subject at hand."

Dragons.

It was fairly easy to find Tiamaris, when all was said and done. From about two blocks away—where blocks in this case were mostly defined by the charred remnants of what had previously been some of the sturdier buildings in the fief—Kaylin could see the strangers. They didn't walk the way the rest of the mortals in the fief did; they walked as if they owned, or intended to own, the streets. They bristled with weapons, and although their armor wasn't in the best of repair, it was a damn sight better than what the rest of the citizens were wearing.

Not that there *were* any "rest of" anywhere in sight.

If, however, the strangers had suddenly decided to become meek and terrified, it would still have been easy to find Tiamaris at this distance because he was, at the moment, a very large Dragon. She glanced at Sanabalis, who didn't appear to have noticed.

"Is he always like this?"

"Frequently. The Dragon form is more robust."

They made their way down the street, which attracted attention. It was easy to see why; they were the only more or less human-looking people who were actually *approaching*. "Please don't tell me that they're serving as his personal guard."

"It is…an informal guard."

"Great." The very large sword that was being lowered in their general direction sure as hells didn't look informal. It did, however, make Kaylin and Severn stop much farther away than guards or thugs usually did; whatever Barren had managed to scrape off the streets had seldom been an actual threat. She lifted both hands, and turned them, palms out, toward the two men who had lowered their weapons; Severn did the same, although his hands were closer to his weapons. The two eight-foot-tall giants exchanged a few words and started to head toward the taller outline of Tiamaris.

Sanabalis, however, had decided that waiting wasn't in the cards. He *roared*. The two men stiffened, which gave Kaylin a moment of petty satisfaction. Tiamaris turned.

"You'll have to teach me how to do that," Kaylin muttered.

"If it were even possible, I would still refuse," Sanabalis replied. "Lord Diarmat would find it...impertinent."

Tiamaris parted the crowd of armed strangers by turning. They didn't rush to get out of his way; they moved. For all their apparent bulk, they moved quickly. As they cleared enough street for a Dragon with folded wings, Kaylin saw Tara. Tara was, in fact, wearing her gardening clothes, and Morse was walking by her side, looking about as happy at this new set of guards as Kaylin felt.

Morse had been a lieutenant of the previous fieflord, but she'd made the transition to Tiamaris without much trouble. Beside Tara, she looked like a thug in the true sense of the word; her hair was still a very short, shorn crop, and her face still bore scars from earlier fights. When she smiled at all, it was a grim, black smile, and it usually meant someone was about to die. Or it had meant that. She did smile at Tara, but usually only when she thought no one else was watching.

Tara broke into a wide grin as Kaylin met her eyes. Kaylin knew that Tara could be aware of her presence the instant she set foot on the right side of the Ablayne, but she often seemed so surprised and delighted, the thought held no weight. She broke into a run, which ended with her arms around Kaylin, and Kaylin's arms around her.

"Lord Sanabalis said you would come," Tara said when she at last stepped back. "Hello, Corporal Handred."

Severn also smiled, and it was an unguarded smile. "Lady," he said, bowing to the fief's title, and not the name Kaylin had given her.

"Did he explain the difficulty?" Tara asked.

"No. Now that the fief is Tiamaris's, he feels any information has to come from Tiamaris."

"Why?"

"Don't ask me. I'm not a Dragon." She did add when she heard Sanabalis's snort, "I think it's something to do with the etiquette of hoard law. Dragons are, by simple human standards, *insanely unreasonable* about their hoards."

"Ah. It's possible that he is entirely correct then." She turned and smiled at Sanabalis, who appeared unimpressed with Kaylin's description. "Thank you."

He bowed to her. He bowed damn low.

Kaylin raised a brow at Morse, and Morse responded with a pure fief shrug. "What's happening?" Kaylin asked Morse, stepping to the side to add a little distance between them and anyone who might be listening.

"We have three thousand eight-foot-tall people who can't speak Elantran and have no place to live. They also have no sense of humor."

"Neither do you."

"Exactly. Consider the source of the comment."

Kaylin chuckled—but she also winced. "Sanabalis implied there were other difficulties."

"That's how he worded it? 'Other difficulties'?" Morse spit to one side.

Kaylin frowned. "How bad is it?"

"There are two problems. One, we're trying to track down, but even the Lady is having some trouble; we're not sure why."

"That would be the subtle Shadow that Sanabalis also mentioned?"

"That's not what we call it, but yeah. You're here to help with that?"

Kaylin frowned, and then nodded. "That's my guess. What's the other problem?"

"The border boundary," Morse said, voice flat. There were four possible borders that defined the fief of Tiamaris—but only one was a threat to the fief's existence: the one that faced into the unclaimed shadow that lay in the center of the fiefs.

Kaylin almost froze. "The border's supposed to be stable."

"Oh, it's holding. If it weren't, we'd all—*all*—be dead by now. But the freaking Shadow across the fucking border is puking out whatever it can. Nothing small and easily killed, either; apparently the bigger one-offs can survive the 'transition' with some of their power intact."

Kaylin sucked in air. "When the hells did this start happening?"

"Pretty much the same day *they* did," Morse replied, jerking her thumb in the direction of the strangers.

"Believe," Kaylin said after an uncomfortably sharp silence, "that they didn't bring the Shadows with them."

"Oh?"

"If I understood what was said correctly, they were fleeing from them."

"And being followed."

"I was *there,* Morse. If great chunks of Shadowy one-offs had followed them into Elani, believe I would have noticed." But she hesitated. Morse, no fool, noticed.

"What?"

"When they arrived, they did this funny thing with a bunch of drums and a lot of loud chanting. It was supposed to be some sort of purification ritual, but the end result? The Dragons—all four of them—took flight over the city while they did it." Kaylin shook her head, glancing briefly at two of those four: Tiamaris, in full scales and wings, and Sanabalis, in slightly drab but official clothing. "And...the chanting was magical, somehow."

This admission of the use of magic by obviously dangerous giants did nothing positive for Morse's mood.

"But...something *answered* them. Something in the fiefs. If I had to guess," she added quietly, "something from the heart of the fiefs."

"What, it was some kind of fucking *challenge?*" Morse's brows rose toward the nearly shaved dome of her head. "Are they *insane?*"

From a fief perspective, there could only be one answer to that question. But...this fief had become, almost overnight, an exception to the rules that generally governed the fiefs. Kaylin glanced at the large huddle of strangers—she'd have to ask Sanabalis what their own name for their race was because "strangers" wasn't going to cut it—and said, "Not insane. I think they're used to fighting a war with the Shadows, rather than locking the doors and praying a bunch."

"Great." Morse glanced at Tara, who seemed to be involved in a serious discussion with Sanabalis, while Tiamaris, over her shoulder—well, part of his jaw, at any rate—looked on. Severn was beside the older Dragon, listening intently.

Kaylin frowned.

"What?" Morse said sharply.

"There's something I don't understand."

She was rewarded by something that was halfway between snort and grunt; the sarcastic comment that would have usually followed failed to emerge. For Morse, this was a big improvement. "What?"

"Tiamaris *is* fieflord in a way that Barren wasn't."

"You can say that again."

Fair enough. "Barren didn't hold the Tower. Tiamaris does."

"And?"

"Holding the Tower at all should prevent your one-offs from getting through."

Morse shrugged. "The Ferals get through."

"I know; they get through everywhere. I'm not sure why."

"Time to find out?"

"Well past." Kaylin turned toward the discussion that was even now taking place without them, and as she did, Tara froze. It was a very particular stillness, and it reminded anyone who happened to be standing close by that Tara's physical form, the form of her birth, was made of stone.

It was warning enough for Kaylin, but if it hadn't been, there was another one that followed less than thirty seconds later: the strangers began to shout, and weapons began to catch sunlight and reflect it in a way that spoke of movement.

Morse swore. Loudly. But her brief word wasn't equal to the task of carrying over the cries and shouts—directed, not panicked—of the strangers. "Kaylin!" she shouted.

Kaylin turned.

"Incoming!"

Sanabalis's eyes turned instantly orange as Tiamaris swiveled his head and roared. Kaylin's ears were still ringing when the fieflord spread wings, bunched legs, and pushed himself off the ground; it was a miracle of grace and movement that prevented those wings from knocking anyone *else* flying. Tiamaris roared again as he rose above the heights of the standing structures erected along the border—they were few, and they were clearly meant as lookouts and not living quarters.

Severn had already unwound his weapon chain; Morse had a sword in hand. But Morse remained close by Tara, rather than running to join the giants. After a brief glance at Severn, Kaylin headed toward those giants, her own daggers still sheathed. Severn joined her; Sanabalis did not. But Tiamaris's shadow passed above them as the drums began their rolling thunder.

What kind of people carried drums into a war zone anyway?

Kaylin noticed, as she approached the main body of the strangers, that there were no children here. There were men—and women—who looked as if they'd left youth behind, but they carried their weapons with the same grim determination that the younger men and women did. If any of them had ever survived to *be* elderly, they were also nowhere in sight.

They noticed her, but they were accustomed to a lack of clear communication from the humans and made no attempt to question her; they did, however, let her pass into their midst. She briefly regretted her armor; it was hard to shove it out of the way, and as she couldn't, she couldn't expose the marks on her arms with any ease. Those marks, the strangers did recognize in some fashion.

But Severn spoke a single curt word. "Bracer."

Her reply was less civil. She shed splints, exposing the heavy golden manacle, and she crushed gems in sequence to open the damn thing. It clicked, she removed it and tossed it over her shoulder, remembering after it had left her hand that there were enough people behind her that it might actually hit someone. No one, however, shouted in outrage, and better yet, no one attempted to remove her head from her shoulders, so she moved in the direction of the drumming itself.

The drummers were standing behind a line of men and women who faced the interior of the fiefs; there were four drums in total that Kaylin could count. The men who beat them had weapons at their feet, but they were otherwise intent on stretched skin, not incoming danger. The four drums circled three people, however, and Kaylin recognized one of them: Mejrah. She was the oldest stranger present, she was about a foot shorter than the People standing beside her, and her eyes were all whites.

CHAPTER 4

Mejrah was not a door ward, but the hair on the back of Kaylin's neck began to rise, and the marks on her skin began to ache in their usual protest at the presence of magic. Her exposed arm was also, damn it, glowing softly; the runes were a pale blue. At the moment, however, the visible marks gave her one solid advantage: no one stood in her way, and anyone who happened to be there moved.

Severn crowded her back to take advantage of the brief openings; he moved, as he often did, like a cat.

"Kaylin, twelve o'clock."

Twelve o'clock, like positions ten to one, was occupied by large, weapon-wielding men; it was also briefly illuminated by bursts of angry, orange flames. The flames were close enough that Kaylin could feel their instant heat, and far enough away that she didn't burn. But in the wake of fire, she could see the shape of something dark and ungainly rising above a horizon composed of tall warriors. Whatever the creature was, it was *not* small.

Size, in Shadows, wasn't necessarily directly proportional to their power. But appearance was often an indicator. The creature was not being helpful in this regard: it didn't seem to have *a* form. Instead, Shadow rose and fell, like black snowdrifts in a very bad storm. Like snow, the blackness accreted. Dragonfire seemed to cause it some damage—but not enough to stop it or destroy it.

The men spoke in short, sharp bursts; they were clearly giving orders in harsh, guttural syllables. Mejrah's voice soared above them, twining as it did with the two voices of the men who stood on either side of her, as sightless as she. Their voices formed words, and these words were tantalizingly familiar to Kaylin; she couldn't understand them, but she felt as if she should. She glanced at Mejrah, and from her to the air just above the old woman's hands; it was wavering, as if it had substance and texture.

Kaylin expected to see words form in that air: ancient words. True words. Instead, light grew, curling in on itself as if it was a trapped, compressed cloud.

The creature drew closer and closer to the boundaries, and as it did, it opened what might—*might*—have been a mouth, and it began to speak. To Kaylin's surprise, she recognized some of the language. Not enough to understand it, of course—that would have been too easy. It wasn't the ancient tongue, though—it was the tongue that the strangers spoke, and were speaking even now.

They were shouting *at* the creature, and from their stances, it appeared that they were *taunting* it. Had she not been so much on edge, her jaw would have hit the ground and bounced. Every instinctive reaction she'd developed over the course of her life screamed in protest: this was suicide. Then again, so was standing still, which they were notably *all* doing.

Had they been anyone else—in particular, people who

would understand a word she shouted—she would have started
to shout orders of her own. As it was, she reminded herself,
firmly, that they had spent most of their lives fighting Shadows in one way or another. If they were standing there while
Mejrah was doing a complicated form of magic that would
have had the Imperial mages looking down their noses in
contempt, they had to have a reason for it.

Tiamaris roared and the men on the ground took up his cry;
she thought they were attempting to repeat what he'd said.
The timbre of their voices suited their size; it wasn't Dragon,
but it had enough strength behind it not to make a mockery
of the word itself. The drumbeats began to pick up speed until
all sound was a collision: Mejrah, Tiamaris, the warriors on
the ground, and the pounding beat of the skins themselves.

And then, suddenly, there was silence. Light leaped from sky
to ground, passing *through* the raised weapons of the strangers.
The blades absorbed light instead of reflecting it, as if they
were being anointed.

The Shadow roared; it was not a dragon roar—but it was as
loud, as intense, as Tiamaris at his peak. It was also cold and
dark enough to devour light and the things that came with it.
Kaylin took a step back, although she wasn't in the front line;
the warriors, however, didn't.

The Shadow continued to roar, and as it did, the ground
around it began to heave. That ground, the surface of the
street, and the hint of the buildings that had once occupied
it, were black and white, leeched of color. They were soon
leeched of their form, as well; they shimmered and began to
fold in on themselves, condensing as they did into vastly less-
stationary shapes. She'd seen something similar once before,
on the very edge of the fief of Nightshade. Where the moving,
shambling mass of attenuated Shadow had been, more grew,
separate and distinct from it.

She now understood *why* the front was so heavily occupied; in less than five minutes the whole of the ground on the other side of a border that suddenly felt amorphous and theoretical had literally risen in fury. The newer shapes took on a solidity of form that the central Shadow hadn't: they stretched to eight feet in height, growing limbs as they did. For the most part they had two of each—arms and legs—although the little details wobbled if Kaylin examined them for long. They were disturbing because they didn't so much walk as glide, and they were utterly silent.

Then again, the mass at their center was doing enough shouting for a small army, which was convenient for it, as that's what it appeared to be raising. It began to move through the rain of Tiamaris's fire, and Tiamaris, wings spread, flew once over it. The creature *threw* some part of itself, as if a tendril, at the moving Dragon.

He dodged, but Kaylin could see he'd been hit; he didn't bleed, but the Shadow darkened one wing and began to spread. She drew one sharp breath, but before she could shout, the strangers did. Tiamaris banked, breathing fire as he made his way toward the earth on his own side of the border; he landed behind the front line, behind where Kaylin now stood. She glanced over her shoulder to see Tara moving down the street. Given her height, it would have been impossible to see her if she'd actually been walking; she wasn't.

She was flying; her back had sprouted familiar Aerian wings. She headed directly for Tiamaris, and as Kaylin turned back to face the border, the Shadows arrived.

Shadows could, in theory, be stopped by the usual things: swords, clubs, crossbows. The Ferals that had terrorized the night in the fiefs of Kaylin's childhood—and still did—could be killed. They just couldn't be killed *easily,* they were so damn fast.

But the Shadows she'd encountered in the High Halls or in Barren, just before Tiamaris's reign, had been different. They were visually distinct, for one; they were often larger than a good-size horse; they had an indeterminate number of limbs, heads, or jaws, and the jaws could frequently open up at the end of *anything:* tail. Forearm. Stomach. Some had no eyes; some had eyes where every other part of a body would otherwise be. Some could fly, some could float, some seeped like the spread of thick liquid; some could speak.

The speech was always disturbing.

It was disturbing now. It wasn't the tenor of the voice, it wasn't the words—because at the moment, the words were unintelligible to Kaylin. It was the fact that they could speak, think, and communicate *at all.* Ravenous, efficient Ferals felt *almost* natural. Moving, dense mist shouldn't have been *able* to keep up a steady stream of continuous speech, continuous command.

But the words came out of the darkness. It drew closer, and as it finally reached the edge of the border—a border defined entirely by eight-foot-tall warriors—black mist cracked and shattered. It had shattered because what it contained was too large: the thing at its center—still speaking—began to unfold, gaining height and width as it did.

It was tall: half again the height of the warriors it now faced. But unlike many of the one-offs, as Morse called them, *this* one had two arms, two legs; it had, more or less, one head. The head was massive, and it was nauseatingly unstable, the line of mouth and nose and what might have been eyes wavered like a heat mirage. That wasn't what was remarkable about it, though.

It wore armor.

And it *was* recognizably armor. It was chitinous, but so was Dragon armor when worn in human form; it was sleek, and it covered the whole of the body, except of course the face. It shone, reflecting light rather than absorbing it. The Shadow had continued to speak as it unfolded, revealing itself to the men and women who now waited in grim silence. But when at last it drew its weapon, it, too, fell silent, signaling an end to speech.

An end, Kaylin thought, drawing her daggers to life. She watched the giant raise his sword in two hands, lifting it over his head and exposing the whole of his chest to do so.

And she watched the bolts that flew—from where, she wasn't certain—to strike that chest and that armor. All but one bounced; one snapped. The sword plunged toward the earth, and the men who stood beneath it; they had raised their own weapons, but they weren't fools; they *moved*. The sword crashed into the ground, literally breaking it.

Kaylin leaped to one side of the fissure that was opening beneath her feet, cursing in full Leontine. Nothing she had seen when Barren had ruled this fief and the borders had gone *down* had been as bad as this.

Mejrah shouted; her voice was higher and rougher than the voices of the men, and it carried. The warriors regrouped a few yards away from the armored giant, standing their ground as the Shadows that he had summoned poured toward them.

This shouldn't be happening. Kaylin knew it. The Tower was active, and it *had* a Lord; that had been the whole damn point. She backed up—it was that or be trampled—and she saw that the Shadows had changed their formation: they were flowing *into* the fissure the sword had made, following the damage done.

Fully half the warriors on either side of the gap in the ground now turned their weapons upon the invaders, and those weapons—lit, still, by the brilliance of the odd light Me-jrah and her two companions had chanted into existence—cut through Shadow as if it were insubstantial mist. But insubstantial or no, the Shadow burned.

It also attacked. This army of summoned Shadow was in no way as impressive as the summoner, but it didn't have to be: it was still chaotic, amorphous, unpredictable. The uniformity of form that had existed before the lesser Shadows had attempted to cross the border through the breach melted away, and the Shadowy forms that had echoed the warriors were lost. The separation between the forms was lost, as well, as the warriors struck; the Shadows began to bleed into one another, combining and congealing into something vastly less human in appearance.

It was almost a relief. She lifted a dagger, reversed her grip on it, and threw it cleanly toward an emerging eye; Shadow eyes, in her experience, generally did more than just see things. The throw was mediocre; the dagger embedded itself into the iris, not the pupil. In a normal creature, this would have been fine, but the Shadow had pupils the size of Kaylin's fist. It couldn't see her from that eye, but it turned the bulk of its moving form—which was legless—in her direction, while the warriors hacked bits and pieces off its body.

Those pieces dissolved, seeping into the crevice itself; the Shadow continued to move toward Kaylin. Her dagger slowly disappeared into the damaged eye, as the eye transformed itself into a bleeding mouth. *Damn it.* She leaped back as another eye began to emerge; this time, it was lidded, and this time, her dagger bounced. As it did, the lid snapped open.

Damn it! Eyebeams lanced the ground. Clods of dirt and broken stone rose in chunks, and a shout went up from the warriors, one of whom hadn't been lucky enough to dodge in time. He went down; the rest of his companions, instead of running for cover—which was admittedly a lost cause this close to the border—formed up. They *parried* the damn beams.

No fool she, she threw herself forward, rolled between two of them, and came to her feet. Or tried.

The ground shook, causing her to stumble; the armored giant had once again brought his sword crashing into the packed dirt and cracked stonework on the edge of the border itself; the rupture traveled across the boundary. The giant, however, did not. No, Kaylin thought, watching him. He *couldn't*. And the only purchase his Shadows had were in the crevices themselves, at least until the barrier was breached.

She turned to look for Tara and found her easily. The Avatar was glowing. She still had wings, but her face looked like alabaster: white, cold, and hard. Gone were the dirt-stained, slightly oversize clothes of a fledgling gardener; the Avatar's clothing, it appeared, was whatever she desired it to be. At her side, but grounded, stood Tiamaris, and at his side, still encumbered by the frailer human form, stood Sanabalis. Severn was on the other side of the first crevice, and he was working his chain and its terminating blades.

Tiamaris left the warriors as they hacked away at both eye-beams and the physical body that was shooting them so chaotically. He turned his attention to one of the three new breaks that straddled the edge of his fief; Tara flew to a different one. Sanabalis grimaced, and then walked—quickly for a man who affected age—toward the last. He still hadn't bothered to shed the human form, but he didn't need to be in Dragon form to breathe fire.

Clearly age made some difference; the fire was white, and it was hot enough to cause the ground to glow red. The small amount of Shadow that had leaked into the crevice over which Sanabalis kept watch began to smolder, and black smoke rose as it screamed. For a puddle, it made a *lot* of noise. Morse joined Sanabalis; she had a long sword, but she stayed behind the Dragon Lord, watching the ground intently. When tendrils rose up the sides and tried to find purchase in the ground above, she cut them down without blinking.

Kaylin cursed as the earth shook again. This was getting them nowhere; the giant could make cracks in the ground all damn day and he didn't seem to be running out of Shadow to fill them. He couldn't cross the border; that much was clear. He tried; she could see him straining to move, and she could see the sudden stillness that made his failure clear.

Her arms and legs were aching now, which she expected, given the magic. What she didn't expect, as she turned her full attention to the armored giant, was the way her vision began to blur. This was *not* the time to pass out, and as she'd had some experience with that on her drinking binges with Teela and Tain, she recognized some of the signs.

But she hadn't been drinking with the two Barrani Hawks in months; she *certainly* hadn't been drinking today. She forced herself to focus, and as she did, the whole of the armored giant snapped into place with a sharp clarity that was so sudden it made her teeth rattle. It wasn't his size or his shape or the way his blade—which she doubted she could even lift—was drinking in both Shadow and light; it wasn't the way his armor glowed, or even the way his eyes did—because he had eyes and she could suddenly see them.

It wasn't even the movement of his mouth, the way his lips formed a continuing chain of syllables that she couldn't quite force into words. It was his *name*. She could see it as clearly as she had ever seen a name before, but for the first time, she actually understood what it was she was seeing. The border that he struggled against was also completely visible to Kaylin as she watched him. It, like his name, had form and shape in a way that it had never had before.

It was hard to look away, and she could only manage it for a few seconds. But the brief glance the effort afforded made at least one thing clear: the Shadows that crossed the border had no similar words at their heart; they had no substance. Which was a stupid thing to think of creatures that could destroy anything standing in their way.

Then again, so could tidal waves and earthquakes, and no one tried to reason with *them*.

She turned back to the giant, and to the word that was at his heart. The rune itself wasn't dark, and it wasn't ugly; it was, just as any other ancient word she'd glimpsed, composed of familiar broad strokes, fine lines, dots, and hatches. Its meaning wasn't reflected in its visible shape. It wasn't necessary. She could read it. What she couldn't easily do was tease meaning out of it, which was what reading was supposed to be about.

"Kaylin!" Severn shouted. Something was wrong with his voice, although it took her a minute to figure out what it was: it was the only shout she could hear; all the rest of the noise had vanished. The movement of blades, the shouting of indecipherable orders, the crackling of Dragon breath, had suddenly gone mute. She turned—tried to turn—in Severn's direction, but her legs had locked in place. She couldn't take her eyes off the rune. Even the form that enclosed it on all sides was now a translucent black with shiny bits. The weapon that extended from both of the giant's long arms was the only other part of it that was as solid as the word—but the two weren't connected.

She squinted, looking at the sword, in part because she could. There, along the flat of the blade she could see carved—and glowing—runes. They were, like the giant's name, ancient words. She cursed in Leontine, but the words apparently failed to leave her mouth, because she couldn't hear them, either.

What *could* she hear?

The movement of a giant. The whistling fall of his sword. The muted movement of Shadow, which sounded like the rustle and gather of fallen, dead leaves in a dry wind. The earth, in the universe her ears now inhabited, was not being broken; the Shadows, in the same universe, weren't speaking.

She was still frozen in place, although time hadn't stopped. She tried to step back, tried—again—to turn, with no effect. Taking a deep breath, she accepted the inevitable and took a step forward. Forward worked. Of course, forward led her to, and not away from, the giant; forward led her to, and not away from, the border. She was momentarily glad that she couldn't hear anyone else because she was fairly certain at least a handful of people were now shouting choice phrases at her in their native tongues.

But the border yielded to her in a way that it didn't yield to the would-be invaders: with ease, and without the necessity of a lot of collateral destruction. The landscape didn't magically change with the crossing; the colors didn't return; neither did sound. But the runes developed a texture and a dimension as she approached them, which made the sword look decidedly more unwieldy.

The giant noticed her only when she was five yards away. His eyes widened slightly, and his sword arm—well, arms, given the overhand swing—stilled. He then turned toward her; the word at his core didn't shift at all.

But it wasn't a complicated word. It wasn't like the name of the Outcaste Dragon; it wasn't as immense as the name of a world. Kaylin began, as the giant slowly ambled toward her, to speak it. To speak his name, even though she couldn't understand what she was saying.

Speech was now an act of instinct. She wasn't speaking to make herself heard or to be understood; she wasn't speaking to communicate. She *was* buying time, because she had no doubt at all that if the giant reached her, speech would be impossible. Breathing might also be an issue.

Names in the old tongue had syllables that, in any other language, would compose an entire paragraph's worth of words. Or a page. Or a book. They couldn't be spoken quickly in a breathless rush; enunciating them at all was like trying to speak with a mouth full of molasses. It was messy, it took effort, and it was probably unpleasant to watch.

But as the syllables came, the giant's steps slowed and faltered, as if he was keeping time to her awkward struggle to speak. To speak, she realized, to him. The giant was, or had once been, a man. Not a human; humans didn't have names like this at their core. But inasmuch as Dragons and Barrani were alive, he had once been alive.

His sword was no longer raised above his head; he lowered it, letting one hand fall away. The free hand, he raised in her direction, where it tapered from fist to point. She continued to speak, but as she did, he began to speak, as well. His voice was the low rumble of moving earth—a Dragon's human voice, but slightly deeper and slightly fuller.

She couldn't understand a word of it.

But even as she thought it, she realized that understanding what he meant to say wasn't quite the same as understanding its effect: he was trying to *tell her* his name. He was trying, as she was, to speak the whole of it even as he closed the distance. He was also going to kill her if he could; that was clear. But he *knew* that if she knew his true name, she could prevent him. This utterance was the whole of his attempt at self-control.

And he wanted it.

His desire gave her strength; his speech gave her attempt a more solid foundation. She continued to speak, but as she did, she understood why Mejrah and her companions chanted in unison: she was speaking his name as a harmony to his speech.

It was like song, like music, like a chorus of two. It grew louder as she grew more certain; it came faster, because she was no longer struggling to find, to *feel,* the syllables. Every syllable spoken caused him to lose height.

When he at last reached her, he was a mere eight feet—or eight and a half—in height, and his blade was no longer so big it could stave in rooftops. And as she spoke what she knew were the last three syllables, the blade fell from his hands, landing on the ground between their feet.

She looked at him. The armor still girded him, but he was now the size and shape of…of a refugee. He wasn't young; he might have been older than Severn, but it was hard to tell; if he had a *name,* he should be immortal.

At least in this world.

His hands were shaking as he lifted them and removed his helm. In the dark light of altered vision, the helm shone like polished ebony as it rested in the crook of his arm. His eyes were clear, and they were a shade of gold that looked both familiar and wrong in his face. He spoke again, and this time, she lifted a hand and walked toward him slowly, until she could touch what she could still clearly see: his name, the name he had spoken with her, and by speaking, had given into her keeping. When she touched it, she could hear his voice so clearly it was almost a song.

"Chosen," he said softly. "You are Chosen."

Kaylin nodded; her arms were glowing so strongly the runes could be seen.

"But you are not of the People."

"Not of your people, no. Do you know where you are?"

"I am in the heartland," he replied. It made, of the word *heart,* something to be dreaded or loathed.

"Do you know what you were doing?"

"Yes. I was summoning my forces to do battle against the

fortress of...our enemy." He lifted a mailed hand, and re-moved, with effort, a gauntlet. His hands were callused and scarred; he lifted them to those startling eyes, dimming them a moment.

"Call them back."

He nodded, and lifted the mailed hand. "I cannot hold them for long," he told her. "Not as I...am." He bowed to her then. "I can send them from the border for now."

"And what will you do?"

"I will be called, sooner or later, and I will follow."

"You can't—"

"Can you give me back my name, Chosen? Can you, when you cannot take it and use it as your own? I would serve you, could you hold me. But the name is not known to you alone."

Even as he spoke, she heard the whispers of a distant voice. "Maggaron," she said softly. And then, in the silence of thought, *Maggaron*. It wasn't the whole of his name as she'd struggled to pronounce it, but it was the expression of what she'd achieved. Just as Nightshade's name had been, and was, although this was the first time she understood the fact *as* fact.

He smiled; it was a pained, tortured expression. *Yes.* The mental bond came with the true name.

Are you alive?

Is this life? I would not be considered alive by the People.

Could they cleanse you?

Ah. No. It is not...an infestation or a contamination of that nature, Chosen. I am used against myself; nothing else is required.

Kaylin snorted. "You're not a twenty-foot-tall giant; you didn't get that on your own. You've been living in shadow, in the Shadows, for how long?"

"What does time signify here?"

"Spoken like an Immortal," she snorted. She heard shouting, voices, and one loud roar, as the world suddenly returned; she turned to meet it.

The road was a mess because it wasn't really *road* anymore; there were patches of it that were still glowing an unpleasant orange, and whole new ditches that would kill any horses anyone was stupid enough to drive this far into the fief's interior. But there were only a few bodies on the ground, and most of those were moving, albeit not without help.

Morse was bleeding; something had lanced her cheek. She didn't appear to notice, and not even Tara fussed over Morse when she decided an injury was beneath contempt. But it was Mejrah's voice that was clearest, because Mejrah was shouting or crying—or both—as she pointed at Kaylin.

No, not at Kaylin. At the man who stood before her in his odd armor, his name exposed and held beneath the flat of her open palm.

CHAPTER 5

"Kaylin." Tiamaris's voice was the low rumble of moving earth. "Step back across the border."

Kaylin frowned. From where she was standing, she could no longer see it—not that it had ever been all that clear when there wasn't a small army of Shadows waiting along its edge. "Can I bring him with me?"

Smoke—a literal stream of it, forcefully expelled—eddied around her feet. Before the fieflord could follow it with words, Mejrah approached Kaylin, her hands lifted and turned palms out as if to imply that she was helpless. She spoke to the armored man, her voice low enough that it broke on syllables.

The man, still facing Kaylin, moved his head toward the old woman. His expression as he did could have broken stone hearts. Mejrah, however, turned to Kaylin and spoke rapid, agitated words—none of which made any sense. Language lessons had never seemed so profoundly important; unfortunately, no one present was yet expert enough to teach them.

"What is she saying?" Kaylin asked Maggaron.

"Can you not understand her words?"

"I wouldn't be asking if I could."

His brows rose in genuine surprise. "But—you are Chosen."

"I can't walk on water," she replied tersely. "And you clearly understand her. What did she say?"

"She wishes to know if what you have done is stable."

"Tell her I have no idea."

He did. Kaylin was running through Leontine phrases in her mind.

"She asks if you know who I am."

"Tell her—" Kaylin bit back the flippant response. "Does she know who you are?"

He didn't repeat the question; instead, he nodded. When he began to speak again—to Mejrah—Kaylin listened. But she listened, if it were possible, with her hands; she listened to the word that she hadn't released. It was warm, and it was bright; if she looked at it too long it burned itself into her vision, the way the sun could at the wrong height.

"Ascendant," Mejrah said. Kaylin could hear two words overlapping each other as the older woman spoke. It wasn't cacophony, but it was disturbing. "How is it that you come to be here?"

"Do you not understand? You are here."

"We came through the emptiness. We—all of our people that could be gathered—walked the gray space and the hungering void. We *are* here. But you..." She hesitated.

"I fell in battle."

"Yes. On plains far from these streets and this...city. But even here, the Shadows exist." This last was said with resignation and bitterness.

"Yes."

"They are not so strong here; the war in these lands has

barely begun. We will fight," she added, her voice a low growl.

Maggaron's smile was sharp and brief. He raised an arm in salute.

But the older woman was not yet done. "We did not think to see Ascendants again. How did you travel here?"

"I...did not travel here."

Mejrah was silent for a long moment. When she spoke again, her voice was harder—but it was also more brittle. "How is it that you command the darkness? How is it that you fight at the behest of our enemy?"

He flinched and turned away from her—but turned back as if shorn of will. "There is truth," he finally said, "in the stories of the Ancients. The Shadows spoke my name, and they knew me, and when they bid me follow, I could not disobey for long, although I did struggle. I came, at last, to the heart of the Shadow—and it is the heart of the world, Mejrah. What I have seen—what I have touched—" He fell silent. "I have fallen. But there is beauty and majesty in the Shadows; there is—there could be—freedom."

"If you were free," Kaylin asked, "would you stay in the Shadow?"

His smile was bitter. "No, Chosen. There is no freedom for me now. What they have, they hold, and they will hold it—"

"Until they're destroyed."

He shook his head, and his face developed the expression that Kaylin most loathed: pity. "They cannot be destroyed. They are eternal; they live and breathe and move and change. They defy death, just as—"

"As you do."

"No, Chosen. Their will is stronger than any other force they have encountered. They live in the web of the knowledge of worlds, and they feed from it. They move along its strands, and they change whatever they touch. They speak all languages, they can live in any environment. They require no breath, no warmth, no food."

"If they were that powerful, all worlds would already be Shadow. All of them. We can fight them. There are people here who are also powerful and ancient." She was acutely aware she wasn't one of them.

He did not speak; instead, he looked toward Tiamaris and Sanabalis. And then, to her great surprise, he bowed. His armor clanked. She wondered, given its weight, if he'd be able to stand up again without teetering, because she doubted she could have. "They are Dragons," he whispered.

"Yes."

He rose with an enviable ease. "They are the firstborn, and the oldest. Do you not understand what they are?"

A brief memory of Diarmat's first class came to mind. It was hard to feel any awe for someone you wanted to strangle so badly. "They're Dragons," she said.

"*Kaylin.*"

Kaylin turned to the fieflord. His eyes weren't orange; they were an unfortunate shade of red. Sanabalis was now standing by Tiamaris's side; *his* eyes were orange. And unlidded.

"I have his name," she told them. And then, after a pause, "He has one."

The two Dragons exchanged a glance. Sanabalis said almost gently, "I do not believe that is possible if he is of the People."

"Why?"

"They are mortal. They age and they die."

"So am I, and *I* have one."

The Dragons exchanged a more familiar glance. It was Tiamaris who answered. "And that is, of course, information that is best shouted loudly at the edge of a fief, where Shadows are

dominant." His breath was a plume of bright-colored flame.
"Do you *hold* his name?"

"Yes. But so do they."

"They?"

Actually, that was a damn good question. She didn't have an
answer, but hazarded one anyway. "The Shadows." Frowning,
she added, "What does happen if more than one person holds
a true name?"

"It depends," Tiamaris replied. He glanced at Sanabalis, and
Kaylin could almost see him passing the question off.

Sanabalis ran a hand through the long strands of thin beard.
"It would depend. Let us assume that you speak of only two
entities: yourself, in this case, and the Shadow. If you have
opposing goals—and again, we will assume for the sake of
simplification, that this is true—you will exert the force of
your will upon the name.

"The name will not break; it is not a physical object. But
the man will be pulled in two directions. The best that can
be achieved in that case is that he will be rendered immobile
and will do nothing."

"And the worst?"

"You sleep. You are easily distracted. You are not accustomed to enforcing your will and your desire upon others. I
do not believe any of these three things can be said of your
enemy. Kill him, if it is possible for you to do so; leave him, if
it is not. If he follows you now—and I believe he will—there
is no guarantee that he will not turn upon you, or upon any
of *us,* the moment your will flags.

"And he will be dangerous then. The power that he can
easily reach will be lessened, but he will be able to draw it;
he will be a window from the heart of the fiefs into the fief
of Tiamaris, and we are *already* undermined by some Shadow
we cannot yet locate."

She turned back to Maggaron. He smiled. It was not a happy smile, but unlike most smiles one saw in the fiefs, it wasn't cruel, either. Bending at the knee, he retrieved the sword that had fallen between them. "Chosen," he said. "Learn to speak the tongue of the People. Ask Mejrah what the Ascendants are, and how they are born.

"If I understood the Dragon Lord correctly, *you* bear a name much like mine, but you are, like the People, a thing of flesh and mortality. Take this. It will serve you well in your coming war."

She looked at the runed sword in his hand. It was no longer the greatsword of a giant; it had lost that form and shape when he had lost the same. But at its size it was still something even Severn would have difficulty wielding with any grace; it was a weapon of brute force.

"Take it, Chosen. Take it, or it will serve *me,* as it has done."

She shook her head. "I can't—"

But Mejrah shouted in her ear loudly enough that her teeth were rattling by the end of it. She didn't need to understand the language of the People to understand exactly what the old woman's demands were. She wanted Kaylin to take the sword. Kaylin's sword training was such that she was competent; she doubted she would ever be *good*.

And she didn't doubt, looking at the blade whose runes still glowed, that good was what *this* sword deserved. But she lifted her hand, and Maggaron placed the sword across her palm hard enough that the blade bit the skin of the single hand she'd lifted; the second was occupied. She wasn't willing to release him yet, and she therefore kept her hand around his name.

He shuddered once as the sword left him, and then took a step back.

Mejrah shouted at him.

Tiamaris, however, roared at Mejrah, and the old woman stilled. She didn't, however, shut up; instead, she lowered her voice and spoke quietly to Kaylin. Quiet didn't have the force of imperative behind it. "What is she saying?" she asked Maggaron. She couldn't focus clearly enough to pick up the language again.

His smile was slow and sweet around the edges; it was also sad. He shook his head. "Go with her, Chosen."

"Maggaron—"

"She wishes you to bring me to the People here. I cannot take that risk."

"You can't destroy yourself."

"No. But...the Shadows have less purchase here, and I do not think they will send me to the outlands again." He bowed. "I must go. Can you not hear them?"

Kaylin frowned. The rune beneath her palm was still warm, but it felt...less solid. "No," she told him, staring at the hatches and curved strokes beneath her palm. She began to speak the word again, and it gained brilliance, as if her syllables were filling it. His brows rose, and his eyes took on that light.

"How important is this?" she asked him. "Ask Mejrah."

Mejrah replied almost before he'd finished the sentence.

"She says it is very important, Chosen."

Kaylin nodded. "Tiamaris!"

The Dragon rumbled, his language as unintelligible for the moment as Mejrah's. "He's been to the heart of the Shadows; he knows something about them that we don't—or can't— know safely. I think it's worth taking the risk—but it's not my fief."

"Good of you to remember," the Dragon Lord replied. She couldn't see what he did next, but she heard steps, and Sanabalis entered her peripheral vision. "How strong is your hold?"

"I *don't know,* Sanabalis. I haven't fought many wars *inside* a living person before."

"If you aren't careful, you'll cut your hand in half," he observed. He walked past her until he stood like the third point of a very tight triangle, the other two of which were Kaylin and Maggaron. "I am aware of your dislike for magic," he told her calmly. "Unfortunately, some magic is now required."

She nodded. While she couldn't hear what Maggaron clearly could, she could *feel* it beneath her hand; the texture of the rune was shifting and changing. Not the word itself—the parts didn't bend, split, or fold. But it was, once again, losing solidity. She knew that when it became permeable enough, he'd be gone.

Sanabalis had given her warning. As usual, he had mastered the art of understatement. If she'd plastered her entire body—both sides, bottom of feet and top of head—against the most extreme door ward in the Imperial Palace, it would have tickled in comparison. She bit something—her tongue, her lip—and her mouth filled with the familiar and unpleasant salt of her own blood.

It was followed by the worst Leontine phrase she knew; it was all she could do not to drop the sword *and* the damn name simultaneously.

Sanabalis didn't seem to be particularly concerned—at least not with her. But he studied Maggaron's face, and as he did, Maggaron's eyes began to shift colors in a rapid cycle. She'd never seen anything like it before, and had she, she would have immediately assumed the person possessing those eyes was dangerously insane. But Maggaron's expression didn't change at all; he continued to stare at Kaylin. It was very disturbing.

"Sanabalis," she said, forcing the syllables through gritted teeth, "is this entirely necessary?"

"It is."

"Will-it-be-over-soon?"

"Yes."

She didn't even ask him what he was doing because his answer might have prolonged the casting. But her eyes began to water, and her vision began to blur; she saw two or three of Maggaron begin to separate as she watched. The blood in her mouth did *not* help. People began to speak—shout, cry, babble, and *hiss*—in a way that destroyed the actual weight of syllables. She bent slightly into her knees to brace herself, and then bent slightly more, because if her legs were too stiff she'd probably topple, and folding usually left fewer bruises.

She could barely see Maggaron now; she could see—and feel—his name, and she clung to that, tightening her fingers into rigid claws. Unfortunately for Kaylin, her suspicion that the sensation of hand-on-rune was a metaphor that didn't *actually* involve her real hands was proved correct. It didn't hold her up.

Nothing did; she felt as if she were walking—slowly—through the portal in Castle Nightshade. Or rather, that Sanabalis had uprooted said portal and had dropped it, in one go, on her head.

Kaylin. The single word was cool and clear, and none of its syllables—all two—clashed with anything else. Even given the source, it was a relief.

Nightshade?

Where are you?

In Tiamaris.

You are not in Tiamaris, was his edged reply.

I am—she stopped. *I'm less than ten yards from the border of the fief.*

Return to the fief. Now.

So much for relief. *We have a bit of a situation here,* she said as tersely as she could, given that she wasn't actually speaking any of this aloud. *I'm leaving the heartland as soon as Sanabalis stops—*

Stops what?

Whatever the bleeding hells he's doing.

What is he doing? Kaylin—what are you doing?

I'm falling over.

Nightshade had never had a sense of humor. He did, however, have a temper. He also had the universal condescending arrogance of the Immortal everywhere. She *felt* his frustration and his annoyance.

Tell Lord Sanabalis to stop whatever it is he's doing. Tell him to stop now. There is a danger.

She couldn't even *see* Sanabalis by this point, and what she'd had of breakfast was threatening to revolt; telling a Dragon Lord—even one as tolerant as Sanabalis—what to do was so far out of the question it hadn't even occurred as a possibility. The frosty and furious arrogance of the Barrani wasn't Kaylin's by birth or inclination.

She started to think as much—saying it was beyond her—but the flow of defensive thought was interrupted by something a lot less pleasant: thunder and the flash of something that looked like black lightning.

She heard Nightshade curse, and she understood the meaning. The syllables themselves were—or would have been in any other circumstance—a delight of discovery because they were Barrani, and Barrani, to her knowledge, didn't *have* curse words. But delight at that discovery was swamped by the sudden certainty that the danger that Nightshade feared was about to arrive.

On the heels of Nightshade's sharp word, she felt the pain and the disorientation recede in a rush, as if someone had pulled the plug. That someone was Sanabalis. As the pain and the visual distortion fled, she felt two things: the physical, full-body trembling that was often the result of portal crossing, and the hair-raising, sharp pain that was *also* the result of strong magic in such proximity.

Her hand was somehow still clasped around the broadest of strokes that comprised Maggaron's name and she blinked rapidly as his multiple wavering images coalesced into a single shape again. She turned, still holding his name, and also holding the sword he had handed into her keeping by the blade, which would have caused any number of sword experts to deafen her in their rush to have her handle it properly. Since it had, in fact, cut her palm, she didn't require this. She set the blade on the ground, and picked it up again by its hilt.

It was, of course, in her off-hand, but at this point, it didn't matter; the hair on the back of her neck was rigid. She was afraid to release Maggaron's name, and that fear was just a bit stronger than her fear of being unarmed. Adjusting the sword, she turned. Oddly enough, her grip on the name itself didn't change at all, even though Maggaron was now behind her. She could see the word; she couldn't see him. This meant something. She wasn't certain what.

At the moment, it didn't matter. She could see a black, amorphous cloud rising—coalescing—in the not-far-enough distance; it was the source of the dark lightning.

Tiamaris roared a warning in all-out Dragon, and Sanabalis roared back. Before Kaylin could speak—or react—at all, Sanabalis lifted her with ease and leaped toward the border, where Tiamaris and Tara were standing. The People had pulled back, and huddled more or less behind them. Kaylin noted that Sanabalis had also picked up Mejrah, who was, in theory, too large and cumbersome to be tossed around like a sack of potatoes.

Maggaron, however, didn't move. Kaylin tried to shout

his name, and then, remembering what she held, thought it instead. *Maggaron.*

No, Chosen.

She cursed him in every language she could—which now included Barrani. *Maggaron, cross the border,* damn you.

It is not safe, Chosen—

It's not safe to stand there—you don't understand what that *is.*

Of all unexpected things, he laughed. It was a wild roar, just slightly quieter than the Dragons' normal speaking voices would have been. *"I?"* he shouted. "*I* do not understand what *that* is?" He swept an arm toward the approaching cloud; as Kaylin watched it, she saw that it was *eating* the ground it passed over.

His laughter grew wilder, and she heard pain break free of amusement. "It is the Shadowstorm, Chosen. What do you think I was born for? What do you think the Ascendants *are?*"

Crazy. She didn't say the word. And then cursed as his laughter deepened. *We don't have time for this.*

You cannot take the risk of—

Yes, damn it, I can. She took a deep breath as Sanabalis deposited her more or less on her feet beside the Avatar of the Tower. Tara was glowing. The whole of her form—winged, an echo of Aerians—was made of shining alabaster. But stone or not, she moved; Tiamaris didn't.

"Tara," he said, speaking in sharp Elantran, "do not risk too much."

"It is a test," was the cool reply, "of the boundaries and the area over which my responsibility lies. Kaylin," she added in a tone of voice that no friendly, itinerant gardener should have been able to use, "bring your follower across the border."

"I'm *trying.* He's afraid that the Shadow—"

"I *am* the Tower. I am the border. Bring him; the responsibility will be on my head."

On her head, Kaylin thought, but if she failed—if Maggaron was right—it would be writ in the bodies of the People and the humans who still lived in the fief of Tiamaris. She was willing to take that risk; she'd already attempted to call Maggaron. At Nightshade's insistence she had done that before—to him—and she had felt his counter.

No; it wasn't the same. She had *called*. She hadn't commanded.

She'd never truly attempted to impose her will on Maggaron in a way that she didn't try to force it on anyone else in her life—by shouting, pleading, swearing, cajoling, even demanding. What the name gave her meant that she *could* do more.

Would she? If he stood in the streets in the path of a storm that could—if the Dragons were right—literally unmake, remake, or worse—everything that he was, could she *force* him to do what she desired?

Maggaron!

He didn't, and wouldn't, move. Everyone was shouting now. Mejrah, in Kaylin's ear, as if volume could compensate for lack of comprehension. Tiamaris was roaring, and if it wasn't in her ear, he was less than ten feet away, so it had the same effect.

Swallowing air and strengthening resolve, Kaylin looked at Maggaron, and his name flashed like lightning or gold. Yes, she thought grimly. Yes, *I would.* He had given her the ability. His folly gave her the *right.* She called his name as if his name were part of her, and she *pulled* him, focusing all her will on the simple act of motion: his.

It hurt her. It hurt, and she almost stopped. But Maggaron had moved, taking drunken steps toward Kaylin—and, more important, away from the moving cloud.

She heard Nightshade's chuckle as she hesitated. *Do you think that power is taken—or practiced—free of cost, little one?*

Since the answer was more or less *yes,* and since he now already knew it, she didn't reply. Instead, she looked at Maggaron and said, *Don't make me do this. Please.*

She could see his eyes so clearly they might have been inches from her face. *If you cannot do even this, Chosen, how will you protect them from me, should the time come?*

Damn you, she thought, hating him for testing her this way. *Damn it, if it comes down to their lives, I can. But this isn't their lives—it's yours. Maggaron, please.*

She felt his laughter; it was sharp and unkind. But he wasn't wholly unkind; he did as she all but begged. He walked— quickly—toward where she now stood, his name in her hand. She grimaced, and then, as if letting go of a security blanket, she removed her hand from the rune; it remained in her vision, something Nightshade's name had never done.

Kaylin, Nightshade said. He, too, was laughing. *You are far too weak for the power you have been granted. But you will learn.*

The first thing Tiamaris did was order a retreat from the edge of the border. Everyone obeyed—and given he spoke Dragon, Kaylin was surprised that the People understood his command. Then again, she didn't understand Dragon, either, and she had. Severn was waiting—always, and in his usual grim silence.

But Severn wasn't looking at Maggaron, although the rest of the People sure as hells were. He was looking at Kaylin. More accurately, he was looking at the sword in her hand. She glanced at it, and her gaze stuck. It had changed shape. The blade was shorter—not long-knife short, but short-sword short; the hilt was practical and almost unadorned. It was straight and it looked—to her eyes—like a normal weapon, except for the obvious runes along the flat.

Her first thought was, *I broke it.*

Her second thought was, on the other hand, *Maggaron.* He was watching her, his eyes a flat shade between blue and brown. "Your enemies will not hesitate to do what you could not do."

"If I have to do it, I'll do it."

To say he looked dubious was an understatement. She started to speak, and stopped as Tara touched her shoulder.

"Kaylin," the Avatar said. "Come."

"Where?"

In answer, Tara led her to the edge of the border, which had once again become an invisible, theoretical line across the ground. The storm that she had seen so clearly was still moving, and it moved toward where the People had gathered. Kaylin tried to see not the cloud itself, but what its passage left behind; she couldn't. The billowing darkness was too dense.

"What are you doing?" she asked Tara.

"Containing the storm," was the reply. "There is a reason that the Shadowstorms do not leave the fiefs."

"Wait—are you always aware of the storms?"

"No. Not always. But even were I not sensitive to their proximity, I could hardly fail to notice this one." She lifted her arms. Her wings spread and their tips rose, framing her. They also almost knocked Kaylin off her feet.

"Watch," Tara said as Kaylin adjusted both her stance and her distance.

"Watch what?"

"The storm. I do not see as you see, Chosen. I see as a Tower sees. Watch. My Lord watches, as well."

"Not at a very safe distance."

"He is behind the border. The storm will *not* pass me."

CHAPTER 6

The storm drew closer. Kaylin took an involuntary step back, and felt Severn's hand on her shoulder, steadying her. She smiled; he couldn't see it, but it didn't matter; he could feel the hand she lifted and placed over his. The clouds were thick and as they approached, the darkness revealed itself as a gray-green haze. They looked like thunderclouds to Kaylin, although she'd never seen them this close before.

But thunderclouds moving at a distance were impersonal; only the lightning they shed was a danger. These clouds, similar in color, contained a more immediate threat. She had seen the Devourer as a void or a spreading darkness; she saw these clouds as something entirely different. Their moving folds hinted at shapes—both familiar and new—breaking and distorting them before Kaylin could fully catch or name them.

She heard Dragon conversation, but at a remove, as if it were thunder.

Which was strange. She realized this storm and its clouds were *silent*. Shapes continued to unfurl as they approached

Tara, blocking out sunlight and shadowing her white visage. White, pale, it was as giving as stone.

Stone could tell a story if one understood its cracks and the way it wore over time. But this stone was new. Kaylin thought, watching Tara, that it hadn't yet been tested. Or maybe it had, and it had faltered once. As if she could hear the thought, Tara tensed and her wings flexed.

The clouds hit then.

All sense that they had anything in common with the storms that occasionally covered the city skies vanished; they battered the air above and in front of the Avatar, stretching and thinning as they did. Stretched and thin, they were blacker, darker; they lost the tantalizing hint of moving forms, and for a moment, became two large hands, fingers pressed and curved against nothing.

The storm roared, as if it were a disembodied dragon; there was both agony and fury in the sound. Through it all, Tara stood like a wall, lifting her chin as she gazed into its heart in defiance.

The heart of the storm gazed *back*. Kaylin could see its eyes, disembodied but visceral, present. She could see a mouth, made of dense shadow, forming words that she couldn't understand but could almost see.

Tara's response was clearer; it was more solid. Seen more than heard, runes filled the space between the two: Tower and destroyer. The ground beneath the Tower's feet shifted, cobbles melting and reforming over and over again as the storm sought purchase and Tara defied it. Denied ground, it rose, warping the heavens. Above the storm the sky became what opals might have been if they had been truly repulsive. And cold.

Lightning sheared stone, but this lightning, from that sky, wasn't a flash of white: it was a lance of many colors and those colors bled, like chaos, into the ground itself, defining the hard line of the border in a way that nothing else had. Where the Tower's Avatar stood, the known, the reliable, held sway; where the storm raged, nothing did.

Kaylin looked toward Sanabalis, who hadn't yet gone Dragon, although his eyes were *almost* red, and his nostrils— in human form—were flared. He'd also managed to singe his beard, something she'd've bet was impossible. "Sanabalis, is this—"

He lifted a hand, swatting her words to one side. Given the color of his eyes, she let them go, and turned, reluctantly, back to the storm. It was *screaming.*

Severn caught her wrist and yanked her around, stepping to the side to avoid the flailing edge of the sword she hadn't dropped. He pulled her into his arms, her back to his chest, and held her tightly, lowering his jaw until it rested close to her right ear. She knew he was speaking. But she felt his words as a tickle of breath and a sensation; she couldn't *hear* anything but the sound of the storm itself.

The storm and her own answering cries.

She wanted to run to it. To run *into* it. Hadn't she done that once, already? Maybe this time, maybe *this time,* she could travel back to the night that Steffi and Jade had died. And this time, she would be armed. This time she wasn't thirteen. This time she *knew* what would happen. She could *change* it. She could *unmake* it. She could do what she'd failed to do then.

She swallowed her screams, opened her eyes, forced herself to *look.*

Why doesn't it affect you the same way? she asked Severn in the silence and privacy she almost never used.

I'm not you. She felt his smile. *It's almost passed,* he added, and she opened eyes that she hadn't realized she'd closed. The sky was still the wrong color above the angry mass of darkness, but the darkness itself was dissipating, and its screams had faded into attenuated cries that still broke the heart.

She preferred multi-eyed demonic heads with obsidian claws and mouths in their butt ends.

"When will the sky return to normal?" she asked as Severn released her almost reluctantly and stepped back.

"Normal?" Tara lifted her head, her eyes narrowing briefly. "Ah. Not, I think, anytime soon. It is…a statement, Kaylin."

"Of what?"

"The sky is…off limits? Is that you how say it?"

Kaylin nodded.

"The sky is off limits for my Lord, should he choose to attempt to cross the border in that fashion."

"What will happen to him if he does?"

"No one can say. But we can be certain that *something* will."

Kaylin hesitated, and then said, "The Shadows aren't fond of the storm, either."

Tara frowned, and then inclined her head, lowering her wings and folding them across her back. Silence descended, and as it did, the wings folded themselves into the shades of brown that were the Avatar's gardening clothing. It was a surprisingly effective indication that the conflict—and its inherent danger—was over. "No," she told Kaylin, her gaze still fixed at a point beyond her own borders, "they are not."

"Then you don't know for certain what might happen."

"No. We know only that there is change, and it is neither predictable nor, in the end, desired by those who have been changed. Our history is…incomplete."

"But I came to you, at your awakening."

"Yes." Tara still spoke in a voice better suited to the height of cold stone fortification than the gardening clothes she wore.

"And I came through the storm."

"No."

"But Tiamaris called it—"

"He was incorrect."

"Does he *know* he was wrong?"

"Yes. The borders and their defense are the reason I was... born. They are not, however, the sole reason I was *reborn*. I want this life," she added, and as she did, her voice softened, and her eyes lost the hard flint of steel. She now looked exhausted. "We've discussed this at length. My Lord felt that the storm—that what he had identified as storm—had not only proved fortuitous, but, in some fashion, benevolent."

This stretched Kaylin's strict definition of benevolent, although she couldn't argue with the eventual outcome.

"He thus argued that the storms themselves ultimately had some greater purpose, and that some faith or trust might be placed in them. He is willing to risk much," she added, voice soft, expression pensive. Then she shook herself, reminding Kaylin very much of one of the women who worked three days a week in the office as she did—which wasn't generally something she thought of when she thought of ancient, god-touched edifices.

"You *know* it wasn't a storm."

"Yes."

"But in shape—"

"And in *look*, yes. There were reasons that my Lord made his assumption, Kaylin. This," she said, pointing to the now empty and still air in front of her, "was a storm. Can you see the difference?"

The urge to be humorous came and went. "Yes," Kaylin replied. She did so slowly enough that Tara raised a single impatient brow. "The first storm we encountered had no voice."

"Voice?"

"You couldn't hear this one? It was *screaming*, Tara."

"I told you, Chosen; I do not perceive Shadow the way you perceive it." Her eyes closed for a few seconds. "Nor does my Lord."

Morse joined Tara. The former fieflord's lieutenant had taken one new gash across her forearm, which had destroyed padding but had managed to break very little skin.

"So," Kaylin asked her, "this happen often?"

"Every other day."

Tara frowned. "Morse, it doesn't happen every other—"

"Figure of speech," Morse broke in quickly. Kaylin stifled even the hint of a smile. "Believe it or not, it's better than it was before the fieflord."

"The—oh, you mean Tiamaris."

"I don't mean Barren." Morse spit.

Tara watched her covertly, as if fascinated by the gesture, and then turned back to Kaylin.

"I understood what Morse meant," Kaylin said quickly. "These border attacks happen frequently." She glanced at the People.

Tara frowned. "Illien is still within my Tower, as my Lord's guest. I remember Illien, and I remember the feel of the borders of his domain before...I could no longer sense them. You can cross the border," she added. "And at the moment, it is safe; the storm has driven the Shadows from them, and they will return slowly, if at all today. I do not think you will notice the difference, if you travel farther up the road; the road here has been destroyed by the storm, and it will be a while before it once again looks like the other half of a street, at least to mortal vision."

"It'll—it'll go back to what it once was?"

"Yes."

"The fief's streets didn't. And the buildings that were half consumed or transformed by Shadows—those didn't, either."

"No. That is one of the differences between the Shadow-lands and your own. Your lands—my Lord's lands—are solid; they exist.

"The Shadowlands are more malleable; they do not take scars in the same way. Where Shadows are strong, the land-scape on that side of the border will respond to the weight of its call, the force of its power. The buildings will shift and change, growing or sinking or fading; the streets will become molten pools or gaping pits. But when the Shadow passes, so does the changes it made.

"Were *I* to likewise make such drastic changes in the geog-raphy of my fief, when the battle was over, what would remain would be those destroyed buildings, the molten rock, and the fissures."

"Can I ask how you know this?"

Tara raised a brow. "The knowledge was built into me," she finally replied. "And when I close my eyes, I can see the dim and faded image of ancient battles; I can hear their attenuated battle cries." She smiled then, and it was an almost bitter smile. "I am not what you are, Kaylin. Why do you need to know?"

Kaylin shook her head. "I want to know—which is different from need—because it's always a good idea to have as much knowledge of your enemy as possible. It'd be better if any of it made any sense." Saying this, she lifted the sword that was still, against all odds, in her hands. "Take this, for instance. I would swear it was a greatsword meant for a giant when I first laid eyes on it."

Tara said nothing.

"...please don't tell me you recognize this weapon."

"I do not recognize the weapon," was the Tower's reply. It was evasive, and honestly? While Tara had learned many things about interacting with people, she wasn't actually *good* at some of them. Which, given she could take you apart and find her way—with ease—to the darkest and most painful of your memories, said something. Kaylin, at this moment, wasn't sure what.

"What do the runes on the blade say?"

"Runes?" The Tower frowned. Glancing at Tiamaris, who was now waiting, wings folded, in the still streets, she said, "My Lord, I believe the danger has passed for the moment. May we retire?"

His eyes shifted color. "You are injured?"

"No! No. But the storms are tiring."

"I will remain. Morse!"

Morse nodded. It wouldn't pass muster as respectful anywhere but the fiefs, but since that's where they were standing, it worked. "You want me to keep watch on the construction?"

"The People are here. Escort the Lady home."

Tara pointed at Maggaron, and Tiamaris's brows constricted; they were silent for a long moment, but at length, he nodded.

The Lady's escort was not confined to Morse; Kaylin and Severn traveled with her, at her request, Maggaron walking to their left in subdued silence. Subdued or no, he still wore armor, and he was still eight feet–plus in height; he cleared streets just by existing.

Lord Sanabalis, however, remained—in human form—at the side of his former student. His gaze flickered rapidly over the sword in Kaylin's hands, but he chose not to say a word. Loudly, and with an expression that implied that all the words he held in abeyance would be put to better use later.

The border streets grew smaller as they walked, and the streets themselves were, not surprisingly, empty of anyone that wasn't about eight feet tall. Even the children of the new arrivals remained out of sight. Morse, in the absence of Tiamaris, relaxed. She didn't so much walk as move while slouching.

"So. This happens a lot?" Kaylin asked, picking up the strands of their previous conversation, if it could be called that.

"Not the storm. But the Shadows have gone *nuts* in the last couple of days."

"Since the People arrived?"

"The giants?"

"Is that what they're called hereabouts?"

"Nah. We call them the Norannir."

"Why?"

"It's what they call themselves." Morse grinned. "It's more or less what they call anyone who isn't a Shadow, and we adopted it. The other Imperial guy—"

"Sanabalis." When Severn cleared his throat, Kaylin added, "Lord Sanabalis."

"He's attempting to learn some of their language, and attempting to at least teach their kids some of ours. The kids pick it up faster."

"What else have the Norannir been doing?"

"Anything. I mean *anything* they're asked to do, if we can make it clear. But…they're not afraid of the Shadow. They hate it, don't get me wrong, but they don't fear it. They don't fear the Ferals, either; they make camp *beside* the damn border, and they watch." She grimaced. "Truth is, they make the streets safer just by living there.

"But our people? They're fuckin' mice. They scatter at the sight of the Norannir."

"Big surprise. They were generally smart enough to scatter at the sight of you, and you weren't eight feet tall and wielding an ax they probably couldn't lift on a good day."

Morse was willing to concede this, but only barely. "I *wanted* them to be afraid. I *was* a threat. Avoiding me? Made sense. But avoiding the Norannir makes none."

Clearly, life in Tiamaris—the fief, not the Dragon—agreed with Morse; she'd never cared much whether people made sense before.

"They'll stay if the Lady's with them, though. They love her more than they fear the Norannir."

"We can probably work with that."

Tara, who had been walking in silence toward the Tower—with the odd stop to look at dirt or grass—turned to look at Kaylin. She raised a brow to make clear she'd heard the words and wanted details.

"The Norannir are going to be living in the fief. They may make their way out in ones and twos—I did, Severn did—but this is where most of them are going to stay. The rest of the People who already live here don't have much choice, and even if they thought they did, they wouldn't say anything.

"But they trust you now." In truth, it had taken much, much less time for that trust to build than Kaylin would have guessed. "If they trust you *enough* that they're willing to risk their lives in the presence of the strangers, we can work with that. We can make the strangers seem less, well, strange."

"How?" Morse demanded.

"I don't know how much time Tara has, but…these language lessons. Sanabalis has a good idea once in a while; he's trying to teach the kids. What if we do it in the other direction?"

"What?"

"We teach the human kids the Norannir language. Tara can be there to help. It doesn't have to be much, and it doesn't have to be useful right away. But the kids'll spend time with the Norannir, and anything that doesn't terrify kids…"

"Who's going to volunteer their kids?"

Kaylin said, "I don't know. But we won't be the ones asking—Tara will. Besides, not all the kids have living parents. Offer them a meal and they'll come." Morse nodded and they both looked at Tara.

Tara, however, looked ahead to the Tower. "Come," she said quietly. "You asked me about the sword."

"You said you didn't—"

"I don't. I don't, but I can—in the words of the fief— guess."

The Tower doors still boasted no door wards, and this, more than anything else, made it instantly feel like home. Or as much a home as a rising pillar of white stone, surrounded by carrot, beet, and potato gardens could ever be. The doors rolled inward as Tara approached them, but many, many of the fancier buildings in the City had doors that did that, as well. Here, she bowed to Maggaron.

"You will be safe within," she told him.

"What I see—"

"You will be safe. You cannot harm *me*. And if I do not wish you to leave, you will remain within the Tower for the rest of your natural existence."

He didn't find this as off-putting as Kaylin might have were she in his shoes. Instead, he nodded. "I have no weapon to offer," he added, as if this made sense. Clearly, to the Norannir, it did. Tara nodded.

Kaylin, on the other hand, said, "This sword—"

"It is yours," was his grave reply.

"Yes, I got that. But—did it happen to come with a sheath?"

His brows, which were pale, rose in an arch that almost touched his hairline.

"I'll take that as a no."

Maggaron looked to Tara; Tara said nothing. Together, they entered the Tower, shadowed by Morse. Kaylin and Severn pulled up the rear.

As Towers went, this one—at least in the front—was stable. The foyer looked the same as it had any other time Kaylin had crossed the threshold, and the long wide halls still looked as if a Dragon in native form could comfortably maneuver them. The doors were doubled, and wide, where they could be seen at all. Given the changing nature of Castle Nightshade, this brought Kaylin some comfort.

Maggaron had no difficulty entering the doors; nor did he find the halls themselves in any way cramped or confining.

"Where are we going?" Kaylin asked when Tara opened the doors that led into the main—or what Kaylin assumed was the main—halls.

"To the mirror," was the quiet reply.

Kaylin managed to hide a grimace, in large part because Tara had already turned and begun to walk away. The mirror within the Tower wasn't an actual mirror; it was a small pool whose still water was reflective. Kaylin's previous experience with said mirror hadn't exactly been comforting.

Tara raised a brow, as if she could hear the thought; given who she was and where they were, she probably could. "I think you will find the visit less exciting this time," she offered.

"Think?"

"You are unusual, so there is always the possibility that something entirely unforeseen could occur."

"This has something to do with the sword?"

"No. Not directly."

"With Maggaron?"

"No. I find him curious," Tara added, "because it is clear

to me that he is *not* immortal; it is clear, as well, that he has a true name. These two things should not be able to coexist."

Kaylin cleared her throat.

Tara raised a brow. "I am aware of your claims, Kaylin. I am aware of what you carry. I am not yet aware of how it affects either you, or the name itself; nor am I certain whether or not the name can be used against you, as true names can otherwise be used.

"But in the case of this man, the name *can* be so used; it is part of him."

"You can tell that just by looking?"

"You cannot?"

"Never mind." Kaylin turned to Maggaron and said, "Mejrah called you Ascendant. What does that mean?"

It was his turn to look confused. "You do not understand what an Ascendant *is?* But you—you are Chosen."

"I'm what passes for Chosen in *this* world. And in *this* world, until a few weeks ago, there were no Norannir. And no Ascendants, either."

"I do not understand."

Join the club, Kaylin thought. "The Norannir now live in a world that's mostly populated by people like me. Or like my companion, Corporal Handred."

"And Dragons."

"There aren't so many Dragons as all that," Kaylin replied. "One of them is the Lord of this fief. I think there are five Dragons in total; one of those five is Emperor, so he'd be considered the Lord of the fief *I* live in. Which is not this one."

"And this Tower? Is it not yours?"

"No, it is definitely *not* mine. It's the home of Lord Tiamaris—the one with the large wings, the long neck, and the impressive set of teeth." Pausing, she added, "What are Dragons to the Norannir? I get the impression you didn't have them at home."

"Our stories of our own home are best told by the elder: she is the keeper of our tales." He had stopped walking, but so had Tara, and she'd tilted her chin in that particular way that meant she was paying attention.

Kaylin watched his expression as she asked her next question. "The Norannir clearly hadn't seen Dragons before they came here. They were really…uncomfortable…about their transformation to and from Dragon form the first time they saw it—they thought the Dragons might be Shadows.

"But you saw Tiamaris and recognized him. Maggaron, you knew Dragons."

CHAPTER 7

Tara approached the closed double doors at the hall's end. They were exactly as Kaylin remembered them, as was the rest of the hall. They rolled open into a room that was also familiar: runes glowed on the walls, separated by standing pillars; these pillars surrounded a shallow, circular pool of water that was absolutely still.

Maggaron hesitated, still pinned by Kaylin's gaze. At length he turned and followed where Tara led. He hadn't answered the question; Kaylin *knew* it was because he would have lied. Which made no sense. "Maggaron—"

"If you want an answer I am sworn not to give, you have the option of forcing it from me."

She cursed briefly, and in Barrani. This cheered her up; she was going to have so much fun at the office with that word.

They entered the room, Severn pulling up the rear, and the doors rolled quietly—but not ominously—shut behind them. Every part of this building was in some way part of Tara; it *was* her physical form, her body. Sanabalis might not understand why the citizens of the fief didn't fear the Avatar, but Kaylin did; Tara, at her most terrifying, stood against things that had demonstrably killed—or worse—people's neighbors in the past few months. While people had famously short memories, they weren't *that* short.

"Kaylin?" Tara asked.

She lifted the sword that was still entirely without a scabbard.

Tara frowned. "Do you wish me to take it? You don't mind?"

Something about the way she asked the question caused an answering frown across Kaylin's lips. "Should I?" She held the weapon out. It was, absent runes, a sword. It looked decently forged, decently put together; the hilt was fancier than Kaylin would have ideally liked, because fancy hilts were a total pain in the butt to keep clean.

Tara held out a hand, and Kaylin put the sword's hilt—not the blade, as Maggaron had done—into her palm. Tara was watching her face closely. "You feel…nothing?"

"Should I?"

"I don't know. I would have said, had I been asked, that you must." She turned to Maggaron. "You gave her this blade."

He nodded, and then his glance bounced off her gaze and landed somewhere on the wall just past her shoulder. "I did."

"Did you not feel its pull?"

He was silent.

Tara frowned again. She lifted the sword, examining the runes along the blade as if she were reading a letter.

"What do they say?" Kaylin asked her.

Tara was silent, absorbed in her inspection. When she spoke again, it was to the Norannir. "Could you have given her this blade at all if your name were entirely your own?"

He grimaced. "I do not know, Lady. The blades call *us*

when we are finished our training and we are taken to the spire of ascension. If we are not called, we go no further, although many who have failed the test of sword have gone on to lead, and lead well."

"When you say call, what do you mean? Do the swords literally speak?" This question, Kaylin could have asked. She hadn't, but she was interested in the answer.

His answer was quiet, and long in coming. "Yes," he finally said.

Kaylin glanced at the blade that now rested in Tara's hand. "It didn't speak to me," she told the Avatar. "It changed shape, but it didn't speak."

Tara examined the sword once more. After a pause she spoke, and the word traveled down Kaylin's spine as if it had been hissed in her ear. The sword's runes began to glow, the color shifting from pale blue to a white gold that was hard to look at for long. Tara's eyes, when she looked up, were literal stone, which happened when she forgot to maintain their appearance. The rest of her face looked normal. "Tara, what do the runes say?"

Tara was silent for a long moment, scrutinizing the blade's flat. At length she said, "I cannot read them. I cannot *see* them clearly, Kaylin. I can sense that they are there, no more. The sword—it did not speak to you."

"No. Should it have?"

"But it took a shape that you could more easily wield. Maggaron, did the sword speak to you?"

"I answered—"

"No, not upon your ascension. Today. In the streets of the heartlands."

Once again, he turned away. "Yes, Lady."

"When? I apologize if this is uncomfortable," she added. The words were not gently spoken.

"When she spoke my name," was the soft reply. "When the Chosen spoke my name, the sword spoke to me." He started to speak, stopped, and turned away completely, but his expression was so wounded Kaylin reached out and caught Tara's shoulder, pulling her back.

Tara, eyes still marbled stone with no whites, no pupils, and no irises, frowned. "If we do not understand the nature of the weapon's interaction with this man, we will not understand the weapon itself."

"It doesn't matter," Kaylin said, pitching her voice as low as possible. "I think we can guess at the answer to at least that question."

Tara hesitated, and then color returned to her eyes as they lost that disturbing appearance of carved rock. "Can I ask him what the last thing the sword said was?"

Kaylin, looking at the blade, could also guess the answer. "I think—I think the sword told him to give it to—to someone else."

"To give it, Chosen, to you," was the soft reply. "I have not heard her voice for so long—" He shook himself then. "She must be speaking to you; her shape is now yours. You cannot hear her?"

"No."

"Have you tried?"

"Well, no. It's a sword—I didn't expect it to try to hold a conversation."

He appeared to be genuinely scandalized; it made him look younger. "Please—try. She *has* a voice, and if you hear it once—" his voice broke, but this time he continued "—you will hear it until you fall."

"As you did."

"As I did."

"And you can't hear her now?" It was hard, to give a sword a gender.

"No, Chosen. She is no longer mine, and I—I am no longer hers."

Tara, mindful of Kaylin's words, said, "But you carried her into the Shadow, and she absorbed some of what you absorbed."

He nodded.

"And you're certain the sword is both whole and safe?"

"Safe? She is as you see her."

"Safe to use. Uncorrupted."

"She cannot be corrupted." There was no doubt at all in his words.

Kaylin lifted a hand. "She might not be corruptible," she pointed out, "but the fact is you used her to cleave great chunks of ground to open a crevice that passed beneath the borders here. It doesn't matter if she can't be *changed* if you can use her at the command of Shadows."

He said nothing.

"Maggaron—"

"I will not speak of it further unless you force the words from me," he replied. "But she is—as she always was—blameless. I could not cast her away; the weakness was mine. She is now in your hands. Mejrah knows; take her to Mejrah and she will begin to teach you."

Tara shook her head. "I do not like this," she finally said.

"The sword?"

"Or the connection between the sword and the bearer. There is something that is not quite right here." She turned to Kaylin. "I suggest that you do not wield the weapon until more of its nature is understood."

Kaylin shrugged. "I'm not great with a sword, anyway. Do you want to keep it for now?"

Tara hesitated again, and then nodded. She carried the sword to the still, and untouched, surface of the mirror, and lowered it gently toward the water. The mirror's surface began to ripple. Tara spoke slowly as she held the sword—Kaylin couldn't understand a word of the speech. But the rhythm of the words implied ritual, not conversation.

The water began to rise, and the Avatar frowned. She spoke again, and this time the cadence was different—but Kaylin saw no images reflected in the water's surface; there was too much turbulence. "Tara?"

Tara frowned. She shifted her grip on the hilt and brought it down into the water in one sudden rush of movement.

The water *parted*. Anywhere where the sword's edge was, it wasn't.

"Tara, the water's not supposed to do that, is it?"

"It is not entirely water, and as you have apparently surmised, no."

"You weren't going to leave it *in* the water, were you?"

"No, Kaylin. But I wished to access information about the runes on the blade itself."

"You can't."

"I cannot access any information relevant to this weapon at all. The mirror does not…see it…clearly."

Kaylin wasn't certain how mirrors—of any kind—"saw." It wasn't one of the technical details explained in Magical Theory 101; if it had been, she'd probably have paid a lot more attention. But as a student in that particular class, she'd been expected to accept as incontrovertible truth whatever the teacher laid down as "fact."

What she'd taken out of the class, however, was basic: when magic was working properly, things were fine. When magic broke down—like, say, carriage joists—things went downhill very quickly, and not in entirely predictable ways. "Maybe we shouldn't try."

Tara lifted a brow. "Perhaps. But I find the sword disturbing. I am aware of the ways in which weapons were imbued with magic; with the oldest of magics, the enchantments were not entirely predictable. Even so, there is something about this blade that is strange. I will keep it for the moment."

Kaylin, however, shook her head and glanced pointedly at the roiling water. "It hasn't hurt me, yet," she told the Tower's Avatar. "And it hasn't had any effect on me that I can see. But it's certainly having an effect on the Tower. I'll keep it." She grimaced. "And try to find a damn sheath for it." Turning to Maggaron, she said, "What did you use for a sheath?"

"A…sheath?" He stared at her for a moment, and then said in a clear and distinct voice, "What have I done? What did you ask me to do?"

She realized that he was speaking not to her but to the sword that currently rested in Tara's hands. What was disturbing was the attenuated sound of a disembodied *snicker*.

Tara returned the sword to Kaylin. "Perhaps you are correct," she said quietly. "But…be careful if you decide to use the blade." She stepped away from the pool and then said, "Have you eaten?"

Maggaron accompanied them into a hall that branched off the main one. He was silent in the way that badly shaken people are. Kaylin, who'd been perfectly serious about a sheath for the weapon, couldn't bring herself to ask again. But there were other questions she wanted to ask.

"Maggaron, how long have you been trapped in the—the heartlands?"

"I do not know, Chosen. Time does not pass in the Shadows the way it does in my homeland. The sun rises and sets in a manner that makes no sense, and night is oft long." He hesitated, and then added, "She would know."

He meant the sword. "She's not speaking to me, yet; I don't think she'd answer the question. How much can you clearly remember?"

"Enough. I was not always aware of where I was or what I did when under compulsion. I can be controlled; I can contain the Shadows, but only when controlled; they will not otherwise come at my call."

"Do you understand how they're called?"

He frowned. "No. I understand that they are both individual and connected somehow; they speak, but they speak through or past me. They are aware of what I am, and some handful have attempted to attack me directly; they fail.

"But beneath the ground in some areas of the heartland, the Shadows lay fallow. They are seeded there, dormant, and they rise when called. They do not always don the same forms, but when they are finished, they always dissipate; the ground once again absorbs them."

"Are they aware of you when they're in the ground?"

"I do not know."

"If they're not called, they don't attack?"

"They do not attack me, Chosen; there is no point. At best, they could destroy me, but I would then be of little use."

"What do they want from you?"

"What do they want from any? They will corrupt any land that borders their own; what they cannot corrupt, they destroy. But when the land is transformed, those that cannot be transformed wither and die; it will no longer sustain them. That is history," he added with just a faint hint of reproach.

"They didn't destroy you," she pointed out.

He stopped walking. His expression when he turned to her was both gaunt and hollow. "Did they not?" he whispered.

She decided to take her own advice to Tara, and fell silent.

Tara led Maggaron to a set of doors that were, as all doors in the Tower, quite wide. "Maggaron," she said quietly. She gestured and the doors rolled open. "There is a window; it doesn't look out into the streets or the gardens."

He glanced at it.

"The doors are not warded, but they are...sensitive. If you are willing to remain here as my guest, remain here."

"I—"

"Tomorrow, when my Lord and I return to the borders, we will bespeak Mejrah and discuss your fate. For the remainder of the day, however, the Chosen and my Lord have much to discuss; she was not summoned to these lands in order to contain you, but rather, in order to serve my Lord."

"I—are you certain it is safe, Lady?"

"I am certain. While you are in this Tower, you are safe. Not even Kaylin could use your name against you here if I did not desire its use."

He lowered his head. "I will rest here," he said. "The room is large enough, and the bed—"

"It was designed for the use of the Norannir."

He was silent.

"Maggaron, how long has it been since you slept?" Kaylin asked softly.

"Slept?" he asked, as if it were a foreign concept.

"Sleep now, if you can."

He nodded. It looked as though a bad puppeteer had pulled strings to achieve the effect. "She is no longer mine," was his quiet reply as he headed awkwardly toward the bed. "Maybe, now, I will sleep."

★ ★ ★

Tara had clearly learned about dining from an Imperial Dragon who attended large, formal state dinners and regularly fed hundreds of people in one sitting. Since this was not the first time that Tara had offered Kaylin food, the room that appeared when the doors rolled open was a bit of a shock. It was, for one, huge; the ceilings were high, the walls were adorned with tapestries that could have been used for an entire mansion's worth of walls.

There was one very, very long table. Broken in two, it would have served in the mess hall if it weren't so very fine; it gleamed, and if the usual boredom-induced engravings were anywhere on its surface, they didn't show at this distance. There were plates, glasses—three for each setting—and an enormous number of knives, forks, and spoons. There were even plates on top of the plates. What there wasn't, at the moment, was food.

Severn cleared his throat, and Tara turned immediately toward him. Gone was the dispassionate and ancient defender; in her place was a slightly apprehensive woman of middling height. "Yes?"

"We're underdressed for a meal of this formality." It wasn't even *dinner*. It was lunch. Probably late lunch, but still. Lunch.

"Oh. I could fix that," she said, brightening up.

Over my dead body, Kaylin thought.

"Why?"

Morse suppressed a laugh, mostly by coughing. "I'm on duty," Kaylin replied.

"Why don't you like formal clothing?"

Kaylin gave up. "It's not me."

"No, of course not—it's clothing. You wear armor, yes? And the tabard where it's appropriate? You wear things to sleep in and different shoes or boots depending on weather and terrain. None of these things are you."

Morse was having an all-out coughing fit.

"Morse can explain it," Kaylin said sweetly.

"Morse can't," was the flat reply. "I've asked her several times."

Kaylin looked at Severn, who gave her the empty hands-up, indicating she was on her own. She grimaced. "Powerful people tend to dress in really fancy clothing. It's supposed to make a statement."

"About what?"

"Fancy clothing costs a *lot* of money. Most of us can't afford to wear anything fancy *and* pay rent."

"But you don't have to pay to be clothed appropriately in *this* Tower," Tara reasonably replied.

A very different snort came from the open doors; for one, it had smoke in it.

"Tiamaris, help!"

He chuckled. "It is my intention, in a future which might be far enough away that it won't be a concern of yours, to entertain in the fief. Some of the people I hope to entertain will be of high standing in the Merchants' Guild, among others; they expect to be treated as men of power, if not rank. This is therefore a necessary endeavor."

"I won't be here when you're entertaining them," Kaylin told Tara.

Tara nodded, but it was too much to hope it would be left there. "Why?"

"I don't know enough about how to eat with powerful people." Or speak with them, if it came to that, "and I've got so much to learn—"

"Lord Diarmat is teaching you, though," was the response. "So you'll have to learn anyway."

Kaylin wilted and surrendered with as much grace as she ever did. "No fancy clothing," she told the Tower's Avatar, "but you can tell me which of the four dozen utensils I'm *supposed* to be using."

Tiamaris joined them for dinner, and, to Kaylin's surprise, he at least went through the motions of eating. She couldn't recall ever seeing a Dragon eat before, and had often wondered what they ate when they did. He didn't apparently *enjoy* the experience, but he made no complaints. He was not, however, focused on the food.

"Lord Sanabalis informed us that you've been seconded to his service for the near future."

She nodded. Tara informed her politely that the large fork was not yet appropriate as she turned toward Tiamaris. "Is the border always that heavily contested?"

"Always?"

"Morse implied that it's gotten worse since the Norannir moved in." Kaylin snuck a glance at Morse, who had taken up a position by the far wall.

"Implied? That's more subtle than Morse generally is."

"Is it true?" Kaylin asked, leaving his accurate observation alone.

"It is."

"Do you know why?"

"I have some suspicion, yes. Lord Sanabalis, however, is the better person to ask."

"Meaning you won't tell me."

"Meaning his idle speculation in this case matches my own. We have, on the other hand, more serious difficulties."

Kaylin, having seen the border skirmish, stilled.

"Tara," Tiamaris added, "although it is not generally done in a more formal gathering, I believe at the moment our discussion requires a mirror." He lifted a brow in Kaylin's direction and added, "What are you doing with that fork?"

She lifted one right back. "Eating."

"You are conveying food to your mouth, yes," was the severe reply. "That is, however, not the way a fork is held."

"Does it *matter*?"

If anyone had ever told Kaylin in her early days with the Hawks that a meeting of this seriousness could be delayed over instructions on how to hold a fork, she would have bet every coin in her possession against it. Tiamaris, however, would have lost her that bet, and then some.

"It must be nice to be rich enough that you worry about how you hold a fork to eat," she muttered, "rather than how you get enough food to not starve."

Tara, however, said, "Lord Sanabalis suggested that you eat with us while you're working here. He said it would make your lessons with Lord Diarmat less difficult. For you."

The thought of the head of the Imperial Guard instructing her on the use of utensils made all arguments wither. She practiced while Tara brought a mirror into the hall. Interestingly enough, she literally carried it; she didn't just wave a hand or bend a thought and cause one to materialize in a useful position.

"I can't," Tara told her, although Kaylin hadn't made the observation out loud. "Not with mirrors. I can with chairs or walls or some of the tables. Not all of them, though."

"Why?"

Tara frowned. "Why?"

"Why can't you? And why not the tables?"

"Well, this table," she said, "is very large. I don't believe it would survive the transition. But the mirrors are connected magically to external mirrors, and the connections are tenuous."

"Connected how?"

"Magically," the Avatar repeated. "The magic does not originate with the Tower."

"It was tricky," Tiamaris added, "to allow the mirror connection to breach the Tower defenses. Lord Sanabalis found it quite challenging."

"Nightshade does it."

"Indeed. I imagine he also found it challenging. I would be curious to know his point of connection to the external city."

"You can probably ask him. I think it's likely he'd answer."

"Not without some cost on my part, and at the moment, we cannot afford that; there are, as I mentioned, difficulties in the fief." He turned to the mirror, which Tara had placed in front of him. It was a standing oval, in shape and size very similar to the one in the Hawklord's Tower, except that the stable, flat length of its base had been replaced by a platform with wheels.

Tara came to stand to the left of where he sat. He didn't immediately invoke the mirror or its images, however. "You are aware that I am in the process of building a small force which would police the fief."

She nodded.

"We are faced with a few difficulties. We have no citizens with any experience in that regard; some very few had parents whose experience with the Law was perhaps not one we wish to repeat. We also now have a large number of citizens who are not yet familiar with the style of law I wish to put into practice, and who further cannot speak either Elantran or Barrani."

"You're not going to write laws in High Barrani."

"I fail to see why not; it has worked admirably for a force

composed almost entirely of mortals for some hundreds of years."

"Most of the people you'd be employing can't *read* it."

"Neither, if I recall correctly, could you."

Morse snorted.

"The point I am attempting to make," Tiamaris continued, "is that there is no such force in place at the moment. The investigations, such as they are, will have no support structures outside of the information Tara—or myself—can provide. Lord Sanabalis has offered his services should you require them; he will, however, be found along the border watch with the linguists. He was willing to see me hand the investigation to you in its entirety, however."

"And you?"

"I concur. Your methods and your general lack of tact will not harm you; nor, at this moment in time, will it harm my own reputation."

"What," Kaylin asked, "are we investigating, exactly?"

"On the surface of things, a series of murders."

"Murders."

"You *are* familiar with the term?"

She heard Morse snicker and ignored it; if she didn't it was going to be a long day. Or week. Or month. "It's not generally in use in the fiefs," was her clipped reply. "And frankly, when bodies are discovered, unless they're of import to the fieflord's authority, it's not generally considered a problem."

His eyes shaded instantly to an orange bronze. "That would be because your previous experience of the fiefs involved Lords who were notoriously underfocused. The people who have died are my citizens and my subjects. Mine. If I'm not of a mind to kill them myself, no one else will do so without repercussions."

Now, *that* sounded like a Dragon. Kaylin frowned. "You're

versed in the practices of the Investigative branches of the Halls of Law—you've worked with the Hawks before."

He nodded and rose. Glancing at the mirror he said—thankfully, in High Barrani—"Records."

CHAPTER 8

The mirror, which had reflected the Dragon Lord's image until he spoke the word, seemed to shatter; shards flew out from its surface. But Tiamaris didn't move, and after the initial harsh crack, neither did the shards. He stepped back, gestured, and they began to coalesce—beyond the mirror's surface. Kaylin, who'd seen her share of mirrors, had never seen one that did this; the only one that had come close in her experience had also then been put strictly *off* limits as dangerous.

Tiamaris was as expressive as Dragons usually were; he never looked snide, he never looked smug. Mostly he looked dispassionate or annoyed. There was, however, just the hint of a smile as he spoke to the mirror again.

"Map, Capstone."

Kaylin frowned. Capstone was one of the longer roads in the fief. "Morse, isn't that where—"

"Yeah. Great big one-off Shadow on your first day back in the fief."

"Burned down the building? There, near Holdstock?"

Morse nodded.

"Is it part of the reconstruction?"

"It is part of the planned reconstruction," Tiamaris replied. "But at the moment, rebuilding border towers and defenses are a priority. Capstone and Holdstock," he continued, and the rather large and almost featureless lines of road coalesced into images that resembled the fief as it actually was. "The first body was discovered here."

"That's the burned-out building."

"Actually, it's the one to the side; Barren wasn't concerned with containing fire."

"Badly scorched?"

"That was one of the unusual things about the victim. No."

She frowned. "So the person died there after the fire?"

He was silent.

"Records," Kaylin said sharply. Tiamaris nodded to Tara, and the mirror rotated to face Kaylin. "Image of body discovered at 84 Capstone."

"I should warn you," Tiamaris said, "that Barren did not see fit to operate a morgue."

"So you don't have the bodies anywhere."

"We do now, but if others died in a similar fashion during the encroachment under Barren's reign, we have no records or information about their deaths beyond what Tara herself remembers—"

"My memories of that time are incomplete," was the quiet reply. "My memories of the later period of Illien are likewise incomplete. My memories of Tiamaris, however, are not."

"None of your memories contain anything relevant?"

Tara hesitated. "I am not certain," she said at last.

The mirror had divulged the standing image of a young woman. She was clothed in a style that Kaylin didn't recognize— and it *was* a style; it wasn't the desperate hand-me-downs of most of Kaylin's early life in Nightshade or Barren. For one, it wasn't torn, and it seemed to fit the girl perfectly; it was a deep shade of blue, although the sleeves were edged in something that looked like dirt-covered gold thread. She'd apparently only had luck in dresses; her feet were bare; her hands were also bare of rings or any discoloration that might have indicated they'd once existed.

"Cause of death?" Kaylin asked softly. She approached the image that floated beyond the mirror's surface and examined it. She could walk around the body; she didn't try to touch it. But there was no blood on the dress, nothing that indicated fatal wounding; her neck was not mottled or bruised; her face was not marked. The back of her head did not look crushed, and she had none of the bloat that Kaylin associated with a drowning death; her fingernails were clean, and what Kaylin could see of her wrists appeared to be unbruised.

Tiamaris said, "We have no coroner. And no, before you ask, my expertise at dismemberment rarely involved careful examination of the dead."

"Magic?"

Tiamaris glanced at Tara. Tara said, "I'm not certain."

It wasn't a no. "We'll head that way first. Is the building structurally sound?"

"On the west side, yes. Which is where the body was found. There is, before you leave, more."

"Who found the body?"

"A young boy; he was chasing a ball or a stone, against the wishes of the old woman who was serving as his guardian."

"And word reached you?"

"Not directly," Tiamaris replied, nodding at Tara.

"Where was the dress made?" Severn asked quietly, reminding everyone that he was still in the room.

"An interesting question," Tiamaris replied. "Why do you ask?"

"The shade of blue is unusual; I'm not conversant with all our dyes, but it can't be common."

Morse was looking at the side of Severn's head. Turning to Kaylin, she said, "Did he really come out of the fiefs?"

Kaylin nodded. "Same one that produced me."

"Mirror: mark first victim," Tiamaris said.

"Victim's name?" Kaylin asked.

"She doesn't appear to have had one," was the reply.

"No one was willing to identify her?"

Tiamaris and Tara exchanged a glance. It was Tara who answered. "No one recognized her."

In the fiefs, that was pretty common; no one knew *anything* that could get them in trouble. They forgot their own names, their homes, and their families if anyone they didn't trust asked. "No one you asked?"

"No one who spoke of the incident at all," was the calm reply. After a pause, she added, "I listened."

Kaylin could see clearly why Sanabalis found her alarming. She grimaced. While it wouldn't be the first time she'd marked a corpse as Victim Number something, it always irritated her. "How many victims in total?"

Tiamaris didn't reply. Not directly. "Mirror," he said. "Capstone and Enclave."

The silent, standing corpse disintegrated into almost instant particles of light that shed color and shifted position. When they reintegrated, Kaylin was looking at a topographical map of Capstone and Enclave. It wasn't one of the streets she'd frequented at Barren's behest in her six months in Barren, but she was familiar with the intersection; among other things, it housed a well.

The map now centered *on* the well, and Kaylin looked away. "In the water?" she asked quietly.

"Very good, Private. There was a difficulty with the water itself, and it was brought—quickly—to my attention. The corpse was in the water."

"Drowned?"

"That would be the reasonable assumption. It is not, for reasons which will be obvious, the correct one in my opinion. Mirror, second victim."

Once again the three-dimensional image disintegrated, and light rippled out in concentric spheres, changing shape and color. When it finally stilled, Kaylin frowned. "Mirror," she said, "second victim."

The image didn't change. She turned to Tara. "The mirror—"

"The mirror is relaying the correct information," the Tower replied.

"But—but it's the same woman."

Severn began to walk around the standing-dead-simulacra. "It seems to be the same woman," he told Kaylin, "but the *dress* has clearly been in the water for some small time."

"It's the same dress, too."

Tiamaris nodded.

"Did you see this corpse?"

He nodded again.

"Did you see the first one?"

"Yes. The Lady was present and examined both of the bodies."

"I don't know how refined the Lady's sense of smell is. I know Dragons are close to Leontines. Was there any way to distinguish them?"

Tiamaris lifted a hand. "Both were dead."

"I'll take that as an inconclusive. When the bodies were

unclothed were there any identifying marks—birthmarks, old scars, missing teeth—that you could use to tell them apart?"

"Mirror. Victim one and victim two."

Both women now appeared as standing—and naked—corpses. They were oriented in the same position, but their eyelids had been pulled up, and their mouths opened to reveal even rows of teeth. Kaylin had watched Red in the morgue; she'd seen her share of unclothed, and often partially disassembled, bodies. They often bothered new recruits; they'd never bothered Kaylin as much. The people were dead; they felt no shame, no pain, and no fear.

Neither did these women.

Both she and Severn walked around their fronts and backs, but they spent most of their time looking at the women's teeth. Not only did both women have all of them, but the teeth themselves seemed, admittedly to their inexpert eye, to be the same set in each mouth.

"Notice any identifying marks on either?" Kaylin asked Severn, because she could find none. Severn shook his head. Almost everyone had some sort of blemish, freckle, birthmark, mole, or scar by these women's ages. Neither woman appeared to have read that memo.

Morse watched, but said nothing.

"Tara, did anyone recognize this woman? The second victim?"

"No. But they were a great deal more upset because of where her body was found. There was some anger."

"I bet." Killing someone was frowned on. Killing someone and dumping their corpse into the well, however, was making your personal vendetta everyone else's grief, and only the fieflord could get away with that for long. "I think we need to head down to Capstone."

Tiamaris lifted a hand. "I have not yet made the extent of the difficulty clear."

"There's more?"

"There is, as you so elegantly put it, more."

"Tell me."

"There are five more victims."

"Five?"

He nodded.

"Are they *all* the same woman?"

"Yes."

Two hours later, all the mirror images had been examined; notes had been taken as Tiamaris talked. The first two deaths—if indeed the victims had died where they'd been found—had been on Capstone, but almost at opposite ends of the street. The other five had been spread across the fief.

"I understand why Sanabalis called this subtle," Kaylin finally said. "There doesn't seem to be *any* obvious cause of death. There weren't, as far as we can tell, any encroachments of Shadow anywhere near the vicinity?"

"None," Tara said. The single word was definitive because it could be; if she was certain, it was true.

"The first of the bodies was discovered after the Norannir arrived?"

"Yes."

"But they haven't been connected with the Norannir at all."

"No. If there were obvious violence, obvious physical damage, it would be...difficult. But no."

"And there's no chance at all that this is somehow the *same* corpse and it's just been moved around?"

"None. The Lady houses our de facto morgue at the moment. I did not feel it wise to contain the bodies within the heart of the Tower; she feels it is safe to house them in the spaces in which we entertain. There are, at present, seven bodies laid out. Magic has been used to both safeguard and preserve them, and if you wish to examine the actual—"

"I do." She didn't, but that was true of half the things her job required.

"Tiamaris, has anyone else gone missing?" Kaylin asked as they walked at a brisk clip down the wide halls.

"How, precisely, would we determine this?"

She cursed. In Leontine. There was no missing persons department in the fief. There was no official way of making reports, and even if there had been, no one would actually make them.

As if he could read her mind, he said, "Within the next two years, a full and official census will be taken, and the records that result will be housed in the Town Hall."

"The *what?*"

Tiamaris raised a brow. "While I understand that human hearing is not as acute as one could desire, I believe you heard me."

Kaylin turned to Morse. Morse offered a very fieflike shrug. He was the boss; she wasn't arguing.

"We will also," he added, "build a more martial hall which will house my police force. Neither project is viable at the moment, given the manpower being diverted to the interior border—but we are still left with this particular problem."

"The first death occurred—or rather, was discovered—how long after the Norannir arrived?"

"A day."

"Tiamaris, they've only been here for what, two days? Three?"

"Three."

"So the rest of the bodies—"

"Yes. All of the seven have been discovered in the past two days."

"Do you think you've missed any?"

"Possibly. The Lady judged it unwise to stir unrest in this regard, and a more thorough investigation would almost certainly cause unrest at this point."

Kaylin snorted. "Morse?"

"I've asked a few questions in the right—or what used to be the right—places." She shrugged. "So far, nothing—but it's only been a day, and I've mostly been at the borders, same as the rest."

Kaylin nodded. Tiamaris and Tara now stopped in front of a door that was as wide as any of the others in the Tower; it was less ornate. It, like the other doors, was completely free of door wards; it was also free of handle or knob. This wasn't a problem for Tara, who merely nodded at it. It opened.

Going from a dining hall that the Imperial Palace might boast to a room with corpses lying across two of three large stone slabs—in a lower than normal temperature—was a little like arriving as a guest and being thrown into the dungeon. Straightening her shoulders, Kaylin took one short breath, expelled it, and headed toward the bodies.

Severn joined her. They were fully clothed, and at that, in the same dress; the dresses themselves had taken some damage, although most of it was cosmetic. "Nothing changed when you removed the dresses?"

Tara frowned. "No. Not noticeably."

Severn cut a piece of cloth from the hem of one dress, marked it, and slid it into his pouch. He did this with the hem of each of the dresses. Kaylin clipped hair samples. "So, at the moment we have no clear idea if anyone else has disappeared."

"Many people are missing; many died in the incursions.

There is no system in place at the moment to account for them all."

"Have you consulted the Norannir?"

Tiamaris raised a brow. "No. Why?"

She shook her head. "I don't want to tie these deaths—if they are that—to the Norannir, but the timing seems suspicious."

"The dead woman is—or was—human, a race that they'd not encountered before their arrival here."

Kaylin nodded. Severn marked the hesitance "You're going to need some sort of uniform for your policing forces," she told the Dragon Lord.

"The thought had occurred to me. It is not a practical concern at the moment."

"It will be," was Kaylin's resigned reply. "Because we're going to need to wear something when we hit the street." She glanced at Severn and added, "We'll need a few things, and I want to consult with some people in the office before we start asking questions. Will that work for you?"

Tiamaris nodded. "I will expect a report of your findings."

The seven identical women had been arranged in a standard corpse pose, arms to the side, legs straight, neck straight—and in their two rows, they looked like macabre dolls. They also looked entirely real. If they had been examined without clothing, the clothing had been returned to them. Humor drained from her voice; she turned to Tiamaris, one-time Hawk and now Dragon fieflord. "Have you done a cursory exam?"

"Magical?"

She nodded.

"Yes."

"And?"

"It revealed nothing—to me. I am not as subtle as Lord

Sanabalis, and Lord Sanabalis, for political reasons, chooses to absent himself from the Tower."

"Will you do a cursory scan now?"

"This is something," Tiamaris said as he now approached the row of four bodies to Kaylin's left, "you should be able to do in the very near future. How is the candle going?"

Her answer was a very short Leontine word; it made him chuckle.

"You are inordinately gifted, in ways none of us fully understand. But the candle—"

"Bodies?" she said pointedly.

He nodded, losing the brief grin. Lifting his hands, he held them palm down over the two middle bodies laid out on the center slab. This wasn't, strictly speaking, necessary, but every mage had their own small tics or focus-aids, and at least he wasn't using a physical object like a wand. Then again, he had once had Sanabalis as a teacher, and anyone who tried that with Sanabalis would probably be missing limbs.

She watched him carefully. He murmured mantric, repetitive syllables, softly enough she had to strain to catch them. "He discovered nothing the first time," Tara told her.

Kaylin nodded and kept on watching.

"What do you think you'll see that he doesn't?"

"I don't."

"Then why—"

"Every mage sees magic in a different way. Even me. Don't ask me why. Sanabalis says we interpret what we see because if we didn't, we'd probably go mad. But—if someone is really bookish or word based, he most often sees letters or words or symbols. If someone has really acute visual sensitivity, he'll see colors. Someone who has a strong sense of touch or smell will feel or scent things. It's more complicated than that. But according to Sanabalis, they're all seeing the same thing—they just…comprehend it differently." It had sounded lame to her the first time she heard it; it sounded less lame now, but she sympathized with the expression on Tara's face.

"So. You believe that your…interpretation…and my Lord's differ in significant ways?"

Tiamaris, who should have been so focused he wasn't listening, gave a suspiciously well-timed snort.

"It's why you'll often see more than one mage at important Imperial investigations. We're not entirely certain how much our interpretations differ, but they will, and something in our paradigm might give us insight or information that the others lack. The reverse is also true." She grimaced and added, "That's the theory. Let's see how well it works in practice."

In practice, as it turned out, it didn't work at all. Although Tiamaris was in fact drawing enough magical power that Kaylin's skin began to goose bump, nothing rose from the corpses: no nimbus of light, no runic sigils. Because she wasn't the one casting the detection spell, she was free to move, and did.

"What is it?" Severn asked.

She glanced at him.

"You're frowning."

"Was I?"

"Yes. In the way that produces pronounced furrows across the bridge of your nose."

"Oh." Kaylin didn't pay all that much attention to her facial expressions because she couldn't see them herself.

"There's no obvious—"

"No sigil, no. No obvious artifacting. No shadow. But…" She shook her head.

"You notice something," Tiamaris said.

"Yes—but if you ask me what, I'm not sure I can answer." This had never been popular with any of her fellow Hawks.

"Try," was his terse and familiar response.

Everything looked the same to Kaylin. There wasn't anything she could put her finger on. "Are you doing the whole sweep or is it local to the actual corpse?"

"Both the corpse and the dress."

She nodded again. For fifteen minutes she poked—literally—and prodded, and she was no closer to an answer. "Turn it off," she told him, still staring. He did. She knew the exact moment when he did because something subtle *faded*.

"Tiamaris, can you do the scan again?"

He rumbled. She took that as a yes, and kept her eyes locked on the face of corpse number four. "What do you see?"

"They're—they're brighter when you're casting."

"Brighter?"

"It's subtle. But the color of the skin and hair—it's more vivid."

He came to stand beside her. "Is it the same across all the bodies?"

"I think so." She glanced at Severn. He shook his head. "Tara, did you notice anything?"

Tara was frowning. She was concentrating hard enough that her eyes once again resembled onyx, rather than the usual mortal variety.

Tiamaris began to cast, and this time, Tara, like Kaylin, watched. Kaylin had no idea at all if a Tower could actually see and understand the whole of what was there without somehow translating it into an unknown frame of reference.

Kaylin was frustrated; the actual *casting* of the spell made no obvious difference, but when the spell was allowed to fade, something *did* drain away. Tiamaris noticed it this time.

"It is subtle," he said. They were the wrong words for the sudden shift of his tone. Kaylin glanced over her shoulder and froze; his eyes had gone at once from a pale, comfortable gold, to the burning edge of orange. The wrong edge. Pushing Kaylin aside, he bent over the corpse and lifted the closed lids of her eyes.

To Tara—in a *very* quiet voice—Kaylin said, "You said you'd examined the bodies?"

Tara nodded, but her gaze was now affixed to Tiamaris's face.

"Was there anything unnatural about the eyes?"

"You saw them."

"I mean, to you."

"No."

Tiamaris held the lids open between two fingers and began his spell of detection and identification for the third time that day. It was impossible not to look at the eyes of the corpse. They were, like the eyes of any corpse Kaylin had seen, cloudy; the original hazel color of the iris was still evident, but very murky.

Tiamaris spoke the syllables of his focus in the deep and rumbling bass of true Dragon; she could feel it in the soles of her feet. As Kaylin watched the eyes he held open between two large and careful fingers, she stopped breathing. The cloudiness receded; they looked, for a moment, like living, sightless eyes. The pupils didn't shift shape or position; the eyes themselves didn't move.

But the irises were now a completely clear and brilliant gold.

They stayed that way for another fifteen minutes before Tiamaris let the spell drop; she knew the moment he did because clouds overtook the corpse's eyes and the color dimmed, once again, into a very human hazel. Kaylin had seen a handful of Dragons in her life, and by law, they were required to be in their more or less human forms; no Dragons she had ever met had hazel-colored eyes.

No human she had ever met had eyes that shade of gold.

She waited until he once again drew the lids down over the dead woman's eyes. His own were now a heated orange; he was agitated. He didn't, however, show it in any other way; his voice was brisk, his expression smooth and neutral.

There was a lot of awkward silence packed into the longest five minutes ever. Kaylin finally broke it. "You can't think she was a Dragon?"

"That would not have been my first thought. It would not, given our initial examination of the bodies, have been my hundredth."

"And now?"

"I...do not know, Kaylin." He stepped away from the bodies. "Magically unaugmented, she is human, perhaps five years older than you are now. I do not know what the eyes signify." He shook his head, as if to clear it.

Kaylin looked at the dead woman. Or at one of them. "I would never have guessed," she finally said. "But I've never seen a female Dragon before."

"There is a reason for that. However, it is quite probable you have *not* seen one now."

The Other Dragon, as she'd called him, was waiting outside the Tower grounds when Kaylin and Severn emerged. Tiamaris and Tara had chosen to escort them out.

Sanabalis offered Tiamaris and Tara a deep bow. "On the morrow," he told his former student. Tiamaris grimaced, but nodded and turned back toward the interior of the Tower.

Sanabalis rose. "Well?" he asked Kaylin.

"Tara's determined to teach me proper table manners."

He raised a white brow. "While that was not entirely

what I meant, I approve. Did the subject of the investigation come up?"

"Yes."

"And?"

She hesitated; the sudden change in the color of Tiamaris's eyes urged her to be cautious. "Why did you call this a subtle Shadow incursion?"

"I am not convinced that it is not."

"I'm not convinced that it *is*."

"Then you will approach the investigation with an open mind."

"There's something you're not telling me."

"There is always something I am not, as you put it, telling you. Suffice it to say, the investigation is, to my mind, enough of a priority that even Lord Diarmat will accept the necessity, should the matter arise."

"Sanabalis—"

"And before you make pointless accusations," he said, lifting a hand, "let me assure you that none of the information I am currently refusing to part with has any direct bearing on the investigation itself. I admit that I find it disturbing."

"Good. Disturbing enough to help me leverage a small item or two out of the Imperial mages?"

He raised one brow. "That, I feel, is a matter for the Sergeant to decide."

"The Sergeant will say no—the fiefs aren't in his jurisdiction."

"Possibly. What, exactly, do you hope to leverage—as you put it—out of the Imperial mages?"

"Just a crystal. A small one."

Both his brows rose. "You want a projection crystal."

"Just one."

"Private Neya, Sergeant Kassan would in all likelihood

deny the request if you were working on the investigation into the Exchequer himself. Do you have any idea of the expense you would be incurring?"

"No," she replied, entirely truthfully. "But I know they're both rare and useful."

"The reason they are rare in spite of the fact that they're demonstrably useful is the expense and difficulty of their creation. What, exactly, do you hope to demonstrate?"

"Not demonstrate, exactly. I want to take it into the streets and I want to show people what she—what they—looked like when they were alive. I have two things in mind to start. One, we cast it entirely as an important missing person and two, we *also* attempt to find out if anyone has gone missing within the last three days."

"Why?"

She shrugged. "Even if the corpses *are* corpses—and I want Red to come and inspect them, or I want them exported to the Halls—that *can't* be what they originally looked like. Sanabalis, there are seven *identical* bodies. Even if they were somehow sisters, there would be distinguishing birthmarks, moles, differences in teeth—something. There isn't." She hesitated again, and Sanabalis's eyes narrowed. "You've done a magical analysis?"

"I? No. I have not entered the Tower where the bodies are kept."

"But you've seen the bodies?"

"I've seen three of them."

"And?"

Sanabalis, however, had run out of patience. He now adopted his teacher voice. "You were in the Tower. You were no doubt allowed to inspect the bodies. You have already, in the course of your duties, displayed an uncanny sensitivity to magic. Did you, or did you not, notice anything of significance that would indicate the bodies themselves were enspelled?"

His eyes had gone from gold to bronze, and his expression was very pinched.

She had no ready answer. His eyes narrowed, but his gaze remained a steady and comforting bronze. This wasn't the usual definition of comfort when dealing with Dragons, but in comparison to the livid near-red of Tiamaris, it would do.

"What, exactly, were you looking for?"

She grimaced. "Sigils. Signatures."

"You did not, of course, find them."

"No."

"What does this tell you?"

"It doesn't tell us that magic isn't involved," she said firmly.

"No?"

"No."

"Private Neya, while it is entirely true that I fail to tell you everything that might satisfy your apparently boundless curiosity, this is not a situation in which turnabout is, to coin a human phrase, fair play. What occurred in the Tower?"

"Tiamaris had already examined the bodies for vestiges of magic."

One pale brow rose. "Of course he had."

"He said he found nothing. But I asked him to cast the spell again, in my presence."

"Good. The results?"

"I…don't understand the results," she admitted. "But he wasn't very happy with them."

"You said he had cast the spell once and received no useful information."

"Yes. But—"

"You will be the death of either yourself or me. My preference at this point is obviously yourself." Sanabalis began to walk, and Kaylin joined him. Severn walked to her left.

"Usually I notice sigils, physical signatures. That wasn't the case here. I almost noticed nothing."

"Almost?"

"There was no difference. When the spell was invoked, I noticed no change. It was when the spell faded that I did. But when I mentioned this to Tiamaris, he cast the spell again— and this time, *he* looked. But he—he looked at the woman's eyes."

He lifted one hand. "Thank you, Private."

CHAPTER 9

"You already know what he saw." Kaylin kept accusation out of her voice with effort. She stopped walking, however.

Sanabalis didn't. She had to jog to catch up. "No. I did not know until you spoke."

"You suspected?"

"No, Kaylin."

"Do you think she's supposed to be a dead Dragon?"

"An interesting choice of words."

Glancing at his profile she saw that his inner eye membranes were up. Even with their opacity, his eyes were now a bright orange. "We will go directly to the Palace," he told her. "Corporal?"

Severn nodded.

"Private Neya's visual memory is not always as…crisp…as it could be. Yours, on record, is excellent."

Severn raised a brow, but it was Kaylin who said, "You're going to give us the crystal."

"Not precisely," was the clipped response. "The availability of necessary materials within the Imperial Order is not guaranteed, and the process of requisition requires some entanglement with the Order's very fine bureaucracy."

"But?"

"The necessary materials—without the paperwork—can be found in only one place in the Palace. I leave it to your very fine mind to deduce where."

The Palace, at the moment, was not where Kaylin wanted to be, although her next session with Diarmat wasn't scheduled until tomorrow night. The Dragon to her right, on the other hand, was not someone she wanted to argue with, and since he was much closer, she headed—in silence—to the Palace.

The guards did not seem thrilled at the prospect of the naked-short-blade in Kaylin's hand, and they seemed both underimpressed and derisive when they noted that she wore no sheath for it. It set her teeth on edge, but she failed to comment. Sanabalis, however, had no difficulty excusing its presence, and clearly he outranked them; they let her pass.

Word of this exception must have traveled, because no one else gave her trouble. Everyone else, on the other hand, *did* notice the sword.

"We will have to do something about that," Sanabalis said under his breath. "Find a makeshift sheath for now if you will not leave the blade somewhere safe."

"By now, you mean after we've finished speaking with the Arkon?"

"Don't be clever, Kaylin. It's been a very trying week."

"Yes, Sanabalis."

"Let me speak," he cautioned her once they'd passed the officious man at the doors and the usual gauntlet of Imperial

Guards, and had entered the wide, tall halls of the Palace proper.

"Unless he demands an answer, he's all yours."

"If he demands an answer, I will answer."

She snorted, and wished, briefly, that the noise was also accompanied by smoke and a little fire. For someone with perfect memory—and all Immortals pretty much laid claim to that—his was certainly convenient; he'd clearly forgotten what the Arkon was like.

But at least when he approached the closed Library doors, Sanabalis was considerate enough to press his palms into the door wards; he didn't demand that Kaylin do it herself. The doors rolled open.

Although the Library was the Arkon's in any way that mattered, it was nonetheless staffed by mostly human attendants; set a few yards from the door was a long and impressive desk behind which one such employee sat. He looked up as the doors opened, his somewhat forbidding expression shifting when he saw who'd entered. He rose immediately and bowed.

"Lord Sanabalis," he said as he rose. "I don't believe the Arkon is expecting you."

"No."

This wasn't the hoped-for answer, but the man nodded. Reaching for something beneath the lip of the desk's surface, he said, "I will send word that you've arrived. Is it urgent?"

"It is not—at the moment—an emergency. If it is more convenient," he added as a much younger man appeared from behind a long row of shelving, "I will approach him myself. Has he given orders he is not to be interrupted?"

"They're standing orders," was the slightly grim reply. "The Royal Librarian lost much valuable archival time during the last crisis."

The younger man made his way to the front of the desk

and stood in front of the older one, who was clearly—in the absence of the Arkon—in charge. But the older man grimaced. "Never mind, Wills. Lord Sanabalis has a message he wishes to convey in person. Lord Sanabalis, you will find the Arkon in the third hall of artifacts. The Hawks?"

"They are with me. They understand the rules of the Library. I will personally deal with any infractions."

"Thank you, Lord Sanabalis." He cleared his throat before they'd taken two steps, and the Dragon Lord turned back.

"Yes?"

"The Private," he said, indicating Kaylin.

"What about her?"

"She is carrying a sword."

Sanabalis glanced at the blade that Maggaron had given her. "My apologies," he told the Librarian. "We wish the Arkon to examine it, and I believe he will find it of interest, but for the moment, we will leave it at the desk in your care."

Turning to Kaylin, he added, "If that is acceptable to you?"

"It is." She hesitated, and then said, "But I don't think it's safe for anyone else to actually attempt to wield it."

"No one will wield it," was the Librarian's response. But he looked at the blade with distinctly less comfort. "No one will touch it. If you will bring it to the back of the desk?"

Behind the desk was what looked like a long counter. Its gleaming wooden surface caught light, which it then scattered because the Librarian lifted it. It was hinged, and beneath its surface was something that looked very much like glass casing. It made Kaylin queasy as she approached, which made it clear that it was magical.

"When artifacts are brought to the Arkon," the man explained, motioning toward the empty case without once attempting to touch the sword in her hands, "this is where they are kept if they are deemed either fragile or magical and of unknown origin. I will remain here until you leave the Library. No one else, besides the Arkon, can open the case. If you will?"

Half relieved, she set the sword down and took a step back. He dropped the countertop, and it once again looked like normal, necessary desk space.

"Let me guess. The Arkon is not in the best of moods," Kaylin ventured when they were out of the normal human earshot of the supervisor.

"He has certainly been in worse in your direct experience," Sanabalis replied. "But he has been attempting to ascertain that no damage was done during the recent magical surge, and this takes both time and very focused attention to detail. He does not like," he added, "to be disturbed."

He had never *liked* to be disturbed. In the time she'd known him, he'd left the Palace exactly once, and that had involved the possible end of the world.

The Arkon was working in the third hall of artifacts, as the man at the desk had called it. Kaylin didn't consider what was essentially a closed, dark room to be a hall. There were no windows, or at least if there were, none of them let any light in. She'd been in a similar room in the bowels of the Library before; the walls were mostly lined with shelves, and there were standing items that only spiders appeared to have touched in the intervening centuries since they'd been collected. Sanabalis was considerate enough to retrieve lamps for their use; the usual magical lights were forbidden.

The Arkon had already left off work when the light from the open door alerted him to their presence. He looked like a moving antique; the dust and the cobwebs that time and spiders had deposited clung to his robes and the edge of his beard. His eyes were a shade of unfortunate orange, but given both Tiamaris and Sanabalis today, he seemed relatively calm.

"This," he told Sanabalis in a rumble of a voice that implied he was speaking Barrani out of a minimal courtesy that could vanish at any second, "had better be important."

"In my opinion, it is," Sanabalis replied.

"Obviously." The Arkon now condescended to notice the two silent Hawks who had accompanied Sanabalis. He sighed, which sounded suspiciously like a snort, with about the same smoke content. "I have not failed to notice, Private Neya," he said as he all but shoved them out of the doors and back into the light, "that Lord Sanabalis's disdain for my orders that I remain undisturbed frequently intersect with his interactions with *you*."

The Arkon's annoyance at the interruption was not, sadly, improved by the nature of Sanabalis's request. It did, however, leave him speechless and slightly openmouthed for at least thirty seconds. Sanabalis's expression could have been carved out of stone; he didn't even blink.

"I assume you have a more than adequate reason for this request?"

"I do. And it is, I believe, a situation in which time—in the mortal sense—is of the essence. The usual process for requisitions of note from the Imperial Order—which I will, of course, begin immediately—will require more time than we have."

The Arkon was not impressed. Dusting his hands on the folds of his robes, he snorted more smoke. "This had better at least be interesting, Sanabalis. I have discovered some possible damage to some of the more unusual items in the collection, and I am not pleased."

There wasn't a colloquial phrase or curse that went something like "may your day be full of angry dragons" or "may every dragon you meet today be pissed off," but there should have been. Had the floors not been so solid, the Arkon would have left footprints in the stone.

"Where is he going?" Kaylin asked as Sanabalis began to follow.

"Probably one of the conference rooms. The artifacts in the third hall are delicate, and shouting—in our native tongue— might cause them harm."

The Arkon did indeed lead them to one of the almost featureless rooms several halls and a few doors away. It contained a table that was flat, long and practical; chairs were tucked beneath its surface. The walls were bare. The door was warded, or appeared to be warded, but the Arkon didn't bother to touch it; he barked at it and it flew open. Even the inanimate objects in the Library apparently knew enough to try to stay on his good side.

The door slammed shut the minute Sanabalis entered the room behind Kaylin.

"Well?" the Arkon said, folding his arms across the trailing edge of his unkempt beard.

"There is a problem in the fief of Tiamaris."

This didn't seem to mollify the Arkon. "Given the known problems that occur in lands that border the fiefs, I fail to see how a projection crystal is justified. It is not a useful teaching tool." He referred, Kaylin realized belatedly, to Sanabalis's work with the Norannir. "Nor is it a shield against the incursions of Shadow. It is a fine research tool," he added, "and any grant from my library will of course decrease the effective ability to do research *here*."

Kaylin cleared her throat.

"Yes?"

"It's also an effective tool for investigations."

"It is, and the *usual* method for requisitioning such equipment results—on occasion—in a grant of a crystal for those purposes. Has the Hawklord acceded to your request?"

Silence.

"Ah, no, of *course* not. The fief of Tiamaris is not considered Imperial territory, and any investigations would not fall under the jurisdiction of the Halls of Law. Sanabalis," he added, losing the honorific that he usually used, at least when in the presence of mere mortals. "Explain yourself. Now."

"There have been a series of highly unusual murders in the fief of Tiamaris. While we are all aware that the general conditions of rule in the fiefs are somewhat lacking—" He glanced at Kaylin, who had clamped her jaw shut. She'd become used to the roundabout understatements of people who'd never actually had to live in the fiefs, but she was never going to like them. "There are indications that a subtle magic is involved."

Mindful of Sanabalis's orders to let him do the talking, Kaylin said nothing. She was, however, Kaylin; she said nothing *loudly*.

It was not to Kaylin that the Arkon turned, however; it was to the almost invisible Severn. "Corporal Handred," he said in his succinct and biting High Barrani, "I have been impressed with your calm and your sense of order in trying and difficult times. You accompanied Private Neya on this excursion into Tiamaris?"

"I did."

"Good. I would like to hear your version of the difficulty, and your opinion about the use of the crystal." When Severn did not immediately launch into speech, he added "Now."

In very sparse words, and in an entirely even and matter-of-fact tone, Severn offered the Arkon an account of events. He made clear, in the same tone, that the only hands-on investigation either he or Kaylin had done so far was a brief and cursory examination of the bodies.

"On the morrow," he added in his flawless High Barrani, "we will visit the discovery sites and attempt to discern what the victims may—or may not—have in common."

But the Arkon had fallen utterly silent; he didn't even seem to be breathing. "You are certain," he finally said, "that all the bodies were identical? Mortals often look very similar."

Kaylin winced; Severn didn't. He nodded smoothly. "There are known cases of multiple births that result in children who appear—to strangers—to be identical. There are always distinguishing marks or differences that yield to a closer inspection."

"You have reason to suspect that the seven discovered will not be the last?"

"No. Given the discovery of seven in such a short span of time, however, I feel it unlikely."

"You do not possess the magical sensitivity that Private Neya has demonstrated."

"No, Arkon."

"Private Neya." He glanced once at Sanabalis, and added, "You were not present, Lord Sanabalis. Your word will not carry the weight of hers here, no matter how carefully you speak. Or how carelessly she does." He turned back to Kaylin. "You will wait here. I will return with the object you have requested."

"Thank you."

The Arkon raised a brow. "I am certain that when we are done you will be markedly less thankful. There is a second reason that the crystals are not deemed suitable for frequent use."

★ ★ ★

When the Arkon had exited the room, Sanabalis ran his fingers through his beard. "That did not go well," he finally said.

"I tried, Sanabalis. What did he mean, I won't be happy?"

"Imbuing the crystal with an image that can be seen directly by those with no magical training or inclination requires magic."

"Yes. That's why it's a *magic* crystal."

"Very amusing. What it also requires," he continued, "is a process that is somewhat similar to the one used to imbue memory crystals. You *are* familiar with memory crystals?"

"Intimately," she said, her shoulders sloping toward the ground. "I don't suppose Corporal Handred can be the imaging source?"

"He can be *one* of the sources, yes. I highly doubt he will be the only one." The Dragon Lord was frowning.

"Sanabalis, what do you think is happening in the fiefs?"

"I am not entirely certain," was his reply. "Let us leave the question of the subtle difficulty for the Arkon's return. I have a different one. What possessed you to cross the border into the Shadows on the edge of Tiamaris?"

"Maggaron. He wouldn't come to us."

"I have a few questions about the nature of Maggaron," Sanabalis replied.

"So do I. I don't think we're going to get all the relevant answers until we can speak to Mejrah."

Sanabalis frowned. "I have not asked Ybelline to enter the fief. For obvious reasons, I consider the danger to the castelord to be too high to justify the request; she is, however, the single most adept speaker of the Norannir tongue. Very well." He looked as if he would say more, but the door opened and the Arkon walked in. He was holding a crystal the size of a coin in his hand; it was smaller than the memory crystals Kaylin had, on several occasions, been required to carry. Its base color seemed to be a transparent blue, or possibly a faded purple; it was hard to tell.

He set it on the tabletop and spoke a single word. An image rose, like solid mist, from the heart of the crystal, spreading both up and out until it occupied a much larger space. The image was, oddly enough, a Dragon in draconic form. It was obviously scaled down, but even so, was about the size of a normal person, stretched lengthwise. It was also taller.

The Dragon was a cobalt blue. Its miniature scales caught and reflected the room's diffuse light as if they were solid. The Arkon spoke another—much louder—word and the Dragon lifted its neck and spread its wings to their full span.

"With your permission?" Severn said to the Arkon, who raised a brow and then nodded brusquely. He then approached the miniature Dragon and extended a hand. The Dragon attempted to remove it; Kaylin heard the snap of jaws that suddenly didn't seem so small and harmless as the Corporal quickly withdrew.

Sanabalis snorted. "It cannot actually harm you. The sounds and the visual representation of movement are present. The tactile components—unless one is in direct contact with the crystal—are not."

Severn nodded, but didn't offer the image his hand again. "If I were holding the crystal?"

"You would experience the physical sensation, but unless you were a mage with a great natural talent and no control whatsoever, you wouldn't be bleeding. Contact with the crystal also gives you more direct control over the image and its presentation." The Arkon spoke again, and this time, the miniature Dragon answered. Kaylin did not clap hands over her ears because she'd been expecting it.

"Will training the crystal require the loss of this image?" Severn asked quietly.

The Arkon lifted a brow. "No. In a lesser crystal, the answer would be different and in that case, I would cede you one over my ashes. This, and a handful of others like it, were created before the Empire. This image," he added, his voice inexplicably softening, "is the oldest it contains, and the strongest. If you do nothing, or if your focus is not strong, this is the image that you will present when you hold and invoke it."

Sanabalis was staring at the miniature Dragon in a very odd way. His eyes were, momentarily, gold—and most of the gold Kaylin had seen today had been in the eyes of a corpse. "Who is it?" she asked Sanabalis.

He didn't seem to hear her. "Arkon, I feel it germane to remind you of the unpredictable nature of the Private's magic."

"If the crystal is damaged, the unpredictable nature of her power—and the unfortunate squabbles about her training— will no longer be an issue," was the unpromising reply. "But I would prefer that Corporal Handred be both its keeper and its invoker for the time being." He gestured and the image of the Dragon was sucked back into the heart of the blue gem. "Please," he added, indicating the crystal. "Corporal."

Severn nodded, and without hesitation, picked up the crystal and held it cupped in his right palm.

"You will feel the crystal's power," the Arkon said. "It is not unlike brief contact with the Tha'alani. It *is* intrusive."

Severn nodded again.

"Concentrate on the central image—or related images— you wish the crystal to store. When you wish to begin recording, inform me."

Severn closed his eyes. His grip on the crystal didn't change. Kaylin, hands behind her back, watched as the hair on the back of her neck began to rise. It was her usual physical reaction to the sudden influx of magic, which was odd: the image of the Dragon itself had caused no discomfort.

Nothing discernible happened to either Severn or the crystal, but her skin began to tingle. The Arkon nodded to himself, but said nothing and did nothing. Minutes passed and extended. There was no easy way to mark the passage of time in the featureless, windowless room. Kaylin began to pace, her hands still locked behind her back.

The crystal in Severn's hand finally began to glow. Severn's eyes were still closed, but his grip on the crystal tightened involuntarily, and the line of his jaw tensed. His knuckles also whitened. Kaylin took a step toward him that was just as involuntary, and Sanabalis caught—and held—her arm. She quieted instantly, but the Dragon Lord didn't let go.

"How long is this going to go on?" she demanded.

"For as long as it takes. It will not cause the Corporal any permanent harm."

As long as it takes, in Dragon parlance, was almost three hours. Kaylin, who *had* experienced the sting of melding with a memory crystal, decided then and there that she was never, ever going to requisition one of these things again, unless her career depended on it. Memory crystals, while sharp and painful, took no time. Added to that was the fact that Severn's face was the color of white cheese by the end of those hours.

The crystal, on the other hand, looked unchanged.

"Good, Corporal. Concentrate on the image now, and let me see whether or not the impression you've made is a solid one."

"It had better be," Kaylin muttered. The piercing and entirely unfriendly look she immediately received from the Arkon was a reminder that Dragon hearing was superior to human hearing.

Severn closed his eyes. The heart of the crystal began to

glow, and light spread out through its hard sides in narrow filaments that looked disturbingly like tendrils. They slithered—that really was the word for it—toward each other, intertwining as they moved, and merging, at last, into a central standing figure in a familiar blue dress.

The dress itself was a perfect replica of the seven similar dresses that Kaylin had seen; the woman, however, took longer to come into focus; the edges of her jaw and nose were blurred, as were the contours of her cheekbones, the hollows of her eyes. They radiated light, bleaching her skin of color. Sanabalis let go of Kaylin's arm and she moved away from him, toward both Severn and the image that was solidifying above his hand.

Her own visual memory of the dead woman—all seven of them—was not so clear that she could have painted a picture; it was clear enough that she could tell Severn what she thought was missing. But even as she opened her mouth to do just that, the image suddenly sharpened.

"That's it," she said softly. "That's her. Or one of her. I don't think she'd be that pale if she were alive."

Severn nodded. He was sweating, and his jaw was locked in place; she couldn't have wedged words out of him had she tried. She didn't. She meant to ask Severn about the woman's eye color, because the crystal was meant to imply that this was a *living*, missing person. Her eyes were closed.

When they opened, they were a liquid, perfect gold, and Kaylin was momentarily deafened by the Arkon's sudden roar.

The roar was wordless, but it went on for at least a minute, shorn of syllables, of anything that would elevate it above the dangerously bestial. His familiar eyes had shaded to a red that was almost deeper than Tiamaris's eyes had gone. Familiarity with the booming voices of Dragons speaking in their native tongue meant she didn't immediately dive for cover under the room's only table, but it was close.

Severn, on the other hand, seemed unfazed. He was closer to the Arkon and he waited with what seemed to be his usual calm. He was faking.

"If this is some attempt at humor," the Arkon finally said, literal fire around the edges of his words, "you have survived it. You will not, however, continue to do so if you do not cease."

Kaylin glanced back at Sanabalis, whose eyes were a very dark shade of orange. He, however, was as outwardly calm as Severn; if it weren't for his eyes, she wouldn't have known he was worried at all. "Arkon," he said in quiet High Barrani.

The Arkon swiveled. This time, he didn't bother to contain his fire; he roared, and it hit Sanabalis full on. Apparently, this is what enraged Dragons did—to each other—because Sanabalis flinched as his robes blackened, but he didn't otherwise move or spew fire in return.

This would be a very, very good time to leave, Kaylin thought. On the other hand, it would only catch his attention. The underside of the table was looking better and better all the time. Sanabalis opened his mouth and drew a longer-than-usual breath, which gave Kaylin just enough time to cover her ears. Not that it helped.

Severn took a step back, toward the wall farthest from where the two Dragons were now shouting at each other and not incidentally blocking the room's only known door. The two Hawks exchanged a glance—words wouldn't carry—and Severn's lips turned up in a brief grimace. He mouthed the words *This was your idea, remember,* as they settled in to wait.

Dragon wings did not magically unfurl and native forms did not magically appear, which, given the size and the thick stone walls of a room that would have trouble accommodating one Dragon, never mind two, was a damn good thing. But it was clear that the Arkon was actually upset. Or enraged. He focused the full force of his ire on Sanabalis for the duration of a turbulent hour before he heaved one more fiery breath and stormed out of the room, slamming the door behind him.

Sanabalis, in robes that were mostly ash, now readjusted his clothing into a more Dragon military style: scales grew out of the folds of his flesh and more or less armored him. It was disturbing to watch, but it was probably a touch *less* disturbing than watching him walk through the Library butt naked would have been.

"You couldn't have warned us?" Kaylin asked, although she kept her voice as low as she could.

"Demonstrably not. He will have to consider what he has seen, and we will have to wait until he has." He turned to Severn as if this sort of thing happened every day, and said, "Bring the crystal to the table. I would like to examine it more closely now that we have leisure to do so."

"Leisure?"

"We can't do anything else," he pointed out. "The door has been magically sealed."

"Why?"

"I believe the Arkon does wish to discuss this with you both—eventually. At the moment, if we are very lucky, he will not march straight to the Emperor."

"The...Emperor."

"Indeed. I will say that the last time he was in this much of a fury he staved in a wall somewhere beyond the actual Library proper." He glanced at them both and added, "It was well before either of you were born, and before you ask, no—no one was stupid enough to be standing between the Arkon and the wall. Any wall.

"If this newest crop of librarians has any wisdom at all—and for the most part, he chooses them, so it would be highly likely that this is the case—there will be no nonstructural casualties."

Severn set the crystal down; the image didn't dissipate. Sanabalis approached it with caution, although he knew it was entirely a projection. Sanabalis's eyes were orange, but his inner membranes were up. Kaylin watched him. The Arkon was the oldest of the Imperial Dragons, and clearly this woman—or her eyes—meant something to him. Tiamaris was the youngest, and it had also clearly meant something to him.

But Tiamaris, if you believed the Dragons, was the racial equivalent of Kaylin in terms of temperament. Sanabalis was not.

"You said you saw three of the corpses?" she said, forcing the last syllable up to make it a question.

"I did."

"And you noted nothing strange?"

"Beyond the fact that they were identical, down to the lack of visible distinguishing marks and any obvious cause of death?"

"Beyond that, yes. That wasn't what sent the Arkon off to rearrange architecture."

He snorted. "No. Nor did Tiamaris, and he had in his possession all seven." Sanabalis was silent. There was clearly no point in asking him what he'd suspected, and Kaylin was restrained enough not to try.

"If the Arkon had seen the seven?"

"I think it possible that the Arkon's reaction would have been very different than either of our initial reactions. He had already begun to descend before the image's eyes opened."

"Who does he think she is, or was?"

"That would be the question," was the quiet reply. "Tiamaris will not, now, cede any of the corpses to the Halls or the Emperor. But you have some influence with the Lady. Use it, Kaylin. If the corpse cannot be brought to the Halls, you have the dubious privilege of convincing the Hawklord to second Red to the fiefs for an autopsy."

"Given Tiamaris's reaction, I'm not sure performing an autopsy is in the cards. We *need* Red," she added. "I could try to get Mallory sent in his place."

Sanabalis snorted. So did Severn.

"What do you think he'll find?" she finally asked.

"I don't know," Sanabalis replied. "But we now need the information. You will not understand why," he added softly, "but I am almost certain that these deaths—if they are, indeed, deaths—are entirely a product of the Shadows that lie at the heart of *Ravellon*. And they are spread throughout the fief of Tiamaris."

"You think they might be spread throughout the rest of the fiefs, as well." It wasn't a question.

"The situation in Tiamaris is different," he replied, but it took him at least a minute. "Only Tiamaris has a Dragon for a Lord. I do not know if that was the intent of the Tower's creators or not; I know that something at the heart of *Ravellon* has now turned an eye upon the newest of the fieflords. If there were no similar identical corpses to be found in any other fief, it would not surprise me."

"And if there were?"

He was silent. It wasn't a particularly *good* silence.

"Sanabalis, I've never met a female Dragon."

"No."

"Aren't there any?"

"That is not a topic of discussion that will prove fruitful," he replied, and as he glanced at her, she concurred, because his eyes had dipped to a shade that was almost—but not quite—

red. She had the usual vested interest in making sure they didn't get there. "I will speak with Lord Grammayre on the morrow."

"Sanabalis—"

"I do not know, Kaylin. Today was more...eventful...than even I had guessed it would be. Diarmat's lesson tomorrow, however, must not be missed. Unless you are severely injured. Minor injuries, sadly, will count for little. But you have failed to mention Maggaron to the Arkon; you have also failed to mention your sword."

CHAPTER 10

Sanabalis grimaced. "This is not the time to be careless in the presence of magical weapons, especially not if you claim to own said weapon." His eyes were now a pale orange. "You will, of course, procure a sheath before you meet with Diarmat again, if it is at all possible. I assume the weapon didn't come with a sheath?"

"Given the reaction of the previous owner to the question, I'm assuming the answer is no."

"He was angry?"

"Horrified. I don't want to ask him again. I got the impression the question itself was hideously disrespectful."

He glanced toward the unadorned ceiling in much the same way her Sergeant had when she'd been younger. "It is no small wonder to me that your lives are so short," he finally said. "They are far, far too crowded with immediate catastrophe; if the whole of my life had been this eventful, I'm not sure I wouldn't have considered mortality a distinct boon." He turned his back on the figure that stood, unmoving, just above the crystal Severn had set on the table.

"Sanabalis—"

He cleared his throat.

"Lord Sanabalis."

"Yes?"

"What did the four of you *say* when you were flying over the City?"

Sanabalis didn't reply.

"What did you hear?"

Severn stepped in and carefully tapped her shoulder. She turned. "If it's a matter of the Dragon Court, think carefully about how much you want the answer. Lord Diarmat is unlikely to approve."

"And if we need it?"

"If you require the answer," Sanabalis replied heavily, "you will know." He started to speak, stopped, and made a show of straightening out his beard.

The door flew open, framing the Arkon, whose eyes were now an even, simmering orange. They darkened when he glanced at the figure that adorned the tabletop, but this time no flame accompanied his exhalation.

"Arkon," Kaylin said quietly. She felt Sanabalis's warning glare drill the side of her cheek, and ignored it. Nothing she'd ever said had caused the ancient Librarian to spout flame in the middle of his hoard, after all. "Her eyes were only golden when the bodies were examined under spell. In normal conditions we believe they were brown or hazel."

"Whose spell?" he asked, voice sharp.

"Tiamaris's."

The glance that the Arkon shot at Sanabalis was far from friendly, but he seemed satisfied with the answer. "My apologies for my outburst," he said. "I was...surprised. I also interrupted the details of your investigation thus far, and I am now ready to entertain *all* those missing details. Private?"

When she had finished answering his questions, she felt as if she was sitting in on an interrogation. Her own. But the Arkon had turned his attention to Severn. "You took samples of the cloth?"

Severn nodded.

"I would like to examine them."

Without blinking, Severn took them out of his satchel and set them on the table to one side of the crystal.

"Why did you cut these?"

"The dye," Severn replied after a careful pause. "It's an unusual shade of blue. Blue dyes aren't common, and they're expensive; they're not readily found anywhere in the fiefs. If the fabric was made in the Empire, we should be able to find out where."

"Leave one sample with me."

Severn nodded again.

"I would also appreciate a report—in person, and off the record—of your findings in this particular investigation. Lord Diarmat was mildly skeptical about the necessity of your presence in the fiefs. *I* will set his doubts *permanently* to rest."

"Arkon," Sanabalis began.

"If he wishes to argue, he may."

"Can he do it when I'm nowhere near the Palace?" Kaylin asked.

Both Dragons turned to look at her, and she had the grace to redden. "There are a couple of other things that we haven't had the time to mention."

The Arkon's brows rose quickly enough there was some chance they'd detach.

"It has," Sanabalis told the Arkon, "been a very complicated day."

Before they'd finished in the Library, the Arkon took a few moments to examine the sword Kaylin had left at the front desk with a man who was now understandably entirely absent. The sword, however, was where she had placed it, boxed in on all sides by glass, wood, and magic.

His mind was clearly not on the sword itself, but his inspection wasn't cursory; it just wasn't magical. He asked Sanabalis for details—in, thankfully, High Barrani; Sanabalis supplied them. Kaylin glanced around; nothing *seemed* to be on fire, and nothing had been staved in.

Sanabalis raised a brow. "You don't think he'd damage any part of the *Library,* do you?"

Because she thought better of answering that question where anyone might hear her, she didn't fall further afoul of the Arkon. Unfortunately, before he dismissed the Hawks, he asked several pointed questions, and he didn't seem entirely satisfied with the answers. Given that Kaylin surrendered everything she knew of relevance to Maggaron, Ascendants, magical swords, and fief borders, she thought it a touch unfair. Especially since he didn't seem to consider any of *her* questions pertinent or worth answering in return.

But after what felt like hours, he rose. "You will take the crystal, Corporal. Use it as you see fit in the confines of your investigation. Because you are both so young and at least one of you defines lack of wisdom by her actions, I will tell you to use that crystal as far from the Dragon Court as it is possible to do." He took the swatch of cloth Severn had left him and said, "I will begin my own investigations here; we may confer at the end of tomorrow."

Kaylin lifted a hand.

"Private?"

"I have lessons with Lord Diarmat tomorrow when I return from the fiefs."

"Yes. But Corporal Handred does not. You may join us if you survive your lesson."

There was only one stop left—the Halls of Law. It was now dark enough that the office, with its gossip, betting pools, and paperwork, would be relatively quiet. Given the day, this was a good thing.

Marcus, on the other hand, was still in the office. The mirror on his desk—a small, unobtrusive oval on iron legs—was putting on a light show that made Kaylin turn to look at the schedule posted on the board. But Teela, Tain, and a half dozen of the other Barrani Hawks were also in the office; quiet wasn't in the cards.

Teela looked up as Kaylin, sidling around Marcus's desk, approached. Barrani didn't need much sleep or food—unless you counted alcohol—but this didn't show on Teela's face; she looked peaked. "Kitling," she said. "Corporal." Peaked changed to something with less approval in it. "What are you carrying, Kaylin?"

"A sword."

"With no sheath."

"It didn't come with a sheath." She laid it across the surface of an almost-clean desk and draped herself over the back of the nearest empty chair. Marcus hadn't even growled when she'd entered, which was always a bad sign.

"Where did it come from?"

"The fiefs. It's—it's a magic sword."

If she'd expected Teela to snort or laugh, she was disappointed; the Barrani Hawk was staring at the sword as if she expected it to stand up and dance. "Yes," she finally said. "It is."

Tain walked by, dropped a stack of papers to one side of Teela's elbows, and said, "Lord Grammayre expects us within an hour."

"An hour from now?" Kaylin asked.

"An hour from now."

She watched Tain leave, and then turned to Teela. "The Exchequer?"

Teela nodded. It was a curt, grim motion.

"How 'not well' is the investigation going?"

"There's some possibility that the Arcanum is indirectly involved."

Severn whistled.

"And how is the fief of Tiamaris?" Teela asked, as if a change of subject could bring momentary relief.

Kaylin's shrug was less graceful than Teela's, but not by much. This caused Teela to raise one dark brow over eyes that were a little too blue to be emerald. "Lord Diarmat has petitioned the Hawklord for your services."

"I know."

"Ah, no, you don't. He sent a second request in, directly, by his personal courier, citing the lack of legal jurisdiction for your current deployment."

Kaylin grimaced. "I think that'll be withdrawn."

"You have information you can bring to bear on Diarmat?" the Barrani Hawk said as her second brow joined the first in its high arch above her eyes. "Spill."

Kaylin almost laughed. "I have no information that I could use against Diarmat, and even if I did, I wouldn't touch it—I like breathing. But there's something going on in the fiefs of Tiamaris, and I think it's important."

"Diarmat is not going to care what you think."

"I think it's important because the Arkon thinks it's important."

"Better. How important?"

"He was...intemperate enough...to breathe fire on the only person in the room it wouldn't kill?"

"That's important," was the grave reply. "Anything else?"

Kaylin leaned over her folded arms. "We spent an hour at the interior borders in Tiamaris. The Shadows were there—and focused—in an all-out attack."

Teela stilled. "The borders held?"

"Yes. But as far as I can tell, that's the point of the borders."

"That's the public point of the borders, yes. But, kitling, you've seen the borders before, albeit in Nightshade, not Tiamaris. Was there an obvious, physical barrier then?"

"No."

"Did Shadows cross the Nightshade border?"

"Yes."

"And you weren't alarmed."

"I was almost *killed,* Teela. How much alarm do I have to show?"

Teela laughed, and reaching out, she ruffled Kaylin's hair. Kaylin, used to this, didn't resent it as much as she probably should have. "No. I wasn't alarmed by the crossing. I didn't know what purpose the Towers served at the time."

"And now?"

Kaylin was thoughtful. "Now? I think Nightshade must have allowed them to cross."

"You need to rethink that."

"You weren't there."

"No. But, Kaylin, think on this: the Shadows are contained or confined unless the borders become destabilized."

"I know that."

"Not everything that can speak to—or hear—Shadow is entirely *of* it. It's why the Dragon Outcaste is considered such a threat. He can move between the borders of the fiefs and into the Empire, should he so choose, because he *is* a Dragon. His power is not in its entirety of the Shadow."

She thought about this for a moment. "And the Leontines?"

"The same. They are not, or were not, entirely of the Shadow, but they were very, very vulnerable to its voice and its words." Teela shook her head.

"And Ferals?"

Teela shrugged. "They were probably once rats; they certainly have, or had, a physical, mortal component."

"Which is why they can come to the fiefs."

"Yes. It is also why they aren't a danger." Kaylin glared; Teela was so preoccupied, she didn't notice.

Kaylin leaned even farther over her arms, tilting the chair to bring herself closer to Teela. "I wanted to ask you a question."

"No, really?"

"Have you ever taken someone else's name?"

If she'd asked a mortal that question, she would have been talking about marriage—itself a hot topic on any given day in the office, as some people were trying to avoid it, some were actively courting it, and some were in the midst of discovering that they hadn't really learned anything from their previous mistakes. True, some of the naming customs were race and class dependent, itself a topic for some heat when the days were slow and the Sergeant was somewhere else, but it still had that meaning.

She was talking to a Barrani, an Immortal, and a Lord of the High Court.

"Kitling," that Lord said, "this is not the time for that discussion. And, in case you're slouching on Barrani social custom—"

"No classes covered this."

"It's not unlike asking for the explicit details of your sex life. But more offensive." All of this was said in Elantran. "I know you, and I've known you for years, so I *choose* not to take offense. For now. What might solidify that position would be your careful explanation about *why you're asking.*"

"Because I don't understand how it works."

"Clearly. What I don't understand is why it's relevant." She lifted a hand. "What you know—or do not know—is something you had best keep to yourself. Why are you asking what I know?"

Kaylin hesitated. Teela's eyes shaded toward a blue that had no green in it. "Kitling, I asked you a question."

"I...accepted...the name of a man who came out of the Shadows on the wrong side of the border."

Teela stared at her as if she'd grown two extra heads, neither of which had the brains she clearly thought Kaylin was missing. "Is 'accept' a human euphemism for 'take'?"

"...Maybe."

Teela was silent for a minute. Her eyes didn't get any greener as the time passed. "When you say he came out of Shadow, what exactly do you mean? Was he fleeing the Shadows? Had he somehow wandered across the border without realizing it?" Her tone made it clear that she found this improbable.

"Not exactly."

"*Kaylin.*"

"He was kind of leading the attack."

Teela looked at Severn, who nodded. "You took his name presumably to end the attack?"

"Yes."

Teela raised a brow.

"Mostly."

"Kaylin."

"I took his name because he wanted me to take his name, Teela. I'm not the only one who holds it—and the other person, persons, or unknown entities were what caused him to start the attack in the first place. He didn't *want* to be fighting *for* the Shadows; his people hate them."

"His people?" Teela frowned. "Are you telling me he's one of the refugees?"

"Yes. And no. He was, but I think his role was special."

"So he arrived here with his people—Kaylin, they're mortal as far as I can tell. They don't *have* names. He then wandered across the border where he gave a name he shouldn't be able to possess to the Shadows on the other side?"

"No."

Tain had come to stand to one side of Teela, and was gazing pointedly at the untouched reports by her elbow when he inserted his stare into the conversation.

"He says he fell in battle while in his own world."

"And he ended up here how?"

"I don't know."

"Kaylin, did it not occur to you that he was *lying?*"

"He couldn't."

"Because?"

"I held his name."

"You understand," Teela said, rising and grabbing the stack of papers that needed her attention, "that this is not like taking in a mangy stray, unless the stray just happens to be rabid? If he is indeed bound to the Shadows, your binding takes precedence if and only if you *enforce* it. Your will against theirs, for as long as the person being pulled between you survives." She shoved her chair to one side, glanced at the papers in a hand that was now almost fist, and then said, "Where is he now?"

"I left him in the Tower of Tiamaris."

This seemed to be the right answer, even if it plainly followed a host of the wrong ones. "You can't hold him," Teela said, voice flat.

Tain touched her shoulder, and she flicked his hand aside without even looking at him.

"If I can't hold him, the Shadows have—"

"An agent in the heart of the fiefs, yes."

"I don't know how to let his name go," Kaylin finally said, after a long pause. "I don't know how to just forget I know it."

Tain coughed, and this time, Teela did look at him. It wasn't particularly friendly. "You can't," was her flat, cool reply. "If you are ever in a position where you need to break the binding of a name, there is only one option available to both you and the named. You kill him. Or her.

"There's more—much more—that needs to be said, and I don't have the time if I want to keep my job and if the Hawklord wants to mollify the Emperor. But, kitling, do *not* do anything stupid in the fiefs. You are playing with something you don't understand."

"It's not the only name—"

"That you've seen?" She raised a hand. "What I suspect, I suspect, and it is best left—if you value *my* life—as mere suspicion. But let me remind you of the most basic truth about True Names: if you seek to *use* the name against the person who gives it life and force, you will have to have, and sustain, the greater will, and all of your focus must be upon the destruction of any spirit or free will standing between you and domination.

"Any. The stories in which the knowledge itself is enough are just that—stories. Only mortals believe them. You do not have the force of will to take and use any of the names you might possibly have seen in the past.

"I have to go. But—inasmuch as I understand the Towers, and really, I don't, the Tower is possibly the safest place in the Empire to leave him for the moment. Until you have a better grasp of what you've started, *leave him there.*" Her eyes were almost midnight blue as she suddenly looked at the sword. "This blade—did it come from your servitor?"

"...Yes."

"And you're *carrying it unsheathed?*"

Since the answer was obvious, Teela didn't wait for it. Instead, she stormed off into an office that had, apparently, fallen as silent as the office ever fell.

"Well, that could have gone better," Kaylin said as she rose.

"It could have gone worse. You're still standing, and there's no blood." Severn nodded in Marcus's direction. "Come on."

"She was pissed off."

"Yes. She's worried."

Kaylin exhaled. "The Exchequer—"

"Not about the Exchequer, Kaylin," Severn replied, raising a brow. "About you."

Before Kaylin could reply, he walked toward Marcus's desk, where the mirror could be heard conveying someone's raised voice. Or voices.

Sergeant Kassan looked as if he'd gained a lot of weight, but Leontines looked like that when their fur was almost standing on end. His eyes, the best indicator of mood, were a wary, but pale, orange. "If it's not life-threatening, I don't have time," he said, before he looked up.

The person on the other end of the mirror looked surprisingly official by dress and age. Kaylin didn't recognize him.

Marcus, however, considered Kaylin's presence life-threatening enough. "Please excuse me, Councilor. A matter of some import has come up."

"More important than this?" was the loud and angry reply.

Marcus exhaled on a low growl. "It had better be." The mirror's image froze, and he turned to his Private and his Corporal who, to their credit, were not trying to become instantly invisible. "Did I tell you to report in?"

"Yes, sir."

"Shoot me. Lord Diarmat wasn't pleased with your current assignment."

"No, sir. I have some good news on that front, though."

"Good. Good news is in rare supply at the moment. What is it?"

"The Arkon's convinced that the current assignment is necessary."

"This is obviously a definition of good you didn't learn in the Halls," was the sour reply. "What else are you going to drag away from my department into a realm 'outside of my jurisdiction'?"

"We'd like to borrow Red for a few hours tomorrow morning."

His brows rose. His ears stiffened. "Red specializes in things that can't move. In particular, corpses."

"Yes, sir."

"Then I suggest you bring whatever you want him to examine *to the Halls*."

Kaylin was prepared for this. "We would, but the bodies in

question are possibly magical in nature. To a cursory external examination, they look human."

"And the bodies already in the morgue *also* look human. The bodies that will no doubt pile up the minute he steps out of those doors will undoubtedly look human, as well. Get to the point, Private. While I appreciate a break from the conversation I was having, I have limited time and zero patience."

"We have seven corpses, collected over the course of two days."

"Not my problem."

"They're identical. Not the cause of death—frankly, we can't find one—but the bodies themselves. They are all, as near as we can determine, the same woman."

The Sergeant didn't even blink. "And nothing in your fancy Dragon-run fief is capable of pointing out the reasons that's impossible?"

"No, sir. Without the magic inherent in the Tower, we wouldn't have a morgue capable of stopping the bodies from rotting." Kaylin didn't add that she suspected magic wasn't the only reason they hadn't started to decay; Marcus was in a bad enough mood she was willing to leave that to Red, poor sod. "Tiamaris has no formal missing-persons reports because there's no one to report *to,* and even if an agency that could take reports existed, no one would talk to them anyway, so there's no fast way of checking the dead against reports.

"On the other hand, if Tiamaris *had* an Exchequer and he thought the Exchequer was causing him trouble? There wouldn't be a lot of hassle about due legal process. He'd just eat him."

"If it weren't for the fact that due legal process pays the bills," came the growl of a reply, "I'd consider agitating for the lack, myself." He exhaled, ran his hands over his eyes, and said, "How serious is this?" in an entirely different tone of voice.

"My guess?"

Marcus nodded.

"It's serious. It's not possible that the same woman could have died—without cause—seven times that we know of, so there's got to be magic involved. What we don't—or won't— know is how extensive that magic is."

"What do you think?"

"I think you can't make bodies out of nothing. It's not an illusion; magical scans would detect that instantly, and Tiamaris is more than capable of that level of magic. The change—and I'm assuming that some bodies somewhere were magically altered—is physical, real, and finished."

"You think these bodies started out looking entirely different?"

"I can't think of any other explanation. Tiamaris can't, either..." She hesitated again.

"Spit it out," the Sergeant growled.

"The Arkon was *very* upset. I've never seen him so—"

"Unhappy?"

"Enraged. I think he melted some of the floor—the *stone* floor."

The Sergeant whistled.

"It's possible that there *is* some underlying explanation for the seven identical bodies that we're not privy to at the moment."

"Unlikely."

"That's what we think. So we're looking for missing people of approximately the same gender, shape, and age in a fief that has no method of making those disappearances easily accessible. Best case, we find a mage who's transforming other people. Worst case, they're not actually corpses at all, but something different."

"So far, there's no reason the corpses can't come *here*."

"Since we have no idea how they died or how they were created, for want of a better word, we've got no guarantees that we don't cart the corpses out of the fief and have them come to life on Red's slab. If they do, they're not likely to be our friends."

Marcus nodded then. "You've got him. Tell him when and where you want him to be—I'll raise him on mirror and give him some warning. But, Private?" he added as she and Severn turned to head toward the morgue. "Lose him, and you'll be paying for the rest of your short career."

"Yes, sir."

Red was working in the morgue. Kaylin, at an early age, had been both fascinated and horrified by vivisection, and Red—like many of the Hawks—had been patient enough to tolerate her presence at his elbow. How, she didn't know. Red's job had never, as far as Kaylin knew, involved patrolling the streets of any part of the City, although she thought he'd be good at it; he was patient with idiots.

He was untying the apron he wore, and glancing balefully at the mirror that adorned the full length of the wall opposite the door, when they entered.

"Ironjaw said you had an on-site assignment for me," he said as he sponged his hands clean.

Kaylin nodded.

"How much metal am I going to need?"

"All of it."

"What kind of records access will I have?"

"Portable."

Red grimaced. "Where?"

"That's the trickier part. It's in the fiefs."

"The fiefs. Now I've seen everything." He shook his head. "How old is the body?"

"Bodies. Two or three days, on the surface of things."

"Preserved?"

"More or less. Tiamaris has done some time with the Hawks, and he's the one running the morgue. He doesn't have a staff of consulting mages, though."

"That's probably an advantage," was the curt reply. Red began to pack his things, and Kaylin obligingly carried the bag into which he was dropping them. "I won't have much time," he said as he slid scalpels of varying widths into their leather cases.

"You're expecting a corpse here?"

"If they can find him, yes. Some people are holding out hope that if we do, he won't be a corpse."

"Who?"

"I don't know his name," was the serious and quiet reply. "But he is—or was—a key witness in the Exchequer investigation."

"Any reason you're betting on a corpse?"

"Yeah. What was left of his home wasn't pretty. It *was* magically demolished, but the trace was contaminated."

"How?"

"He was a mage, of sorts. Most of the strong signatures are his."

"He didn't destroy his own home."

"He could have. Doesn't seem sane or likely. But, well. Mage."

"And if I ask how a mage was involved in the investigation as a witness—"

"Don't. Let's just say he was a junior Arcanist and leave it at that. You can bother Ironjaw if you're feeling suicidal, but it's not going to get you any answers. Until he calls you in—and I think we could have used you for the on-site investigation of the wreckage—it's locked down." He finished his cursory inspection of his traveling gear, and nodded. "You'll be here in the morning?"

"On time, even. Promise."

"Good. I'd bet on it, but at the moment, the office betting pools are being neglected. Anything else?"

"No."

"Yes," Severn said. "Not a corpse."

"Good. A little variety never hurt anyone. What is it?"

Reaching into his pouch, Severn pulled out the swatches of cloth he'd cut from six of the dresses; the seventh piece was in the Imperial Library under the Arkon's ferocious glare. Red frowned and held out a hand. "These are from what?"

"Dresses. Seven identical dresses, or as near to identical as they could be, given external factors."

"This is silk," Red said. "But the color—"

Severn nodded as Red fished out a jeweler's glass. He barked a single word and the lights in the room brightened. "You want me to figure out how it's dyed?"

"Yes. That might tell us where it was dyed; I don't think the color is all that common."

"I'll see what I can do—I'm not sure I'll have what you need for tomorrow; it depends on what happens for the rest of the day. Or night."

"Night?" Kaylin's voice rose slightly.

"I'm on call."

"Since when?"

Red looked down at her. "Since the investigation into the Exchequer was blown by your theoretical fraud on Elani. It's gotten uglier by the minute, and I'm not sure the Halls are going to drag themselves out of this mess smelling like roses. But at the moment, I'm free. You want to watch?"

Kaylin did. But she also wanted to sleep. "I did say I would get here first thing in the morning, and on time."

He chuckled. It was a weary chuckle but it would do.

Severn volunteered to walk Kaylin home. In and of itself, that wasn't unusual. She expected him to bring up Nightshade, but he was kind. He didn't. He didn't speak much at all, but it wasn't a cold or hostile silence. When they reached her room, she crawled under the bed and retrieved the egg crate.

He watched, leaning against the wall nearest the door, a comfortable shadow in the moonlight.

"Can you check my mirror?"

"It's gray."

"Good." She was busy unwinding the scraps of fabric that she hoped kept the egg warm in her absence. Having done that, she carefully pulled the egg out of its temporary home. "Do you—do you want to stay?"

"I don't think there's enough room in the bed for you, me, and a fragile egg," he replied. He was smiling; she could hear it in the words, even if she couldn't see it. "How is the egg?"

"It's—I think it's harder. Or rougher. I'm not sure."

"You should take it to Evanton."

"In my copious free time, I'll be sure to do that." She began to peel off clothing; the night was cool. Tonight, because Severn was standing there, she actually folded it as neatly as she could in the dark and left it in a small standing pile near the foot of the bed. Then she curled up on her side around the egg, wrapping her arms across it just before she pulled the blankets up beneath her chin.

"I'll come by in the morning," he said. "With food."

"Bracer?"

"If it's come home by now, I'll leave it. I'm tired of water stains on my furniture."

"I promise I'll stop throwing the damn thing into the Ablayne."

"Don't make promises you can't keep. I'll see you in the morning."

She drifted off even before she heard the click of the door's lock.

CHAPTER 11

Red was punctual. Since Severn was absolutely true to his word and had shown up with food at the crack of dawn—if you could call something as dark as that dawn—so was Kaylin. Her sleep had been the usual broken affair. It was why she valued exhaustion so highly; if she fell over face-first the minute she hit the bed, she was likely to sleep like the dead for at least four hours. It was seldom that she slept for longer without waking from dream or nightmare.

On the other hand, the last week had pretty much been one waking nightmare after another; if this kept up, her dreams wouldn't have the power to terrify her.

"Here," Red said, handing Kaylin one very heavy leather bag. Its handles were worn and shiny. "Be useful."

Some minor changes in Red's uniform were hastily made before they picked up the carriage in the yards and headed toward the bridge that led to Tiamaris.

"Sergeant Kassan requested that we mirror the Halls when

we arrive. I take it we *can* mirror the Halls from wherever it is we're going?"

"We can."

"Good. I think his sleep has been poor enough that he regretted yesterday's decision; I thought I wouldn't make it out the doors. We're to mirror when I arrive, when I leave, and if I find anything significant. If there's trouble crossing, he'll send Swords to meet us on the way out."

Kaylin groaned. "Just what we need."

"He also asked me to remind you that you have an etiquette lesson tonight. He doesn't care if we discover the probable end of the world—Corporal Handred and I can stay. *You* can't."

Tara was gardening. Morse was standing a couple of yards away from where Tara was moving clods of dirt around, trying to look useful. She even looked grateful at the arrival of the carriage, because it gave her something to do.

"Lord Tiamaris is waiting for you. Lord Sanabalis arrived half an hour ago."

"Was he supposed to be here? He told me he doesn't enter the Tower—"

"He doesn't. I didn't ask." Morse gave Red the once-over, but didn't give him trouble; instead, she sauntered toward the Tower's door. Red, to his credit, didn't spend much time gawking. He walked up to the door, lifted his hand, and looked confused. Kaylin wanted to laugh.

"This door doesn't have wards," she told him.

"I...can see that."

"Tiamaris's a Dragon; no one's going to waltz in and steal stuff. Even if they did, they wouldn't get far; the Tower would probably eat them before Tiamaris could."

Tara suddenly poked her head up from whatever patch of dirt held her attention. "Oh, I would never do that," she said as she unfolded and began to wipe her hands on an apron that was already mostly dirt. "Not without my Lord's permission."

"Red," Kaylin said. "This is Tara. She's the Avatar of the Tower. Tara, this is Red."

"He's the coroner?"

"Yes." To Red, she said, "She can sort of read stray thoughts, so you'll probably want to keep yours relatively clean."

"Relative to what?"

"Oh, Morse's."

Morse told them all what they could do as Tara laughed. She made her way to the doors—which were still closed—and offered Red a not very clean hand. Red enveloped it, anyway. "I don't meet many friends of Kaylin's," she told him. "Besides Severn, I think you're the first family member she's brought to visit."

"Uh, we're not exactly related—"

"You're a Hawk, no?"

"Yes, but—"

"Tara's just confused about family," Kaylin said in a rush. The doors began to roll open, which would hopefully save her any other embarrassment.

Tiamaris stood ten feet from the doors. He wore armor—Dragon scale—and a tabard; he was prepared to fight. But he raised a brow. "Red."

"Lord Tiamaris." Red didn't skip a beat. "Lord Sanabalis?"

"He is in the morgue. Follow."

"Is there a mirror I can use there?"

"Yes. Briefly."

Marcus couldn't actually be seen when the mirror activated, but he could be clearly heard; he was growling around syllables.

"Seven bodies, Sergeant. This may be awhile. But there were no incidents on the way."

"Good. Mirror before you leave. If you need any assistance—"

Lord Sanabalis lifted a hand, and then let it drop, since Marcus couldn't see it anyway. "Sergeant Kassan," he said in a deep rumble that was probably the Dragon equivalent of growling, "I will personally escort your coroner back across the Ablayne when he has finished his duties here to *my* satisfaction. The Emperor expresses his gratitude at your understanding during this difficult time."

After which, Marcus had very little to say. The mirror went flat, shivered for a second, and then became reflective. Sanabalis then turned to the coroner. "The Emperor also wishes to convey his approval of funds to hire—and train—appropriately skilled apprentices to work in the morgue in the Halls of Law. While he understands the pressures facing the Halls at this time, he requests that such training be expedited."

Red bowed. He didn't, however, respond.

Instead, he began to set up in Tiamaris's morgue, opening his bag and spreading his tools across the only flat surface that wasn't a slab. He almost never left the Halls, but it wasn't the first time Kaylin had seen him do off-site inspections. In general, though, Red went off-site when there wasn't *enough* of a body to bring back to the Halls. This was clearly not one of those times. He donned a large, white apron, tying it loosely behind his back.

He frowned as he began to walk down the small aisle made by two large slabs and seven bodies. He paused in front of one body, and took a mirror out of one of his generous pockets. "Records." The mirror was a very small one. It wasn't generally useful for communication, except in extreme emergencies, but it could record conversation and small images, which would later be archived in the Halls.

"Magical scans have already been done," Tiamaris told him.

"Who was the investigating mage?"

"I was," Tiamaris replied.

Red nodded. "The results?"

"The only enchantment indicated involved the eyes."

"How so?"

"The color of the eyes."

"Preservative?"

Tiamaris shook his head. "Illusion."

"On a corpse? Why?"

The Dragon Lord didn't answer; Red was an old hand. He took the hint. He did open eyelids, and he did the same cursory examination on all the corpses. This took no time. While he worked, with the occasional aside to the mirror, he asked Tiamaris questions; Tiamaris answered. He then walked over to the table on which his various tools lay. "This," he said, "is *not* going to be a short day."

"Will it require more than one?" Tiamaris asked.

"If it doesn't require another three, it'll be a miracle. Not a small one, either."

"And that," Tiamaris said, turning toward the door, "is our invitation to leave."

"Where's Maggaron?" Kaylin asked Tara after the impromptu morgue's doors were firmly shut behind them.

The Avatar blinked, and then said, "He is in his room."

"Awake or asleep?"

"It is hard to tell. I believe he is awake; he is neither moving nor speaking, but his eyes appear to be open."

"What color are they?"

"Blue."

She glanced at Severn. "Are you *certain* it's safe to leave him here?"

"Yes." Tara frowned, and then added, "Perhaps I should ask for clarification before I answer. Safe for him or safe for us?"

"Either."

"It is safe for us. The Shadows cannot breach this Tower."

"His name?"

"Even if they find purchase here through use of his name, you'll sense the struggle. If you're too far away to intercede— and Lord Tiamaris feels that no point in the City is too far away, regardless of fief boundaries—it will not be safe for him, because I will have to kill him. Neither I nor my Lord will be in any significant danger."

"Then I'm going to leave him here."

"I believe Mejrah wishes to speak with you about him."

"Can it wait until tomorrow?"

"Why?"

"Because we're in theory here to investigate the deaths of those seven women, and I'm much more confident of being useful there than I am of talking to strangers near a border that's teeming with Shadow."

"You were of critical use yesterday."

Tiamaris, however, said, "It can wait one day. You, however, will be on your own. I will take Lord Sanabalis and Morse. If you require a map of the fiefs—"

"We don't, if there's mirror access within the fief."

"There are...very few mirrors in much of the fief."

Tara said, "If you will come this way?"

Not even Sanabalis stayed behind. Sanabalis, however, chose to wait outside in the Tower grounds, and headed there immediately, asking only Tiamaris's permission to do so. Kaylin found the interactions of the two Dragon Lords interesting;

Sanabalis was obviously still fond of Tiamaris, but he was not quite at home in the Tower; he was willing to enter it—after receiving an almost formal invitation each time—but he was never going to be a visitor who outstayed his welcome.

If it wasn't Kaylin's second home, it had joined her list of possible candidates.

"This way" sadly, returned them to a very familiar mirror—a flat, clear pool of water that lay in the ground. Tara smiled in what Kaylin presumed was supposed to be an encouraging away. "We're not accessing anything that the normal mirrors through the Tower can't access, so it should be safe."

Famous last words. Kaylin nodded anyway as Tiamaris, with no warning at all, roared. Clearly he'd woken up on the wrong side of the bed this morning, although rumor had it that Dragons didn't actually *need* sleep. She wondered if that was accurate, or if it had been spread by the Barrani. The roar, which left ringing in the ears, also left a shimmering, large image across the whole of the water's surface.

"You will be familiar with these streets?" Tiamaris asked Kaylin.

Kaylin nodded.

"Good."

Morse coughed. "Geography's never been her strong point."

"She has Corporal Handred, a man known for his competence in both navigation and memorization." Tiamaris hadn't looked up, but when he opened his mouth, Kaylin covered her ears.

The bastard grinned and spoke in High Barrani.

The lines on the map began to shift. Or at least it looked that way at first. What shifted, however, was the color in which they were drawn; they went from a bright gold to a rust red. Gold lines then ran across the map, spreading from the central point of the Tower toward the outer edges of the fief. In most cases, the gold overlay the red precisely; in a few cases, it didn't.

"These would be the street changes?"

"Yes." Small white circles materialized in what appeared to be entirely random places. "These would be the areas in which the bodies currently in our keeping were found, along with the dates. Red might be able to give us an idea of how much time passed between death and discovery."

Kaylin shook her head. "I don't think it's going to matter."

"No?"

"What we really need is an idea of how much time passed between the placement of the corpses and their discovery; they could have been killed earlier. I mean, the body found in the well didn't die by drowning; the corpse found in the half-burned ruins didn't die by burning or inhaling smoke." She grimaced. "You see anything like a pattern in the placement of those bodies?"

He frowned. "What do you see?"

"There's no real pattern. But the corpses that were found earliest *seem* to be slightly closer to the interior border." She frowned again.

"Kaylin?"

"It's nothing. Tiamaris, may I?"

He nodded.

"During the breach of the borders, and while you were reestablishing border control, how many storms occurred in the fief?"

"Shadowstorm?"

"Yes."

Tara lifted her head. Her eyes drained of all color that wasn't obsidian, something Kaylin always found unsettling. "That information is not complete in records." She spoke as if she were the voice of the mirror—which, all things considered, she probably was.

"Pardon?"

"Shadowstorm is difficult to capture visually," Tiamaris replied. "It defies objective comprehension. The large storms you've seen resemble regular storms in some fashion."

Small fashion, in Kaylin's opinion.

"But not all storms are immediately visible; nor do they all have immediate effect. What I see and what you see will differ. The effects of the storm can be clearly documented; the areas are defined in records by the effects."

"So, in theory, if there were no effects there was no storm?"

"In theory, yes—as far as the fief records are concerned." His tone made clear what he thought of the theory.

"I don't understand why. You can track every single occurrence of Shadow in the fief, and you can track all areas which have been contaminated. Why not the storms?"

"If it wasn't clear to you yesterday, even the Shadows themselves seem to fear the storms; the storms are not of the Shadows."

"And our keeping strong borders just gives them another reason to hate us, not that they appear to need them?"

He chuckled. "Something like that, yes. The storms are confined to the interior, where only the Shadows and those that serve them need fear their effects."

Tara took a step, knelt, and placed her palm against the surface of the water; this caused Kaylin to flinch, although she didn't look away. Water, unlike the enchanted, silvered glass of most mirrors in the modern world, was more mutable. "You think that these bodies might have appeared because of the storms?"

"I...think it's a possibility," Kaylin replied cautiously.

"Why?"

"Because a storm, Tara, is how I first met you. There's no other way I could have done it."

Tara nodded slowly. "Do you think she was always a corpse?"

"That's what we're hoping to find out. We have an image crystal here; it shows the woman as we think she looked while she was alive. We're going to hit the streets in the areas where the bodies were found to see if we can bribe anyone into telling us if they saw her."

"Do you think you will find that information?"

"I don't know. If you can mark the points where the storms occurred—"

"I cannot mark all of them," was the quiet reply. "Some of my defenses—demonstrably—were compromised in the absence of a Lord. I could not see clearly all that was occurring within the boundaries of the fief at that time." She hesitated and then said, "Lord Illien might know."

Kaylin was silent for a full thirty seconds. "...Severn and I are going to head out to see if we can find *any* leads. If you can mark areas where the storms were known entities, we'll see how much overlap there was. A lot depends on whether or not we can find a single eyewitness anywhere."

Kaylin and Severn weren't wearing the Hawk. This didn't stop doors from being closed—usually on their feet—or, better, failing to be opened at all. The gem, activated, with its stunning but admittedly unusual representation of a well-dressed stranger, had seemed like such a good idea at the time. The Arkon's reaction should have been a big clue.

But in the streets of the fiefs, magic of any kind was more terrifying than weapons. It was probably on par with Ferals, at least in the sunlight hours.

In two hours, they managed to talk to three people in total, the last two because Severn deactivated the gem and described the "missing person" with words.

"We clearly need more obvious magic in these streets," Kaylin muttered as they began to walk toward the well at the end of the road.

"They're probably confusing it with Shadow; they've seen enough of *that* to last a few lifetimes."

"They've probably seen a Dragon, as well—which most of the rest of the city hasn't."

"Ferals."

"Okay, fine, this is going to be harder than it looked." She glanced at the sun's height.

The well was never completely abandoned at this time of day. The streets around the well were about as crowded as fief streets ever got, and children were playing in the streets. Well, technically, four of them were playing and two of them were having a tug-of-war over a stick while practicing street language that would only grow more useful with time.

"This is the well," Severn said quietly.

Kaylin nodded. "I'm surprised there are any people here at all, given the scare about the water."

"The corpse didn't decay—at all. I'm sure it's not worse than drinking any other well water in the fief."

Kaylin wasn't, but was willing to take his word for it. Wells in the fiefs could be claimed by the fieflord or his thugs, and often were. People bartered for water because it was better than broken bones, lost teeth, or severe bruises. Since she wasn't in the best of moods to begin with, she'd been sort of looking forward to knocking a few teeth out of some-one's mouth, but there were no "guards" near the well. There weren't, from a brief scan of the streets, any lookouts of any sort, either.

"Tiamaris has really done a good job with this place," she murmured, taking a seat in the shadows cast by the well itself and placing her back against the stone there. She stretched out both legs and took a deep breath. "Gem?"

Severn tried to hand her the crystal.

"Not falling for that."

He chuckled and activated it. The woman appeared above his palms, as if he were carrying her. This had the advantage of clearing the streets of anyone who wasn't terribly nearsighted. Or old enough to know better.

"Let's see how it goes," Severn told her. "An hour?"

She glanced at the sun. "Two, tops."

It took less than an hour for someone to approach them. The someone was young, which wasn't surprising, and he was sprinting ahead of an older woman who wouldn't make it half a street from Ferals if she were stupid enough to be caught out at night. Young or no, the child hesitated slightly as she approached, but sped up again when she realized that she was about to be snatched off the ground by an increasingly angry caretaker.

Kaylin raised a brow. "You're going to be in deep trouble," she told the girl.

This seemed to mean "Please, jump on my thigh in an attempt to reach Severn" as far as the child was concerned. The girl tried to grab the image. Her hands passed through nothing, and she almost fell over.

Kaylin caught the back of her oversize, thinning shirt. There weren't a lot of polite children in the fiefs, but the girl mumbled a thank-you. This didn't stop her from trying to grab the skirts of the image again.

The old woman who'd been keeping an eye on her stopped at a much safer distance—four yards, give or take—and bowed nervously. "She means no harm," she said, rising. "Give her back to me. I'll make sure she never bothers you again."

"She's not bothering us," Kaylin replied. She didn't bother to speak softly; no point, and in the fiefs at the moment, it would just seem suspicious. The girl had fallen through the image the crystal projected another three times, and only Severn's arm had stopped the last one from ending in a face-plant at the base of the well.

The old woman finally called the child by name. In this case it was Susa, and it was said in the low growl that only elderly voices can achieve. It was ignored, on the other hand, in the way that only the youthful could manage.

"What," the woman said, because a quarter hour of this had made it less strange or less terrifying, "is that?"

"We're members of the Imperial Hawks," Kaylin replied, which wasn't really an answer. "This is one of the tools we use—across the bridge—to find missing people."

"You think someone was stupid enough to run *to* the fiefs?" The last word had squeaked up a register, and was followed by a snort. On the surface, it was the only reasonable fief response to Kaylin's reply.

Kaylin glanced at Severn. For a guy who was better with words, he was way too content to let her fumble through most of the talking. "She's not from Elantra."

"Dressed like that, she's not from Tiamaris, either."

Strike two. "We're here because Lord Tiamaris used to work with the Imperial Hawks before he took the Tower."

This got the old woman's attention. It did not, however, cause her face to go either white or green with fear, and it didn't cause her to instantly collapse to her knees, the nearest door being a little too far to conveniently leap for.

"Lord Tiamaris is currently busy doing two things: securing the border, and overseeing the reconstruction of the fief. So he asked us to look into this, as a favor. I'm Private Neya," she added, "and this is Corporal Handred. We're both Hawks when we cross the bridge."

"Look into? That girl, the one Susa keeps falling through, she's important to the Lord?"

"Yes. We're not sure why," Kaylin added.

"She missing?"

This was technically trickier, since according to Severn, one of the seven bodies had been discovered in the well they were currently leaning against.

"You should ask the Lady. She'll be able to find her if she's here."

"She'd be able to find her," Kaylin said, still cautious, "if she were a citizen of Tiamaris; she's not. She's a visitor."

"From where?" This was sharper.

"To be frank, we're not sure. The Lord did ask the Lady, but it's not something the Lady could find out. We're his backup. We're not certain we can find out, either—but this is part of what we do across the bridge."

"You always find your missing people? Susa, do *not* jump up and down on his legs like that. You'll hurt him."

"Not always, no. Lord Tiamaris is aware of what we can, and can't, promise. If we fail, he's not going to eat us or turn us to ash."

"Well, she doesn't look like one of those foreigners." One wrinkled, bony hand was now rubbing her chin.

"The Norannir?"

"The giants."

"Ah. No, she's not."

"I haven't seen her, not around here." She frowned in an entirely different way, because the inevitable had started to occur. All the children who hadn't been pulled off the street or dragged around a corner began to approach them; Susa had tested the waters, and as she was unbruised and obviously still alive, it meant curiosity was more or less safe.

With the children came their caretakers, many of whom were older, and some of whom were young enough to be older siblings—or at least she hoped they were. They were on that edge of young enough to still need mothers.

Severn said quietly, "You didn't have one at that age."

"Did I say that out loud?"

"Not in so many words."

"Good. Answer it the same way."

An hour and a half later, the crystal had been handed—carefully and with stern warning and near death threats—around the growing group of children. Susa had long since disappeared to scrounge for food, and many of the other children had followed buckets down one street or the other, but they'd all been replaced by equally curious children who were willing to approach strangers in a crowd. Kaylin's legs were cramping because she was sitting on them, and her stomach was beginning to make threats of its own.

But one of the children—a six- or seven-year-old, given fief food—said, "Hey, we saw her!"

Kaylin raised a brow. "You're certain you saw her? Not someone who looked like her?" It was all she could do to stay seated, but leaping to her feet would have scattered the crowd as easily as if they were small birds.

The child frowned. "It was her."

"Did anyone else see her? Any of your friends?"

"My grandfather."

"He's here?"

"Nah. He's back at home."

"And he's the only other person?"

"Don't know. He's the only person who was with me."

"Where did you see her?"

The boy had the grace to pale, although he was dark enough it wasn't immediately obvious. His voice dropped, and the line of his shoulders fell, as if they were drooping. The other children were all watching him with the type of curiosity that small carrion creatures might display if they were actually friendly.

"Here," he finally said, almost inaudibly.

"What do you mean, here?"

He pointed at the well.

"You saw her body in the well?"

"No—she was—no. We didn't put her there!"

Kaylin lifted both hands; Severn lifted one. At the moment, the other was occupied by the crystal. "We don't think you—any of you—put her there. Where did you see her?"

Hesitation again. Kaylin fished a silver coin out of her pocket. She then fished another out, and a third. "Where did you see her?" she asked again.

The boy, no fool, hesitated. Kaylin thought about adding another coin. She didn't because she'd've had to fish it out of Severn's pockets. Instead, she held her palm flat and steady. There was a small chance that one of the other kids would try to grab it and pull a runner, but that might have happened in any street of the city, not just these ones. It was worth the risk.

It was worth the risk because the boy reached out with an unsteady hand, and he did take the silver that had been warmed by its contact with her. "She was walking toward the well," he told Kaylin, having made his decision. "She was drunk."

"You're certain?"

"She was walking like a drunk."

"Did she climb into the well?"

"Hells, no. She fell into the well, though. She stopped just here," he added, pulling himself slightly out of the crowd to approach the well itself. "She looked down. Grandpa tried to stop her, but we were too far away."

"She fell in?"

The boy nodded. "Fell in. Grandpa was worried—it's our well," he added, as if to make clear his grandfather wasn't an idiot humanitarian. "But—she was talking. When she was leaning over the water, she was talking."

"What did she say?"

"We didn't understand it. Some foreign words."

"Did you see where she came from?"

He hesitated again. Then he slid the coins into his pocket and pushed them as far down as they would go. He lifted a hand and pointed. "She came from there."

Kaylin rose for the first time; Severn, however, remained seated. The boy was pointing at a building that looked, from this distance, to be one of the older buildings in the fief. It was stone, although the stone had cracked, and some of its corners had crumbled. There was a roof, although it looked much more recent than the walls. Windows—and it had windows—wore shutters that were warped and faded.

"Can I go now?" the boy asked.

Kaylin nodded. "Thank you. You've helped your Lord and Lady. Severn?"

There weren't a lot of buildings in the fiefs that were unoccupied. In Tiamaris, this was probably more true at the moment than in any other fief. If Kaylin had entertained the vague and hopeful notion that this building would be an exception, it was dashed pretty quickly. Like many of the oldest of buildings, it was set farther back from the street, although in this case, *street* was a charitable word for a mixture of stone and dirt with a lot of weeds thrown in.

There had once been fencing, and the perimeter of the property had been defined by a wall or a demiwall. What remained was crumbled stone that stood at various heights, and rusty spots where fence posts had once resided. Beyond what had probably been the property line, the weeds were higher. There was a door, but it wasn't much of a door, given that only two of three hinges seemed to actually be working; it had had a lock, but that had been removed or destroyed some time ago, as well. It creaked.

"She was alive," Kaylin said as she pushed the door inward.

Severn nodded. He spoke a single word, and the crystal's image immediately winked out. He slid the crystal into the pouch at his hip.

"Do you think it was an illusion of some kind?"

"I don't see why anyone would bother."

Neither did Kaylin. On the other hand, Kaylin didn't understand how there could be seven of her, either. Transformational magic did, in theory, exist, but in practice, she couldn't immediately recall a case in which it had been relevant. Magic that transformed living creatures, on the other hand, was a magic best ascribed to gods. She was fairly certain that any less-than-divine mages who tried it would end up with corpses, regardless of their starting material.

There were, as expected, families in the building. Walls of very dubious construction had been put in place some time ago; they weren't original to the building. Kaylin sighed. "Shall we do this the old-fashioned way?"

Severn nodded.

No one who lived in the building—which is to say, no one who was actually brave enough to answer their door—had seen the woman in question. Kaylin was reasonably certain they were telling the truth, and any investigation of a more magical nature would have to wait for either Sanabalis or Tiamaris; she could sense no magic anywhere in the building. This wasn't unusual for the fiefs.

There was a basement as well as two stories. The basement was the last place they looked because even in the fiefs, people didn't *like* to live in the dark. But there were people, or at least evidence of people, living in the dark here. They weren't home or weren't answering their door. The door was actually locked, and the lock was half-decent.

Kaylin was torn. It wasn't a hard lock to pick, but she didn't have many tools for that kind of work at the moment. On the other hand, she wasn't the Law, here—a little bit of break and enter, if it wasn't accompanied by theft or violence, wouldn't cause paperwork or complaints.

Severn didn't think it was worthwhile. "Now that we know where it is, we can ask Tara to examine it at her leisure—and at a distance. I don't think we'll find anything."

Neither did Kaylin, which is why she didn't insist.

They made it back to the Tower ahead of the Dragons and the Avatar. Given the nature of the Tower, the doors weren't locked. If they didn't roll open on their own as she approached them, they did open with a little help.

Kaylin and Severn made their way to the morgue, where Red was still working.

One look at his expression made clear that he wasn't finished. That, and he wasn't entirely happy with the work in progress, not that happiness per se was ever something you expected to find while cutting into corpses.

"What's wrong?" Kaylin asked.

"I'm going to need another set of scalpels," he replied curtly. "Are you two done for the day?"

"I am," Kaylin said. "I've got another appointment I can't afford to miss. Red, what *is* wrong? Do you know what killed her? Or them?"

"No. I'm not sure anything I do will give us that information, either."

"Why?"

Red hesitated. "I've done enough autopsy work on humans and Tha'alani to understand them; I can work my way around Aerians and Leontines. I've never touched a Barrani, but she's not that—not externally. She looks more or less human to my eye."

"But?"

"She's not."

CHAPTER 12

Kaylin and Severn exchanged a glance. "What is she, then?"

"I'm not entirely certain. You said she passed a magical scan?"

Kaylin nodded.

Red heaved a louder than usual sigh, and stretched both arms. "I want record access," he finally said.

"I'm not sure Marcus'll be happy about that. Ask Sanabalis when and if he gets back here."

"If?"

"He doesn't really like to spend much time in the Tower. I don't know why. I can't wait, though," she added.

"You've got a date?"

"Yes. With a really arrogant Dragon Lord. I'll trade," she added.

"No, thank you. You'll just destroy the corpses."

Kaylin had spent enough time in the streets that she'd have to move quickly to make it to the Palace on time for her second encounter with Lord Diarmat. She tried to leave Severn in the Tower, but that was a lost cause.

"I'm not going to pick a fight or lose my temper on the way to the Palace," she grumbled as they walked quickly toward the bridge.

"No. But you probably won't eat before you hit the Palace, either."

"I don't have time—"

"Eat while you're walking. Talk less." He paused in front of a small stall and quickly purchased the food he meant for her to eat. She was hungry; it had been a long day, and there hadn't been much of a lunch to break it. Sanabalis and Tiamaris hadn't returned by the time she'd all but run out the front doors, which was bad; she had a couple of questions she wanted to ask them.

They'd wait until tomorrow, assuming Diarmat didn't turn her to ash, eat her, or throw her in the local dungeon for insubordination. Or breathing.

Get a grip, Kaylin. He's a teacher. *You spent most of yesterday on the borders of the fief, while Shadows the size of a building tried to squash you flat.* At the remove of a day, those Shadows were infinitely more appealing, and only in part because manners, etiquette, or their opinion of her made no difference at all. She had the option of dodging or dying; nothing she said when she opened her mouth was likely to change that.

Whereas, with Diarmat, there *was* a small chance that something she said could change her whole future, for better or worse—except for the better part.

Ugh. She'd spent so much of her life telling herself—and, more embarrassing, anyone else who would listen—that she didn't *care* what other people thought of her. Her life—much of her life—had revolved around that belief, because she *had* believed it. She was good at her job.

…At all the parts of her job that didn't require her to be anything other than a half-educated kid from the fiefs.

All right, you bastard. I'll learn.

"Kaylin?"

She reddened slightly. "What?"

"You're cracking the cobbles."

"Very funny." She could see the Palace a few blocks away. "Severn, how did you manage it?"

"Manage what?"

"How did you learn the manners and etiquette of the Imperial Court?"

He shrugged. "To start with? I didn't talk much." He still didn't. "I observed. I watched what other people were doing. I watched people react to each other. It's not much different; the nobility use different words and gestures, but the intent's the same."

"Intent?"

"They're politer when they threaten you. They don't call in their thugs when they're pissed off. They don't throw a punch themselves, and they don't pull weapons. But power matters. Once you get used to the *way* they talk, you can figure out what they would have said if they'd lived in the fiefs." He shrugged, a fief shrug. "They're not better or worse than fief-lings. You've learned to speak Barrani; you can speak passable Leontine and Aerian. Consider the difference between Barrani and High Barrani.

"The difference between Court Elantran and street Elantran is similar, but larger."

She thought about it for two seconds. "The big difference is that there isn't anyone to observe but Diarmat. His guards don't breathe when he's there. No one speaks to him unless he speaks first."

"That's still something. Until you have some feel for what

he's saying, say as little as possible, as politely as possible. Speak High Barrani exclusively. You don't need to smile. You don't need to be friendly. He doesn't have to like you."

"He's never going to like me."

"No, he isn't. Give up on that. It's easier. You don't have to charm him. You don't have to impress him. You just have to survive him."

"Can I ask for a small favor?"

"How small?"

"Take this home for me?" She handed him the sword.

When Kaylin entered the very large room that she'd been escorted to the last time, she realized how much easier said than done that was. She also became acutely aware of just how much dirt and dust had accumulated on her clothing during the long day in the fief the minute she crossed the threshold.

Diarmat was seated behind his desk at the far wall. He didn't look up as she entered; he appeared to be engrossed in his writing. But this part of the drill, she knew. She walked briskly to his desk and stood in front of it, fighting the urge to lift her chin and expose her throat, since that didn't seem to mean to Dragons what it meant to Leontines.

There, as much at attention as she could force herself to be, she waited. And waited. And waited. She looked at a point just above his left shoulder and listened to the rhythmic sound of quill against paper. Even, deep breaths kept her calm. She understood this particular test; she'd learned how to pass it before she'd actually been inducted and taken the Imperial Oath. There was no way that Diarmat could make her fail this, and she took some comfort in that.

If he kept her standing here for three hours, she could go home without disgracing herself. It would be a long three hours, but the consolation prize would be the tiny sense of victory she'd take with her.

Clearly, Diarmat was aware of this.

"Private Neya."

She looked down. "Lord Diarmat."

He rose and handed her an envelope. "Please deliver this to Lord Sanabalis."

She nodded sharply and turned to head toward the door. He cleared his throat. It was a remarkably deep and unfriendly sound. "Lord Sanabalis is not currently within the Palace; deliver it to him on your own time."

"Lord Diarmat." She slid the envelope into her shirt's interior pocket, where it was just long enough it would bother her for the rest of the evening.

He rose and came out from behind the desk. She stood her ground.

"What," he asked, in a cool voice, "is your business with the Emperor?"

"Whatever he wants it to be."

The Dragon Lord raised a brow. His eyes were a shade of bronze, but Kaylin doubted she'd ever see gold in this particular face. "Elaborate."

"I have no personal reason to see the Emperor, Lord Diarmat. I have no personal desire to see the Emperor."

"You dislike him?"

Oh, please. Kaylin almost resented the transparency of the question. Actually, she did resent it. She therefore kept her face as stiff as possible. If her words were a bit chilly, he probably wouldn't notice. Or care. "The Emperor is the Commander of the Lords of Law. His laws are the only laws I enforce and follow." Grinding her teeth, she took a deep breath and then slowly exhaled. "I don't know the Emperor well enough to either like or dislike him, because it's not relevant. I respect and admire his laws. The Lord of Hawks meets regularly with the Emperor, and any commands he receives, we receive. We don't need to know more than that."

"Do you know why he created the Law you uphold?"

"Yes, sir." Damn. "Yes, Lord Diarmat."

"Where did you learn this?"

"In the Halls of Law."

"You were not a noteworthy student in any positive sense of the word. Please elaborate what you feel you were taught."

This was the type of test Kaylin abhorred. Abhorrence warred with her desire to have a job that was also a duty, a responsibility, and a vocation. Desire won, but it was close; it had been a long day. She was certain Diarmat knew, word for damn word, what she'd been taught; the problem was, she didn't. What she knew was now a blend of every other conversation, every other argument, and every other experience she'd had as a Hawk.

None of which mattered to Diarmat.

"The Eternal Emperor is a Dragon, the Lord of Dragons. He was born during the wars between the Barrani and the Dragon flights, and much of the territory now known as the Empire was taken during these wars. The Barrani and the Dragons weren't the only people living on those lands, although many of the mortals served one or the other in some capacity." She hesitated, and then said more quietly, "They were often slaves."

Lord Diarmat inclined his head, that was all. His eyes didn't shift color in either direction, and his expression was as cold and disdainful as it always was.

"They died in greater numbers than either of the Immortal races."

"That would be a given. They exist in greater numbers, and they breed quickly. Continue."

Here, she hesitated. What she knew of Hoard Law hadn't been taught in any class. Diarmat was probably the Mallory of the Imperial Palace; accuracy wasn't as essential as following the rules. Which meant the classroom lectures. Damn it. History of this kind had never seemed important; it wasn't relevant to her ability to do her job.

"The Eternal Emperor must have valued the mortal races. He summoned the leaders of the Caste Courts, where they existed—the Leontine leadership is spread out, and diffuse; the human leadership is similar—and they came. He built the Imperial Palace here, and he built it as a dwelling which could house any race. He asked the Caste Courts to do the same thing, and they agreed."

"Why did they agree?"

"They wanted to survive."

"Indeed. You ascribe no nobility of purpose to their decision, then?"

She stopped herself from shrugging with difficulty, but she did stop. "I think some nobility of purpose may have been present, but even absent anything but desperation, they did as he requested. He then told them what he would, and would not, tolerate within the City. It was not so different from what he would tolerate in the rest of the Empire."

"Meaning?"

"If it didn't bother him, he didn't care what happened."

Diarmat's eyes did change color then, and not in a good way. High Barrani, damn it. Do *not* let it slide again.

"There were difficulties integrating the races within the Imperial City. The Emperor told the Caste Courts that they were to deal with any infractions of his rules. They failed. He then had the choice of dealing with the difficulties himself."

"And?"

"He did this initially. It was a slaughter, and it didn't diminish the behavior that annoyed him; he hadn't killed all the people responsible for crimes against his rule, but he *had* killed hundreds who upheld it. The random deaths of those innocent of any crime had a negative effect. During this period, Barrani Arcanists made use of the chaos to attempt to dethrone the Emperor, relying on the mortals—mostly human—who felt they had been wronged. They failed." Had she been speaking to anyone but Diarmat—anyone at all—she would have added a few colloquialisms at this juncture.

"At this point, he had the choice of torching the entire City, or of establishing some sort of martial law. He chose to establish martial law."

"For what reason?"

She towed the party line. "He valued the citizens of his Empire enough to make the attempt to preserve them. He understood that mortals are more flexible and less experienced than Immortals; the Barrani kept out of his way." Reading between the lines, they'd done this by more or less manipulating stupid mortals into the front lines, but Kaylin was pretty certain Diarmat didn't read between the lines and wouldn't appreciate the observation. "The imposition of martial law—and the influx of a large number of armed soldiers—restored some order to the City.

"The soldiers, however, created the difficulty that any standing army will create. There was a sharp division between soldier and civilian, and the soldiers became a distinct and separate entity. They weren't trusted; they were feared. They weren't feared as much as the Dragons would have been feared because they weren't capable of doing as much damage; they *did* damage, on the other hand."

"And this was not to the Emperor's liking?"

"No. He therefore dispersed the small army."

"How?"

"We weren't taught that." She could guess; she didn't offer. "The partial success of the largely mortal army suggested an alternate course to the Emperor. He understood that the army itself stood above the civilians, but they did it by force of arms. In some cases, this was an advantage, but the advantage was temporary. He desired a body of men and women who could supervise said civilians by force of law. He therefore retired for some months with members of the various Caste Courts, and when he once again returned to the Palace, he had the first draft for Imperial Law as it now stands.

"Having the Law didn't instantly mean he had a way of enforcing it; he'd had a much less comprehensive set of rules prior to these, and enforcing those had proved problematic, if the goal was preservation of life. He therefore decreed that one building—and one alone—would be built in such a way that it could occupy the same space and height that the Palace did. This building, with its three towers, is now the Halls of Law.

"The Emperor needed a force of arms that he could command when such force proved necessary. He therefore created the Swords, and tasked them with preserving the peace when peace was not upmost in the minds of his citizens. Mindful of the resentment of the populace at the death of people who were innocent, he then created the Hawks. The Hawks were to investigate known breaches of the Law, and apprehend the criminals. The Hawks were therefore tasked with finding both criminals and proof that the accused had committed crimes against the Empire.

"The Imperial Courts—peopled by mortals, although, in theory, Barrani and Dragons could serve, as well—were to evaluate the charges, and if the accused were found guilty, to sentence them or censure them, depending on the severity of the crime.

"In those cases where the criminals were deemed exceptionally dangerous, or in those cases where the criminals escaped the Courts, they were to be hunted and retrieved. He therefore created the third—and the smallest—body of the Halls: the Wolves. The Wolves also served the Halls as investigators of a particular type."

Diarmat didn't appear to be pleased. On the other hand, he wasn't breathing fire. "Why do you suppose the Eternal Emperor went to these extremes? Surely any breach of his orders constituted justification for the annihilation of those who showed such disrespect?"

Kaylin exhaled. Heavily. "That wasn't covered in class," she finally replied. "The fact that the Emperor saw fit to do so was enough. Our teachers aren't paid to second-guess the Emperor."

For the first time ever, Lord Diarmat cracked a smile. It was remarkably chilly, and just as remarkably brief. "Very good, Private. I will now ask you to answer that question, regardless. Your teachers, past and present, will not be held accountable for your response."

"We're part of his hoard."

Diarmat raised a brow. Remembering just how contemptuous he'd been when she'd dared to use the word *hoard* on their first lesson, Kaylin stiffened. "Continue."

Bastard. "I don't understand hoard law well."

"An understatement, but an acceptable demonstration of your awareness of your limitations."

"Because I don't understand hoard law well, I may be misinterpreting. I don't understand how a hoard is defined, or how it's chosen. I know that there's something special about the choosing or gaining of a hoard, and I know it's pretty much permanent. Dragons don't have more than one, and they don't walk away from it; they're carried away in pieces, if at all." She grimaced and slid back into High Barrani, momentarily loathing it. "Because I don't understand how it's chosen, I cannot speculate more on that. But the Emperor's hoard is complicated and it is vast.

"The mortals in the Empire are part of it. He preserves them, as he can, because of that. In my opinion."

"Very well." Diarmat rose. "Your answer is crude and short, but I will accept it for the moment. Tell me, if mortals are part of his hoard, how can he destroy you so easily if you displease him?"

Beats me. Kaylin stopped herself from shrugging. Again. "Just because we're part of his hoard doesn't mean we decide how we're valued and how we're either kept or tossed away."

"Elucidate."

She almost surrendered. Almost. Still speaking in less formal language, and trying to choose her words with care, she continued. "It's like—say we're apples."

"Apples."

She nodded. "You can generally tell when an apple is bruised just by looking at it. But that takes time. Even if you have that time, you can't tell which apples are rotten at the core until you cut them. The apples that are rotten aren't useful in any way. Those can be discarded. But if you want apples, you can't discard *all* of them because some of them might be rotten. Or have worms. We don't live for all that long. Our time, from birth to death, might pass without ever crossing the Emperor's path.

"But in our view, the life from birth to death is long. We'll see things the Emperor won't have the opportunity to see. We don't make all the decisions, but we're part of the process. Maybe he guards mortals the same way he'd pick apples."

Diarmat said nothing, but his eyes were once again bronze. Kaylin took this as a good sign, and continued. "Some of the mortals in the Empire find favor in the Emperor's eyes. The Imperial Playwright, for instance. There are also positions for poets and various artists—sculptors, painters. There's a position for a Mage Emeritus, as well." She knew that the list was longer, and that Severn would probably be able to name each and every such position. "Even if the mortal's life is brief, things can be created which last—and they come out of the mortal condition. There's no way to know, at birth, which mortals will have those talents. There's no indication, or no clear indication, by which to judge babies. We're therefore all theoretically valuable because that potential exists."

"Indeed. It is possible your reputation as a student is not entirely deserved. Very well. I have heard that your duties in the fief of Tiamaris are both onerous and necessary. I am therefore satisfied for this evening. I expect you to be on time two nights hence. I will have a few more questions, but at that time I will also begin to explain suitable methods of Imperial Address for those in your social position."

Shock kept Kaylin suitably silent until she reached the main hall. She had no escort to direct her through those halls. The Palace Guard didn't stop or question her, and she made it to the entrance without incident. The man who habitually greeted guests stopped her before she could escape.

"Private Neya," he said in his clipped and well-enunciated speech, "Lord Sanabalis has requested a moment of your time."

"Should I follow you?" she asked in Elantran. "I know the way."

"He will be waiting in his function rooms, if you wish to proceed there directly."

Sanabalis was waiting, as promised. Food, however, was also waiting, and it was infinitely more welcome than a dour

Dragon Lord. She handed over the letter, which he received without comment, and took the chair he indicated—the one closest to said food—and began to eat. She was aware, as only an evening with Diarmat could make clear, just how lucky she was to spend time with a Dragon who didn't demand formality.

"You appear to have survived your second etiquette lesson."

"There wasn't much etiquette involved," she replied around a mouthful of soft bread. "But Lord Diarmat's eyes stayed pretty much in the bronze range for most of it."

"What was discussed?"

"The founding of Imperial Law and the Halls of Law."

"I see. Did he ask about the subject of your investigation at all?"

"No. He said he'd heard it was necessary."

"Good. You are never to bring it up. If he asks, you are to answer both truthfully *and* minimally. Is that understood?"

She nodded.

"You are not, however, to withhold information from me."

"Yes, Sanabalis."

"I had no chance to speak with Corporal Handred. The difficulty along the border was notably less…intense. It was not, however, absent, and it has slowed the accumulation of language significantly. Did you discover any information of note in the fiefs?"

"Yes, but I'm not sure what it means, yet."

"I am far too weary for games of caution; given your evening with Lord Diarmat, I am deeply surprised that *you* are not equally weary." In case his meaning wasn't clear, he added, "Tell me. If I am required to wait until you *are* certain, I might, in the parlance of the mortals, lose my temper."

She cleared her throat, looked for water, and drank some of it. It didn't really help. Wine might have, but that hadn't been supplied with the snack. "Red says the corpses only look human. I think he's blunted his scalpels. He's going to request any information on nonmortal autopsies to bring back to the fief when he returns." Seeing the color of Sanabalis's eyes, she added, "I'm answering as fast as I can, Sanabalis.

"In our first foray into the streets for information, we heard something we haven't been able to confirm."

"And that?"

"She was alive. At least one of the seven women was alive when she arrived in the streets of the fief."

"If you were unable to confirm this rumor, how did you come by this information?"

"There was an eyewitness. Two."

"And they are credible?"

"No. It's the fiefs. But they've got no reason to lie about this. Given it's the fiefs, their best bet is to shut up, and stay quiet."

"Did you bribe them?"

"Yes."

"And you don't consider the bribe sufficient reason to lie?"

She did, but there were factors that made the lie very risky. "It wasn't enough money to take that kind of risk. Tara can't—and couldn't—find this woman in the streets; she *can* find almost anyone else if she puts her mind to it. People are nervous about the Norannir; people are nervous about the Dragon. But…they seem to really like the Lady. We've put out word that this is being done on *her* behalf, and we're waiting to see if any other word is delivered to the Tower."

"Very well. Speak to the Arkon before you leave."

It was too damn bad the windows here were invulnerable, because Kaylin considered falling to her death from them would be marginally less painful. The door wards to the Library were fully active, and Sanabalis didn't bother to touch them; he left that to Kaylin. Her left arm was numb when the doors rolled open, but at least this time she didn't have to push them.

The Arkon, however, wasn't snorting fire in one of the distant rooms of his huge collection; nor was he consulting the hidden, liquid mirror at the very heart of the Imperial Palace. He was sitting behind the front desk—itself longer than the largest of the offices in the Halls of Law. He looked up as they entered, and waved. It wasn't a greeting; the doors rolled close behind their backs. They didn't close quietly.

Kaylin wondered if Dragon eyes in the Palace were ever going to be gold again. The Arkon's were bronze, and it seemed, at a safe distant, that they were also bloodshot, something she would have bet against being possible. "Private," the Arkon said, lifting his wizened face. She'd heard the word *cockroach* said in a friendlier tone, but as his hostility couldn't hold a candle to Diarmat's, she didn't mind.

"Private Neya has a brief report to tend before she leaves the Palace," Sanabalis said in quiet High Barrani.

The Arkon nodded. He set aside the small stack of cards he'd been writing on and rose.

"The corpses of the seven identical women don't appear to be human. Or at least two of them; the coroner hasn't finished his examinations of the rest."

"I am aware of that," was the frosty reply. "I received an unusual request from the Records in the Halls of Law, and I have yet to decide how to answer it." Given his tone, one of the answers might be total destruction of said Records. Kaylin, no fool, didn't ask what the request was; she could guess.

"Two witnesses in the fiefs claimed to have seen the woman whose image we captured in the crystal," Kaylin said, moving right along. "They saw her before she died."

The Arkon said nothing. It was a loud, brittle nothing and Kaylin wanted to be home and under her bed before it shattered.

"Did they hear her speak?"

"Yes, but she wasn't speaking a language they understood. They thought she was drunk," she added. "Because she seemed to be unsteady. She fell into the well, and by the time she was retrieved, she was dead. We're attempting to find out if any of the other six were sighted, moving—or speaking—before their deaths. But..."

"Yes, Private?"

"The Tower thinks there is some small possibility that the arrival of the women occurred during the Shadowstorms that appeared in the fief before Tiamaris took the Tower. Tara's memory of what occurred before Tiamaris became the Tower's Lord isn't clear or precise, so we've been collating what she does know."

"You think it's likely that *seven* storms appeared beyond the borders during Barren's reign?"

Kaylin nodded.

"They are unlikely to occur again. Very well, Private. Thank you for your information; you may leave now. If any other corpses appear, you are to notify me *immediately*. I do not care about the hour; I do not even care if the Court itself is in session. Do I make myself clear?"

"Yes, Arkon." Still in one piece—and not notably deafened—Kaylin retreated.

Marcus hadn't given explicit orders to report for debriefing. Kaylin was grateful. She went straight home. She even considered flagging down a carriage to get there faster, but she was short on funds, and the streets, at this time, were short on carriages. They were also short on open stalls and

most pedestrian traffic. It was quiet and peaceful, and she'd
been lacking both in the last few days. Days? Weeks. Maybe
months.

She therefore walked slowly toward home, trading moments
of peace for moments of sleep, something she rarely did. Her
usual anxiety didn't catch up with her until she'd unlocked her
own door and stood in its frame, looking toward her mirror.
Only when she saw its flat, reflective surface did she relax.
There'd been no emergencies. The midwives hadn't called
her. Marrin hadn't mirrored, which meant all was well in the
Foundling Hall.

She made her way to her bed, crawled beneath it, and fished
out the crate that still held the egg. Unwrapping it with care,
she placed it on her pillow. She was awake enough to undress
and fold her clothing; she was awake enough to wash herself—
quickly, because the water was cold—and towel herself dry.

Then she slipped into bed, wrapped herself carefully around
the egg, and listened, pressing her ear gently against its shell. It
felt warm. She smiled because it felt warm, and slowly drifted
off, wondering what would hatch from it, if anything ever
would.

CHAPTER 13

Severn woke her in the morning. Morning, given the previous evening, wasn't as much of an enemy as it usually was, and she woke to the aroma of food. Severn was cooking. He was also whistling something, and even whistling on-key. He stood where sunlight could reach him, and sun was streaming in through the open windows; his shadow was long.

"Teela dropped by," he said without turning. "She tried to wake you up."

Kaylin had no memory of that at all. "Are you sure?"

"I stopped her from upending the bed, if that helps."

Kaylin laughed. "Was Tain with her?"

"No—but she had a message from Evanton she wanted to pass on."

"Evanton?"

"Apparently."

"He couldn't mirror?"

"Apparently not." He turned then; he was grinning. "Physical objects don't travel well through mirrors."

"Of course not—that would be useful. What did she bring?"

"It's on the counter."

Curiosity was a better incentive than work; Kaylin slid out of bed and slid into clothing. While she dressed, Severn said, "She seemed a bit surprised by the egg."

"Surprised how?"

"She wanted me to explain biology to you." He was smiling broadly. It wasn't genuine.

"What did she say?"

"She *did* say that. But she touched the egg, Kaylin."

"And?"

"It turned red."

"Red."

He nodded. "Red, orange, gold; it looked like a small, contained fire."

"Did it—did it burn her?"

"Got it in one. It didn't burn you, though—and you were in direct contact with it the entire time. She's not happy," he added.

"What did she say?"

"Oh, some Leontine, some Aerian, some Elantran. Strictly non-Barrani for about two minutes."

Kaylin examined the egg; it looked the same as it always did in the morning. She placed it back in its crate, wrapped it with care, and shoved it back under the bed. "Does she know what it is?"

"No. She wants you to get rid of it, though."

"Big surprise. What did she bring?"

Severn reached across the counter and lifted something: it was a sheath.

"How the hells did he know?" Kaylin asked as she crossed the room to take it from his hands.

"He's Evanton. If I had to bet, Teela probably told him."

She lifted the sword that she had taken from Maggaron, and took the opportunity to examine it closely. The blade was still much shorter than it had been the first time she'd seen it, but aside from that one huge shift in shape and form, it was solid. It was a clean, gleaming steel that held a perfect edge when inspected with the naked eye. Runes, however, had been carved in the flat of the blade on both sides.

"I'm glad Teela left," Kaylin murmured as she swung the short sword experimentally in the air a few times. She could fight with long knives, but long knives and short swords weren't the same species of weapon, and her sword training, given that she'd started it so late, was minimal.

"She wasn't."

"She's a core part of the Exchequer investigation. Marcus is enough on edge about that he'll rip out her throat for the usual minor infractions."

Severn shrugged because it was true.

Kaylin picked up the sheath sent by Evanton. It was wrapped in what felt like leather, except at both lip and tip; those were steel of some sort. There were no words on the leather, and no engraving on the steel; nothing set the scabbard apart from any other utilitarian scabbard she'd ever seen. It suited her.

It did not, unfortunately, seem to suit the *sword*. Kaylin had sheathed many weapons in her life; she'd never before had the privilege of fighting with said weapon when she tried.

"Kaylin!" Severn shouted. "The sword's glowing!"

The sword wasn't. The runes were. Severn could be forgiven for skipping the details. He could also be forgiven for jumping as far out of the way as her small apartment allowed before he hit the wall. The sword swung her arm. It hit her chair. It cut her table. It separated parts of the mangy rug she used to absorb the sound of creaking floorboards. She hoped like hells that it hadn't actually split the floor.

She wasn't weak; she spent at least three days of any given week drilling and lifting weights. That probably saved some of her furniture, because she began to fight the sword for control of its direction. She wouldn't have been surprised if the damn thing had started to speak, but it didn't. Instead, it started to change shape, which was *so* not what she wanted.

Cursing in Leontine, and wishing she had the bulk that usually came with the language, she grabbed the hilt with her other hand and tried very, very hard to keep it still enough to put it *in* the sheath.

It took twenty minutes and some very cautious help from Severn before she managed to slide the weapon home. Only when she'd managed it did it suddenly cease to struggle.

"I want words with Evanton," she said. She'd managed to bite her lip because one of the directions the sword had swung had connected her knuckles with the underside of her chin. Because she was in her apartment and no one, in theory, cleaned it but her, she didn't spit the blood out.

"They're going to have to wait," Severn replied. "So is breakfast."

They weren't late. They weren't late by a very small margin and a very fast run. Kaylin's new scabbard hung off her waist by a thick and serviceable belt; she tried not to stare at it with either annoyance or suspicion when she walked between the guards that led into the Halls.

They went on a quick flyby of the office; Marcus was shouting at the mirror, which was a good sign for Marcus and a bad sign for whomever it was he was speaking to. She would have cleared the office after sign-in, but Caitlin caught up with her.

"Lord Sanabalis is waiting in the carriage."

"What carriage?"

"The Imperial Carriage. Red is with him."

Figured. "Where's Teela?"

"The Barrani are in the Tower with the Hawklord."

At least something was going right this morning. Kaylin tried to be grateful. "Tell Marcus Lord Diarmat's not screaming for my head, yet."

"That's good to hear, dear. Marcus is screaming for his coroner back. Do you think Red will be finished sometime today?"

"Not according to Red. Sorry, Caitlin."

Caitlin winced. "It's fine, dear. Lord Sanabalis delivered a personal letter from the Arkon. Red's duties in the fiefs are to be treated as emergency work."

"Do they come before or after the investigation into the Exchequer?"

"I believe the Arkon considers them more important. The Emperor, however, has failed to mention them at all. Try to remember to eat lunch," she added, giving Kaylin a push toward the doors.

Sanabalis was waiting. He was waiting attached to eyes that were a pale copper. Red was utterly silent; he didn't see a lot of Sanabalis, but he wasn't stupid; he knew the color of the Dragon's eyes meant Bad Mood. Kaylin, who had seen them tint orange more often than she liked, wasn't as worried, but the carriage ride was tense and silent.

Also? The scabbard was making her legs itch. She wondered if this was the real reason Maggaron had looked so shocked when she'd asked him about a sheath for the sword. She'd have to ask him, if she had the chance.

★ ★ ★

They didn't take the carriage all the way to the Tower;
Sanabalis rapped three times on the roof as they approached
the Ablayne, and a bridge that was, once again, congested.
They got out, Red carrying a larger bag than he had the previous day, and began to make their way across the bridge on
foot. Since a wagon was also making that crossing, and the
bridge was lamentably narrow, it took ten minutes.

Sanabalis was snorting smoke by the time they hit cobbles
again.

Kaylin waited until the air was clear to speak to him. "Are
you heading out to the interior border?"

He failed to hear her. Given Dragon hearing, she didn't ask
again.

Morse was waiting for them when they reached the Tower.
So was Tara; she'd been in the gardens, and it showed; she
wore heavy gardening gloves, an apron that was more brown
and green than the off-white it had been at some point, and a
kerchief to keep her hair out of her eyes. Her eyes, however,
were almost entirely obsidian when she approached. Given the
color of Sanabalis's eyes, this was not a comfort.

Kaylin hugged her anyway.

"My Lord is not happy," Tara told her as she returned the
hug. Someone could have said the same thing about either a
husband or an injured puppy, in the same tone of voice.

"Neither is Sanabalis. And my Sergeant is practically spitting
fur."

"Oh? Why?"

"Because Red is here, and we need him in the Halls.
Among other things. Sorry," she added. "None of that is
your fault. I have no idea, on the other hand, what's irritating
Sanabalis. Um, how is the border?"

"The Norannir guard the border at the moment. It is…
stable…but the storms have been heavy."

"The borders keep the storms contained, don't they?"

Tara nodded gravely. "They have, in the past. But I cannot recall another time since my awakening when the storms
on our borders have been so fierce, and so consistent." She
looked up at Sanabalis, who stood to Kaylin's left and a few
yards behind. "You will remain in the Tower today?"

"If it is acceptable to Lord Tiamaris."

Tara said nothing. Instead, she removed her gloves and
handed them to Morse, who seemed to be expecting them.
"He is waiting," Tara told them. "Red?"

Red detached himself from Sanabalis—and safety—and
approached. "Lady."

"Why do you hate the name Reginald so much?"

If there'd been a nearby wall, Kaylin would have hit it.
With her head.

"Is this an inappropriate question?" Tara asked her when
Red failed to answer.

"Ye-es." Kaylin all but hissed.

"Why?"

"Because almost no one *knows* that that's the name he was
given at birth, Tara. He wouldn't be called Red if he wanted
them to know it."

"Oh." She turned to Red, who'd remained silent, and said,
"Please accept my apologies. I am trying to listen less deliberately, now."

His brows rose.

"She *is* the Tower," Kaylin told him. She didn't bother
to whisper, because Tara was almost impossible to offend.
"You're standing on part of her. When you do that, she can
pretty much read your mind. Think of the entire Tower, and
the ground it stands on, as if they were Tha'alani stalks."

Clearly, he visualized what Kaylin had just said, and the information didn't exactly comfort him. "There are some parts of my mind it is not safe, by Imperial Dictate, to read," Red told Tara. Tara blinked.

"But Imperial Dictate has no meaning in the fief."

"Lord Tiamaris remains a member of the Dragon Court."

"He does."

"Imperial Dictate governs some part of his actions. I can't—clearly—stop you from retrieving information, but before you speak of any of it, speak with Lord Tiamaris first. He knows the Emperor's mind and the Emperor's will better than anyone in the Empire who isn't a Dragon. It's important that you understand what is, and what is not, public knowledge."

Kaylin caught the coroner's arm as the doors rolled open, and she all but dragged him from the steps. She didn't really want to have to explain the concept of public knowledge to Tara, because in Tara's world, the only important secrets revolved around her duties to keep the fief free of Shadow, and she'd probably spend the better part of an hour—if Red was lucky—attempting to figure out why *he* equated the two. Explaining that he didn't would take time; Kaylin knew this from personal experience.

Tara trailed after them, and Sanabalis and Severn pulled up the rear. Severn said something to Morse and Morse snorted; she waited outside.

Tiamaris was in the morgue. His eyes were a shade darker than Sanabalis's, and if Kaylin had to guess, for about the same reason.

"It is," Tara said quietly.

Both of the Dragons glanced at Tara, but reserved the brunt of their obvious glares for—who else?—Kaylin. Kaylin who had no idea what the actual *cause* of their unhappiness was, and had been relying, in silence, on base intuition.

"Red," Tiamaris said, prying the glare from Kaylin's face and adjusting his expression to one that was more neutral and vastly more respectful.

Red *bowed*. Kaylin was torn between shock and envy, because the bow wasn't awkward, didn't seem forced, and was likely to be one of the many, many things she would have to learn to do *perfectly* if she didn't want to be Diarmat's next meal. Which, she grimaced, Tara might take as literal fear.

"Oh, no," Tara said, on cue. "I know the Dragons don't actually *eat* mortals."

Red walked to one of the empty slabs and opened his bag; he took out the long, cloth roll in which he kept scalpels, tweezers, pliers, and gods only knew what else. Kaylin frowned. Red had been silent in the carriage, which she expected given Sanabalis's mood. But he'd been remarkably subdued when Tara had pretty much announced the most hated word in his past vocabulary, and he'd bowed to Tiamaris.

"Red," she said, clearing her throat.

He continued to lay out scalpels, and he also drew a small mirror from the depths of his bag, which he laid beside them. "Private?"

"Did you get the Records information you were looking for?"

"Yes." It was a curt, cool word. That tone of voice would usually have muted any further conversation, because Red, like Caitlin, had ways of making a person suffer when they'd annoyed him. It muted Kaylin for entirely different reasons, and it made his deep bow suspicious in exactly the wrong way.

But she no longer had the desire to pester Red while he worked; she had, instead, the much stronger desire to grab Severn's arm and drag him into the streets of the fief, where they could do the work they were, in theory, meant to do while they were here. It was always a bonus when you could hide cowardice behind the facade of responsibility.

She chanced a look at Sanabalis; to her relief, he didn't immediately return it. Red, however, had most of his attention, and Red moved very, *very* cautiously toward one of the bodies that he hadn't yet touched. His scalpel hand was, to Kaylin's genuine surprise, shaking—and he hadn't even picked up a scalpel, yet.

Instead, he said, "Private, bring me my mirror." She did exactly as ordered, which brought her closer to the body and the man under the glare of two pairs of Dragon eyes than she'd've liked. "Records."

The small mirror flared in a brief, blue flash, its edges glittering in the dull and steady light of the morgue. Kaylin was surprised when marks on her arm began their low, distinct itch. Mirror magic didn't generally cause her pain the way stronger magics did. She said nothing, although she had to force herself not to absently rub her sleeves against the skin of her inner arms.

Images began to form in the mirror, then. In the past, Kaylin had pulled up a stool while Red worked; he'd explain what he was doing and what he was looking for, so she knew what the inner cavity of a human body looked like. She knew more or less what bruises looked like beneath skin; she knew what damaged organs looked like. She didn't really have that strong a sense of what living, healthy organs looked like; seeing parts of someone's internal organs spill out was one of her personal nightmares.

But dead people were dead people. They felt no pain. They felt no shame or humiliation. She reminded herself of this when she lost the detachment necessary to function in a job that saw so many deliberate deaths. Still, watching the image form on the smaller mirror surface made her squint, because it looked...wrong, somehow.

"Red?"

He was silent; they were both looking at the same image.

"Red, what is that supposed to be?"

"Private," Sanabalis barked. "Let the coroner do his job." The words were very loud; they echoed in the chamber.

Red spoke a few more words to the mirror; they were technical enough that Kaylin didn't immediately recognize them—which she guessed was his intent. She watched the mirror as the images shifted; in one case the mirror came up entirely gray, which was a mirror's version of "no clue in hells."

"Coroner, will it be enough?" Sanabalis asked.

Red nodded. He then took the scalpel and began to cut into the skin just below the corpse's exposed breasts. Kaylin, who'd seen this done many times, was surprised because the woman's skin seemed to resist the blade's edge. Either that or it was very, very blunt, and given Red, this was unlikely.

Red then motioned the two Dragon Lords toward the slab. He ordered the mirror to change its orientation, which was just lazy, because he could have rotated it himself; the Dragons, however, studied the image in the mirror.

They then studied the cut—the two cuts—that Red had made, watching as he pulled the skin back.

Kaylin understood, then. She couldn't figure out why it had taken her so long.

"Yes," Sanabalis said. "Your guess was correct. She is—or was—a Dragon."

Kaylin was the first person to speak, as she so often was, and the words that fell unplanned out of her mouth weren't particularly bright. "But—that's impossible. There's no way—"

"Oh?" Sanabalis said, proving that fiery breath and icy chill were not, in fact, incompatible.

Tara turned to Kaylin. "Why?"

"Dragons have scales. You've seen Tiamaris when he's wearing them in his human form—it's armor, and it'd blunt most swords produced in the Empire."

"Only by mortals," she replied.

"The scalpels Red's using were created by mortals, Tara. And if it wasn't easy, they did cut skin."

Tara tilted her head to one side. It was mimicry of a human gesture, and it was off. Before Tara could speak, Kaylin said, "Because it looks deliberate, Tara, and I'll explain more later. Sanabalis will turn me to ash otherwise."

She frowned and then nodded. "It is true, though. There should be scales." Her frown deepened, and she said what Kaylin was thinking. "Unless female Dragons have substantially different forms or physical rules?"

"They don't," was Sanabalis's curt reply. "I am sorry, Lord Tiamaris. We must either move the bodies, or bring the Arkon here; I do not think the portable mirror and its recall will prove satisfactory to him."

"Move them," Kaylin said, thinking of Marcus and the general relief he'd feel to have this particular set of autopsies off-loaded to someone—anyone—else.

"Bring him here," Tiamaris said, at about the same time.

They exchanged a glance. Sanabalis intervened. "Lord Tiamaris is correct, Private. The Arkon has had some small suspicion about the results of this autopsy, but matters within the Palace at the moment are such that he has not—that *we* have not—chosen to disturb the Emperor. Nor will we, unless the Arkon feels there is sufficient cause."

"Dead Dragons wouldn't be sufficient cause?"

"Ah, you mistake me. Yes, they would. But the objections

you voiced are entirely reasonable, and without the Arkon's aid, it is likely that they will not be addressed. The fiefs are not, as you are aware, part of the Empire. The Emperor does not control them and he does not claim them.

"The bodies were discovered in the fief of Tiamaris. We have no idea whether similar bodies have appeared elsewhere, although some attempt to confirm or deny is being made. You," he added, "are part of that attempt. We wish you to speak with Lord Nightshade at your earliest convenience.

"In the meantime, we will send word—by mirror—to the Palace. The Arkon's part in the other investigations is minimal."

"If the fiefs are outside of Imperial Law and control..."

"You can't even finish the thought. Yes, even if they are outside of his control, should our suspicion prove correct, the Emperor may feel a need to act upon this discovery." He turned to Severn. "Corporal. Private. Please proceed from here to Nightshade. Gather what information you can, but be brief and to the point. I will return to the Imperial Palace and fetch the Arkon."

"I don't understand why in the hells we can't just have proper mirror access in the gods-cursed fiefs!"

"At the rate you're stamping along the streets, we won't have much left of the roads in the fiefs, never mind mirrors."

"If we *had* mirror access I wouldn't be *in* the streets."

"No. You'd be in the morgue with one disturbed Dragon, one extremely worried Red, and a completely silent and immobile Avatar. Oh, and seven identical corpses."

"That's better than Nightshade."

"There's no reason mirror access couldn't be negotiated, but it would *be* a negotiation. I believe Tiamaris is considering it now—but it means allowing full access to Imperial mages, and not for an insignificant period of time."

Every so often, conversations like this were necessary to remind Kaylin that mages did, indeed, serve useful and necessary functions.

"We're only going to ask one question," he reminded her.

"It's never just one question with Nightshade."

"Kaylin." Severn stopped walking. "What are you so afraid of?"

She lifted one hand to her cheek, and touched the mark there. It was easy to forget it existed on most days—but not on the ones that saw her heading into the fief of the Barrani who had placed it there. "I'm not afraid." It was more or less true.

But she *was* nervous. Nervous enough that thoughts of Nightshade displaced hunger or thirst and caused her hands to drop to her dagger hilts for simple comfort's sake. Severn started to walk and she fell in beside him; they traveled a few blocks before she spoke again. "I don't understand what he wants from me."

"Don't you?"

She shook her head. "I understand part of what I think he wants."

"Is it greatly different from part of what I want?"

"Severn—"

He lifted a hand. "Sorry, that was unfair and uncalled for."

"But it's not—it's not wrong. I understand that part. Sort of. Barrani aren't generally interested in mortals. There are stories and legends, yes—but in reality? We're brief, boring, timid lives that go by too quickly. We're old before we're fully interesting, and we're never going to be beautiful or strong the way Barrani are. The only interest, historically speaking, that the Barrani have showed in mortals usually involves slavery or benign servitude; it frequently involves bizarre ritual murders. It seldom involves just…sex.

"It's not the Barrani who were crossing the bridges into Barren's fief, after all."

"Nightshade's interest is not that simple."

"No."

"And yours?"

This was the question she had wanted to avoid. No, in truth, it was the question she *had* avoided. She didn't lie to Severn; she ran away from him. But she could only run so far from herself. "I…I don't know, Severn. I don't know that I want to know. If I could, I'd avoid him. I avoid him as much as possible. But my life seems to lead to his castle, over and over again.

"I've been a fieflord's lapdog. And worse. I *never* want to be in that position again."

"It's not the same."

"No," she said, feeling hunted. "It's not. I don't know why—but it's not."

"You're not thirteen. You're not helpless. You're not alone. There are many, many reasons why it's different." He spoke calmly and softly, the way he usually did when she was upset—but she could feel the thread of his own unease twisting beneath the spoken words; it was the first bad thing giving him her name had exposed. She didn't want it. She thought he might be either jealous or hurt, and—she didn't want that.

Which was strange, because she'd wanted to *kill* Severn for years, and that hadn't bothered her at all.

"Sometimes, when he's close, I can't breathe. I'm afraid, but it's not just fear. But sometimes, Severn, sometimes—he's just so far above me. There's nothing *I* can do that'll hurt him. Nothing I can do that can kill him or indirectly cause his death. He's just impervious."

"You'll never be responsible for him?"

"How could I be? I don't know what he'll do, and even if I did, I couldn't stop him. I can't control him. I can't even ask—" She shook her head. "Sometimes I think the reason he's almost attractive is that. He's untouchable."

"And I'm not."

She closed her eyes. Stubbed her toes. Opened them again, biting back a curse. "No. You're not. I don't want to lose you. I don't want you to die. I don't want to be unable to save you."

"I can take care of myself, Kaylin."

"I know that. But I don't *know* it. Not the same way." She hesitated, and then added, "Is it stupid?"

"To be attracted to someone because he can't be harmed?" She nodded.

"I don't know. And given the number of bets you lose, stupidity probably doesn't matter."

"The thing is, he's not Barren. What he wants—it's complicated, but it's not what Barren wanted. Barren wanted power over me. He wanted me to know how little power I had. Nightshade wants power. He even wants *my* power, I think. But not like that."

"Do you think he loves you?"

"What does that mean to a Barrani? I'm not even sure they have a native *word* for it." Aware that more was wanted, she added, "No. I'm certain he doesn't."

The border between Tiamaris and Nightshade was invisible; all the fief borders, as far as Kaylin knew—and that was only two fiefs' worth at the moment—were. But crossing borders was strictly forbidden on either side of the boundary that only residents clearly knew or understood. For that reason, they took the long way—crossing the Ablayne into the City proper and walking the length of the road that followed it until they reached another bridge.

That bridge led to Nightshade, and unlike the crossing to Tiamaris it was deserted, as it had almost always been. Kaylin stopped at its height and gazed into the river running beneath it. The sound of water against either bank was like a muted, continuous whisper; as a child, she had thought it a language of its own. Once conquered, she could understand the secrets of living a happy life, because a happy life was guaranteed to anyone who made it to the other side.

So much for the dreams of childhood.

"I'm sorry," she said to Severn without looking away from the water.

"For what?"

"I can talk to Nightshade from a distance, but I...I hate it. I don't do it unless it's an emergency. It just feels...wrong."

"Kaylin." He caught her face in his hands and turned it toward him. "Believe that you never need to apologize for that." His smile was gentle, its edges softened by something that almost felt like relief. His hands were warm and callused, his face scarred in ways Nightshade's would never be. He gave her five more minutes before he let her go.

CHAPTER 14

The streets of Nightshade really hadn't changed much, but the lack of change drove home just how much the streets of Tiamaris had. There were no carpenters here, and no wagons; the roaming groups of would-be thugs were both common and undirected. It had never occurred to Kaylin, while begging and stealing scraps of food in these streets, to wonder how it was that anyone survived in them. In Tiamaris, the thugs were either dead or now served Tiamaris, and the terms of his service usually meant they were the unofficial guards of construction sites.

Some construction *was* done in Nightshade, often by people who lived in the buildings that lined the streets, but it was repair work, and generally shoddy. Peeling paint, cracked boarding, warped shutters—these were streetside adornments. Through some of those warped shutters, people watched as Severn and Kaylin walked toward the castle that most of the residents avoided. Kaylin had once been one of those people; she wondered if they were children.

But children did play, both in Nightshade and in Tiamaris. In Tiamaris, however, they didn't avoid the Tower. They never avoided Tara. They did avoid the Norannir, but hopefully time would change that. Time, Kaylin thought, or a better grasp on the part of the newcomers of appropriate weaponry. Still, Tara took pains to make clear that the Norannir were dying on the borders in order to defend the fief, and Kaylin thought Tara's words would carry weight.

She hoped they would.

Nightshade knew she was coming; she felt his presence as she approached the Castle, and was certain that he'd been aware of hers for longer—probably the moment she crossed the Ablayne and stepped across his border.

"Heads up," Severn said quietly as they approached.

She smiled; she could see Lord Andellen waiting for them a few yards from the fake portcullis. Her smile froze when he bowed. It wasn't a bow that she could execute in that much armor if she didn't want to topple into the person before whom she was bowing. He rose before she could say as much.

"Lord Kaylin," he said, voice grave. His visor rose over emerald eyes that had a little too much blue in them to indicate happiness. "Lord Nightshade will join you shortly."

"I can enter the portcullis," she replied. "The danger's been contained."

"I merely follow my Lord's orders."

She grimaced. It wasn't that she was eager to cross the Castle threshold; she wasn't. The portcullis always landed her on her knees, and she always had to fight the horrible nausea that accompanied its passage. But there were some conversations she didn't want to have in the open street, and the back door into the Castle involved a long drop into an unused well.

"We've heard of the difficulties facing Lord Tiamaris,"

Andellen said as Kaylin more or less shuffled her feet. She stopped.

"From who?"

It wasn't a question that Andellen would answer. Fair enough; she was the one who had come, like a beggar, for information. "Tiamaris has a few difficulties. Some of them—the introduction of a few thousand foreigners—are mostly under control."

"The border?"

"It's solid. What's attempting to break the barrier is pretty damn solid, too—but so far, the Tower is winning." She hesitated for a moment and then added, "The storms are bad, though."

"Have they been markedly worse since the introduction of your foreigners?"

"They're not *my* foreigners."

"Ah."

"It is a figure of speech that can surely be forgiven," a new voice said. A new, *familiar* voice. Lord Nightshade, in perfect silence, had arrived through the portcullis. Unlike Andellen, he wore no armor; he wore dark robes and a long cape that was the same night black of his hair. His eyes were a mix of green and blue, and even at this distance, Kaylin had the distinctly uncomfortable impression that she could see her reflection in them.

But he nodded to Severn. "Corporal Handred."

Severn nodded—a bit stiffly—back. "Lord Nightshade."

"You have a personal interest in the fief of Tiamaris, do you not?" the Lord of Nightshade asked, as if his greeting, once offered, could be entirely discarded.

Kaylin stopped herself from shrugging. "I do."

"It is interesting. I have watched the borders with care since Lord Tiamaris took the Tower. He appears to be building."

"He's been building."

"To what end?"

"He wants a different fief than the one occupied by either Illien or Barren. Not more, not less."

"He has, if rumor is true, cut off the source of most of Barren's previous wealth."

"It's true."

"What, then, does he do to fund his…reconstruction?"

"You can ask him. I'm not an accountant."

Nightshade's eyes shaded to a more definite blue. It distanced him. She wanted that. "I had not expected Lord Tiamaris to show such an unnatural concern for mortals."

Kaylin bridled, but managed to say nothing. Not that it mattered; Nightshade generally knew what she was thinking. Then again, so did Diarmat, and he gave her points for strict adherence to the forms of protocol. It was, she told herself grimly, good practice.

"The borders of Tiamaris are not the only borders to see an increase of activity. Yet they are the only borders to face such a proliferation of Shadowstorm. Do you—or does Lord Tiamaris—have any opinion as to why?"

"No."

"And that is not why you have come."

"No. It probably should be," she added.

He raised a brow, no more. "Come," he finally said. "I will escort you through the portal. I have wine and sweet water, if you will take either, and some refreshments have been prepared."

By "escort," Nightshade meant carry. It should have been more uncomfortable; Severn wasn't happy with it. But while Kaylin was in his arms, the portal became a dark passage, no more, no less; Nightshade made himself a barrier through which the worst of the portal's magical effects appeared to be too terrified to pass.

It is not the portal, he told her, *but the Castle; I am its Lord. I control it when I so choose.*

They exited the portal in the foyer, as they always did. It was almost obscenely brilliant, and if she felt no nausea and none of the usual disorientation, she still had to close her eyes. Nightshade, taking little notice of her weight—and even less of her dignity—continued to move. She opened her eyes as quickly as possible, and asked him to put her down.

He did, and he did it gracefully. He then led them to the room in which he often entertained Kaylin; she assumed it was where he entertained any other guests he didn't intend to torture to death as an example for the rest of the fief. She held on to that thought as if her life depended on it.

"Welcome," Nightshade said, "to my Castle. Corporal, Private, please take a seat and make yourselves comfortable."

Food had been arranged in the usual artful, sparse way on several small dishes that ran the length of the low table. Kaylin sunk into the long couch. Severn hesitated for a minute and then joined her. Nightshade waited until they were as settled as they were going to be before he also sat.

"Kaylin, when you faced the Devourer, or perhaps directly afterward, you were in the streets. Did you understand the singular nature of what you witnessed?"

Thinking of streets packed with near-giants, all bristling with completely practical weaponry—if one happened to be that large—she nodded.

He raised a brow. "The foreigners were, I admit, unusual, but it was not of their arrival that I spoke. It was of the flight of the Dragon Court, absent only the Emperor and the Arkon."

"Oh. That. Yes, I saw it." She could still see it if she closed her eyes and concentrated, although the image was growing fuzzy. What remained in memory in a way that time couldn't dislodge was the sound of their voices, the trumpeting roar of defiance or anger or—something.

"Were you aware of the reason for their flight?"

Frowning, she nodded. "Something rose from the fiefs."

"From the heart of the fiefs, Kaylin."

"I saw it. It looked like smoke or shadow."

"You heard it. What did it sound like to you?"

She closed her eyes. "Roaring."

"Yes."

"...Dragon's roar."

"Yes, I believe so. I heard it," he added quietly. "And *Meliannos,* my sword, heard it, as well. It was the voice of the Outcaste Dragon."

"It wasn't." Kaylin had heard the Outcaste. She'd almost been flattened into bone paste by him. She knew his voice.

"It was."

"I'm telling you it couldn't have been. You've seen him. You've fought him. He was a *Dragon.*"

"And I am telling you that *Meliannos* recognized his voice. It was the Outcaste." He reached for the crystal decanter in which a dark, burgundy wine was airing. From it, he poured a few ounces into each of three crystal glasses. He offered them to Kaylin and Severn. Kaylin took one almost absently; Severn accepted one, but set it on the table untouched.

"How could he be Shadow? He's alive. I'd bet everything I own, he's alive. He's not like the undying immortals, if the Dragons have ever had those."

"He exists in the heart of the fief. He does not own it; he does not rule it."

"How can you be so certain?"

"The same way I was certain that Barren was not the Lord

of his Tower. There is only one name that comes across the border, and it is *Ravellon*. If the Outcaste finds some method of holding the fief's heart as his own, it is not that name I will hear."

"But he—"

"Yes. He has already beguiled Shadow in some fashion; it is clear now that Shadow has also beguiled him. They are joined; I cannot clearly see how. But perhaps that is not why you chose to pay this visit?"

She crushed the irritation the question produced as quickly as she could. "No, it's not." She hated people who insisted on asking questions when they already knew the answer.

"And the question?"

"In the past week, several corpses have appeared in Tiamaris."

"Given the activity along your borders, that is not surprising."

"The corpses didn't appear along the border—if they had, they'd be less alarming. Not less suspicious, on the other hand. These bodies appeared throughout the fief, and I'm here to ask if you've made similar discoveries."

"People have died in the fief within the last week," was the noncommittal reply.

Kaylin turned to Severn; Severn nodded and pulled the memory crystal out of his pouch. He set it in the curve of his palm and spoke the activating words. The image flowered instantly within the confines of the room, and as it did, it leeched light from everything else. Kaylin, who'd watched the image for hours the previous day, didn't remember that particular effect.

Nightshade's eyes were now an almost royal blue, although Kaylin thought that was an artifact of shadow, not mood.

"Who," the fieflord said after long moments in which he looked at nothing else, "is this?"

"We don't know."

"And it is her corpse that you found?"

"It's her corpse that was found, yes. Seven times."

Severn set the crystal in the center of the table, carefully rearranging the dishes that had been laid out first. "Do you recognize her?" he asked.

"I? No. Not precisely."

"Have you found a similar corpse?"

Nightshade was silent for a long moment, at the end of which he answered. "No. Is she mortal?"

"An odd question." Severn glanced at Kaylin, and handed the rest of the conversation off to her.

"We assumed she was, initially."

"How did she die?"

"We're uncertain. The bodies are being examined now." After a pause, Kaylin added, "I don't think we're going to get any answers from that examination, though."

Nightshade leaned forward. Lifting his hand, he reached out; his palm stopped an inch from the image's face. "Her style of dress is unusual."

"Not as unusual as the fact there are—or were—seven of her."

"Agreed." He lifted his glass and looked through the dark wine. "What do you suspect, Kaylin?"

"I don't know. But there's a possibility that she is—and is not—a Dragon."

She'd surprised him. Nightshade didn't particularly *like* to be surprised. "This is why Tiamaris sent you?"

"This is why I chose to come here, yes."

"Kaylin, I cannot play games with words for the whole of the day. Tell me what you know and what you suspect."

"If there are none of her corpses in this fief, it's not relevant."

His eyes flashed blue. "And you will absent yourself entirely from the fief of Tiamaris until any present danger is past?"

"No."

"Then it is not irrelevant." He walked around the table, examining the image. "Seven corpses appeared."

"Yes. There's some reason to suspect that they didn't arrive in the fief *as* corpses, but they didn't survive for long."

His eyes widened; that much surprise he couldn't conceal. Turning, he said, "Where and when? You told me the borders of Tiamaris are secure."

"They are now. But during the end of Barren's crumbling reign, they weren't. I think there's some chance that there were small, localized Shadowstorms in the actual streets of the fief, not beyond its border. There are certainly storms beyond its border now."

"And you think the storms are responsible for the corpses?"

"I can't think of anything else that would be. The corpses don't radiate magic, and they would if they'd been transformed after death. If they'd somehow been transformed before death, I don't think they'd radiate magic—but I do think they'd be tainted with very detectable Shadow."

"Shadow?"

"There's no magic I know of offhand that can entirely transform a living body. None except Shadow. Tara would know if that had happened. A dead body's been transformed in small ways before, but that leaves visible traces, regardless."

"Are you so certain that this is as true of Dragon bodies as it is of mortal ones?"

She hadn't mentioned Dragon corpses. "No. Would it be true of Barrani corpses?"

"...No. Do not pursue that avenue of questioning any further. It is irrelevant if, as you claim, the victim arrived alive and died shortly thereafter; it was not her corpse that was transformed."

"Do you think the Shadowstorms behind the barriers and the storms that escaped into the fief are related?"

"Kaylin, it may come as a surprise to you, but my familiarity with the effects of storms is of necessity scant. I cannot answer the question, even to surmise. I will, however, say this: if she is recognized in some fashion as a Dragon by the Dragons, there will be difficulties." He frowned. "That sword."

She glanced at the scabbard. "Yes?"

"It is not your usual weaponry."

"No. It's—it's new."

"May I examine it?"

"No." She really, *really* did not want to have to force the sword into the scabbard a second time.

"The scabbard?"

Damn it. "The scabbard came from Evanton. The Keeper. The sword came from the heart of the fiefs. It was the weapon wielded by the man whose name I now hold."

"Not even you could be foolish enough to take a weapon from the heart of the fiefs." The words were flat and cold. They also contained a thread of very strong doubt.

"The sword didn't come from the heart of the fiefs originally; it was carried there by a man who was possessed by the Shadows. In his world."

"Corporal, I believe the crystal can be deactivated," the fieflord said as he took a seat and poured himself another glass of wine. This he drank as if it were water. "Private, please explain what exactly you mean by the phrase 'his world.'"

"I think—and there's some minor translational difficulty—
that the man who carried this sword, the man whose name I
now hold, originally came from the same world as the rest of
the Norannir—which is what we're now calling the refugees.
They either recognized him or recognized what he's supposed
to be."

"He traveled with them?"

"No. He was lost to Shadows during their war in their own
lands."

"Yet he is here now and this did not alarm you?"

"It didn't overly alarm anyone else."

"By anyone, I assume you refer to the Dragons."

She thought about this; it hadn't alarmed Severn or Morse,
either, but she knew Nightshade wouldn't consider this significant. "Yes, I mean the Dragons. And the Tower."

"The Dragons may well be viscerally preoccupied with your
investigation."

"We know there are other worlds."

"Yes."

"We suspect that *Ravellon* is the place where those worlds
overlap."

"Yes, you suspect that."

"...That seemed to explain his presence."

"At *this* time? After the traveler found this particular world
for his people? After the challenge issued by the Outcaste and
answered in full fury by the Dragon Court?" All traces of the
usual possessiveness that underlaid his communications with
Kaylin had momentarily vanished. He turned to Severn and
said, "Corporal, if you would, I would hear your thoughts on
this matter."

Severn was silent. He intended to let Kaylin speak. Either
that or he was disinclined to aid Nightshade; it was hard to
tell. Kaylin, however, didn't speak. She was—and was sur-

prised to be—angry. At herself, certainly, because Nightshade was right. At Nightshade because, well, he was right. She wondered if his eyes would ever be emerald again. It was a stray thought.

Wine was once again poured; Nightshade didn't bother to offer any of it to either of the Hawks because neither of them had touched theirs. "Let me ask you an entirely different question, then. Where—and by whom—was the sword you now carry made?"

"I—I don't know."

"I suggest, if possible, you attempt to find an answer to that question. It may be relevant to many of your investigations." He lifted a hand to his eyes. "While I have never been as… ambitious as Lord Tiamaris, there is work that my fief requires. I will ask you now to pay careful attention to two things. The Dragons and the sword."

"The man who carried the sword?"

"Because he is a source of information, he, too, is to be watched."

Kaylin rose. "Lord Nightshade," she said, matching his use of "Private." "I wish to ask one question."

"I am not inclined to either stop you or answer."

She asked anyway. "How do I release a name?"

"How do you forget speech? How do you forget how to breathe?" His brows had once again lifted, but only slightly. "There is only one certain way that I am aware of, Private. It involves your death. Or his."

So not the answer she wanted.

"We do not, however, always get what we desire—if indeed such a trivial impulse can truly be classified as desire." He set his empty glass down on the table. "And yes, I am not being entirely truthful; I have no idea how you contain the name, but you do; there is therefore a possibility that *you* could release it. I could not. No more could the Dragons.

"In return for the information I have provided, I will ask one favor. I have information for your Sergeant Kassan, which I will trouble myself to deliver in person. It is consequential in one of the investigations which you find so troubling—and in which you are not currently involved."

"Which investigation, exactly?" Kaylin asked, although she had a sinking feeling that implied her subconscious, at least, already knew the answer.

"There is, if my information is correct, some difficulty with the Imperial Exchequer?"

Damn it.

"The information I provide, however, comes at a cost."

"And that cost?"

"I wish you to travel to the West March."

"P-pardon?"

"With me."

"But you *can't* travel to the West March—you're Outcaste, or have you forgotten?"

"It will require a leave of absence on your part. The Sergeant, or perhaps the Lord of Hawks, will grant it, or I have nothing to offer them."

Nightshade was annoyed enough that Kaylin was left to find her own way out of his Castle, which meant about twenty minutes of wobbling legs and intermittent nausea. Severn accommodated her by walking slowly until she'd fully recovered.

"I don't like it," he said. Since that was pretty much a given, Kaylin nodded. "Why the West March?"

"I have no idea. Well, not a good one."

"And the bad one?"

"He once said something about the stories told in the West March. They're not stories like ours—they're like the stories told to the Leontines at the dawn of their creation."

"And he wants you to hear them."

"Looks like." She was particularly grateful that she'd been too tense to eat. "We're heading back to Tiamaris."

Severn nodded.

"What do you think Marcus'll do?"

"Need a new desk."

She chuckled, even if she'd be the one who was responsible for the desk's purchase. "Beyond that?"

"He'll take it to the Hawklord. The Hawklord will agree; if the information isn't useful at all, he'll ignore his agreement."

"So I'm to pray for useless information?"

It was Severn's turn to shrug. "The investigation is going badly enough a solid lead would be worth the absence of one Hawk. If the lead comes from Nightshade, it's a sure bet there are Arcanists involved."

"Not necessarily. Nightshade gets a lot of the same traffic Barren used to get; all we can say for certain is members of the Human Caste Court are involved."

"Betting?"

"...No."

He laughed. It was not one of his happier laughs. "Don't ask me what to pray for. Don't," he added, "ask me what I'm praying for, either."

"I'm personally looking at the very near future," she offered. "And I'm praying that the Arkon was too damn busy to haul his ass to the fiefs."

Gods sucked.

Morse—and only Morse—met them at the Tower's open

doors. "We've got another Dragon here," she said the minute Kaylin entered the foyer.

"What color were his eyes?"

"Before or after?"

"Now."

"Now? Pretty close to red."

"Did Tara tell him we've arrived?"

"I'm not sure."

"Good. Can you take us to where Maggaron is staying?"

"Instead of the morgue?"

Kaylin nodded. "We'll hit the morgue right after we've finished speaking with him."

"Good. I'll stay with you two."

Maggaron's door was closed; it was not, however, locked. It opened into rooms that looked larger than Kaylin remembered them being the first time she'd seen them. That, on the other hand, wasn't unexpected for a Tower.

He wasn't sleeping. Instead, he was sitting in a chair that faced the room's tall, long window, looking out. If he heard the door open—and since he'd failed to hear the loud knocking that preceded it, Kaylin wasn't certain he had—it wasn't obvious.

"Maggaron." He didn't move. He might have been carved of stone; she couldn't clearly see any indication that he was breathing. She approached the chair he sat in and then glanced out the window. There, she froze. She heard Severn call her name, but it was a faint, attenuated sound; it belonged in a different world.

It certainly didn't belong in the world the window now exposed. For one, the sky was the wrong shade. It was blue, but the blue seemed too purple. Even if the blue had been the right color, the ground beneath it lacked streets. It lacked all but a single building, and that building was in the far distance, surrounded by trees and the distant glint of sunlight on water. Flags were flying at the building's odd height, but they were far enough away that they were anonymous.

"Is this your world?" she asked him. They were the first words she'd spoken that evoked any response.

"It was. But this window—it's a window into the past. It is not a window into anything that can be reached now." He lifted his head. His hair was no longer braided; it fell down his shoulders, thinning at the ends, in a rich, tangled brown. He looked as if he hadn't eaten for days; his eyes were sunken, his cheeks hollow.

"Maggaron, I don't intend for you to die here."

"Does it matter where I die?" His voice was soft and almost uninflected; it was shorn of hope, and it made acceptance something reached only at the end of all endurance. Because she recognized it, she flinched.

"It matters to me."

"Why?"

"I don't know. Does there have to be a reason?"

"If there were a reason, I would hold on to it with what little life I have left." His glance went back to the window. "This is not what your world looks like."

"Not mine, no. Mine is made of buildings and cobbled streets and people of different races. And crime. A lot of crime." She placed one hand on his left shoulder. "Maggaron, I need to ask a question."

"Ask. If you command it, I will answer."

"Can we just skip the command?"

"It depends on the question."

"It's about the sword."

"Has she spoken to you at all?"

"No."

"Then she has not accepted you, Chosen." Although the words were neutral, a tiny thread of happiness ran through them. Kaylin wasn't certain how to answer that, and decided not to bother.

"I need to ask you who made this sword. And how they made it."

"It is one of the swords that define the Ascendants," Maggaron replied. It wasn't an answer. She felt his indecision, and she lowered herself to the ground—not to kneel, but to sit. Her knees she gathered beneath her chin as she moved to face him.

"I'm never going to be an Ascendant," Kaylin told him. "I only want to be an Imperial Hawk. That's it. That's all I've ever wanted. I don't consider myself the wielder of the sword; I consider myself its—its guardian. Its keeper."

"For what, or for whom, will you keep it?"

There wasn't a good answer to that question. "I don't know. I don't know enough about the sword. Tell me what you know. Or tell me what you were told."

"I cannot, unless you compel. There are mysteries that I cannot reveal."

This was the answer she expected. She knew she could force him to answer. She also knew that short of that, he wouldn't. "Tell me what any of your people would know, then."

"Chosen, I cannot separate what I know from what an outsider knows—not anymore. If you cannot bear to command me, speak with Mejrah, the elder. She will tell you what any exceptionally promising child is told before he leaves on the pilgrimage of a candidate for ascendancy."

Kaylin looked to Severn. Severn nodded. "We should have the time."

"If I could release you, I would," Kaylin told him.

"If you could release me," he replied, "I would test the

very bounds of my nature; I would try to die, here, where the Shadows cannot call me."

She rose and headed toward Severn, Morse, and the door. But in the door frame, she turned for one last glance out the window; his reflection, pale and ghostly, looked back.

"You should just put him out of his misery," Morse said, but only after the door was firmly shut. Morse had never had a lot of patience with despair. "He sits around the room all day—when he isn't sleeping. Makes me want to kick his ass."

"Sitting around in the room all day means he's one less thing I have to worry about—or did you forget what he looked like when the Shadows had a grip on him?" Kaylin said.

Morse shrugged. "Morgue?"

"Sadly, yes."

The door of the morgue opened before Morse could touch it. While Kaylin appreciated this far more than traditional door wards, she still found it slightly creepy, and given the contents of the room, a little time spent opening the door meant a few seconds less time in the company of angry Dragons, which was never a bad thing.

No sound escaped into the hall. "Are they still there?" Kaylin whispered.

"Yeah." Morse entered the room. Kaylin and Severn had little choice but to follow her lead; cowardice was one thing, but obvious cowardice was quite another. The first thing Kaylin noticed was Red. He was sitting in an armchair that looked entirely at odds with the rest of the morgue's decor; it had a high, tall back that gleamed. His arms lay against the armrests, and he'd gotten rid of the smock in which he normally worked.

She started toward him, caught his expression, and stopped.

Turning, she noted the rest of the room. The seven corpses were now covered, head to toe; nothing could be seen, not even the women's hair. Standing between the two large tables that served as almost communal slabs were the Dragons: Tiamaris, Sanabalis, and the Arkon. Tara was nowhere in sight. The color of the Dragons' eyes was, as Morse had reported, Not Good.

Six orange eyes now turned toward her. "Private," the Arkon said. If he'd said it in Leontine, it would have sounded like a curse.

She folded in the middle immediately. "Arkon." She didn't even bother to look up from the very uninteresting floor, boring being preferable to painful. He didn't tell her to rise.

"Did you speak with Lord Nightshade?"

"Yes, Arkon."

"And?"

"No similar corpses were found in the fief of Nightshade."

"He is certain?"

"We showed him the contents of the memory crystal you prepared, Arkon."

"Good. Stand up," he added, growling. "And do not test my patience in this fashion again. You may play these games with Lord Diarmat. He has had centuries of training humans, and obviously has the tolerance for it."

If she'd opened her mouth, she would have choked on her tongue. She did, however, rise. The Arkon was no longer looking at her, and she was now looking at the back of his robes. She could see Tiamaris and Sanabalis because they were more or less facing her. They weren't stupid; they were looking at the Arkon.

"You have no contacts in the other fiefs?"

"No, Arkon."

"I dislike making assumptions on so little information."

"Yes, Arkon."

"Sanabalis?"

Sanabalis cleared his throat. The sound was pure Dragon. Kaylin had the very sick feeling that Dragon conversation was about to erupt, but she kept her hands dutifully by her sides. "Inasmuch as it is safe to make any assumptions in the fiefs, I feel it is safe to make this one. The corpses appeared in Tiamaris, and only in Tiamaris."

"An artifact of the crumbling barriers?"

Tiamaris nodded. "That is Tara's suspicion. She has marked, in as much detail as possible, the locations of the storms that escaped the boundaries during the end of Barren's reign. There is no immediate correlation between those locations and the locations at which the corpses were found, but if the… women…emerged alive and died after the fact, that would make some sense."

The Arkon broke a bit of stone off one of the slabs, and proceeded to crumble it into fine powder. Kaylin couldn't see his expression, and was grateful. "There is no doubt," he finally said. "The internal organs are exactly what we would expect if the victim was a genuine Dragon.

"The skin was thicker than mortal skin, with the possible exception of Leontines in their prime, but there are no internal scales, nothing to indicate that scales could have once existed. I dislike it intensely. Yes, Private?"

"It's—it's nothing, Arkon."

He turned. Kaylin was surprised the floor beneath his feet didn't crack; she was also surprised it wasn't blackened, charred, or molten. "Perhaps I did not indicate how severe my lack of patience is. If you have a comment or a question, I am willing to hear it. Barely."

"All of the members of the Dragon Court I've met look

distinctly individual when in their mortal forms. Can that be altered?"

"Our mortal appearances? Yes. Not with ease, and not without cause, but, yes. We gravitate toward specific experiences naturally, however; color of hair, shape of face, height."

"So…it's possible that these could, in fact, be seven different corpses?"

"They are clearly seven distinct corpses." His voice was Winter, a reminder that people froze to death just by being outside.

"I mean they could, when alive, have been seven distinct Dragons."

The Arkon's silence was chillier than his words.

Sanabalis, however, answered. "It is possible." Kaylin seldom heard such a lukewarm acknowledgment of possibility, and filed this as a No.

"Is there any evidence that she *ever* had scales?"

The Arkon exhaled smoke with a bit of fire in it. "Not," he finally said, "according to your coroner. The coroner, of course, has no actual experience dissecting Dragons; it is possible that he is incorrect."

"Possible," Tiamaris said quietly, "but doubtful."

"Then…what does this mean? Do you think she came *from* the heart of the fiefs?"

"We do not have any metric for predicting what Shadowstorms will do," Tiamaris said before the Arkon could exhale again. "You know, or should know, this. We have no method of determining how she arrived or from where she traveled."

Kaylin's frown deepened. She opened her mouth to ask another question, and then snapped it shut as she felt Severn tug at her. It wasn't a physical tug; it was far more personal. But he was worried for her, and he wanted her to stop Right Now.

Kaylin edged her way across the floor to where Red sat.

Lowering her voice as much as possible, she said, "You're done here?"

He nodded; his hands on the armrest tightened. She'd seen Red examine corpses that would have made anyone with a shred of sanity run screaming from the room, and he did it without working up a sweat; this was the first time she'd seen him this disturbed. Turning to where the Dragons stood, she said, "Arkon, may we escort the coroner back to the Halls of Law? We've an entirely unrelated message to pass on to the Lord of Hawks from Nightshade."

"You may. The bodies will remain in Tiamaris. No formal report of the work done here is to be entered into Records at the Halls of Law; to that end, we will retain the coroner's personal mirror. No verbal report is to be tendered to either the Lord of Hawks or the Sergeant."

Red nodded. Kaylin winced, but nodded, as well. She could just imagine how happy that was going to make Marcus. The Hawklord was always more resigned when it came to random Imperial Fiat. Then again, the Hawklord actually spoke *with* the Emperor, something Marcus had never done, to Kaylin's knowledge. On the other hand, she'd never seriously asked.

"And you, Private, are to return to the fief when you have finished your errand."

"Yes, Arkon."

CHAPTER 15

When they were well away from the Tower, Kaylin turned to Red. "How bad was it?"

"I think my hearing is slowly returning."

She winced. "I didn't even feel the shouting."

"Pardon?"

"When the Dragon Court is having an argument, it shakes the whole damn Palace."

"I guess the Tower is better constructed." Red fell silent. He carried his bag as if it had gained ten pounds over the course of the day.

"Red, can I ask a question?"

"I don't know. Lord Tiamaris said the Tower can listen in on any conversation that occurs in the fief—are you going to ask a question that's not safe for me to answer?"

"Given the Arkon's current mood, 'Would you like something to drink' would probably be punishable by death."

"Then, no. No questions."

"Red?"

He sighed. "Kitling," he began, never a good sign, "you've had more exposure to Dragons than anyone in the Halls except the Lords, and possibly, the Barrani. Maybe you're used to them; I'm not. I don't think I could do an autopsy today without making a mess of the corpse. I'm still shaking. I want to go back to the office and deal with normal crimes, normal bodies, and even a very pissed-off Sergeant." He grimaced as a little color returned to his face. "Scratch the last one."

"That's probably the only thing you can count on."

He even dredged up a chuckle. "What was the question?"

"Did you get any sense from the angry Dragons that it was possible to separate a Dragon's mortal form from its Draconic one?"

"Kitling." Again with the diminutive. "Stay away from this one. Trust me. You don't want to get any more involved than you currently are." Because she was waiting, he added, "Half their conversation was conducted in Dragon, and I didn't understand a word. After a few sentences, it didn't matter; I don't think I could hear anything else."

Red accompanied Kaylin into the office, something he didn't normally do. This caused a bit of a stir, but only in the parts of the office nearest Marcus's desk; the other parts were busy—or chatty—enough not to have noticed. Caitlin, however, looked up. "Red."

He stopped by her desk. Kaylin and Severn paused, as well, although Marcus was clearly aware of their return.

"Is your work in the fiefs done?" Caitlin asked when Red failed to find even pleasant nothings to say.

"Unless the Dragons say otherwise, it is. Unfortunately, the Dragons have decided that the work I've done is to remain entirely off the record, and out of any reports."

"Meaning you won't be filing one."

"Correct," Red replied, dropping his bag and folding his arms across his chest. "But I still expect to get paid."

Kaylin's brows rose a fraction. "Does that work?" she asked him.

"It had better." To Caitlin, he said, "Do you want me to deliver that happy bit of news to Sergeant Kassan, or can I pull a runner and leave it in your hands?"

"Leave it in my hands, dear. You look like you're in definite need of lunch."

"Lunch won't be necessary," said the coroner, who was famed throughout all three branches of the Halls of Law for his iron stomach. "I think I'll have an appetite somewhere around dinner. Were there any emergencies?"

"Not more than the usual."

"Good. I'll be in my office if Marcus wants to frustrate himself in person."

Marcus was *not* in a good mood. The Sergeant—and any casually working Barrani—had of course heard every word that Red had spoken to Caitlin. His eyes had shaded from gold to bronze by the time Kaylin and Severn had pushed off from Caitlin's desk and approached his.

"Why," he growled, "are you here?"

"We escorted Red out of the fiefs, sir."

"And now he's back. Is Sanabalis finished with you?"

"No, sir."

"Then get lost; some of us are busy."

Kaylin cleared her throat and lifted her chin. Marcus gouged a deeper runnel into the surface of his desk. Red was right—he was in bad need of a new one; it was a wonder the claws hadn't gone through the desktop by now. Kaylin mentally added buying another inexpensive desk to the list of things she had to do Right Now.

"Private."

"Sir."

"Why are you *still here?*"

She thought about retreating without mentioning Night-shade at all. It seemed the least career-limiting option. But if what Nightshade had implied was true, he had information about the Exchequer—or at least involving the Exchequer—and the Halls were in desperate want of solid, useful information. If there was a decent chance Nightshade was right, they needed it.

"Don't move your lips when you're adding things up in your head," the Sergeant growled. "It's a terrible habit. *What* do you need to speak with me about so urgently?"

"Lord Nightshade."

"Is he in his own fief?"

"Yes, sir."

"Has he stayed there?"

"Yes, sir."

"Do you have any reason to suspect that he intends to engage in illegal activities in Elantra?"

"Nothing illegal short of breathing, sir."

"Then I don't need to hear it right now."

"He says he has information that you might be interested in, and he's willing to discuss it with you in person."

"I see. And you think this is information we need?"

"He mentioned the Imperial Exchequer, sir."

Marcus's eyes went copper; Kaylin's chin went higher. Wood shavings appeared beneath his extended claws. "He's willing to discuss it out of the goodness of his heart?"

"…No, sir."

"How much does he want?"

For the first time, she glanced at Severn.

Marcus turned to Severn. "Corporal?"

"He's requested a leave of absence—for Private Neya."

"I'm not interested." Marcus made a show of turning back to his paperwork, which didn't involve much actual movement, given there was so much of it.

Not for the first time, Kaylin hated her lack of involvement in what had become the department's most important investigation to date. Had she been, she could have agreed and negotiated in Nightshade. As it was, she knew about as much as Nightshade did—or demonstrably less—and it galled her.

"Sergeant."

Marcus's facial fur was now standing on end, as were the tufts of his ears.

"Nightshade didn't tell me either the information or its source. But I think you should at least listen to what he has to say. If you don't want to negotiate with him directly, let the Hawklord do it."

"I'm *not interested,* Private."

That might have been the end of it, given the color of Marcus's eyes, but Teela—and a slightly more cautious Tain—sauntered over to his desk. Like Marcus, they'd probably heard everything. Unlike Marcus, they were pragmatic. Braving a face full of angry Leontine, Teela spoke first.

"Sergeant."

Marcus didn't bother with orders; he growled. It wasn't a quiet growl, and the background noise in the office took a nosedive in its wake.

Teela was unfazed. Her eyes, however, were distinctly blue. "At this point, we can't afford to turn away any possible leads."

"What leads can a fieflord give us?"

"We won't know until we hear him out. He's not asking for money."

"If it were money, I'd listen."

"He's not asking you to fire her."

"What the hells is he asking then?"

They both turned to look at Kaylin. Blue and orange weren't colors that went well together, especially not given the expressions that surrounded the eyes. "He wants me to go to the West March with him."

Teela's thin brows rose. When they fell again, her eyes had narrowed. "Why?"

"I don't know."

Teela slid into High Barrani. Mostly. "Kitling, Lord Nightshade has oft played dangerous games. The reservations of the Sergeant—"

"Those aren't reservations; they're an outright refusal."

"The reservations of the Sergeant are not unfounded. When did Lord Nightshade ask for your company?"

"He hasn't given a date."

"I have some suspicion of the dates. It is not, however, a *short* leave of absence, and if I'm not mistaken, you have very little experience traveling." She frowned. "Very well, Sergeant. I offer this. If, as I suspect, Lord Nightshade intends to travel for the gathering, I will also be in attendance."

"He said only me," Kaylin began.

"Indeed. And only you would be required to take a leave of absence. The Barrani Hawks, however—"

Tain cleared his throat; Teela glared at him. "The Barrani *Lords,* however, are given a leave of absence for important cultural events. I am a Barrani Lord. I had not intended to attend the gathering, although I have, of course, been invited. I will change my plans," she told Marcus. "If Nightshade's information warrants it. Technically, you would not be in violation of his request, if you agree to fulfill it."

"I'm not sure she's any safer with you around," the Sergeant growled. But his eyes were less lividly orange. "No drinking."

"Can we compromise and say no brawls?"

"I'll leave that to the Hawklord."

Teela lifted one delicate brow and dropped back into Elantran. "I'd prefer that his information be entirely laughable."

"Oh?"

"I dislike travel. The West March is interesting if you're inclined to revere plant and insect life."

Marcus rose. "Caitlin," he shouted. "Mirror Grammayre and tell him we're on our way up."

"Yes, Marcus."

"And you two," he added, glaring at Kaylin and Severn. "Get back to work if you don't want your pay docked. Did Nightshade happen to say when he'd be dropping by?"

"No, sir."

"Fine. Get lost. I mean it this time."

He'd meant it the first time, as well. Kaylin hesitated.

Severn bent and whispered, "It's not our case, Private. We've got a lot of ground to cover today. Let's go."

Kaylin took one deep breath, expelled it, and shook herself. She headed toward the door and Severn fell in to her side. "It's not that I don't want to leave," she said, lying, "but we're supposed to head back to the Arkon before we do anything else."

"Given his mood, obedience is probably the only option. Cheer up; he's unlikely to eat us."

Tara answered the door when they arrived.

"Where's Morse?" Kaylin asked.

"Morse is delivering a message," was the noncommittal reply.

"Do you still have a room full of Dragons?"

Tara frowned.

"Sorry," Kaylin said, because she really didn't want to explain the nature of metaphors for the hundredth time. "What

I meant was, are the Arkon and Sanabalis still here, and still in the morgue?"

Tara nodded thoughtfully. "Your question was shorter the first time, but inaccurate. Is it really true that Morse or Tiamaris would have understood what you meant?"

"Yes," Kaylin replied. She continued the explanation that Tara wanted as they made their way down the hall, promising herself to be literal when speaking to Tara, at least for the rest of the day. Sadly, she'd probably forget, because it was too easy to forget. If Tara didn't exactly look normal, she didn't radiate that aura of power that would have otherwise forced Kaylin to be careful with her words. This unspoken observation branched into an entirely different explanation.

Severn was silently laughing by the time they reached the morgue—which was good, as nothing *in* the morgue was liable to be cause for mirth.

Case in point: the Arkon met them as the doors rolled open. Kaylin didn't remember the morgue having double doors, but this was an ancient magical building, and things like that changed without warning or notice. The Arkon didn't appear to care one way or the other.

Lord Sanabalis and Lord Tiamaris were standing as far away from the Arkon as the room allowed, attempting to look busy. Kaylin thought this both cowardly and unfair—although it was probably, given the color of the older Dragon's eyes, also wise. She bowed; so did Severn. The Arkon's smoke wafted over their heads.

"I see you've deigned to return," he said. His voice had dipped into Dragon scale; it was low and very loud. He was not, however, roaring.

"Yes, Arkon," Kaylin said in the tone of voice she generally reserved for Marcus in a foul mood.

"Good. You are to continue your investigation, but you will be accompanied by the Tower's Avatar for the duration."

Kaylin rose and glanced at Tara, who seemed entirely undisturbed.

"There is a reasonable chance that we are missing two bodies," he continued, ignoring the question in the glance. "If possible—if at all possible—you are to find witnesses who heard anything that the woman said before she collapsed."

"She wasn't speaking a language they recognized—"

"That," was the autocratic reply, "is what we have the Tha'alani for."

Kaylin thought about her career, and the application in particular for her promotion, and winced. Opening her mouth was not a good idea.

"Yes, Private?"

Then again, having facial expressions also apparently sucked. "If it's true that the deceased arrived because of small, localized Shadowstorm, it's unlikely that we're going to find many more of her. The borders have been effectively closed. Tara—the Avatar," she said, quickly correcting herself, given the ripple of lines in the Arkon's brow, "says the Shadow is once again entirely contained."

"Yes. There's been some discussion about that."

Kaylin looked past the Arkon to Tiamaris. Whatever the discussion had been, the youngest of the Dragons didn't like it.

"You will go now. I have taken a very small leave of absence from my library while I oversee this investigation; you will report to me at the end of the day."

"Yes, Arkon."

Tara took very little time to prepare, which in this case meant changing into her gardening clothing. Kaylin and

Severn took less. They exited the morgue as quickly as they could; neither Tiamaris nor Sanabalis had uttered as much as a squeak.

"That's not true," Tara said as she closed the Tower doors behind them and stepped onto the garden path. "They spoke quite a lot before you arrived."

"In Elantran?"

"In Dragon."

"What were they discussing?"

"The possibility of lowering the barrier for a few days." Tara's eyes were ebony as she said this.

"Did you join in the discussion at all?"

"My Lord felt it unwise. But he did speak on my behalf."

"*Can* you join the discussion?" Kaylin didn't ask what Tiamaris had said on Tara's behalf; she knew what the answer would be. She was surprised that Tara seemed so calm about the request.

"Oh, yes. Dragon is not difficult to speak; it requires a shift of vocal cords, but that's relatively minor." She began to follow as Kaylin took the lead. "Where are we going first?"

"We're going to the border."

"But the bodies weren't discovered there."

"No. But I need to speak with Mejrah as soon as possible."

"But the Arkon—"

"I know what he said. But anything that keeps us out of his way right now is a good thing. Trust me on this."

"Do you find him frightening?"

"You don't?"

"No. He *is* very agitated. And I find it difficult to read his thoughts."

"Well," Kaylin said as she turned a corner and headed down the widest street that led to the borders of the fief, "he probably can't turn you to ash just by breathing."

"No," was the grave reply. "But I don't think he'd try. Or is that a figure of speech?"

"I wish."

The fief of Tiamaris had almost become two distinctly separate fiefs. There were streets the normal humans traveled, and given it was only afternoon, those streets were nowhere near empty. But the streets where the Norannir patrolled might have existed in an entirely different world; the only visible humans in easy or direct sight were Kaylin and Severn. Even the buildings that girded the street had begun to look different as the Norannir decorated them.

"Oh, those aren't decorations," Tara said when Kaylin pointed them out.

"No?"

"No. They're warding charms. And alarms. They change color in the presence of Shadow. The Norannir want to put them up on every door or wall in the fief; you'll note that some of the streets have also been painted."

Kaylin could imagine how well *that* would go over.

"My Lord doesn't think it's necessary."

"What do you think?"

Tara shrugged. It was such a fief gesture, Kaylin's brows rose. But then again, the Avatar's most constant companion was Morse, a woman who'd perfected the art of the shrug before Kaylin had been born. "I don't think it would be harmful, but I don't think the panic it might cause would be helpful."

"I think the rest of the citizens of Tiamaris would accept the wards if the Norannir would agree to disarm a bit."

Tara looked surprised. "Why would they want to do that?"

"They clearly don't. But weapons like that ax, for instance—half the people in the fief probably couldn't even lift it." She pointed at one of the larger—and older—men in a patrolling group of four. The gesture attracted his attention.

"Yes. But they aren't required to lift it. Without weapons, the Norannir patrols can't deal with the Shadows they might find. They certainly can't kill the Ferals as easily."

"Yes, well. The problem with weapons is they're neutral. Yes, they can be used to kill Ferals, but in the wrong hands, they can do a bang-up job on people, as well."

"But they're not trying to kill people."

"I know that. But even I find them intimidating." The patrol approached as Kaylin finished the words. Tara took a step forward. In her gardening clothing, she really didn't cut much of an imposing figure, but the Norannir clearly recognized her; they stopped their advance, and they knelt on one knee, resting the weapons under discussion against the flat ground.

Tara spoke to them. She spoke in their tongue. Kaylin recognized the word *Mejrah;* she didn't recognize much else.

"They'll take us to the Elders," Tara said cheerfully. "Although they did say Mejrah is very busy."

Mejrah was, as advertised, very busy. And as an older woman, being busy and having a wealth of patience were at odds. One of the men—the one who'd drawn the short straw by his expression—approached the three tents that had been erected at the end of the street; he came back with Mejrah and two of the bearded older men that Kaylin vaguely recognized in tow.

Mejrah had wrinkles in the corners of both mouth and eyes that looked chiseled there as she turned toward the rest of the patrol; the poor unfortunate who'd been sent to retrieve her joined them. These men were uniformly taller than she was, but tall men were capable of cowering on command, even when they were also much better armed.

"She's not happy to be interrupted," Tara said.

Even though Kaylin couldn't catch a word of the rapid-fire exchange, she could tell. "You can understand her?"

"I understand much of what she—or any of the Norannir—now say. My memory is augmented by my ability to sense people and events that occur within the boundaries of my fief. It is not perfect, and if the conversation is specialized, I will not understand the exact words. Mejrah is often annoyed, so these words are very familiar to me now." After a brief pause that was mostly filled with Mejrah's voice, Tara added, "She's angry that they didn't recognize you."

"Me?"

"You're the Chosen," Tara said serenely. "You should be recognized."

"I'm not wearing a sign," Kaylin began. She then looked down at her arms—her sleeve-covered arms—and winced. She was, in fact, wearing a sign; it just happened to be hidden.

Tara nodded, as if Kaylin had spoken. Her ability to read thoughts didn't extend past the Tower itself, but she was acutely observant. Her interpretations of what she observed were often unusual, on the other hand. "It would be good if you could leave at least your arms exposed."

This was a definition of good that had always been extremely bad in Kaylin's experience.

"Mejrah—and the Norannir—feel that the Chosen is worthy of respect. Lack of respect is dishonorable. Dishonor is death, or should be. There are mitigating circumstances; I don't think she'll demand that these people kill themselves."

"So…I'm exposing my arms to prevent them from having to commit suicide?"

"Something like that," Tara replied. "Would you like help with the sleeves?"

"No."

"The reason I wear these clothes," Tara continued, indicating the smock, the kerchief, and the somewhat dirt-covered gardening gloves, "is because it makes me easy to spot."

There were so many better ways to be spotted Kaylin didn't even know where to begin. But before she could start, she considered Tara with more care. Yes, there were better ways to make herself known—she could sprout wings, for gods' sake—but were there really any better ways to make herself accessible? As the Avatar, she could have been a truly terrifying figure with very little effort.

But she didn't want that. Maybe this was the best she could do, after all. Kaylin grimaced and unbuttoned the cuffs of her sleeves. Severn stepped in to help her roll them up. "I'll try," she told Tara.

"I know. You always do."

"I'd like to succeed more often."

"According to my Lord, that only comes with time. He's explained the advantages of being feared. But…he's feared already. Even the people of the fief, who know that he fights for their safety, hide if they see him coming. I don't need to be feared because *he's* feared. But maybe it's different across the river."

Kaylin, her sleeves now rolled up and resting around her elbows, turned to Mejrah, who had fallen to one knee. She reached out and took Mejrah's hand in hers and lifted her off that knee; she couldn't exactly lift her to her feet, given the differences in their size. Mejrah then led Kaylin toward the tents that stood on the very edge of the border. There, she shouted Effaron out of a tent. He was never going to be terribly intimidating, even given his height, but he smiled broadly—and with a bit of relief—when he saw the reason Mejrah had demanded his immediate presence.

This relief didn't stop him from falling to one knee, but

his watchful eye was on the Elder, not Kaylin. Mejrah finally said something curt and he rose. He then tendered a deep and respectful bow to Tara, who returned a nod—and a very encouraging and sympathetic smile. No, Kaylin thought, Tara was not terrifying—not like this. Even though the Norannir had seen her in her full defensive glory, the image of her winged, implacable form faded from memory in the presence of much more common gardening clothes.

Effaron offered Kaylin a hand; she took it gratefully. Direct contact between Kaylin and this one Norannir allowed them to speak to each other; Kaylin had no idea why. But understand it or no, she heard his words in Elantran, except for the odd word that had no Elantran analog; Effaron heard Kaylin in his own tongue, with the same exception.

"Your Lord Sanabalis has made progress," Effaron said. "And the children do learn your words more easily than the Elders. It's not always *wise* to learn things more easily than the Elders," he added with a grimace. "But we've not seen Lord Sanabalis teaching for the past two days. Is he well?"

Thinking about the last expression she'd seen on Sanabalis's face, Kaylin shrugged. "He's in good health."

"And you?"

"I'm in good health for the moment. There's a task or two that Lord Sanabalis wants done pretty much yesterday; I'm indirectly here because of that."

"We are to help the Dragon Lord?"

"Well, no. Not directly. I need Mejrah to tell me about the origins of the Ascendants. I need to know how they became Ascendants. And, um, how they got these swords." She touched the one that hung in the scabbard it so detested on her belt. Effaron's brows disappeared into his shaggy hairline. Clearly, Maggaron was not the only person who considered a sheath for this particular sword sacrilegious.

"Perhaps it would be better to ask the Ascendant himself?"

"I tried that first. Apparently, since I'm not Ascendant, there are things he can't tell me. He suggested Mejrah would be the best source for the things that *can* be told."

"I think she will find it annoying to tell children's stories so close to the stronghold of the enemy."

"We can move."

Effaron winced. "Never mind, Chosen. I'll ask her."

Mejrah was, as Effaron expected, ill pleased, but Kaylin didn't think it was simple anger. It wasn't. .

"She expects you to understand these things," he explained, "and she finds the lack of understanding unsettling. She's willing to accept that the Chosen in *this* world merely has mystical understanding of events in this world." He raised a brow.

"Try not to disillusion her too badly if you think it'll get me killed."

He laughed. "The attempt would likely cause me more harm than it would cause you." Holding her hand, he bowed to Mejrah; Mejrah then stalked into her tent and came out holding a small rug. She unrolled this and sat, cross-legged, on one of its edges, inviting Kaylin, Tara, Effaron, and Severn to do the same. Tara chose to sit on the edge of the rug Kaylin also occupied; her gaze wandered past the tents and the Norannir to the border that was, in the end, the reason for her existence.

The Elder spoke to Effaron, and Effaron translated, which in this case merely meant he repeated what she said. Kaylin, in turn, repeated what she'd heard so that Severn could understand it.

"Mejrah wants you to understand that this is a story that is told to children; it's not special, it has no innate power, and it requires no guarantee or oath to receive. Although a variant of the story is used in more formal circumstances, it's not that different." He cleared his throat. One of the Elders, who was lingering at the edge of the carpet, disappeared and returned with a jug of water and some heavy, clay mugs. He handed these to Effaron, who was clearly expected to serve himself.

"Once, when the world was new, there were no Shadows, and the Norannir traversed all the lands in freedom. There, they hunted and gathered without fear. They built cities, in time, and they grew learned, and they spoke with the Ancients."

Kaylin lifted one hand. "Wait. You said Ancients?"

Effaron nodded; Mejrah was less quick to halt her speech. "The Ancients created the world," he explained. "Did they not create yours?"

"They did. Or we're told they did. I just wonder if it was the same Ancients. Sorry. I'll try not to interrupt."

"Among the Ancients were those who were called Shapers. It was the Shapers who came to us with the promise of knowledge."

"And power?"

"Of course. They offered this knowledge to the Norannir, and the Norannir accepted. But not all the races were pleased, and there was conflict. The Immortal ones felt that the knowledge was too dangerous or too costly."

So much for not interrupting. "Which Immortal ones?"

"You have seen them. Here, in your lands, they walk among us."

"Dragons?"

"Dragons," he whispered. The word itself was reverent. "They were not many, and they were fierce; in their displeasure, they were deadly. But they were the wisest of the Peoples. They were proven wiser, in the end, than even the Ancients, for the Shadows came when the doors were opened."

"Wait, which doors?"

"The doors that lead to enlightenment and knowledge; the doors that lead to languages and lands beyond our ken. The Norannir as they exist now have only words to describe it; there are no images, no paintings, no ruins. To hear of it, it was a marvel, but it was also an impossibility: a place that existed in all places, at once. We do not know how, or why, but that place began to twist and unravel, and if the knowledge was there, the People could not reach it without also becoming twisted and changed, and those people emerged into our world and began the spread of Shadow.

"We did not recognize it at first; it was new to us. But the Dragons understood what it presaged, and they fought—and fell—while around them the world was unmade.

"In the end, the Dragons were all but destroyed, and the Shadows held sway over much of our world, in endless night; our people were infected as if Shadow were a disease that did not kill, but defiled. The Dragons taught us what they could, not of the nature of Shadow, for that they did not entirely understand—perhaps deliberately—but rather how to recognize it, how to fight it, where that was possible.

"Among Dragonkind there was one who was considered the Queen of her race; she was ancient, but when she chose to speak to us, she was beautiful and graceful. We called her Bellusdeo. Her breath was not fire, not ice; it was the storm itself, and where it struck Shadow, Shadow withered for a time. But she could not be everywhere, and she could not see everything, and to her sorrow, those whom she had taught aged and died in her absence, becoming weak, infirm.

"As the numbers of the Dragons dwindled even further, it was the Dragon Queen who came to the Norannir, and she offered the Norannir this one blessing.

"'Choose among your kin the young and the most promising, and send them to me. I will teach them, and I will train them, and I will shape them in such a way that they might know life that is as long as a Dragon's. Understand that they will not, and cannot, return to you as the children they once were; they will become mine. But they will return to you as shields and swords, and there will be no more effective way of combating the Shadows; they will remember where they were born, and how they were raised, and they will love you as kin. Until they fall, you will not fall.'

"The People did as she asked; she traveled the lands that had not yet fallen and spoke these words to all the Elders. In villages and in the remaining two cities, the Elders began to test children when they came of age."

"But didn't she ask for children?"

Effaron frowned. "Indeed."

"Then why would you wait to test them until they'd come of age? Wouldn't that be too old?"

His brows furrowed and then rose. "When you say 'of age,' what do you mean?"

"When they become adult—or as close to adult as the Laws demand."

"Ah! Then we have three 'ages' that we mark. The first is the age at which the children are deemed healthy enough that they are unlikely to die unexpectedly. They would have been five years of age."

That, to Kaylin's mind, was too damn young.

"We did not understand what Bellusdeo was searching for, but we trusted her with our children, and our children were gathered in the fortress at the foot of her Aerie. There, they were trained. They were taught. They learned to speak the languages of man, and to understand some of the language of the Dragons. They learned to wield weapons, and to forge them; they learned many, many things.

"All the while, the Dragons flew at her command, and they fought, and they fell. The years passed, and when the children reached the age of the sword, one of two things happened: they were sent back to their people—if their people and their villages still survived—as warriors and teachers, or they vanished. They were taken by Bellusdeo and they were transformed and they became the Ascendants; the men and women among us who could transcend our mortality and our limitations."

It was pointless to ask how, but Kaylin asked anyway.

Effaron frowned. "It is not part of our tales, Chosen. We do not know. No more do we know, in truth, how we ourselves were created. We know that the Dragons were born from the bones of the world, or the many worlds, and that they were granted a mortal form so that they might, when they so chose, live among mortals without crushing them in their carelessness."

"So...Maggaron was one of those children."

"Yes. But he was not one of the first. He was one of the last, perhaps the last. The first ascended when the Dragons still lived; the last did not."

"And the weapons?"

"They are the weapons of the Ascendants. We call them swords, Chosen, but they are much, much more than that; they understand the heart of their wielder, and they become the weapon of their wielder's choice. They cannot be broken; they cannot be stained."

"So the Ascendants always have these weapons?"

"Yes."

Kaylin frowned. "How were the weapons made?"

"It is not recorded, Chosen."

"But the Dragons made them?"

"The Dragons gifted the Ascendants with the weapons."

It wasn't quite the same thing, but they clearly didn't have the answer. She glanced at Severn. Severn then asked the next question. "Ask Mejrah if she was trained as a possible Ascendant."

Kaylin repeated the question.

Effaron shook his head. "Bellusdeo trained the Ascendants. When she was lost to us, the Elders attempted to teach what they had been taught. But without Bellusdeo there could be no more Ascendants, just the knowledge passed down from the Elders who had once almost been chosen. Mejrah was schooled in that tradition."

"When Mejrah was taught, was she ever shown images of the Dragon Queen? Were there paintings or sculptures or tapestries?" Severn said.

Kaylin repeated that one, as well, feeling more sympathy for Effaron's position as translator than she had in the past.

Mejrah's frown was more ferocious than Effaron's.

"She wants to know why you ask."

"Funny," Kaylin replied, "so do I. Severn?"

His answer was both unexpected and, in the end, unsurprising. He removed the crystal the Arkon had constructed from its pouch at his side. This, he set between his knees on the carpet. "You might want to warn them," he told Kaylin.

Kaylin did as he suggested, watching Mejrah carefully. Mejrah was grumbling at one of the Elders when the crystal's image emerged and unfolded in front of Severn.

The old woman's eyes widened so much they became half white; her mouth opened, and she stared, slack jawed, for one frozen moment.

"Well," Kaylin murmured. "I guess that answers that question."

Severn nodded.

CHAPTER 16

Picking up the crystal again was more difficult than either Severn or Kaylin had considered when Severn had set it down. Mejrah's voice returned, and it was higher and louder than usual—which said something, because Mejrah had the makings of a Sergeant. It was also much faster. Effaron was shocked enough that he dropped Kaylin's hand, which meant Mejrah had to repeat it all once he'd recovered his grip on both his composure and said hand.

What it boiled down to was this: Mejrah wanted to keep it. Emphatically and forcefully.

In any other circumstance Kaylin would have let her have it, even given the cost of its creation. Unfortunately, the crystal had come from the Arkon, and the Arkon had made it very clear he wanted it *back*. Effaron understood every word Kaylin said. Mejrah understood every word Effaron said. Something, however, appeared to have been lost in the translation. Mejrah descended into pleading, which was far worse—on Kaylin's nerves—than threats or demands would have been.

It was also clearly shocking for most of the Norannir who were anywhere nearby. Given Mejrah's general mood, the Norannir were better at pretending they weren't eavesdropping than, say, the Office Barrani, but they *were* people. The two men that Kaylin also thought of as Elders didn't bother with the pretense. They joined Mejrah, kneeling to either side of her on the increasingly small rug.

After some very awkward back-and-forth, Kaylin turned to Severn. "You caught all that?"

He nodded.

"Okay. As near as I can tell, they understand that a) this is very important to one of *our* Dragons and, b) their reverence for *their* Dragon trumps our desire to save our own necks. Am I missing something?"

Severn chuckled; it was pained, but he was genuinely amused. Easy for him, on the other hand; the Arkon never raised his voice at Severn. "I think they assume that our reverence for our Dragons is nonexistent in comparison to their reverence for theirs. They don't hold Sanabalis or Tiamaris in the same reverence—or awe—they clearly feel for Bellusdeo."

"Probably because they never met her," Kaylin muttered. The only Norannir who could understand what she said grimaced. He didn't, on the other hand, repeat what she'd said so Mejrah could hear it, which meant she owed him one.

In the end, it was decided that Severn would leave the crystal with Mejrah until Lord Sanabalis—or the Arkon himself—returned, because Kaylin had no doubt whatsoever that one or both of the Dragons would want to speak with Mejrah about Bellusdeo. Kaylin took great pains to make sure Mejrah—and anyone else in hearing range of Effaron—understood that the crystal was on loan; it was not a gift, because neither she nor Severn owned it. The Elders could make their case to the

Arkon, a Dragon who did not believe—in any way—that possession was nine-tenths of the Law.

But watching Mejrah's face as the old woman gathered the crystal in her shaking hands killed anything as petty as irritation. Her eyes were wide with something too painful to be wonder; they filmed in that particular way that eyes did when a person was determined not to cry and only partly succeeding. The two older men were silent, but one wept openly.

It was almost worth the Arkon's ire. She promised herself she'd try to remember this when she was actually exposed to it.

Tara spoke once they were far enough away from the Norannir border post. "I don't think the Arkon will approve."

"I wouldn't take that bet," Kaylin replied. "But…you saw their faces, Tara."

"I did. I think we should return to the Tower."

"We haven't even begun. The Arkon thinks we're missing two bodies."

"We didn't search for the other seven; they came to us."

"No. But no one's mentioned eight or nine; I think the Arkon believes that they either haven't appeared yet, or they aren't corpses yet."

"You saw the reaction the Norannir had to the crystal."

Kaylin nodded. "If they find her corpse now, I'm not sure what will happen—but they'll certainly let us know. If they find her alive, somehow, their reaction will be exactly the opposite of most of the rest of the fief. Come on. We have two areas marked in the fief where the probability of storms while the borders were down were highest. Severn and I will head there. Do you want to go back to the Tower?"

"…No."

★ ★ ★

The fief of Tiamaris was not the fief of Barren. The streets had more or less the same shape—and the same names, although Tara said that was going to change sometime in the near future. The buildings were more or less the same, where they still existed. Here and there, gaps yawned between standing structures. Tara obligingly explained why it had been necessary to demolish the missing buildings; they were infested. Some of the Shadows that had worked their way across the weakened boundaries had nested in those buildings—and often in the people who'd holed up in them.

"There are still some problems," she added. "My Lord, with the aid of the Norannir, has hunted down most of the remaining Shadows—but one or two are subtle. I'm not entirely certain they're still in the fief."

Heart sinking, Kaylin said, "You don't think they've returned to the heart of the fiefs, do you?"

"No. I think it's possible they've crossed the bridge. The only boundaries that cause them difficulty are the boundaries that the Towers make."

There were others, as well, but Kaylin didn't see a reason to quibble. She glanced at Severn and mentally added it to the list of things that had probably already gone wrong when they weren't looking. She then took a look at a more literal note she'd made. "We want to hit Whetstone and Tanner. The streets," she added.

Whetstone and Tanner were on the way to what Tiamaris hoped would eventually be the fief's market. Three blocks from the heaviest construction in the fief, if you didn't count the border towers, three buildings had gone missing. "Tara?"

"We didn't destroy those," was the Avatar's quiet reply. "If you look, you'll see. There's no sign of fire, no sign of burning."

"There's no sign of building, either. I only lived here for three months, but I remember at least one of those buildings really well."

"It vanished."

"Vanished."

Tara nodded. "There was a storm here, I think. It would have passed through just before my Lord claimed the fief. The foundations and the basements are still here," she added.

Kaylin, who had walked to the edge of the road nearest the missing buildings, could now see that for herself. A small, unpainted fence had been erected along what had once been three buildings' facades. It looked as if the walls had been sheared off at ground level. "Was there *any* debris?"

"No."

"Severn, give me a hand."

Severn nodded. He shrugged the pack he was wearing off his shoulders, opened it, and took out a very flat rope. "I'll hold it if you want to climb down."

"Thanks."

He smiled. "You've always been better at climbing than I have."

"Better at falling, too," she murmured. She hopped over the fence with care; it was a *very* thin fence. Taking the rope, she slipped it around her waist. "This is new."

Severn nodded. "A gift from Evanton. It's strong, but it's not bulky. It won't give you rope burns, and with luck, it won't bisect you if you fall too far." This was a not-so-subtle criticism of Kaylin's choice of knot.

"That's what I like about Evanton," she said as she peered down the ten feet or so of wall that led to packed and oiled

dirt. "He uses magic for practical things. If all mages were like
Evanton, we'd be—"

"Out of a job?"

She snorted. "I won't need the rope," she told him.

"It can't hurt."

Easy for Severn to say. Had she not been wearing the damn
thing, she could have jumped and rolled if necessary; as it
was, she had to half skid down the wall itself. When she did
find her footing, she turned and headed away from the street.
"Severn?"

"I'm here. Do you want me to join you?"

"Not exactly. I think I've found body number eight."

"You're certain?"

"No. But I see a pretty familiar shade of blue in a huddle
against the far wall." She slowed as she approached it, and
heard a soft thump at her back. Glancing over her shoulder,
she saw that Tara had chosen to join her.

"It's the same," the Avatar said, standing beside—and
slightly behind—Kaylin.

The cloth *was* huddled; the skirts rose and fell in a way
that implied knees that were drawn to the chest. Arms were
wrapped around those legs, but the fabric completely covered
her feet. Strands of gold fell to either side of the dress, as if
parted; the top of the woman's head was dusty but distinct.

Kaylin's skin began to tingle. She wondered if that was
due to Severn's rope, but the dagger sheaths that Evanton had
crafted for her didn't cause her magic-sense to start itching;
even the sheath she now wore—which had really pissed off
or panicked the sword—was comfortable. "Tara, be careful."

Tara nodded.

Kaylin took two steps forward. Both made the tingling

slightly worse. She'd seen seven corpses and none of them had had this effect on her. "Severn, I don't think this is a body."

The pile of blue cloth moved; the sleeves fell. As they did, Kaylin saw the movement of hands, the pale color of skin. She froze as the woman lifted her head. Her eyes were a natural hazel with flecks of pure gold; they weren't the gold that the autopsy scan had revealed. They were also wide and unblinking as they stared at Kaylin.

Kaylin hesitated and then, guided by instinct, she turned her inner arms toward the woman who sat curled against the remnant of the wall. The marks on her arms began to glow a faint and steady blue, and the woman's eyes widened further. Her mouth opened in a soundless *O*.

"Kaylin," Tara said, her voice cooler, the edges of the word pronounced. It was meant as warning.

The woman tried to push herself off the packed dirt and onto very unsteady legs. Without thinking—something that she was too good at —Kaylin rushed forward. She didn't mark the moment the runes on her skin began to ache; she didn't have time. She managed to catch the woman before she collapsed. As Kaylin's arms stiffened to support the unexpectedly heavy weight, the woman grabbed her wrists.

She had a grip like a drillmaster's, even though her hands were a lot prettier. "Chosen," she said. "Chosen, hear me. I have little time."

"Don't speak," Kaylin told her firmly. "We'll get help. We can—"

But the woman shook her head. "You bear the sword," she said. "I can hear it. You must kill me, Chosen."

Kaylin stiffened as the woman's grip tightened.

"Chosen."

"What is she saying?" Tara asked.

"You can't understand her?"

"No. She is not speaking native Dragon."

"She can't be. I can still hear her."

"Yes. What is she asking of you?"

"She wants me to—to kill her."

Tara said, after a pause, "I don't think that will be necessary."

"Help me lift her, Tara. If we get her back to the Tower, the Arkon might be able to help her."

Tara nodded; she was grim now. She caught the woman under the arms; the woman struggled. "Chosen," she said, her voice thinner and weaker. "Please, *please*. You must listen. You must do as I ask. Strike while I still have time."

"Tara," Kaylin said through clenched teeth.

The Avatar nodded again, and this time, the cloth she wore transformed in a literal eye blink. Kaylin's arms and legs already ached so badly the Tower's use of magic couldn't make it worse. Wings rose from Tara's back; wings as long and fine as an Aerian's. "I will take Her," she said. "I will take her in haste." She closed her eyes briefly. "My Lord will meet me as I approach. Follow." She lifted the woman as if she were a very small child.

At moments like this, Kaylin understood exactly why Sanabalis thought she was worthy of fear. The stranger's grip on her wrists eased and she began to shudder as Tara leaped straight into the open air.

Kaylin massaged her wrists to get enough feeling in her hands that she could use them to climb. Severn had the rope in hand, and in this case it *was* actually helpful; the tips of her fingers were distinctly bluish in tinge, not a color that looked good on Kaylin. "What happened?"

"She was alive," Kaylin said curtly. "We're to meet Tara

back at the Tower. I think we can safely say we discharged our investigative duties, at least for today."

"We can. That doesn't usually bother you." He fell in beside her, adjusting his stride as she began to speed up. "She spoke?"

Kaylin nodded grimly. "Tara couldn't understand what she was saying."

"You could."

"I showed her my arms."

After a very brief pause, Severn asked why. It was a reasonable question, all things considered. "I was still thinking about what Tara said about the Norannir."

"She's not Norannir, judging by her size."

"No—but Severn, Mejrah recognized her. I thought maybe, just maybe, the marks on my arms would have a similar meaning to her as it did to the Elders. If we were closer to the border, I'd have taken her to Mejrah." She shook her head.

"She recognized them, didn't she?"

Kaylin nodded. She wasn't running—running Hawks tended to cause either panic or congestion in the streets, depending on which streets they were—but she was walking at a very fast clip. "When she grabbed my hands, I could understand her. It worked the same way as it seems to work with Effaron."

"The traveler?"

"Yes. I understood her—but I understood her to be speaking my native tongue. Tara didn't recognize the language." Tara had a Tower's memory; it was probably longer and deeper than the Arkon's. And a lot less temperamental. If Tara didn't recognize it, there was a good chance it had never been spoken in this world. If it hadn't, Kaylin wondered what the Arkon would make of it. "Severn, she wanted me to kill her."

He was silent; she thought her speed had managed to outpace his questions.

"Did it have to be you?"

"What?"

"Did it have to be you who killed her?"

"I don't know—believe it or not, that wasn't the first question that popped into my mind. Mostly, I was wondering why she wanted to die."

"If she does, you're probably the last person in the fief she should ask."

"Severn, no one would have done what she asked. Tara wouldn't. You wouldn't. The Arkon certainly wouldn't."

"True. And?"

"It bothers me. She seemed so desperate. I don't know if she's being hunted; seven corpses certainly implies as much. But something about it felt wrong." Kaylin hesitated again. "I think she recognized Maggaron's sword."

"If Mejrah's not wrong and if the woman's appearance is not a coincidence, that's not as strange as it could be. She'd recognize the sword because she was the one responsible for bestowing it on Maggaron."

"I understand the theory," Kaylin replied as they took the last corner and turned onto Garden Row. "But it's clear that in Maggaron's time—and experience—this sword was never sheathed. How did she recognize it, Severn?"

"I don't know. Maybe she'll be able to explain."

Kaylin nodded. "I don't think it mattered to her who killed her—but I think it mattered how. She wanted to be killed by *this* sword. I just happened to be carrying it."

In the end, the question was to remain unanswered. Kaylin and Severn arrived at the doors of the Tower; they rolled open slowly. Tara stood in the doorway. She was still winged, and her eyes were ebony. She bowed to Kaylin, which was awkward, and not just because of the wings. Kaylin waited until she rose before speaking.

"How is she?"

"She did not survive."

Kaylin uttered a brief word in Leontine. "Was she alive when you arrived?"

"Yes." Tara hesitated. "The Arkon, Tiamaris, and Sanabalis are with her now. They do not wish to be disturbed."

Kaylin was all for not disturbing upset Dragons.

"They did not wish you to leave, however."

This, on the other hand, was less welcome. "What exactly did they want us to do?"

"Wait."

"On the doorstep?"

Tara's expression rippled. "Oh. No, I don't think that's what they meant."

"Do you think we could wait with Maggaron?"

Tara frowned. "You wish to ask him about Bellusdeo?"

"I do. I know this is going to be bad, but do you think you could pry Sanabalis out of that room? We need him to get our memory crystal back."

"I think it will have to wait. You wish to show the crystal's image to Maggaron?"

"Yes." Before Tara could speak, Kaylin hastily added, "But I don't want to show him her corpse."

"Oh? Why not?"

"He's already completely wrecked, Tara. If she's indeed Bellusdeo—or one of a dozen spitting images of her—I think it could push him over the edge." The words left her mouth before her second thoughts could kick in.

"What edge?"

Glum, Kaylin resigned herself to explaining yet another metaphor as Tara stepped out of the door. But Tara was on her own ground now, and she caught the thought before Kaylin could pick out better words to express it. Tara seldom found Kaylin's frustration annoying.

"So you are afraid that you will upset him so much he will not be able to be helpful?"

"Yes."

The Avatar, her eyes like the void, smiled brightly. It was jarring. "I can help."

Maggaron was still sitting by the window. He'd probably only been seated there for a few hours, but they were long damn hours by this point. Kaylin's stomach rumbled; it was like a clock, but embarrassing.

"Are you hungry?" Tara asked.

Since she knew the Tower already knew the answer, she nodded.

"I'm asking," Tara said gravely, "even though I already know the answer because my Lord says this will be important. There are other questions to which I know the answer that I must nonetheless learn to ask."

"Really? Like what?"

Tara frowned. "How is the weather?"

Kaylin snorted. "Tiamaris is teaching you this?"

Tara nodded.

"Do you think he'd teach me at the same time?"

"Tiamaris says this is what Lord Diarmat is teaching you."

"Yes, but there's a difference. Tiamaris doesn't hate the sight of you."

"I'm certain Lord Diarmat doesn't hate the sight of you, either."

Severn cleared his throat, and Kaylin reddened. Maggaron was so silent and still it was almost easy to forget he was sitting right there. Kaylin let the rest of that conversation drop as if it were molten.

"Maggaron," she said softly.

He looked up at the sound of her voice, but his eyes were still empty.

"We need your help."

"I cannot leave this place," was his bitter reply. "You understand why."

"I do. We don't need you to leave. We need you to accompany us."

Maggaron looked at the walls, the floors, and the ceiling without really seeing them. The only thing that drew his attention—and not in a good way—was the scabbard that hung at Kaylin's side. He didn't ask, and she didn't offer the information; there wasn't any point in upsetting him any further.

The halls were familiar; they were wide enough—and tall enough—to allow a Dragon in flight form easy access. The doors at the hall's end were just as wide. They began to open well before anyone had reached them, and they opened into a familiar room.

Maggaron stopped on the threshold, staring at the walls, his eyes wide. They were a shade of emerald green that in Barrani would have been a good sign; Kaylin wasn't completely certain what that color meant in the Norannir. She thought it was surprise. He turned to her. "Those words—"

Kaylin nodded. She lifted an exposed arm.

"Do you understand them, Chosen?"

"No. I'm sorry, I don't."

He deflated, losing about three inches of his height, which was still considerable. Before she could find anything comforting to say—and comfort was, sadly, not her strong suit—he walked to the edge of the shallow pool that served as Tara's mirror. There, he knelt, his knees on the lip of the stone circle. He bowed his head until his chin touched his collarbone, and rested the palms of his hands flat against the tops of his upper thighs.

Tara looked down—barely—at the top of his head. The black drained out of her eyes, leaving them oddly human in the warm light of the room. Lifting a hand, she pressed her palm gently against his head, as if offering a benediction. Or absolution. The line of Maggaron's shoulders relaxed slowly, as did his breathing.

Kaylin wanted to ask Tara what she was doing; she didn't because there wasn't any space in which to wedge the question—not without breaking the very strange communion. She walked to where Severn stood and joined him in silence, waiting for either Tara or Maggaron to speak.

Tara moved first, breaking contact by slowly lifting her hand. She didn't move away from Maggaron, but she didn't have to move—she was at the edge of the still pool. Kaylin cleared her throat, but Tara lifted a hand, demanding silence by gesture alone.

The water began to glow. It rose as Tara nodded, building a familiar image, inch by inch, starting at the feet—or rather, at the edge of blue skirt—and continuing upward until the woman they'd found in the fief stood facing Maggaron.

He whispered a single word. "Bellusdeo."

Kaylin glanced at Severn; Severn was watching Maggaron's expression with something that looked suspiciously like pity.

Tara left the former Ascendant's side and came to stand beside Kaylin. "He recognizes her," she said, although it wasn't necessary. "But, Kaylin, I don't think now is the time to question him."

"No, it probably isn't," was the soft reply.

"He's seen a room very similar to this one before, Kaylin. I believe part of his training occurred in one. She taught there. She chose him."

"How do you know?"

Tara lifted a brow. It was very similar to the expression Kaylin used when someone asked her a question to which the answer was obvious.

"Never mind. Does he have any idea why she wants to die?"

"No; that's not part of his memory."

"What is?"

"She chose him," Tara replied. "And she left him. It is not clear how; it is not clear—to me   why. I believe he understood it."

"You can't touch that?"

"No. I can touch the pain, but the cause is protected. I am reluctant to press him."

Kaylin, remembering her first walk through the Tower at its awakening, flinched but nodded. "It hurt," she said, as if speaking about the weather. "But it helped in a way. It helped me."

"I didn't intend to hurt you."

"I know. You wanted to tell me that you understood what had hurt me in the past. That you understood the pain I was in."

"Yes. I no longer think that's an effective way to communicate understanding," she added. "But it would be that, or nothing; it's buried too deep."

"You could let me ask him a few questions."

Tara shook her head. "Not yet. Look at his expression."

While they'd been conversing, Maggaron had started to cry. He didn't sob; the tears fell in utter silence. He lifted only his face; his hands remained in his lap. The image of Bellusdeo shifted as he gazed at her. Shifted, walking from the center of the pool to the edge. His edge. She knelt on the other side of the pool's lip; only an inch or two of rounded stone separated them. She was taller than Tara; taller than Kaylin.

Kaylin glanced sharply at Tara; Tara nodded, her attention absorbed by what the pool revealed. Or by what Maggaron revealed. Kaylin felt distinctly uncomfortable watching him now, as if she was intruding on something intensely, personally private. The image of Bellusdeo began to speak.

Kaylin recognized the voice. She knew Tara was concentrating, but spoke—quietly—anyway. "Tara—what are you doing? How do you know what she might have said?"

"I don't. *He* does. This is not my image, Kaylin; it is taken from him; I am merely giving it a shape and form that we can also witness."

Maggaron spoke. Even the acoustics of the room failed to magnify his words enough to make them audible to Kaylin. But Bellusdeo was standing inches from where he knelt; she didn't have that problem. She laughed. The sound was a shock of warmth that traveled up Kaylin's spine to her ears, poking her insides on the way there.

"She's beautiful," Kaylin whispered, seeing it clearly for the first time. She would have said more, but the Bellusdeo of Maggaron's memory threw her arms wide and spun in a circle, as if she were a child. No, Kaylin thought, seeing her expression, not a child. The movement was ebullient, but it was deliberate, as well.

Her eyes were perfect gold.

Bellusdeo stepped away from Maggaron, who continued to kneel; when she stood once again above the pool's center, she bowed. To him. Then she laughed again and said something that Kaylin would have paid a week's salary to understand. Two weeks'.

Maggaron's tears had stopped; his face was wet with their

tracks, and his eyes were shadowed by both wonder and apprehension.

Bellusdeo began to transform. Kaylin had seen such a transformation only a few times, because it was, strictly speaking, illegal in the Empire without the Emperor's express permission. If she'd had any questions about the Arkon's visceral reaction, she forgot them: Bellusdeo stretched and elongated, taking at last the shape and form of a Dragon Queen.

CHAPTER 17

She was golden. Her scales were the color of Dragon happiness or Dragon peace; they shone in the room like contained lights, as if she were translucent and had swallowed the sun in her flight. Her wings were folded across her back, and her tail swept past the pool's edge, brushing through the three witnesses like a visible breeze.

"Tara," Kaylin whispered, unable to take her eyes off the Dragon. "Did she speak before she died?"

"Yes."

"What did she say?"

"I didn't understand it," Tara replied.

"Did they?"

"I...I'm not sure. I find Lord Sanabalis and the Arkon very, very difficult to read or understand. The Arkon was upset, if that helps."

"Not really. These days, he's always upset." Kaylin squared her shoulders and left Severn and Tara. She approached Maggaron alone, her hand touching the hilt of the sword she carried. It was cool against her palm; it caused her no pain, no tingling, no itch.

"Maggaron."

He nodded, still staring at the Dragon that Bellusdeo had become. A starving man would have looked at food on a distant table with less longing.

"Is that the Dragon known as Bellusdeo?"

She felt his shock—and his disapproval; he mastered both quickly, remembering that foreigners were allowed to be ignorant. "Yes."

"Is there a reason that she would want to die?"

She expected shock, horror, anger; what she saw instead was sorrow. Sorrow was harder to deal with. She retreated into quiet professionalism instead. "I assume the answer is yes."

Maggaron said nothing.

Kaylin took a deep breath and made a decision. "Maggaron, I think she's trying to reach our world."

He continued to stare at the Dragon. Thankfully, the Dragon's image was silent. "I think she's tried eight times now."

"Chosen—"

"I know this is hard for you. I don't know *how* hard, no. I'm not Norannir, I've never been trained to be an Ascendant. I don't really understand what an Ascendant is. But I know it's hard. I don't want to make it harder—but I don't have much of a choice."

He nodded, but this time he looked away; she could almost see him straining to do it. "Chosen, there are matters that Ascendants do not know. Why do you think that Bellusdeo has attempted to reach this world? And why eight times?"

"Because she's been seen. There were witnesses."

"Were they of the People?" he asked a little too quickly.

"No. One of them," she added as he opened his mouth to speak, "was me."

Clearly the Chosen were considered impeccable witnesses, at least in comparison to unknown outsiders. He glanced once at the mirror's image of his beloved Dragon, but he was torn between agitation and a strange excitement. "Where, Chosen? Where did you see her?"

"In the streets of this fief." Technically, this wasn't entirely accurate, but as Kaylin wasn't writing a report or being debriefed by a cranky Leontine, it was good enough.

"Where is she?"

This was the tricky part. "She wasn't well when we found her. Tara brought her directly to the Tower—and the three Dragons who are currently in it—but she didn't survive. I'm sorry." Watching hope die was difficult; being the one who killed it was worse. Kaylin had been trained to deliver bad news to nervous parents and distraught spouses, but it had always, always been gut-wrenching.

"Was she injured?"

"No. I think she was ill."

"Impossible." He turned away. Turned back. "But it's impossible that she be here at all. You said this was her eighth attempt to reach your world?"

"...Yes."

"She told you this?"

"No, not exactly. The Arkon, a visiting Dragon—and the oldest Dragon in the Empire, as far as we know—implied that there would be nine attempts."

"Nine?"

She nodded. "Is that number significant to you?"

"No."

Damn. "Me, either. Maggaron, we assume there were eight attempts because she died today."

He looked confused, and Kaylin honestly didn't blame him. "This would be the eighth time she's died in the fief of Tiamaris."

★ ★ ★

Not surprisingly, this didn't decrease the Ascendant's confusion at all. "What do you mean?"

"Exactly what I said. The reason we know about her at all is because we discovered her body. And then we discovered her body again. And again. There are seven identical corpses in a magical preservation room in this Tower. I'm not sure where the eighth body is, yet—but it's somewhere in the Tower, as well."

"Chosen, my apologies, but are you certain?" he asked in the tone of voice generally reserved for accusations of insanity.

"Yes. If you want to look at them, we can take you there now." Turning to Tara, she added, "We *can* take him there now, can't we?"

"To the morgue, yes." She lifted her hands; Maggaron shouted. It was wordless, but the meaning was clear. "Ascendant," Tara said quietly, "I will need to use this mirror at some point. But I will leave the image as it stands until that time comes. Will that suffice?"

He lowered both his head and the line of his shoulders. "Yes, Lady. Thank you, Lady."

"Do you fully understand that these images are taken from your memories?"

"Yes, Lady. But it has been *so long*. So long since I have seen her. I cannot now recall her so clearly and so perfectly as your mirror has done; she is buried beneath the weight of other memories." He bowed deeply. When he rose, he smiled at Kaylin; it was a shadowed, fragile smile. "Please, take me to your morgue."

It wasn't her morgue, and she wanted to point this out, but couldn't think of a way of doing so that didn't sound childish or argumentative. She was certain Tiamaris could have done

it, and was mostly certain that Maggaron would escape un-
scathed. It was never a good idea to misattribute ownership
of something that belonged to a Dragon.

But the point was moot. Maggaron was led to the morgue
and when he entered it, he froze in the door. When he started
to move again, he moved slowly and deliberately toward the
seven corpses. As Tara had guessed, the eighth hadn't made its
way here, yet. He walked from corpse to corpse, uncovering
each in turn, but touching nothing except their eyelids.

At last he said, "My apologies for doubting you, Chosen."
He was quiet, and he was visibly jarred, but he wasn't upset.
"Seven. And you've said there was an eighth?"

She nodded. "When we found the eighth she was alive, but
not by much."

"You said your Elder thought there should be nine?"

Kaylin nodded again. "He's not *my* Elder, by the way; he's
a Dragon."

"What do you call him, then? What is his title?"

"We call him any damn thing he wants to be called. At the
moment, that's Arkon. The Arkon."

Maggaron nodded gravely. "My apologies. The Arkon,
then. He said there should be nine bodies?"

"He was slightly upset at the time, and he didn't really
offer much in the way of explanation. You have to understand
something: she doesn't look like a Dragon to us in this form;
even her eyes—"

"Her eyes are wrong, yes. And no."

"I want to hear more about the no; I've heard enough about
the yes."

"The last time I saw her, her eyes were this color."

"I don't understand. It's magical—when we examined the
corpses magically, the eyes were gold. But only then. We can't
dispel the magic." She shook her head and continued. "We

thought she was human. We thought there was a good chance that these bodies were originally seven very different corpses, and that they'd been transformed before death somehow."

He shook his head.

"But the Arkon now believes that she is, in fact, the mortal form of a Dragon in some respects."

"What are his concerns?"

"She has no subcutaneous evidence of scales. Her skin is much thicker than normal human skin, but that's not the defining feature of a Dragon."

"Chosen, you said she was alive when you found her this time."

"Yes."

"Did she speak to you?"

"Yes."

"What did she say?"

Kaylin hesitated, but it was brief. "She asked me to kill her."

This, at least, Maggaron hadn't been expecting.

"I didn't," she added quickly.

"You are Chosen."

He might as well have said "You have blue spots" for all the sense it made. "I don't think she asked me to kill her because I'm Chosen," she told him with a bit more heat than she'd intended. "I think she asked me to kill her because she recognized the sword I'm carrying. She wanted me to kill her with this sword."

"And you refused her?"

"Yes, I refused her. Killing helpless strangers isn't in my job description. Would you have done what she asked?"

He looked at the scabbard that held what had once been a giant's two-handed greatsword. "Did the sword not speak to you?" he finally asked. It wasn't an answer.

Kaylin could guess what his answer would have been,

and she didn't like it much. "No. I've never heard the sword speak."

"You aren't trained to listen."

"No."

"Unsheathe the sword, Chosen."

Kaylin looked dubiously at the sheath, remembering just how much of a hassle it had been to get the sword into it the first time. "She's not here now," she replied, evading the request.

"She is not, no. But you will understand more if you hold the sword." He looked at the sheath again, his eyes narrowing. "The sheath stills her voice. Where did you acquire it?"

"It was a gift."

"It would have been considered a curse—and a great evil—among my kin."

"I got that. Tell me why."

"I...cannot." He turned away.

"You can't? Or you won't?"

"I was trained as an Ascendant candidate. I was chosen to become one of the Ascendants. I was the last. Bellusdeo found me, and Bellusdeo chose me. I've never understood why. I was not the strongest, not the wisest, not the quickest. But she chose."

"And when you were chosen, you were given this sword?"

"Chosen—"

"Look, Maggaron—if the Arkon is right, she's going to arrive here one more time. Only one. I have no idea why he thinks there should be nine of her, but I'm willing to trust him—we have that much history."

"And you and I do not."

"I'm *also* willing to trust him because I don't have any choice." She hesitated and then added, "We don't have a lot of female Dragons in the Empire. By not a lot, I mean none that

I've personally encountered. My instincts are saying that none is pretty close to what the rest of the Dragon Court expected to encounter, and finding one as a corpse—seven times—is not making any of them any happier.

"But the Arkon is old, he's a Dragon, and even the Emperor respects his advice and his opinion. I'm going to trust him; there's a ninth Bellusdeo coming. She might already be here; we might already be too late. You can hide behind secrets all you want, but when you were controlled by the Shadows, don't you think they learned what you know? They had your name."

Maggaron bowed his head.

"If I don't know what I need to know, if I don't understand what's going on, there's a chance I'll screw up. There's a good chance I've *already* screwed up," she added. "But I only get one more chance."

"You have my name," he said.

She flinched. "…Yes."

"Could you not do as others have done, and use that name against me?"

"…Yes."

"It would preserve what little self-respect I have, Chosen."

Kaylin folded her arms across her chest; Severn came to stand beside her. "Can we just skip the part where we torture each other horribly and pretend we've already done it?"

His eyes widened slightly. They were green. This confirmed her suspicion that green was the Norannir version of surprise.

"I don't have a lot of self-respect myself. What I've got, I cling to," she continued. "And forcing the information out of you that way would destroy some of it."

"Why, then, did you take my name?"

"You already know the answer."

Green faded slowly into brown, a color that she seldom saw in the Norannir. "Yes, Chosen. I do. Bellusdeo spoke to you today. But in some fashion that you will not understand, Bellusdeo also chose you."

"I had these marks—"

"Ah, no. You are Chosen for reasons that not even the Dragons can understand. I meant the sword, of course."

She looked at its hilt dubiously.

"If the sword did not desire it, Chosen, you could not have lifted it. Believe that it was tried during my...captivity."

"It was a gigantic greatsword made of Shadow, Maggaron!"

"Yes. It was. Because *I* was its wielder. It is part of me." He looked down; Kaylin had never been so aware of the differences in their height. Somehow, the news she had feared would break him completely had given him strength instead. "Did Mejrah explain what purpose the Ascendants served?"

"More or less."

"She also explained that only a handful were chosen?"

"And the rest were returned to their homes and their families and eventually became Elders, yes."

"Did she tell you that the Ascendants became immortal?"

"Not in so many words, no. But she implied that Bellusdeo had promised to transform or change the children of the Norannir so that they might know a life as long as a Dragon's—which is effectively forever."

He nodded. His eyes had shaded from their unusual brown to a more familiar Norannir blue. "What she did not—what she could not—tell you was how that was achieved. Tell me, do you think the Norannir have true names?"

Kaylin shook her head. "They're mortal."

"Yet you now hold mine. Have you not wondered how it is that I have a name?"

"Well, yes, if you put it that way."

"I was given a part of Bellusdeo's name."

Kaylin stared at him for a long moment. "I want to say that's impossible."

Tara, who hadn't interrupted until this moment said, "It is impossible."

"Lady," Maggaron said, inclining his head to Tara. After a pause, he actually got down on one knee. Kaylin suspected this was less a gesture of supplication than a gesture of respect; it was *hard* to look down from that differential in height while still maintaining awe. "It is not impossible. I am proof of that."

But Tara shook her head. Turning to Kaylin, she said, "I would like to examine the sword more carefully."

Kaylin visibly wilted, but nodded. "You're going to have to help me resheathe it, though." She caught the hilt and pulled it clear of the sheath; it came out so easily she stumbled backward slightly. Severn caught her. Kaylin handed the sword to Tara, or tried; Tara took a step back as the runes on the flat of the blade began to glow. They were a shade between purple and blue.

Tara's eyes lost their whites as she concentrated. Eyes now obsidian, she said, "Maggaron, after Bellusdeo gave you this sword, did you see her again?"

He was silent.

Kaylin, however, asked a slightly different question. "Did Bellusdeo give you this sword?"

"It was left for me," he replied.

"Tara? What do you see?"

"It's not what I see, Kaylin. What do you see? Look carefully."

"I see a sword with engravings on it."

"You don't recognize the runes?"

Kaylin shook her head. "Do you see them?"

"No."

"...What?"

"No. They're fluid to my eye; they have a shape and a line that I should recognize, but I cannot comprehend them visually. I suspect that under the right circumstances, you might."

"What do you mean?"

"Give the Ascendant the sword," was the soft reply.

Maggaron was still on one knee, but his respectful posture gave way to something that reminded Kaylin of subtle cowering. Given he didn't change position at all, this was mildly impressive. "I must decline," he told Tara.

"I don't think she was asking your permission."

"Chosen—" he swallowed "—I cannot—I am not worthy."

"You don't have to keep it—"

He laughed. It was brief, and it was very, very bitter. "You can wield the sword but you cannot understand it; you will always be outside it, if you can say that so easily. If she had not been trapped because of *me,* I would never, ever have surrendered her. Do you not understand? I gave her into your keeping and she allowed it—so that she might be free of *my* entrapment."

She started to speak; stopped herself because the words would have been unkind. He was afraid to take the sword because he wanted it so badly, and Kaylin could understand that. "If you don't want to, I won't force it," she told him quietly. "But Tara thinks it'll tell us—me—something I need to know. Will you try?"

He swallowed. She saw his Adam's apple bob up and down. He didn't trust himself to speak, but he did nod, and he held out both of his hands. They were shaking. Kaylin handed him the sword.

The minute he touched it, it began to change shape, widening and elongating until it looked like a long sword. But way bigger. The runes were clear, bright—and a very steely blue. Kaylin's eyes widened.

"Kaylin?"

Maggaron rose, the sword's blade cradled in his open palms. He was shaking slightly, and Kaylin knew he wouldn't touch the hilt. "Chosen, you must hold the sword, and you *must* listen."

"Or you could tell me what it's saying."

He shook his head, his lips curved in a smile that held both pain and a joy so intense it might as well have been pain, it seemed almost unbearable. "I cannot tell you all that it is saying. But…it is safe, in this Tower. If we leave, I—I cannot guarantee safety." He closed his eyes and whispered a single word. Kaylin heard it as *Bellusdeo.*

She would have given him privacy if she'd thought they had the time. She gave him a few minutes of silence instead. When she spoke, she put on her Hawk's voice and tried to distance herself from what she saw. "The sword—it's part of her, isn't it?"

He nodded.

"That's why the Dragons disappeared." It wasn't a question. "They weren't killed, as the Elders think—they sacrificed themselves."

"It was the only way. She said it was the only way. We're mortal," he added. "We can be killed. We can be transformed—but not easily. But we cannot be unmade and we cannot be rewritten."

Death, in Kaylin's mind, was pretty damn unmade; she didn't point this out. Instead, she stared at the runes on the sword's flat. "They changed," she finally said, speaking to both Tara and Maggaron. "They changed when you took the sword." Her eyes widened.

"How did they change?" Tara asked sharply.

"They became *his* name."

Tara fell silent. At length she said, "I must speak with the Arkon."

Kaylin nodded.

"I would like you to accompany me."

Kaylin cringed. "I'm not finished here, yet."

Tara said to Maggaron, "The sword agreed to allow Kaylin to wield it—or at least lift it—because Kaylin *had* your name. But it is still part of you, Ascendant, and in a way I don't understand. I believe it is safe to leave the sword with you for the moment, but I will ask you to accompany us, as well. I do not wish you to be far from me while you wield it."

Maggaron nodded. He looked both pained and happy, and it was a striking combination. "Chosen—"

"Hold her," Kaylin told him. "While you can. Tell me if she says anything you think I need to hear."

Severn caught up with her in the halls, because Tara and Maggaron walked ahead, side by side. Maggaron didn't sheathe the sword, but then again, he had no sheath for it. She wondered what he did with the sword when he needed to eat. If he needed to eat.

"Tara doesn't look happy," Severn said.

"I think she's confused. I just wish her confusion didn't lead to the Arkon today."

Severn nodded.

"Do you think Nightshade knew?"

"No. I'm not entirely certain the Arkon does, either. But the circumstances were—are—strange enough to warrant close inspection. What do you think is happening?"

"I'm not sure." She hesitated because she always did when she wasn't certain. It was a failing she struggled to overcome, and it was helped by the fact that she'd been wrong before when she *was* certain, and she'd survived that. "His name—the name that the Shadows have—isn't his. He wasn't born with it. He came to it by choice and that choice wasn't entirely his. It's not like mine," she added, aware that she hadn't been born with one, either. "I *took* mine from the Lake, and I don't think that would have been possible if I hadn't been marked already." She lifted her arms, the marks still visible.

"What I don't understand at all is how. It's not, I'd swear it's not, the Dragon's true name. It might be some part of it, but how the hells does that happen? Names are names—they're alive in some fashion. I don't think you can lop off a part of one—it'd be like me chopping off an arm and giving it to you, and expecting you to be able to attach and use it."

He was silent as they walked, but it was a thoughtful silence. It demanded thought on her part, and she gave it.

"In the High Court?"

He nodded.

"The High Lord."

"Yes."

"I don't think it's the same thing."

"No? His name wasn't complete."

I don't think, she continued, shutting her mouth and opening her thoughts, *that we're supposed to be discussing this here. Tara can probably hear us.*

She can probably hear us anyway. I think it necessary if we're to understand what's happening.

It was true.

Tell me why you think it's not the same.

His name wasn't complete. He had a name, but—it wasn't complete...

Until you completed it.

Yes.

But that changed the nature of his name, and that allowed him to free himself from the Shadows who knew it.

...*Yes.* She thought about it. The High Lord—the current High Lord—had failed the test of name that the High Halls demanded of all of its rulers. His name had been revealed to the Shadows over which the High Halls had been constructed. But the High Lord's name had been only part of the whole rune which had been meant for him at birth; it had been enough to breathe life into his still, infant form—but it had never been the whole of what had been intended for him.

Kaylin had found the defining stroke, she had pulled it, whole, from the Barrani Lake of Life, and carried it to where he hid, captive by his choice in his own home.

But that single stroke had *always* been part of his name. And yet...no one had known. Kaylin herself hadn't known until she'd approached him. She didn't understand the genesis of true names. She didn't understand their purpose, beyond the basics: Immortals required them to live. She could recognize them, but how was it even possible that they could be sundered and still somehow function in parts?

Severn followed her thoughts; they were a more forceful version of his own at this point.

What if Bellusdeo was aware of how that might be done in the inverse order? He asked the question at almost the same minute Kaylin did. Neither of them had any answers to give each other.

She couldn't give him a name, he continued, *not in the way you took yours—but what if this was as close as she could come? The sword is, from everything I've seen, part of what he now is. His name is part of hers.*

There's a difference between the High Lord and Maggaron. I mean, a difference between their names. The High Lord owned it all. The part and the whole. It wasn't spread between two; it wasn't given away. Maggaron can't have a name—but he does. Maggaron was immortal because of it. But…I think he has the name when he has the sword. No, that can't be it. He and the sword are bound somehow, even when he's not carrying it. If we could break that, I think he'd be safe.

And the sword?

I don't know. If the sword has a name of its own, it's not owned by Shadow.

She stopped thinking about anything but angry Dragons when Tara stopped outside a set of severe and imposing doors. They were the tallest doors Kaylin had seen in the Tower so far, and they were made of a wood so dark it was almost black. "The doors don't change appearance to reflect your Lord's mood, do they?"

"Yes," Tara answered, her eyes pretty much the same color as said doors.

Kaylin never wanted to live in a place where the decor changed to reflect her mood. Then again, it might keep Teela and Tain out on the bad days.

The doors rolled open. Maggaron looked completely normal when he passed beneath their arch, they were so tall. Tara looked tiny when seen at his side. But although the three Dragon Lords were in their mortal forms, they didn't look in any way insignificant as they turned, eyes orange-red, toward the open doors.

Bellusdeo lay on a bed at the room's far end.

"What," the Arkon said sharply, "do you want?" A little puff of smoke accompanied his words, but at least there were no scorch marks on the floor.

"Not anymore," Tara said pleasantly to Kaylin. She bowed to the Arkon, who looked slightly confused—and not happy to be so—by her comment. "I am correcting a misapprehension on the part of Kaylin."

The Arkon's brows scrunched together. "My apologies, Lady."

"None are required, Arkon. I requested the presence of Corporal Handred and Private Neya; I also requested the presence of Maggaron. It was my desire that they speak with you, not theirs."

Because we're *sane,* Kaylin thought.

"Have you discovered anything further?" the Avatar continued, still directing her words to the Arkon; she generally avoided discussions about sanity or insanity with Kaylin.

"No, Lady. We have been discussing the situation." And he clearly wasn't happy with that discussion. "What have you come to ask?"

She turned to Maggaron. "Please show the Arkon your sword." Maggaron instantly did as bid; it was hard to tell whether it was due to respect for the Avatar, or for the Dragons. He didn't hand the sword over, however; he merely approached and held the blade out for the Dragons' inspection.

"It is the same sword that Private Neya was carrying," the Avatar told them all.

The Arkon raised a brow, but the news didn't seem to surprise him greatly. The blade, however, caused familiar furrows to develop in his brow. He snorted. This time, there was fire in it.

"The blade," Tara said when the Arkon failed to express his annoyance in words, "is some part of the Ascendant's name."

CHAPTER 18

"I beg your pardon?"

When Tara repeated her words, the Arkon turned to Tiamaris. Tiamaris looked grim, but said, "She means what she said literally."

"I cannot decipher the meaning of her words."

"She feels that the sword is physically part of the Ascendant's name—the name that Private Neya knows, and the name that the Shadows used against him."

"The...sword."

"That *is* what she means." Before the Arkon could speak again, Tiamaris added, "The words make little sense to me on the surface; I merely report what the Tower believes. Tara?"

"Kaylin will explain."

The Arkon's brows rose in disbelief. When they fell again, they reached new lows. "Private Neya?"

She glanced at Severn; Severn, however, was studying his boots. "When he's holding the sword—and only then—the runes on the blade take the shape and form of his name." She took a deep breath, expelled it—notably without the smoke that seemed to be unhealthily wafting in this room—and continued, figuring it was better to get possible bad news out of the way. "We think that the sword is part of Bellusdeo's name. Not all of it," she added quickly.

"Lord Sanabalis, has your student become notably more erratic or unstable as of late?"

"No, Arkon."

"Has she undergone some type of trauma that causes damage in mortals?"

"Not to my knowledge, Arkon."

Kaylin cleared her throat. Politely. It was Sanabalis who acknowledged her first. "Kaylin, please explain what you mean."

"We believe that the woman whose body now resides in this room—for the eighth time—is the human form of the Dragon Bellusdeo."

"Bellusdeo?"

"It's what the Norannir called her when they were at home."

The silence that followed this statement was significant. It wasn't pretty. "Tara didn't tell you?" Kaylin finally asked.

"They were not to be disturbed," Tara replied when the Dragons all swiveled to look at her. "Is it a name with which you are familiar?"

"No," Tiamaris replied. He glanced at Sanabalis, who also shook his head. The Arkon was both still and silent.

"Private," Sanabalis said curtly, "please fill us in on the results of the day's investigation."

Kaylin, who had so desperately wanted to avoid mention of the memory crystal in the Arkon's very good hearing, swallowed air and did as Sanabalis had all but ordered. True to form, the Arkon's eyes darkened a shade when she mentioned where the memory crystal now was; Sanabalis, however, promised he would see to its safe return. It only barely molli-fied a Dragon who was already in a foul temper to begin with.

Through it all, she was bookended by Maggaron and Severn, who watched the Dragons warily, but with obvious respect.

"Maggaron was the last person to see Bellusdeo as a Dragon."

"You are certain?"

"No, of course I'm not certain. It's conjecture at this point; I'm not sure we have the resources for more than that. We can't go back to their world, and even if we could, we don't know what we're looking for beyond Gold Dragon."

"Gold."

Kaylin nodded. "Maggaron was willing to go to the Re-cords room in the Tower. I wanted him to see the image of the woman we've now got eight bodies for, and Tara offered to show him; the mirror recorded both his reactions and some of his memories. I believe Tara has captured the image of both forms of Bellusdeo in her personal Records. They both came from the Ascendant."

The Arkon turned to Tiamaris, who nodded gravely. "Please," he said to the Avatar, although it clearly took effort. "Show us."

Tara walked over to the mirror that adorned the room. In shape and size it was similar to the mirror in the Hawk-lord's Tower; it was, however, far more ornate. The frame had clearly been crafted by a man with an obsession for detail, and it appeared, to Kaylin's eye, to be made of polished silver. She lifted a hand and passed it across the mirror's surface; it rippled in response, as if it were water, but vertical.

When the mirror stilled, it was no longer reflective, and the image it showed, framed by perfect silver, was that of the great, golden Dragon before which Maggaron had all but abased himself.

"Ascendant," the Arkon said, although he didn't take his eyes off the image, "this is the Dragon to whom you owe your allegiance?"

He stared at the Dragon, and Kaylin came to the rescue. *Listen through me,* she told him, hating it.

You are certain, Chosen?

Yes. I'm not going to repeat every single word you say just so the Arkon can understand it; it's my head he'll bite off. She did, however, repeat the one question the Arkon had asked. She felt Maggaron as a pressing, sudden presence in the back of her mind and curled her fingernails into her palms to stop from swearing. It helped that he didn't feel entirely comfortable being there, either.

If I...look...I can find the words to speak to your Arkon, and you will not have to speak on my behalf.

Do it.

"Yes, Arkon."

The Arkon didn't even blink at the sound of Maggaron's voice. "And the body on the bed—is it her human form?"

"Yes, Arkon."

"You are certain?"

"I am certain." He opened his mouth as if to say more, and shut it.

"Tell me about this sword that you carry."

"These swords are the symbol—and the strength—of the Ascendants," he replied slowly. "This sword is mine. It is what defines me as Ascendant. I had never been parted from it until I met the Chosen and she took my name."

"But according to the Chosen, it's not *your* name that she took."

Maggaron's brows rose. "It is."

This is why Kaylin hated magic.

"According to the Chosen," the Arkon continued, as if Maggaron hadn't spoken, "the name is part of Bellusdeo's name."

Maggaron was silent. Kaylin gave him a look, which he failed to interpret because he failed—deliberately—to see it. "Maggaron," she whispered.

"I am forbidden to speak of it," he told the Arkon.

Not this again.

You are Chosen. He is not. You found her; she spoke to you. He did not.

It wasn't, apparently, just magic that she was going to hate today. "We can't confirm our suspicions," Kaylin told the Arkon through slightly clenched teeth. "But I believe, given everything, that some part of Bellusdeo exists *in* the sword itself. Some part of her name is what gives the Ascendant his... extended life. It's not his name in the traditional sense of true names; it *is* demonstrably enough to control his actions."

She hesitated. "When the sword came to me, Maggaron said it was mine. It's not. It's still linked to him—and I think it will be until his death." She turned to the Ascendant and added, "Just in case we're not clear, your death isn't an option we're considering."

"Chosen, I have considered—"

"Don't. If I truly hold your name, I'll use it to prevent your suicide."

"Have you considered what the sword requires?"

"Not until this afternoon, and I *am* considering it now, got it? Don't do anything stupid." She turned back to the Arkon. "Mortals don't have names that can be taken, learned, known; they can't be changed or mutated. I think—and I could be entirely wrong—that the purpose of the Ascendants was to be sheath to the sword itself. His presence protected her actions and her power. His was the body controlled by Shadow; *he* controlled the sword, but the Shadows didn't. Maybe they couldn't."

The Arkon blinked. "I will accept that that was the intent, given what little we know of the history of the Norannir. Intent, however, is not ability. What you've described should not be possible without the death of the Dragon—at the very least."

"Why?"

"When we speak of True Names to mortals, we often use the analogy of the soul or spirit. It is an inadequate analogy because there has never been proof that that soul exists. There is more than enough proof that the Names do. Nonetheless, when making this comparison, one conclusion can be drawn that we can both agree on: souls do *not* exist in two places at once."

"I don't see how the Dragon's death changes that."

"If the Dragon dies, the word is no longer encumbered, and if someone could *find* it, it is possible they could dissect it, breaking it down, in the end, to its base parts."

Kaylin glanced at Maggaron, and then at Severn. Severn raised a brow, only that.

"It's been done at least once," she finally said, grateful for the utter lack of Barrani in the Tower. "Once, that I know of, but I've got only twenty years of experience, and no one immortal ever counts that as significant."

"There is a reason for that. Twenty years is not significant. What are you claiming, Private?"

"I don't know how Dragons are given their names. I don't know how Dragons are born, if it comes to that—it's not covered in racial integration classes, and everyone shuts up like a bank the minute I ask. Barrani births aren't covered in any of those classes, either, but I do know how the Barrani receive their names, and by extension their lives. The names are chosen for them, and the names are delivered to them. In one case, the name that was chosen was only partially birthed. It existed as a known entity—one that could be learned and controlled—in its partial form. It *was* a word, with a distinct meaning. It was not, however, the complete name that had been chosen."

Silence.

"I will not insult you by asking how you know this," the Arkon finally said. Turning to Sanabalis, he added, "Do you believe her?"

Someone else was going to have to explain insults to the Arkon, who in this case was obviously not clear on the concept.

Sanabalis was stroking his beard, something he did when deep in thought. Or annoyed. In this case, it was probably both. "Yes," he finally said. "She is a Lord of the High Court, and she clearly has some influence with the Consort."

"Had," was the bitter, mumbled reply. Kaylin had not returned to Court since the disastrous argument with said Consort; she wasn't sure how welcome she'd be, and being thrown out of Barrani digs wasn't high on her list of personal ambitions.

"Regardless, Arkon, yes."

The Arkon frowned; the silence was sulfurous. But the frown failed to produce either rage or fire, and after another long pause, his expression suddenly sharpened. "Tell me, Private—the Barrani who achieved this supposed splitting of the whole of a name—was it someone intimately acquainted with the choosing of names?"

"I'm trying hard not to answer the questions that will get me executed for treason," she replied tartly.

"Failure to answer this question at this time will probably

have the same result; you merely have a choice of whom you commit treason against. It is never wise to owe allegiance to two Lords."

"I owe allegiance to one," she said. Severn prodded her very gently, and she bit down on the rest of the words that wanted to follow. "Yes."

"In this case, you are saying that the whole of the word existed in potential, but the part of it that was not…delivered… remained in the waters of life?"

"Yes."

"As you can see, the situations are gravely different."

Yes. It was clear as mud. "Let me get this straight. You think that what happened in the one case I've cited happened because the Mother of the Race handled the name. You're implying that somehow, she split it, and it survived in its sundered state solely because of her."

"That is a superficial rendering of what I believe, but yes."

"Could Bellusdeo have somehow done the same? Do the Dragons even *have* a mother of their race?"

More silence. "I am not comfortable continuing this discussion in the presence of the mortals," the Arkon finally said. "That includes the Ascendant."

But Tiamaris, not the Arkon, was Lord here. "No, Kaylin, we do not."

"It is not strictly necessary that she know of this," the Arkon told Tiamaris. Clearly, the designation of Lord didn't matter as much to ancient Dragons as it did to Sanabalis.

"Kaylin," Tiamaris said, moving slightly away from the Arkon, "when we entered the Tower for the first time, do you remember what waited at the height of the cliffs?"

She nodded. "An Aerie."

"Yes. With words in the ceiling and twisting, dark tunnels that tapered somewhat."

It had been one of the few pleasantly surprising things the Tower had chosen to reveal. "You said it reminded you of the Aerie of your childhood."

He nodded. "We are not born in our mortal forms; nor are we—as you—born singly."

"So...the Dragon form is the form of your birth?"

"It is."

"But—" She suddenly didn't want to ask any questions while the Arkon was glaring at her. It was Maggaron, surprisingly, who answered.

"The three Lords here were born as Dragons, in form. They lived, flew, and breathed fire before they attained their true names."

Kaylin waited for someone to deny this; no one did. The Barrani babies didn't apparently *wake* without a name; clearly, Dragon babies didn't suffer the same problem. Which brought up the question of why Dragons needed a True Name at all. "Those tunnels a lot of them were people-size."

Tiamaris nodded.

Maggaron continued, as if blithely unaware of the effect his statements were having. Given Maggaron, he probably was. "When young Dragons are judged fit by their Elders, they must earn their name. They must find it."

"What, on their own?"

"We are *not* Barrani," the Arkon said with some heat, and some very real fire for emphasis.

"What if they don't happen to find a name?"

"They will die," Maggaron replied.

She didn't ask how. Instead, she turned to the three Dragon Lords, "When you get your names, you gain your human form?"

After a long pause, it was once again Maggaron who answered. "They do. They must then learn to walk, to speak, and to interact in the smaller body. It is, by all accounts, onerous."

"Why bother, then?"

"Because without that form, they are little more than beasts, according to Bellusdeo."

"Then she gave up the form of her birth?"

"Ah, no. Bellusdeo said female Dragons were different. They are born—they are hatched—in their human forms. They will learn to walk or crawl as mortals. Their thoughts are quicker, but they are different. In order to attain their own completion, they must survive their childhood. This is more difficult.

"But when they find their name—for they are set the same task as their clutchmates—they attain their Dragon form."

No bloody wonder there were so few Dragons. Kaylin looked to Sanabalis. "Is this true?"

"...It is a simplification."

"But it's not wrong."

"It is not entirely wrong, no."

"What happens if the females never find their names?"

"They are not judged dangerous by the standard of the Dragons," he replied. "And they are allowed to live."

"As mortals?"

"Very much as mortals—but they are immortal, Kaylin."

"How is that even possible if they *don't have a name?*"

"They are, even in the weaker form, Dragons. It is not because of the name that we are immortal."

The Ancients *clearly* had a very poor sense of design.

"There is also always the hope that they will find what they lack. As you have often pointed out, they are few."

"If I ask where they're supposed to find those names—"

"Don't."

She shut up and thought for a minute about the wisdom of directing a question—any question—at the Arkon. But she had to ask. "Arkon, you recognized the name Bellusdeo. You probably recognized the human form, if I think about it."

He was silent. He didn't deny it.

"Did you travel a lot between worlds in your youth?"

"I did not. The passage between worlds was considered largely theoretical, even in my youth."

"But Bellusdeo—"

"During one storm—again in my youth—Bellusdeo and a number of the women went missing. Some of the men, as well; they were the guardians of the young. Bellusdeo had not, at that point, found her name; she was to search for it within the year. Shadowstorms hit the Aerie, and many of my kin were…transformed by them. There was much battle and much death. It was assumed by the Elders that she had been destroyed in those battles, but there was some lingering question; no sign of the guardians was found in the aftermath."

"You think this is the same Bellusdeo?"

"I fail to see how it can be; it defies explanation. But yes, Private, that is my belief."

Kaylin drew a longer breath. "Then why, exactly, did you expect us to find nine bodies?"

"Tiamaris, this Tower is secure?"

Tiamaris glanced at Tara, but nodded.

"Very well. I will answer your question because it is relevant. Lord Sanabalis said that the female children were allowed to live if they failed to find their name. He speaks truthfully, but not entirely accurately. They were not hunted down; they were not considered a danger to us. Mortals distrusted them; the Barrani would kill them. But they were not *of* us."

At this very moment, Kaylin hated Dragons. She knew it would pass.

"Bellusdeo and her clutch were different. In a clutch there may be no females; that is most often the case. Clearly, for a clutch to be born at all it requires both parents to possess the life force and will inherent in their names. There is a reason that there are so few clutches, and it is not entirely because of the rarity of female births.

"The Barrani killed the mothers; it was the reason our wars were so bitter. We would have destroyed their breeding grounds had we been able to find them. Before you point out that they exist in the heart of the City, I must caution you; they do not. They are perceived as existing in such a place by those who have the ability to manipulate what the waters contain. Most Barrani could not even *find* the Lake.

"However, on the day of Bellusdeo's birth, nine were born human. Nine in one clutch. It was seen as a great, great blessing to our kind. Most of the hatchlings are not guarded, and they are not protected. But in the case of these nine, exceptions were made."

"Why?"

"Because of the significance of their number."

"All right. I understand that nine girls was very unusual. But you expected to find nine bodies—nine identical bodies. Why?"

"Because, Kaylin, in some fashion, the nine were linked. The Elders did not understand it."

"None of the nine had found their names by the time they vanished?"

"No; they were of an age, almost to the minute. They were all to seek names before they disappeared."

She was silent for a bit, mulling over the information she'd received. It was difficult to process it all because some of it still made no sense to her. "What exactly do you mean when you say they were linked?"

"What I said." His frown was glacial, but it melted slightly. Probably because of the fire. "If one of the nine was hurt, the other eight were instantly aware of it. If one of the nine was injured, the other eight could take some part of those injuries onto their own bodies. They could speak without speaking, but only among each other; the males born to the clutch weren't likewise affected."

"But they weren't identical in appearance, were they?"

His eyes were very orange. "Not at birth, no."

"Then—"

"But as they grew, they were capable of altering their appearance. They did it for fun," he added, his frown deepening. "It alarmed the Elders, and annoyed a small handful of them, as well. They had names that they were known by, and those names were unique to them—but they often changed names as they learned to alter appearance. It is not an ability that the males of the same clutch had."

"Was there ever a clutch of males that were linked in the same way?"

"Yes. But it happened very, very rarely. It was not well-documented until the girls were born and grew into their powers."

"By powers, you mean the link?"

"That, as well."

Kaylin stifled the urge to growl or snarl. "What other powers did they have?"

"They were capable of speaking to the mirrors of the Ancients. They *also* did this for fun."

"Is it unusual to be able to speak to those mirrors?" Kaylin had done it herself on more than one occasion. She glanced at her exposed arms.

The Arkon did likewise, but merely raised a brow before he answered her question. "In the fashion they did, yes. They could speak to the rest of our kin with the voice of the mirrors, Private. It was discomfiting. They were also explorers. They liked to sneak out of the Aerie—often at some danger to themselves—to meet mortals. Or Barrani. They weren't particular at that time." He hesitated for a long, long moment, and then once again asked Tiamaris if the Tower was secure. He received the same answer as he had the previous time he'd asked and fell silent.

"It is my suspicion that they could travel."

"Pardon?"

"You've met the Norannir who guided his people here. You've seen what is preserved in the mirror at the heart of the Palace. You understand what travel, in this case, means."

She did. "But if Bellusdeo disappeared in the wake of a Shadowstorm—"

"Conjecture. But so, too, is my suspicion."

"So you think that the seven—eight—bodies are all part of that clutch?"

He glanced at the corpse that was laid out on the bed, and after a moment, nodded. To Kaylin's eye, she looked exactly the same as the other seven, although this dress was very dusty.

"It looks like at least one of them found their name."

"It does. But the finding and the taking of the name—as one might expect—was obviously untraditional."

"And you think there's a ninth body waiting for us somewhere?"

"I have hope—even if slender—that you will find the ninth alive. The eighth was alive when she arrived here."

Kaylin hesitated, and then said, "The eighth asked me to kill her."

★ ★ ★

"Explain." The word was so sharp it almost cut. Kaylin very carefully explained what had been asked of her.

"You are certain?"

"As certain as mortal memory can make me, yes."

The Arkon's frown was like a chiseled crevice. Several of them.

"From what Maggaron said, and from what you've said here, I think I understand what she wanted."

"The name?"

"I...think so. She was very specific about the weapon I was carrying. I think she wanted me to run her through with the sword that Maggaron is holding. I'm not sure what that would do to her, though. I'm not sure if it would return some part of her name to her and make her whole—or if it would simply kill her and release them both."

"Both?"

"She and Maggaron. I don't understand why he has a True Name at all, but I do understand that his name is some part of hers, and it sustains him."

It sustains us both, Chosen.

Kaylin looked around the room. Her eyes met Maggaron's—they weren't a livid orange, so it was almost reflexive—and stopped there. "Was that the sword?"

He nodded, his eyes wet with unshed tears. "I am not to let you sheathe her again."

"I won't try. Did she hear what we were saying?"

"She heard what I heard, and I," he added, "heard what you heard."

Kaylin sometimes talked to walls—usually rudely. This was the first time she'd ever deliberately tried to talk to a sword's blade.

I am not Bellusdeo, the sword said.

"But you're a part of her, somehow?"

Silence.

"If I kill her while wielding you, what happens to you?"

I do not know.

"What happens to her?"

I do not know.

"Fine. What happens to Maggaron?"

The blade rippled, sheen of steel giving way—briefly—to something vastly less metallic. It was disturbing. Almost as disturbing as the Arkon's demand that she relate—clearly—what was being said.

"That is forbidden," Maggaron told him. He said it as respectfully as one could possibly say words of that nature to an angry Dragon.

The sword snickered and Kaylin realized she'd heard that voice before. Once before. "What will become of Maggaron?" she repeated.

The sword's light rippled again. Clearly, this wasn't a question she—or it—wanted to hear.

Maggaron said, "It doesn't matter."

"No. It doesn't matter to *you*. It matters to me—"

"Why?" He demanded. His eyes shaded to a familiar blue.

"And it matters to the sword," she continued, unwilling to get into that argument in front of the Dragon Lords. If the sword wanted to have that argument, it was fine; the Dragons couldn't hear most of it.

She turned her attention to the blade again. "What did you mean? How does his name sustain you?"

This was apparently a better question to ask. *He bears the brunt of discovery, not I. Where we go, the risk of discovery has always been high.*

"How?"

Chosen, we do not know. But in the heart of Ravellon lies one who can read the whole of what is written—even our most secret selves. One of my kin discovered this, to our lasting regret. We could not engage the enemy without becoming *the enemy.*

We being the Dragons?

The sword fell silent.

"I'm sorry. I don't mean to offend; I don't understand the connection."

"It's not the connection," Maggaron said gently. "The sword is part of me, but it is a distinct entity. Where it came from, how it was forged or birthed—it doesn't matter. It is not a limb or an appendage; it exists." He frowned; clearly, the sword could focus its voice when it chose. "A child—if you ever bear one—will be part of you; without you, it cannot exist. But once it is birthed, once it is free of you, that dependency slowly changes; it becomes a thing separate from you, but influenced in all ways by its birth.

"Thus it is with the sword. The sword is part of *me*," he added. "But it is also not me. When my name fell to our enemy, the sword was trapped within me, but the enemy could not reach her. I could," he added bitterly, "but in the end, I could not change her."

"She was your weapon when you were assaulting our borders," Kaylin pointed out.

"Yes."

"I'm thinking that that wasn't in her plans of action before you were discovered."

"She *is* my sword. No," he added, voice dropping. "She was. I was not all of what she is; she was not all of what I am—but we are bound." He was starting to get frustrated; Kaylin could sympathize. "Bellusdeo understood the danger. But she also understood our need for her. The Dragons convened their great Council, and in the end, they created the Ascendants. For our sake," he added. "For the sake of the People."

"Then the numbers of the Dragons decreased as the numbers of the Ascendants grew?"

He nodded. "It was not widely known," he added. "The Elders would never have accepted such a sacrifice if it were." He lowered the sword slowly. Had it been in Kaylin's hands, it would have hit the ground when she tried to lift it.

To the sword she said, "What would you have me do? Aside from never put you in a sheath again, I mean. Bellusdeo has asked me to kill her—while wielding you. I can do it, but I have some reservations. If you don't know what will happen to either you or Maggaron, what do *you* want me to do?"

The pause that followed was so long, Kaylin almost gave up on getting an answer. But the sword finally said, *Kill her.* It wasn't the answer Kaylin wanted; it was the answer she'd expected.

"Chosen." Maggaron lifted the sword. "I can do as she asks."

But Tara shook her head. "It is not safe for you to leave the Tower, Maggaron."

"The Chosen has my name," he countered.

"She has. But she has shown a strong unwillingness to use it to contain you. If your life is in danger, she will do so—but only in the case that it is immediately *obvious* to her what the danger is. The Shadows are capable of great subtlety, at need."

The line of his shoulders sank and he turned to Kaylin, dropping to one knee—which brought their eyes to about the same level. "Chosen," he said, his voice lower. "I have no right to ask, but I ask it. Please. Let me go where you go. Let me do what must be done."

"I—"

"It is the last thing I can do for either my sword or my Lady. I will accept any consequence; I will welcome any control you exert. I will warn you—"

"You cannot warn her if you are under someone else's control."

No, the sword said. *But I can.*

Kaylin remembered—clearly—the pain she had felt when she attempted to force Maggaron to do something he didn't want to do. But seeing the pain and the bleak hope in his expression was vastly more difficult. "Tara, can you—"

"No. I cannot guard him against the use of his name if we leave the Tower. I *can* destroy him, I believe—although it will be costly to the fief."

"Will you let me make this decision?"

Tiamaris cleared his throat. Loudly. Grimacing, Kaylin turned to her one-time fellow Hawk, and the current fief-lord of the fief. Just as Maggaron had done, she dropped to one knee in full view of the Dragon Lord. "Tiamaris. Lord Tiamaris," she amended.

His eyes were a shade of copper; they were not the livid orange of the Arkon's. "Private Neya?"

"Please allow Maggaron to accompany me."

"Do you understand the risk?"

She nodded.

"Do you understand that you are not the only person at risk? That the citizens of the fief—those who can't defend themselves against either Maggaron or the Shadows—will bear the brunt of your failure if you cannot do what must be done?"

"Yes."

"Do you honestly feel that you are capable of controlling him?"

"...Yes."

He rolled his eyes. Distancing himself from Sanabalis—who was now examining his beard—and the Arkon, he approached Kaylin. "Kaylin, why?"

In reply, she lifted her arms and turned them toward the

fieflord. The runes on her skin were glowing a faint, clear blue. His eyes widened. "This is part of his story, of his history," she told him.

"It is part of ours, and of any whom he might injure or kill should he once again fall under Shadow's sway. The boundary will not protect him, as you should well know."

She shook her head. "This is a part of his story that must be written or told. I'm sorry," she added, feeling more than slightly embarrassed. "I realize it sounds…"

"Foolish."

"I wouldn't go that far. But—the marks."

He nodded slowly. "Tara?"

The Avatar came to where Kaylin knelt, passing by Maggaron, who had also remained in a supplicant posture. "None of us have ever understood the role of the Chosen," she finally said. "If there can be said to be only one role. My Lord, I am willing to allow Kaylin to take this risk."

"I don't like it," Tiamaris replied. Kaylin almost sagged in relief. "But where you are willing to take such a risk, I will follow. Remember, however," he added as Kaylin began to rise, "that there are no laws governing what I do to criminals in my own domain."

CHAPTER 19

The Arkon snorted smoke. "Very well," he said. "Sanabalis, will you remain here, or join us?"

"I wouldn't miss it for the world," Sanabalis replied. "Unless the Private has any objections?"

None that she was stupid enough to voice. "Lord Tiamaris?" she said without much hope.

"I will remain in the Tower. Tara, however, wishes to accompany you."

"Can I point out that we don't *have* a destination as of yet?"

"Given the Arkon's impatience in this matter, I suggest you resolve that difficulty as quickly as humanly possible." He turned to the Arkon. "I would appreciate it if you kept fire to a minimum in my fief."

"Of course, Lord Tiamaris." He fixed Kaylin with a very orange glare. "Private?"

She resisted the urge to pass it on, and instead helped Maggaron halfway to his feet. He bowed to her. "Chosen," he whispered.

"Can you just call me Kaylin? Everyone else does." Strictly speaking, this wasn't true, but the Ascendant nodded anyway. To the sword, she said, "Can you find Bellusdeo if she's alive anywhere in this fief?"

I am not entirely certain. I can find her if we are at all close to her.

"Could you sense her earlier?"

No. The...sheath...all but sundered me from the world.

"I've already said I won't use it again," Kaylin replied in a hurry. "Do you think she'll try to return here a ninth time?"

Yes.

"And is that our last chance to achieve whatever it is she's trying to achieve?"

Yes.

It was hard to believe there was still sunlight when they finally hit the streets. Morse was absent, but that was probably for the best; Kaylin had difficulty with Dragon formality, and Kaylin was an etiquette master when standing beside Morse. Severn, on the other hand, walked between Kaylin and the Arkon; Sanabalis pulled up the other side. Tara walked ahead beside Maggaron, which was fair, as it meant the Dragons had his back in plain sight. If Maggaron found the arrangement uncomfortable, it didn't show.

He looked taller, to Kaylin's eyes; taller and prouder. No, not exactly proud—that was the wrong word for it—but determined or focused. They walked down Avatar Road for several blocks before Tara called a halt. The streets were surprisingly busy, although only in fief terms; there were still people on them. If the people gave them nervous glances, that was to be expected—but Tara's presence seemed to calm them.

Given the size of the sword Maggaron now wielded, that said a lot about Tara, or their faith in her. It had only been a few weeks since Tiamaris had taken the Tower—and through it, the fief—but those weeks had eroded decades of raw fear. Subtle fear would take a lot longer to loose its hold. She glanced at the sun; it was heading toward the horizon.

"Ferals?" Kaylin asked Tara.

"My Lord and Morse will be on patrol within the half hour; so will the Norannir. We've been trying something unusual for the fief."

"Oh?"

"We've been taking the young men and women who want to come with us. We arm them if they aren't armed."

"They hunt Ferals with you?"

"Yes."

Kaylin shook her head. The world had changed.

"They've slowly grown accustomed to the sight of my Lord as a Dragon," Tara added. "It used to upset them more—but word has spread from those young men and women and filtered into the streets; his Dragon form has become synonymous with protection from the things that hunt in the night."

"Was this Tiamaris's idea?"

"Yes."

"Thought so."

Tara smiled. "I approved of it. I still do. No other Lord of the Tower hunted Ferals."

"No other Lord of the Tower considered the fief his hoard."

"Then this hoarding must be a good thing."

Kaylin nodded. "Possibly because it's Tiamaris." A thought struck her. "Sanabalis—" The Arkon cleared his throat, and she quickly appended his title. "Dragon personalities differ hugely; in that, they're not so dissimilar from the rest of us."

A beat of silence followed. "The point of this observation?"

"If a different Dragon had taken the Tower, would he have tried to effect this much change? Would he have cared the same way? The whole fief would still *be* his hoard, no matter who he was."

The Arkon snorted. "Sanabalis," he said sharply, forgetting the title that he demanded Kaylin use, "what have you been teaching the hatchlings?"

Sanabalis fingered his beard. It was his most familiar gesture. "I've been attempting to teach them to make reasoned deductions with the information they have at hand."

"Clearly, you have more work to do."

"Clearly, Arkon." To Kaylin, he said, "Yes, of course it would be different. The whole of Tiamaris's attitude has been informed by his service to the Emperor. He has learned, because of his youth and his ability to accept the Emperor's rule at all, that mortals—such as yourself—have intrinsic value. They are not livestock, they are not cattle, and they are not vermin."

"Arcanists."

"Many of the Arcanists are not mortal."

"Good point."

"It is not an attitude that was…common…in the days of the Arkon's youth."

"Neither was it common in Sanabalis's youth, which is lamentably more recent," the older Dragon interjected.

"Of the Dragons, Lord Tiamaris has had the least difficulty adapting to the Emperor's particular vision. In some ways, the fief is a mirror of the Empire, writ small. It *is* Tiamaris's hoard. It is governed by his desire and his possessiveness. But so, too, are mortal infants, even when their parents' affection is not in doubt.

"It is my suspicion that no other Immortal would have given the Tower the freedom it—she, my pardon, Lady—now has."

"Oh, it's not that," Tara said brightly, smiling at Kaylin. "When Kaylin attempted to help me, to protect me from the

Shadows that had breached my defenses, she gave me some different words."

"So did Tiamaris," Kaylin said softly, remembering the first time they had walked into the Tower together, marked mortal and immortal Dragon. But she returned Tara's smile—it was hard not to. She was like a foundling who'd been adopted by a loving family. Remembering the Foundling Hall, there were more who hadn't, but thanks to Marrin's intervention, those situations didn't last long. At all.

Marrin was family to children who, through no fault of their own, had none. She herself had lost her child. She could have hated children, could have hated people who had what her child didn't: life. But she built.

So did Tiamaris. Maybe it wasn't family in the traditional sense—Kaylin had no idea what a Dragon family was actually like. But if he could protect the people that Kaylin herself had failed so badly, it was enough. More than enough, really. She inhaled and nodded.

Maggaron lifted his sword and they all turned.

"Kaylin," Tara all but shouted.

The Ascendant was stiffening as the syllables faded. Kaylin looked immediately for the color of his eyes; they were almost indigo. "Tara, can you—"

"There is no Shadow here," the Avatar replied as her eyes lost their patina of mortality and became obsidian to his indigo.

But that was irrelevant. Kaylin knew that the Shadows didn't have to be here to call a name that could be heard across whatever it was that divided worlds. She reached for his name, as well, as if drawing a dagger. For the first time since she'd taken—or, to be fair, been all but given—his name, she felt resistance; her attempt to say the name faltered on syllables, as if her voice was sliding across whole scales in an attempt to hit the right key.

No, she thought, as she stopped moving entirely, hers wasn't the only discordance there. Another voice had dropped into the mix. It was a soft, low voice—but in the way that a dog's voice is when said dog has descended from furious, yapping bark to quiet growl. She was bitterly aware that this was exactly what had made Tara so reluctant to let Maggaron out of the Tower. She was even more bitterly aware of her implied promise to protect Maggaron—and indirectly the rest of the fief—from the consequences of a distant Shadow attempting to use his name against him.

She wasn't about to let that happen. But she felt this other voice as if Maggaron's name was a bridge that it had crossed to reach her. She glanced at the sword's blade. It was now a greatsword that seemed to repel sunlight. Etched across the center flat of its blade were Maggaron's runes. They pulsed faintly, as if they were signaling to her, and without thought—the sudden compulsion was so strong—she reached out and placed her palm against them.

Fire shot up her arm. Blue fire. In its wake, the exposed marks of the Chosen began to glow the same brilliant azure. They didn't change shape or form; they didn't rearrange themselves. But she felt them all as distinct and separate entities from the rest of her. Sharp, stabbing, distinctive entities.

She tried, once again, to speak Maggaron's name. It didn't matter where it came from or why it was his; here and now, it *was,* and she had to own it, or the Dragons would be forced to kill him. Given the sword and his size, it would be a slightly more equal battle than Kaylin would be facing—but not, in her opinion, by enough.

Every syllable she spoke—and she realized that was the wrong verb because her lips didn't move at all—made her arm ache. But it was only one arm; the rest of her marks remained untouched by whatever had fired up these ones. Painful or no, the sharp jolts made each syllable a physical sensation. They grounded her.

Maggaron began to shudder; his arms shook and his hands spasmed. Even the hand that held the hilt of the sword— perhaps especially that hand. He fell to one knee and the sword's edge tottered precariously against the cobbles, scraping them in an edge-killing way—if a magical sword had to worry about keeping a sharp edge.

"Maggaron," she said, hand still on the blade, which meant she was now crouched in a much more awkward position, "can you tell me who holds your name?"

The Arkon said, "It is a master-slave connection, Private."

"Yes—but you can't have a totally absent, totally faceless master. I'm not asking Maggaron for his—or her—True Name; I'm asking *if* he knows where or what the other entity *is*."

Maggaron's eyes rolled up toward his skull, exposing whites. *Maggaron.*

Maggaron. What came out wasn't the word Kaylin said; she knew it. It was what she *felt*. The syllables were longer, and there were more of them—but they coalesced, in the same way his foreign tongue did, into a language she knew.

He began to shake. She swore the ground beneath his knees shook with him, as if he were part of the earth, and rooted deeply there. His head swiveled toward the fief's heart. Toward the shadows and the storms and the hidden ancient ruins that had only been barely glimpsed by anyone who now stood in these streets. *Look, Chosen. You've allowed me to hear as you hear. Now, see as I see.*

She did as he asked. She saw the red she usually saw when her eyes were closed; that wasn't helpful. *Maggaron, are your eyes closed?*

Yes, Chosen.

What am I supposed to see if your eyes are closed?

He was silent for a minute; she felt his shock and his frustration. *...Know what I know, then. Feel what I feel. If I try, I can see you; it doesn't matter where I am. You would know that I'm looking if you were paying attention; you could force me not to look. If I try, I can see him. See what I see, Chosen.*

Hand on the flat of his blade—which would have gotten her ears boxed by one of the drillmasters in the Hawks' training ground—she closed her own eyes, as if what she could see on these streets was too small and too confining. Given that it encompassed two Dragons and the Avatar of a fief, this said something.

She was aware of Maggaron's name. In the red darkness behind her lids, she could glimpse it as if it were burned into her vision. She looked at that first because there wasn't much else to look at. It shook, as Maggaron had shaken, as if his movement was an echo of what now rocked the symbol. She reached for it, touched it, and realized that she had no clear sense of where her hands were in the darkness.

As she touched it, as she felt it shrinking away from her figurative palms, she said it clearly. *Maggaron.*

It twisted, as if attempting to avoid her. It couldn't, of course; she knew it. She approached it, rotating it in her mind's eye. It grew larger and larger, until it looked like something produced by a drunk architect's nightmares. It had windows, or at least great translucent patches; it had crevices and sudden openings that seemed to be almost door-shaped. They weren't, however, very welcoming doors; she'd been in condemned buildings on the other side of the river that seemed safer and more welcoming.

Safer and more welcoming, however, wouldn't get the job done, and she knew that she had to enter here. She wondered what other people made of true names and their connections to them, because she realized this was very much like magic, or like the way she saw its effects. It was a metaphor that she could understand.

She entered one of the doors, and was not surprised—although very dismayed—when she discovered it had no floor. She started to fall, and caught herself, remembering that she was firmly ensconced in her own body.

See what I see.

Shadow.

Darkness that was illuminated by patches of chaotic, opalescent colors which all managed to look repulsive. Kaylin was about to take issue with her metaphors when she realized that this was almost a literal vision of formless Shadow; she'd seen things that were very close before. It made her feel cold, but not enlightened; it wasn't telling her anything she didn't already know.

She couldn't walk among the Shadows; it wasn't the way this particular vision worked. It was as if she was looking through an arrow slit in a tall building; she could see out, but she wasn't close enough to be able to change the angle of view. So she watched, waiting for illumination.

When it came, it flew in—almost literally. The Shadows darkened, and they darkened exactly the way any landscape does when something gets between it and sunlight. It was the only thing about the landscape that implied that sun shone here. She watched as the darkness spread, and realized that it was taking shape, and at that, a familiar one.

Not *very* familiar; it couldn't be.

Dragon form was illegal within the bounds of the Empire—not that she'd seen all that much of it—and an act of treason within the borders of the City. But it was unmistakable. A dragon was landing.

She couldn't see where. She couldn't see streets or ruins or even buildings—and she was pretty certain those still existed in the heart of the fiefs. It would have helped, because what she could see caused her to freeze in place, like a particularly stupid rabbit. She recognized this Dragon. She'd seen him twice before.

Makkuron.

The only Outcaste Dragon who still lived. He was dark, his scales obsidian in almost exactly the same way Tara's eyes sometimes were. Flecks of color glinted off those scales, implying that light could change the way they appeared, but not by much. He turned toward her as she stared, and his eyes flared instantly red; she could almost see flame.

"What is this?"

He could see her.

Of course he could see her. She could see him and she had always been aware of his name. Of the size and complexity of it; of the shape and the tone and the architecture. She had seen it once and she had known at that time that to even attempt to speak it was death. It would almost be like attempting to speak the name of a god. Worse, really, because the gods didn't live *here*.

She pulled back, retreating from Maggaron and his name, remembering only as she returned to the world and her eyes snapped open that retreating from him was a very bad idea at this time.

But Maggaron had stopped his teetering shake and his eyes, although blue, had returned to something close to normal for a Norannir. "Chosen," he whispered.

She spoke Maggaron's name like thunder, like a challenge, aware that making him a battlefield with the one Dragon she truly had cause to hate and fear was the act of a coward. The Ascendant was not an object, not a possession; he thought, felt, breathed.

"It is inevitable," he told her softly. "If you cannot control me, if you cannot exert that level of power, people will die."

"Give me your sword," Kaylin told him, holding out both hands. She might have slapped him or beaten him instead; it would have caused less pain. She didn't attempt to force his body to comply with her demand; she simply waited for him.

He understood why she'd made her demand, and he acquiesced without struggle. "I'm sorry," she said when her hands were around the giant hilt. The sword obligingly began to shrink until it was once again the size and shape of a blade meant for someone like Kaylin. "I surprised him; I think that bought us some time. But probably not much."

"You surprised him?"

"Yes."

"You *know* him?"

"Let's just say we've met once or twice. I didn't care for the experience either time." Turning to the Arkon, she said, "I know who holds his name."

The Arkon, who had been listening intently to at least one-half of the conversation, said, "The Outcaste."

Kaylin nodded.

After some discussion between Sanabalis and the Arkon—in Dragon, which Kaylin thought a tad unfair because she only had one free hand and could therefore only attempt to protect the hearing in one ear—the Arkon turned to Tara. Tara, in her gardening clothes, had been listening intently to everything that was said, because Tara understood Dragon. The Arkon must have known this, but chose to address her in High Barrani anyway.

"What we require is a clear idea of *when* the Ascendant lost his name."

"What we need," Kaylin snapped, "is a clear idea of how the Outcaste was able to pick his name out of the air. He's a Dragon, not a god. Last I heard, Dragons weren't particularly adept at reading the True Names of others."

"If we can determine when, Private, it will give the Dragon Court more information with which to work." He placed emphasis on the syllables that involved Dragons and implied Emperor, and Kaylin swallowed the rest of her ill-advised words.

"Does time even work the same way across different worlds?" she asked.

He glowered. Sometimes his ill humor was its own answer; sadly, that answer lacked anything Kaylin could hang a fact on.

But Maggaron rose—unsteadily—to his feet. He looked at the sword in Kaylin's hand. "If you carry the blade," he finally said, "I can...hear less."

"Hear or see?"

"I do not hear my name, Chosen."

"Good." Turning to the Dragons, she said, "Shall we continue?"

The Arkon looked like the definition of the word *no*. Kaylin, who usually let the Arkon make the decisions because she *liked* her job, began to walk anyway. This was because the sword was now pulling at the hand that held it, as if it were an excited orphan at Festival. "It's not me," the Hawk said in a rush. "It's the sword. It's pulling my hand."

"It is almost criminal that you're allowed to touch that sword," the Arkon replied. "Anyone with any sense knows that magical swords cannot be allowed to rule their bearers."

"I don't make the laws, I just enforce them."

"Then remind me to introduce a new set of laws, since the ones we have clearly assume a level of common sense that's lacking."

Knowing the Arkon, who wasn't famous for his sense of humor, he meant it. Kaylin wondered if his proposed new law would be constructed for the general case, or if it would have her name in it somewhere.

Severn joined her; Severn, in silence, surveyed the street at all levels. Most of the windows above ground were shuttered, although many of the shutters had been warped by rain and years of constant temperature shifts. None of them were open at the moment. Kaylin felt herself relaxing as she began to acclimatize herself to the rhythm of the beat. It was a fief beat, to be sure—but there were rules about surviving fief streets; Severn had adopted them as easily as he had adopted the Hawk.

He didn't chide, didn't nag, didn't remind her to do the same. Instead, he did what she should have been doing because she couldn't. The sword was making her arm tingle. It had also made her marks glow; she couldn't turn the light off. But she watched in horrified fascination as that light began to spread to her other arm.

"Severn?"

He nodded without looking at her.

"Please tell me the back of my neck isn't glowing."

He was silent for a beat too long, and then said, "You can't see most of it because of your hair."

"The hair that's pinned up?"

"The hair that needs to be pinned up again, yes."

She said something under her breath in Leontine. The Dragons, who could almost certainly hear—and understand—pretended they couldn't. The Arkon, however, pretended badly. It occurred to Kaylin that in some ways, he lived the emotional life she wanted: he said what he was thinking, he worked on whatever caught his interest, and he mostly scared people who'd interfere out of his territory simply by breathing. It wasn't an entirely comforting thought.

On the other hand, it was better than thinking about the sword, and about the Outcaste Dragon. It was better than thinking about the sudden thunder that started in entirely the wrong direction in an otherwise cloudless, clear sky.

Severn slowed, but this time so did Kaylin. They both turned toward Tara.

"Yes," Tara said quietly.

"Drums?"

"Yes. But not just drums."

If she'd thought the Dragon Lords had looked grim in the room that now housed the eighth corpse of Bellusdeo, she'd been wrong. They looked grim now. The streets, which had been fairly busy by fief standards, suddenly began to empty as people standing close enough to see the Dragons clearly—especially their eyes—now streamed toward doors, and through them. There was a lot of slamming.

This sudden surge of self-preservation clearly met with the Arkon's approval. Tara looked as if she felt vaguely guilty.

"It's not you," Kaylin told her in what she hoped was a reassuring tone of voice.

"No. But…my Lord wants his people to be comfortable in the presence of Dragons."

Kaylin raised a brow at Severn, who as usual said nothing.

"I think your Lord is being overly ambitious." The last syllable was lost to the sound of thunder. "Do you want to head to the border?"

Tara looked torn, and Kaylin pointed at the sword's blade. "We're heading that way anyway, if I had to bet."

"What would you be willing to bet?" the Tower's Avatar asked. She was serious. Betting, as a fief pastime, had caught her interest, but that interest had failed to blossom into actual understanding.

"Not more than a week's pay—but my own money."

"I understand that that phrase means you're very serious." Tara tilted her head to one side. "What I don't understand is what you would bet with otherwise."

"Severn's money."

"Hey!"

"You're teasing me, Kaylin."

"A little. All you really need to understand is that it means I'm fairly certain I won't lose." She began to walk more quickly, which wasn't always the smartest thing to do in the fiefs.

"Private." Sanabalis's voice was on the edge of a growl, or would have been had he been Leontine. She tried to slow down and almost overbalanced.

"Lord Sanabalis?"

"Do you think it unlikely that the Outcaste will seek the border?"

Thunder.

"No."

"Do you think it wise that you carry this sword—and the Ascendant by default—to where he is headed?"

"No."

"Then?"

"I think wisdom in this case won't cut it. If the Arkon is right, and if Maggaron is right, we're headed to the ninth appearance of Bellusdeo. If, for some reason, the Outcaste gets there first, we've lost her." She added because he looked as if he would say more, "We both know that the Outcaste isn't a

Shadow. The border won't keep him out; he can come—and leave—at will."

"That is entirely our concern," Sanabalis replied. Kaylin tried not to meet his gaze because she really didn't like the color of his eyes.

"We know the streets. He doesn't."

"There is a chance that he knows what he is looking for."

"He's probably looking for Maggaron. He has to have a good idea of where Maggaron actually is." The other possibility, that he was now looking for Kaylin, she didn't mention.

Sanabalis, however, wasn't a fool.

"Sanabalis," she said, ditching his title. "Can we afford to let him find her first?"

The Arkon roared. There were syllables in it.

Sanabalis closed his eyes briefly. "Very well. Lead, Private. Lead quickly."

Kaylin nodded. The sword, however, snickered. Easy for the sword; as far as Kaylin could tell, the sword itself was never the one at risk. But in all the stories about magical weapons— magical intelligent weapons—that Kaylin had ever heard, none of the weapons had been reported to display an ounce of humor. She'd never really noticed before. Now probably wasn't the time to start, either, but as she'd pretty much given up on anything but not falling flat on her face, she had the time.

Maggaron kept pace with her, flanking her on the right. Severn remained on her left, his gaze continuing to dart from street to windows and back. The streets widened as they approached the border. They approached it at an angle; the Norannir encampment, such as it was, was farther to the right. But the watchtowers that were the first thing Tiamaris had insisted on reconstructing, given the fall of the previous ones, were mostly manned by the Norannir. The Norannir didn't *like* them—they clearly didn't like being that far off solid ground—but they knew how to sound alarms when necessary, and even if they hadn't, they could make themselves heard for miles. They all had voices like seasoned Swords.

Chosen, the sword said. Kaylin nearly jumped out of her own skin.

Have you been listening to everything?

I have. We are close. Will you risk giving me to Maggaron once again?

Kaylin hesitated. *We're going to have to play that by ear,* she finally said.

What does that mean?

I'll decide when we get there.

We are almost there. Can you see or feel it? the sword asked, sounding almost hopeful.

It? Do you mean her? Kaylin looked up as the sword's pull on her hand—hells, her whole arm—eased.

No.

Kaylin swore. The Dragons, who had been following at a safe distance, did what she assumed was the Dragon equivalent of the same thing; it was certainly louder.

Yes, Kaylin told the sword. *I can see it.*

In the street of the fief—Collande, if she remembered the name correctly—a miniature cloud had formed. Sadly, that description was literal.

CHAPTER 20

"Tara!" Kaylin pivoted, sword in hand, in the direction of the Avatar. Like something emerging from a cocoon, familiar wings erupted from the Avatar's back, moving at a speed that implied danger for even the air around them. They were wide and high, but Tara remained on the ground for the moment.

"It is not," she said, her voice resonating as if it were a Dragon's, "a Shadowstorm."

Given that she was now wearing armor that was every bit as dark as her wings and her eyes, Kaylin inferred that Shadowstorm or no, Tara didn't assume it was safe.

"It is not safe," Tara said, as if she could—this far from the base of her power—still read Kaylin's thoughts. "Storms— ancient storms—bring change, transformation, and often, death."

But Kaylin, sword in hand, stepped toward the cloud. "They also," she said quietly as she passed the Avatar, "brought me to you when you first woke. And brought me back."

"You are not afraid?"

Kaylin lifted her arms; the runes on them were glowing brightly. But the blue had taken on shades of the roiling grays and silvers that comprised the cloud itself. The buildings beyond the barrier of ground-level clouds were dim and hazy.

"Where do you think it will take you?" Tara asked. Both the Arkon and Sanabalis had fallen completely silent. Kaylin was grateful for the silence, although she thought it was probably a bad sign.

"Not me," Kaylin replied softly. "I don't think this storm is for me." She called Maggaron forward, and silent, he came. He was shaking. On the other hand, so was the ground.

"Private," the Arkon said, his voice as deep and rumbling as the movement of stones. "Does the sword speak to you now?"

"Not in so many words."

"What are you being instructed to do?"

"Stand my ground."

"And wait?"

Kaylin glanced at Severn. "And wait," she said in exactly the wrong tone of voice. Severn immediately began to unwind the weapon chain from around his waist.

"Where is the danger coming from?" he asked.

She glanced up, past Maggaron's shoulders, toward a sky that was becoming shades of gray. Severn, to his credit, didn't wince; instead, he became grim and remote. He understood what she feared.

"It is good to know," the Arkon said in a loud and brittle voice, "that the mortals who serve the Emperor's Law with such dedication are so optimistic. That that level of optimism implies insanity is less of a boon. Lord Sanabalis?"

Sanabalis turned not to the Arkon but to the Avatar. "Lady," he said gravely. "I request that you inform your Lord of our situation."

"He is now aware," was the remote reply. "And he has left

the evening defense of the fief in the hands of Morse. He will join us shortly."

"Will he grant us his permission to assume our native forms?"

"Given the gravity of the circumstances, yes. He asks me to remind you both," she added, her voice sliding into the quieter, normal range, "that the Emperor himself has granted dispensation for the breaking of the prohibition where the Outcaste is involved."

Sanabalis stood back from the group. He grimaced, raised a brow in Kaylin's direction, and then turned his back on her. She understood why when he began to disrobe.

"The clothing doesn't survive the transformation," the Arkon told her. "And we have some time. That is generally not the case when we are required, by circumstance, to assume the stronger form."

"Doesn't the Imperial Court cover the costs of lost robes?"

"Of course it does—but the money has to come from somewhere. And at the moment," he added, his eyes narrowing, "the exact amount of money left for such trivial affairs is in question. I assume the Hawks have made no forward progress?"

Kaylin tried not to bristle. "I don't know, Arkon. I'm not part of that investigation, and the information concerning it is given out strictly on a need-to-know basis."

"How surprising."

Before he could say any more, Kaylin took the career risk of cutting him off. "Can I point out—with all due respect—that this is perhaps *not* the time for this discussion?"

"The day you are even *capable* of all respect that is due is the day that Lord Diarmat decides you are ready to graduate. I do not," he added, in case it was necessary, "think that will happen any time soon." His eyes were a pale shade of orange-red, which was odd, given the color of Sanabalis's. "It is my attempt at gallows humor, Private. I hear that mortals are fascinated with humor in difficult situations.

"Sanabalis, are you finished?"

The answer was a roar. Sanabalis stood dead center in the street, his wings folded across his long, long back. He was gray, perhaps a shade darker than he had been the last time she'd seen him take this form—but something in the ambient light made that gray glitter like silver.

The Arkon lifted a brow; his entire expression reminded Kaylin of the midwives' guildmaster's impatience with the young—all of whom were generally older than Kaylin. She avoided saying as much because the cloud in the middle of the street began to condense, which wasn't what she'd been expecting.

The Arkon roared. Kaylin wanted wax to plug her ears; given the amount of time she'd been spending around Dragons, she felt it should be part of her standard kit. Sanabalis roared *back*—and honestly, they were yards apart, was that level of sound *really* necessary?—before he took to the skies.

The Arkon remained on the ground. When Kaylin glanced at him, she was surprised to see his color: he was golden. Apparently Maggaron was surprised by it, as well. In his Dragon form, all pretense of age vanished. Looking at both Sanabalis and the Arkon, it was impossible to tell who was older; the Arkon, in her opinion, was slightly larger, but it could go either way.

"Sanabalis," the Arkon said, choosing to speak his traditional Barrani, but with more growl and depth, "will watch the skies. I believe I hear young Tiamaris, as well."

"You are correct," Tara told him. "My Lord is almost here."

Almost was three seconds away. Tiamaris buzzed ground,

his wings nearly clipping rooftops on the flyby. He was a blur of gleaming red as he rose to meet Sanabalis. A loud blur.

"It serves as warning," Tara said calmly. Her feet were now hovering about a yard off the ground, but she made no attempt to join the Dragons.

"Or challenge," Kaylin pointed out.

"Or challenge," the Arkon agreed.

"You think he'll come?"

"Oh, yes. Guard the ground, Chosen, as you can. I leave you in the care of the Avatar." He growled and picked a few cobbles out of the street. "If Tiamaris is rebuilding," he told the Tower, "have him consider *wider* streets in future."

"I will, Arkon," was the grave—and entirely serious—reply. Tara watched as the Arkon broke free of whatever it was that kept the rest of them bound to ground. The clouds continued to thicken and shrink, and Kaylin's gaze bounced between them and the Ascendant who had, apparently, forgotten how to breathe.

Be ready, Chosen, the sword told her.

Kaylin nodded. She didn't even ask the sword what she was supposed to be ready for, because Maggaron picked that moment to scream. It was loud, but unlike Dragon roars in close quarters, it didn't annoy; it alarmed. He fell to his knees so gracelessly, Kaylin almost dropped the sword to help him stand; the sword yanked itself away from the Ascendant, and Kaylin, still gripping the hilt, staggered in that direction by default.

"Chosen!" Maggaron said, as if he were being throttled. She realized then that he'd thrown himself into as awkward a position as possible, and meant for her to help him maintain it.

"I guess that answers that," Kaylin murmured.

Tara, yards away, replied, "It is not necessary to be in physical proximity to invoke the name."

"Tara—"

"Nonetheless, although your supposition is based on a misunderstanding of the use of the name, I concur. The Outcaste is coming."

So, too, was the shape of the storm.

Kaylin had expected that somehow the ninth form of Bellusdeo would emerge from those silver clouds in much the same way she herself once had. She was wrong. The clouds continued to condense until they looked almost solid. She recognized the shape the clouds had slowly collapsed into: it was hers. Bellusdeo's. Not for the first time, she wondered what in the hells Dragons actually *were*. The gray paled as it turned; for a minute the woman it depicted look carved out of smoky alabaster, if that were possible.

Color began to seep into her skin; her hands became pale and pink, her face pale but sallow; her hair became spun gold. She was not yet wet or covered in ashes or splinters, and as she turned, her skirts still looking like cloud's edge, Kaylin saw the color of her eyes: they were a brown that seemed, at this distance, to be flecked with gold. Maggaron looked up—well, more accurately, across—at the solidifying form of Bellusdeo. He spoke to her in a language that Kaylin didn't understand.

It struck her as strange only a minute later when she realized that Maggaron's words had always sounded like Elantran to her. Bellusdeo had no difficulty understanding what he said, and she answered in the same tongue, or in what sounded, to Kaylin's ears, to be the same.

She saw the Ascendant stiffen. No, she *felt* him stiffen.

The woman who looked like Maggaron's image of Bellusdeo now looked at her. "Chosen," she said. Kaylin's arms were still exposed, and the runes that covered them were glowing. Her eyes widened slightly when she saw the sword in Kaylin's hands, but her expression softened. She stepped forward, and as she did, she seemed to gain the last little bit of solidity. She stumbled. Kaylin caught her; Maggaron was frozen in position.

Kaylin knew why. She could feel the pressure of what might have been syllables pressing against his thoughts.

"Maggaron." Bellusdeo reached out with both hands and gently cupped his cheeks. "It is almost over. You have served me well, and in ways you cannot imagine. It is time now for you to return to your kin."

He couldn't speak while fighting, even if the fight itself involved no physical movement. Kaylin, however, could. "He doesn't *want* to go back to his kin."

A gold brow rose. The woman straightened. "You carry his sword," she finally said.

"I do."

"And his name?"

"...I do."

"Do you understand that he will have no other freedom for the rest of his unnatural existence otherwise?"

Kaylin said nothing for a long moment. She didn't like where the conversation was going. But the sword was humming in her hand, like a beehive, not a singer.

Tiamaris roared in the air above and Bellusdeo's eyes widened in surprise. Her mouth opened in a half O and she looked up, and up again. When she looked down, she closed her eyes briefly. When she opened them, she was calm again. "Chosen," she said, "I haven't much time. You carry the Ascendant's sword. Stab me with it."

Kaylin hesitated.

Sanabalis roared, and this time—this time, fire touched the streets.

"Chosen—"

Kaylin looked up. She could see the undersides and wing-spans of three familiar dragons—but she could also see a fourth. He was distant, but approaching, and his wingspan seemed larger, the reach of his fire longer, than any of the three. "Maggaron—"

The Ascendant bit either tongue or lip; blood trickled from the corners of his mouth. His eyes were wide. Kaylin watched him, her arms aching from the sudden weight the sword in her hand had gained.

Give me to Maggaron, Chosen.

I—

Or do what must be done yourself. We cannot wait.

In the distance, the Outcaste roared; the ground beneath Kaylin's feet shook at the force of the sound. It seemed impossible to her then that the three Dragons she did know could stand against the one that she desperately wished she didn't.

The sword grew heavier and heavier in her hand, its weight pulling her down. *I don't think Maggaron can wield you.*

He can. If you force him, he can.

I can't— She stopped. She *could*. And she felt that it was important, somehow; that's why she'd wanted him to come here in the first place. Her skin began to burn. Or at least that's what it felt like; a casual inspection of her forearms showed that she only got the pain of fire, not the damage.

Maggaron.

He swiveled his head to look at her.

Take the sword.

His hand rose—and fell—at the command. She wasn't the only one who was trying to take control of him. She was the only one who didn't want to succeed—and that had to stop.

He looked at her, his eyes wide, blood still tracing the lines of his chin. Bellusdeo was standing two feet away, her face pale, circles suddenly darkening the undersides of her eyes. There were so many things Kaylin wanted to ask her.

Instead, she dragged the sword toward the Ascendant, and laid the hilt in the palm of one stiff, open hand. It was already far too large for Kaylin to wield. Maggaron's hand spasmed as he sought to close it. Kaylin took a step back as he did. His eyes darkened; they looked disturbingly like Tara's, but without as good a reason.

He rose, shedding the rictus of agony that had all but sculpted his living body. Kaylin closed her eyes. She felt, rather than saw, Severn, all but forgotten, step in front of her. She heard the Dragons in the air above and felt a brief burst of heat somewhere to her left. These were now someone else's problems. She let herself have only one for the moment: Maggaron.

Even with her eyes closed, she could see his name. It was golden, and larger in all ways than she herself felt at this particular moment. She knew its shape, its form; knew its strength and its weaknesses. She reached out to touch it and felt its warmth, felt its pulse. Everything about Maggaron as she knew him was here.

He was afraid. His fear didn't allow for gallows humor; it never had. He had been embarrassingly earnest as a child. She saw it clearly, although she couldn't say how. The only thing he had ever desired was to become an Ascendant; it was both his hope and his fear. He had loved many, many people; had been loved—she felt this clearly—by many people. It humbled him. But he had loved no one the way he had loved—did love—Bellusdeo.

He was afraid now. He was afraid of failing her. No, he was afraid of what his failure had already cost her. He was overjoyed to see her alive—but terrified, as well. He did not want to kill her. He did not believe whatever it was he would do *would* kill her, but he couldn't be certain.

He was also terrified that he couldn't even do that much, because he could feel his body sliding out of his conscious control. She could feel it sliding out of *hers*. And she had it. She had it if she was willing to use it. What he wanted, what he was—it didn't matter; it made no difference to what she could or couldn't do. The whole of who he was, of who he had ever been, was irrelevant.

Kaylin *hated* it.

But hating it, she accepted it; there was no other way. Because what he was didn't matter to the Outcaste, either.

It matters, she heard Maggaron say. *It matters, Chosen. To you. You'll do what's necessary no matter how* much *you hate it because it* does *matter.*

Yes. *Yes, Maggaron. Thank you.*

His hand closed around the hilt of the sword with almost no resistance; this meant the Dragon in the skies wanted it, as well. Maggaron turned toward Bellusdeo, and this, too, met with no resistance. But when he lifted the sword he now carried, he suddenly froze.

He froze because the Outcaste did *not* intend for Bellusdeo to die here. That was information that she was certain someone would be interested in—providing they survived. The air was thick with smoke; she could taste it. Kaylin didn't open her eyes because there was nothing she could do about it.

Maggaron turned like a drunken pillar toward—her. His blade moved—his blade, with glowing runes now edged in black, and he lifted it, struggling against its weight, the imperative of a motion he didn't want. He moved slowly enough that she could dodge, and she did. Even at the speed of his sword, if it connected, the results wouldn't be pretty.

Severn stepped in front of her, his hands around a chain that formed a translucent circle in the air in front of them both. "Don't," he told her. "I'll handle the Ascendant. Do what you have to do—but do it quickly."

Fire strafed the ground to one side of where they stood; it was orange and white, and the stones reddened as it passed. But it didn't come close enough to force either of them to flee because Bellusdeo was in its path, as well. Her eyes looked bruised now. Fear touched her face, and took root. "Chosen," she said, her voice too thin, too mortal. And then, "Maggaron."

He swiveled toward her, and then jerked away; he couldn't speak. But he wanted to—he wanted to speak so badly the inability came close to breaking something in him. She saw it, felt it, understood it—and understood that it didn't matter, either. Broken, whole—he would do what she ordered him to do, if she had more force of will than the Outcaste.

This was how he had lived. He might have ended his life—she saw and felt it clearly in the moment—but even that wasn't allowed him. He had retreated as far inside himself as a person could go; she was honestly surprised he had emerged at all. But he had—for long enough to expose what he knew, not what he *hoped* she might see and take: his name.

Was that all that was left for him? Not freedom, not the ability to think and act on his own recognizance, but rather a transfer to a different master, a different person's ultimate control? She *hated* it. Everything she had ever been afraid of when the word *Tha'alani* had been spoken in her presence Maggaron was living—that, and worse.

"Kaylin!"

She leaped forward as fire once again strafed the street, but it wasn't necessary; Severn's twisting chain caught it and it dissipated. Her brows rose, and her mouth opened on a question, but closed before the question escaped. He'd told her to do what she had to do, and he was *there*.

"Yes," he said, although he watched the sky. "This much I can do." For just a minute, she saw Severn in duplicate: Severn now, Severn years ago. She saw his expression shift, the younger man's more serious, more intent. *I need to be able to protect someone.* She couldn't see who he was speaking to, couldn't hear what that unknown person's answer was.

She shook her head, blinking the vision of the younger Severn out of existence.

Now, in a totally different darkness, she turned and she leaped toward Maggaron, still struggling—and failing—to control the sword of the Ascendant. She wasn't an Immortal; she had twenty years to his centuries. She had no desire for power except as it came in the form of the Hawk. But when she *did* desire power, did it matter if she was twenty or two thousand? Her reasons were at least as good as the Outcaste's— hells, they were *better*. She grabbed Maggaron's solid, shaking arm in one hand and almost left the ground.

She grabbed the pommel of his sword with the other.

Light enveloped the three of them—sword, Ascendant, and Hawk—as her marks suddenly flared. It was as if a flash of lightning had chosen to respond to the bursts of fire across the streets—except the lightning didn't fade into thunder and storm. It grew. It spread until it encompassed not only the three, but also two others: Bellusdeo and Severn.

Bellusdeo was staring at Kaylin. Or at the marks that adorned her exposed arms; Kaylin couldn't really tell the difference. She spoke, she spoke quickly—but it was a confusion of strange syllables and cadences that Kaylin's ears couldn't parse. Maggaron cried out, and Kaylin tightened her grip.

No, she said. *I'm sorry.* She slid her consciousness into his limbs, into his chest, his mouth, his lungs. They became, for a moment, extensions of her, and they felt entirely natural, as if she'd been born in two bodies, not one, even though one was eight feet tall. She felt the Outcaste's presence, as well, but his was shadow and hers? Hers was a light so harsh it burned shadow.

Mine, she snarled.

Mine.

She heard the Outcaste's roar; felt, for a moment, his fury— and his fear.

Taking Maggaron's arms, Maggaron's hands, she readjusted her grip on a sword that, if his story were true and complete, came *from* Bellusdeo. She didn't tell him what to do because it wouldn't have made a difference: she did it instead, using his hands and not her own. She drove the sword into the standing woman who still stared, wide-eyed, at Kaylin.

It was slow. Kaylin had killed with daggers before. She'd killed with the inexplicable and terrible power granted her by the marks. But she hadn't had much training with swords, and using a sword like a dagger wasn't optimal. Bellusdeo stag-gered; she would have fallen, but the sword held her up, and as it entered her farther, Bellusdeo reached up and grabbed the blade in both hands. Blood trailed suddenly out of the corner of motionless lips.

Maggaron was screaming on the inside of his own head.

But Kaylin was screaming on the inside of hers. She watched as Bellusdeo's eyes began to slide shut, and she al-most let go of Maggaron. But that would have been a simple act of cowardice, and it would have given Maggaron over to the Outcaste who waited.

"Kaylin," Severn said, voice low and urgent. "Don't close your eyes. Watch. Watch the sword. Watch Bellusdeo."

She wasn't even aware that her eyes *were* closed; she opened them. Opened them to see the runes on the blade itself: they

were changing. Dimming, yes, but their shapes were wavering
as she watched. She still held the sword's pommel and she slid
her hand down the hilt and toward that blade in a panic, as if
by touch she could somehow preserve them.

But that was impossible.

Worse, she felt Maggaron begin to slip away. Not by
dying—that would have been a blessing for him—but somehow she was losing her grip on his body. His thoughts, which
had been so loud with pain and fear and self-loathing, began
to quiet until she could no longer hear them.

"Maggaron!"

He looked down at the sound of her voice. His eyes were
very wide and very blue—but it was a Norannir blue. They
were his own. He turned toward Bellusdeo and whispered her
name.

Kaylin did the same. Bellusdeo was smiling—at Maggaron.
"Thank you," she said, her voice thin as paper. Kaylin let go
of Maggaron—not the sword—and reached for Bellusdeo; it
wasn't hard because Bellusdeo and the sword were practically
in the same place now.

When she touched the woman's shoulder, she felt the shape
of a word, rather than the curve of flesh over joint. She almost
yanked her hand free, because she'd felt this once before: in the
High Halls of the Barrani, when she had touched the Lake of
Life. Of course, at the time it had looked like a desk. Maybe
for Dragons it looked like a woman?

No. No, Bellusdeo *was* alive. She wouldn't remain that way
for long. Not if Kaylin couldn't do something. She left her
hand where she'd placed it, and closed her eyes. This time,
she saw nothing, but the sense, the feel, of a word remained
in her palm. Not a long stroke, not the missing element of
the High Lord's name, but rather something more refined,
more delicate, and infinitely more complicated. She moved her

hand slowly, hoping she wasn't touching anything embarrassing while she was at it. If she was, Bellusdeo was too absorbed by the sword in her midriff to care.

Yes, the shape was more complicated. But it wasn't the shape the runes on the sword's blade had had—Kaylin would have bet her life on it. Was, she realized, doing exactly that. She could feel the heat of fire and the blackness of rage, but she couldn't see them on the wing. That worried her, but not as much as what she sensed as her touch ranged farther.

The shape of this word was wrong.

Oh, it was written—if true words could be said to be written at all—but it had been written in a hurry, a scrawl; the meaning was sketchy and open to interpretation. She stopped moving. She'd had the thought before actually thinking. How could its meaning be open to interpretation when she didn't even know what it *meant?*

But it *was.* She looked to Bellusdeo, her eyes widening. "How—no, *where,* did you find your name?"

Bellusdeo closed her very mortal eyes. "You understand, Chosen. I…did not, until it was too late."

"No, I *don't* understand." Her hands hurt; the lines and the swirls were shifting beneath them, as if they were slightly unstable.

"He found us. He found us, and he showed us the way." She glanced skyward, although the sky was no longer visible to Kaylin's eyes. She knew that Bellusdeo referred to the Outcaste, and felt cold although she could hear the sharp crackle of flames to either side. "We went to where the words were, at his guidance, and we found our names. We found," she added with a bitter grimace, "our adult forms. We were young, then—and proud, so proud."

"Where—where did he lead you?"

"Through the darkness. Through the heart of the shadow that lies in all worlds."

"And you *followed* him?"

"He was an Elder, and he was strong; we were not yet adult, and we were lost. He was not unkind. He led us to our names. They *are* True Names. But they are not true words."

"And if you lose them?"

Bellusdeo did not answer the question, although she continued to speak. "We discovered his treachery, in time; he could *see* the shape and the form of the names we had chosen for ourselves. It was not simple; it took him time and effort—but he could see. We despaired." Her voice was soft and even, but thinning as the syllables passed. "But we discovered that even his treachery was flawed; the words themselves were mutable and they were not entirely contained." She glanced at Maggaron, and her expression softened.

Kaylin's hardened. She was, for just a moment, furious—with the Arkon, with Sanabalis. Tiamaris escaped her rage because Tiamaris was young and quite possibly ignorant. Then again, maybe not, because he *had* a name. She needed to know to what lake—metaphorically speaking—Dragon children approached to achieve the fusion of form that was their version of adulthood. And she needed to know it *now,* or yesterday.

She couldn't, of course. The Dragons were fighting, quite possibly for their lives, in the skies above. The struggle on the ground might also define and save lives—or conversely, lose them—but they had no time for it. "What's happening to Maggaron?"

"The name is leaving him," Bellusdeo replied. "It is leaving the sword; it returns, at last, to me, where it will be made whole."

"But you said he can—"

"Yes."

"Why?"

"Because I am doomed, regardless, Chosen. And Mag-garon is not. He has lived as less than slave for far too long. I knew where he had traveled. I knew what he had found. I had hoped—" She opened her eyes. Whatever hope she had had, it was gone.

CHAPTER 21

"You wanted to free him."

Bellusdeo nodded. She lifted a hand to his face, and Kaylin saw that his face was wet. She understood why she could no longer control him. But neither could the Outcaste. The sword beneath Kaylin's hand began to dwindle in size, the runes running down the blade as if they'd been written in liquid that hadn't had time to dry.

"Chosen," Bellusdeo said quietly.

Kaylin had often felt like a fraud in her life—as a Hawk, as an adult—but never more than she did now. "I'm Chosen," she said bitterly. "But I've no idea what that *means,* or what it's supposed to mean."

Bellusdeo nodded, as if she'd heard it before. Maybe she had. "I have only met one other who bore marks similar to the ones you now bear. They were not the same marks," she added. "Were it not for his intervention, we would have fallen to Makkuron long ago. The Chosen helped us to understand what we might achieve, and he told us that it wouldn't last.

"But he told me that I might find another of his kind. I searched," she added. The sword was now the size and shape of a dagger—or a letter opener. It was also translucent. "We all searched while we could. He searched, as well—for us. But the Norannir found you. And when they did, we gambled. We, who no longer had the power of flight, or the freedom of it."

"Why—why did they all look like you?"

"Because we are one. We have always been one. Even our names were interconnected in ways that the enemy could not fully perceive, and this bought us much time. He is coming," she added, lifting her face again, her hands still cupped around Maggaron's.

"He can't have you."

"I fail to see what will stop him if they cannot."

Kaylin said, sharply, "I can."

Hope was cruel. It could be an act of torture far more profound than despair. It could cut, and cut, and cut—no one knew this better than Kaylin. She'd tried, in the dark months of Barren, to divest herself of hope entirely, because hope led to pain so directly there were grooves in the path between them.

This, she now inflicted on Bellusdeo.

Kaylin's arms were white. The light shed by the marks on them was now so brilliant she couldn't see skin; she had to squint to make out the individual forms themselves. She swallowed; the sphere that had grown up around them shuddered, and dents appeared in its rounded height, the shape and size of very large claws.

Bellusdeo flinched at the sight of them. Then she grimaced and drew the very small dagger from the wound in her chest—

a wound that was still bleeding. The dagger became a sword—a sword made of glass, or something just as transparent.

"Lady," Maggaron said, his voice breaking between the two syllables. "Let me."

"I cannot anymore, and you know it. Maggaron, you have served me well. You have always served me well. But it is time." He took the sword anyway and set it down on the ground.

What the hells was good about being Chosen, anyway? Kaylin had demanded that Maggaron be allowed to accompany them, and for what reason? Instinct? Fine. But he was here, Bellusdeo had taken a mortal wound, and she had somehow freed him from the curse of a name. The Dragon carried a sword that no longer looked like the sword of an Ascendant, and it was clear to both Kaylin and Maggaron that she meant to use it.

It was clear to both of them that she wouldn't last long. Oh, she'd survive. The Outcaste didn't want her dead. But would her life be any better, in the end, than Maggaron's had been?

Kaylin looked at her exposed arms in an almost helpless frenzy.

Kaylin.

Severn, I don't know what to do.

Don't panic.

She laughed. It was not a happy laugh. The claw-shaped indentations had grown in number, and there were a few new ones that looked as though they might be teeth. But bigger. She felt the ground shake as she heard the Outcaste's roar, and then the sudden incursions stopped.

"Bellusdeo, can you—can you transform now?"

"Transform?"

"Into your Dragon form."

"Not yet, Chosen—but soon."

"No!"

They both glanced at Maggaron.

"Tell her, Lady."

"Enough, Maggaron."

He fell silent. Into his silence came words, and to her surprise, Kaylin was speaking them. She was speaking them just as Sanabalis had once done when he had told the Leontines the ancient story of their birth. There were two words, she thought as she watched them form; she felt their weight in the back of her throat as she struggled to vocalize them. Human throats had clearly not been designed with this in mind.

The words pulled themselves out of the air, gaining shape and size by feeding on the light that Kaylin shed. She'd seen something similar before; she recognized the parts of the runes: the vertical strokes, the horizontal strokes, the dots that crowned them, the squiggles that seemed to flutter at the edges. What she hadn't seen before, however, was their placement: they formed *around* the Ascendant and the Dragon—if either one of them truly fit the descriptions by which they'd lived anymore—like the pristine bars of a golden cage; a songbird's cage in a rich man's house.

Kaylin frowned because she understood that this was an answer, and she couldn't make sense of it.

No, wait… It wasn't an answer.

It was a story. It was a smaller story than the one that had given birth to the Leontine race, but it was a story nonetheless. It wasn't *her* story; it was defined by Bellusdeo and Maggaron. No, she thought as more words began to form around them, it was defined by more than just those two. But they were here now. The other runes floated in the air, rotating and gleaming as they touched one another. They could clearly see them as well as Kaylin could—which the Arkon had implied wasn't possible unless Kaylin touched them. Then again, the last time she had touched the words she'd seen, they'd been *his* words. He'd spoken them.

Here, they were hers.

Bellusdeo lifted a hand and touched one of the interwoven runes. As if she were a glass vessel, the light from the rune began to fill her, or perhaps to drain into her. She turned in wonder to Kaylin, Dragons fighting and roaring above their heads, and said nothing, but her eyes were pure gold. Kaylin was aware that gold was the happy color for Dragon eyes—or for anyone who happened to be *in* the company of said Dragons—but she'd never seen a gold like this.

Bellusdeo reached out with the hand that wasn't touching the word and Maggaron clasped that hand, dwarfing it in his own. Kaylin wasn't surprised to see that same golden light touch him—but it didn't fill his eyes; it didn't change his skin color; it surrounded him like a halo. Without thinking, Kaylin said, "No, Maggaron. That one's not yours."

She cursed as she realized that without their bond, her words would sound like a crash and clatter of syllables and nonsense. Except they didn't. Come to think, Bellusdeo had understood every word she'd spoken. She'd understood, in turn, every word the Dragon had spoken, as well. Maggaron turned to her, unaware that he shouldn't understand what she'd just said. "Mine?" he said, looking mostly confused.

Kaylin nodded. "It's that one. No, the one to the right, the one that's large and very bold." But also spare and simple.

He hesitated, and then turned to Bellusdeo. Bellusdeo smiled for him. At him. Kaylin felt a pang of inexplicable envy at the sight of it.

"You've been part of each other for a very long time," she told them both quietly. Not even the renewed roar of Dragons could drown out the words. "I don't know how it's changed you. I don't even know if it has. But that rune—that one's Maggaron's. Touch it." When he hesitated, she added, "Just touch the damn thing. I know you're humble and you're modest—but we honestly don't have time for either right now."

Maggaron *still* hesitated. Bellusdeo reached up and smacked him. The gesture was so at odds with her expression Kaylin was almost shocked. She started to say something and the words bottomed out as she *felt* Severn's sudden pain. She wheeled and saw that he was standing far, far too close to a melting patch of ground. His weapon's spin wobbled before he gritted teeth and righted it.

Without thought, she reached for him, grabbing his shoulder and pulling him back—and into the light of the words she'd spoken. He tensed as she wrapped her arms around his chest; she could feel his heart beating beneath her glowing arms; could feel his chest rise and fall. "Stay here," she told him. "Just stay here. Stay with me. It's—it's sort of safe."

His weapon slowed; he must have been injured, because it *also* clattered.

"It's proof against the fire," he told her.

"*You're* not."

"No."

She closed her eyes. She could smell fire and sweat and, of all things, *soap*. But she could hear words. Feel them. She opened her mouth and began to speak again, and this time, the words were visible; a thing above and beyond her, but rooted in her, as well, as if they were the crowning branches of a very tall, very ancient tree, and she was, well, dirt.

She opened her eyes and slowly released Severn. Turning to Maggaron, she saw that he had one hand on the thickest and brightest of the vertical strokes of the rune Kaylin had called his. His other hand was still wrapped around the hand of the woman—or Dragon—that he'd served all his life. Kaylin had no idea how long that life had been.

But his eyes began to shift color as he held both the woman and the word. They became gold, as well; gold, however, wasn't the Norannir happy color. Brown was. "Lady," he whispered.

"Chosen," Bellusdeo also whispered.

"It's a story. No, it's *the* story," Kaylin told them both.

"And you are the teller of the tale?"

"Yes."

"Then tell us its ending, who was there at the beginning."

"I can't tell you how it ends, not really; I think...I—I think I can tell you how it finally begins."

She didn't know what she was doing. She knew she was making it up as she went along. She wasn't Rennick, the Imperial Playwright; she couldn't throw out the bits that didn't work—in an ever-increasing pile—and start it again. But she knew, watching the two, Ascendant and Dragon, that they were linked, and she knew, as well, that every single rune she had spoken was part of Bellusdeo.

She counted them.

There were ten.

She really didn't understand how words and names worked; she realized that. She *had* a name and she didn't understand what that meant for her, either. Then again, she didn't understand bureaucracy, and she theoretically worked at the behest of the most powerful bureaucrat in the Empire: the Emperor himself.

"You said that you were always one. The nine of you."

"Yes."

Kaylin took a deep breath. "Then I understand, Bellusdeo, what the rest of the words say."

Bellusdeo wasn't stupid. Her eyes rounded as she, too, counted words that were jostled up against each other in their confined—and comforting—circle. "Chosen—this isn't possible. There is now only one of me."

"Yes. But there were nine, and each and every one of those words is yours."

"How can you know this?"

"I don't know. How can you know how to transform? I *know it*. It's here," she added, lifting her arms and exposing the runes. "Will you trust me?"

"I already have—with my life. With his. But I do not know how I can do what you ask. I am *one;* they are *nine*."

"The others—"

"Are dead. You cannot wake them; they do not sleep."

"It doesn't matter. You were nine, Bellusdeo—and you must be nine again." Kaylin wanted to smack herself to stop the flow of words, because even if she was the one who'd said them, they made no sense if she thought about them for two seconds. Which was about all the time she had.

She cursed—in Leontine, which apparently didn't get translated into ancient and eternal words—and approached the circling runes. She grabbed the ones she could reach and began to push them together, as if the spaces between the individual elements that comprised them were spaces that could be filled by elements that had never been part of their original form at all. As if they were cards and she was shuffling them back into a single deck again before she started to deal them.

She could *feel* Severn wince at the analogy, and it made her laugh.

Bellusdeo was watching her with eyes that were widening as Kaylin worked. She opened her mouth, closed it, opened it again, and then pulled herself closer to Maggaron. That might not have been what she intended, but in her current form—

and at her current weight—that was what happened. She held the rune she had first touched, and she told Maggaron not to let go of his.

Kaylin found that the runes did collapse into each other—but not easily, and not without strain. It was like moving furniture into an apartment that started out empty; it got progressively harder to work with as it filled. Hard wasn't the same as impossible; she reminded herself of this as her arms began to tire; reminded herself again as they started to tremble with exertion. The runes, however, hadn't collapsed into a messy pile of random scribbles, as she'd half feared they might. They had a different shape, a different form, a different density. Some of the lines thinned, some shrunk, some bent—but always in a way that suggested a pattern, an emerging whole.

She wished writing reports worked the same way.

The light had drained out of the marks on her arms as she'd worked; she knew this only because she'd paused for a moment to massage them. The marks were still glowing—but only very faintly. She wouldn't honestly have been surprised had the marks simply vanished with their light, but for perhaps the very first time she would have felt a twinge of regret at the loss.

Sadly, they weren't the only thing the light left; the barrier that had stood as a slender but absolute wall against fire, smoke, and rock that was close to melting had also dimmed. Frustrated, frightened, she cursed herself, wondering if it was somehow *her* power, in the marks, that had maintained that shield—and if it was something she could have learned to do consciously if she'd been a better student.

It didn't matter. If she was to have any hope of saving Bellusdeo and Maggaron now, she needed to finish what she'd started; the anger and the self-recrimination would just have to wait. She'd no doubt she'd return to it later; unlike laundry, she'd never left self-recrimination undone. She took a deep breath, felt its sting in her lungs and at the back of her throat, and struggled.

There were only two runes left standing in their original expressed shape: the ones held by Bellusdeo and Maggaron. The sphere that had been formed of words and light was so thin now Kaylin could see the sky above them; it was red and black. The air sizzled and crackled; liquid was hitting the stones that surrounded them. She wondered if it was rain or blood; the smoke was thick enough she couldn't tell the difference.

She started to push, and this time it wasn't hard—it was impossible. Nothing moved. Nothing so much as shivered. Whatever she'd managed to cobble together was incomplete—but her work, the whole of the work she *could* do, had been done.

"Bellusdeo," she said, voice low and rough, "the rest is up to you. Whatever you took, whatever you absorbed when the Outcaste offered to aid you, it wasn't *real*. This—this could be."

Bellusdeo's eyes were still a bright and shining gold; her expression, however, grew grim. "Understood, Chosen." She hesitated for the first time and then looked at Maggaron. The question was clear in the glance.

"Him, too," Kaylin replied. "I know there are nine parts of what should have been your name—but for reasons I don't understand, his is part of that now. He has to do what I've been doing with his own rune, just as you must."

"And if he succeeds?"

"I don't know." She looked up at the passing shadow that darkened the ground. "Does it matter?"

Bellusdeo hesitated again, which was one answer. And then she started to force her own rune to move, which was another.

Maggaron, to no one's surprise, had already started to push his toward the odd and unfinished jumble that Kaylin had made of the others. His greater size and strength didn't seem to make the task any easier for him than it had been for either Kaylin or Bellusdeo; he was straining to cross an inch or two of ground at a time. Severn's weapon chain was singing at her back; Severn was silent.

She wanted to ask him what he saw.

But what she knew prevented it. If the Arkon's words about Dragon birth were true—and she kind of doubted he could be wrong about something like that, although he wasn't required to be entirely honest—Bellusdeo could fail here. If she failed, Kaylin wasn't certain what would happen, because she wasn't certain what the Outcaste wanted or intended for her. The only possibility—children—she carefully blanked from her thoughts.

She wanted to know how Makkuron had given Bellusdeo something that could serve almost the same function as a True Name, without quite being one.

She wanted to know if this—this amalgamation of nine disparate runes, each complicated and each unique—could replace what she had taken in youthful ignorance without somehow rewriting everything that had come before: her history. Maggaron's. Her role in the life of the Norannir and their war against their encroaching Shadows. She didn't understand, couldn't comprehend, what a True Name meant to those who depended on it. What she knew, watching, was this: she couldn't separate those words again. She couldn't speak them into their former, disparate shapes. Whatever tale they told, it was almost done, and her part as its teller was over. She could witness now; she couldn't be transformed.

They could, if they succeeded, because in the end it was their story.

As Bellusdeo and Maggaron struggled to find a place in the whole for their individual runes, the shape of the various interlocking pieces expanded slightly—only slightly—to give them entry. What had been a mess of disparate elements began to pulse, like a golden heart. It made the whole look dangerously unstable.

Kaylin froze. She had seen one name that was as complicated—as large—as this one, and she'd only seen it once. It was the Outcaste's name. That name and this one weren't the same, but this one was its equal in complexity and form. It looked like the name—like the story—of a small *world*. She had a brief flash of insight as she watched: they were *meant* to be nine. Nine Dragons who were also one Dragon. They were each meant to hold, to capture, to mold one part of this whole until the moment it fused. But...why? How?

Eight of those women, eight of those parts, were dead. But the name itself that now formed was not: it lived, it waited. It was a type of birth.

Above Bellusdeo, the Outcaste could now be clearly seen: he was black, but his scales seemed vaguely opalescent through the haze of smoke and burning buildings. He roared in fury; if he was hurt at all, rage suppressed pain.

The Arkon had landed some distance away, and there was no if about his injuries; she could see the listing wing that couldn't quite fold up on his back. It was torn; there was blood. The fire, on the other hand, didn't seem to bother the Arkon. Sanabalis circled above the Outcaste, but couldn't quite flank him—if that's what he was even trying to do. Tiamaris, however, faced the Outcaste directly, and if the Outcaste's voice embodied fury, it was a very different fury from Tiamaris's. Tiamaris was red. A deep, shining red—the color of new blood or garnets in sunlight. He seemed larger, to Kaylin's eye, than she'd seen him before, and although he was too far above them for his eyes to be visible, she thought they were probably the same color as the rest of him.

And this, she understood. He was in the heart of his hoard. Makkuron threatened it, and nothing short of his removal would still the frenzy.

Kaylin frowned. What she couldn't see was Tara. She started to scan the sky, and then the streets, when she heard Maggaron's cry. It was short, sharp, cut off by the Ascendant himself. Kaylin turned, Tara forgotten, to see that Bellusdeo had collapsed face first into the uneven stones upon which they'd all been standing. Her word had not yet coalesced with the whole; nor had Maggaron's.

Kaylin almost closed her eyes. She moved closer to Bellusdeo—but she was slowed, as if she were running through water or a heavier liquid. Maggaron wasn't encumbered in the same way, but he'd started off much closer. He let go of the word Kaylin had marked as his without any thought or hesitation, and he dropped to the ground, to Bellusdeo's side.

The Dragon's hand still clung to the fading line of the whole rune that had been hers. She lifted her head; her eyes were gold, but they no longer shone, and Kaylin felt utterly certain that when that light guttered completely, she would die.

By the time she reached Bellusdeo's side, Bellusdeo was no longer on the ground; she was in Maggaron's arms, cradled against his chest as if she were a child; given the difference in their sizes, she could have been. Kaylin met the Ascendant's expression and had to look away at what she saw there. But she looked back almost immediately because Maggaron, carrying Bellusdeo, was *also* dragging her rune by default. It moved with her, and it moved far more easily than it had when she'd exerted her own strength and will against it.

"Bellusdeo, can you hear me?" Kaylin said.

"Yes." The Dragon's smile was weak. "You're shouting in my ear."

Kaylin obligingly lowered her voice. "Let Maggaron carry you. But—grab his word the way you're holding yours."

"But, Chosen, you said—"

"I say a lot of stupid things. I told you—I don't know what I'm doing; I make it up as I go along; I reach for what *feels* true, and sometimes, the first time, I miss. It's like I'm locked out of my own place. I've dropped the key down a dark hole. I know the key is in the damn hole, but I'm fumbling around in a space I can't see in an attempt to pick it up. I'm reaching in the right direction but I miss. I keep trying. I know when I've *got* the key." She paused, and then added, "It's like your name. I can see it. I would recognize it if I saw it again—I'm sorry for that—but I can't wrap my mind around the size of it, the shape of it, the *sound*. I can't explain what it is to anyone else—but I *know* what it's supposed to be now that I've seen it. Grab his word."

But Maggaron had already walked to where he had left his standing rune. Of the two, Bellusdeo had made more progress—at least until now, because her rune came with her when he moved. When it did, the whole structure left behind shuddered. Kaylin, in a panic, reached out to hold what was left in place, as if it were physical.

She almost pulled her hands back in shock: the runes felt like living flesh. Not human flesh, not Leontine flesh, not something immediately familiar—but it pulsed, it was warm, and it had that slightly soft give. What it didn't have was anything that remotely resembled a body. Or a cohesive, stable shape. She stiffened her arms as the structure began to bear down on her, grateful that the marks she bore weren't physical shapes like these.

"Maggaron—I can't hold this up forever!" It was unfair

and she knew it; it was also, however, true. She could feel the gaps between the elements of the compressed shape begin to widen. She swore at them in Leontine. And Aerian, for good measure.

Maggaron reached the structure before it collapsed around her like an engineer's worst nightmare. He carried Bellusdeo, and she carried the runes; they were smaller now; denser. They were still, however, the same as they had been when they had been as tall as she was.

"Chosen," he said, "what must I do?"

"What you've done all along. Carry her. Be her shield. Protect her while she does what only she can do."

"I suppose asking you what I can do," Bellusdeo said, her voice thinner and reedier, "wouldn't be helpful."

"You know what you have to do."

"I really don't," the Dragon said, and she laughed. It caused her pain, but it brightened her eyes for a moment. "I'm like you—I've always made it up as I went along." She couldn't touch Maggaron; both of her hands were full. But her voice was gentle. "Carry me as far into the word as you can."

He nodded, tightening his grip briefly. She was, Kaylin could see, exactly what he'd said about her: his life, his reason for living. He didn't want to let go of her. He carried her toward the whole of the shape Kaylin was struggling so hard to preserve, and the runes—the two—preceded her into the whole.

As far into the word as you can, she'd said. Kaylin was surprised at how far that was, because it looked as if there was no space. No space for something the size of either Kaylin or Bellusdeo—who was taller—and certainly no space for the Ascendant. Space or no, he carried her, and it seemed to Kaylin that he carried her *through* the lines, the delicate curves and loops, and the tightly spaced dots. Her word came with her, and when it finally, fully, touched the disparate parts, something snapped into place. No, *everything* snapped into place.

If Kaylin thought the words surrounding Bellusdeo and Maggaron had looked like a gilded cage before, she repented. Now she knew they were inescapable, and she held her breath as they began to shrink, to compress. She had never thought of words as dangerous before. Dangerous to *know*, yes. But in and of themselves? No.

Yet these words—or this nascent word—was. She could see the bleeding that sharp edges caused across the contours of Bellusdeo's cheeks. Her arms fared no better; the dress she wore—the same dress as all the others had worn who now lay in the morgue—began to redden as lines, like swords, pierced cloth and skin at the same time. Kaylin cried out, wordless, and then tried to enter the word itself.

What the Ascendant and the Dragon were allowed, she clearly wasn't. She began to batter the shape with her fists, and someone grabbed her wrist.

It wasn't Severn; Severn's touch, she knew. Severn would never have dragged her away from the word the way she was now dragged. She turned in fury—and fear—and met the eyes of the Arkon. They were orange. Not red. But their edges were gold. She didn't understand, and she hurled short words at him as if he were a stupid, raw recruit—and she were Marcus.

"There is no more you can do, Chosen," he told her, his voice surprisingly gentle, the words—shockingly—in Elantran.

"They'll kill her!"

"They may. They may well kill her. But even if you desired it, they will not kill you; the name is not, and was never meant, to be yours."

"You can see it?"

"No. I cannot see the shape of it at all. It is unfortunate for you that you can." He winced. "If you would stop this senseless struggling, I would be happy to release you."

She stopped instantly. "You're injured."

He raised a brow. "Let me give you a lesson in etiquette that I doubt very much Lord Diarmat—one of the worthiest members of the Court in my opinion—will see the need to teach you; he does not think highly of mortals, but even he cannot always comprehend the extent to which they lack wisdom. When dealing with Immortals it is unwise in the extreme to allude to injuries or infirmities that they themselves refuse to acknowledge."

"I *saw* your wing!"

"Obviously. I, however, have chosen to consider the injury minor. If you attempt to heal it," he added, because she was, in fact, considering it, "I will be forced to discourage you in a more permanent way. Is that understood?"

She nodded and he released her wrist.

"Watch," he told her. "And wait. Waiting is something you will need to learn."

CHAPTER 22

"You *can* see that she's bleeding, right?"

"Yes."

"And you don't think—"

"No, Private, I *do* think. If it were not for the fact that your presence might still be required somehow, I would send you to aid the Avatar."

Kaylin froze.

"She is currently protecting the people who dwelled in the buildings on this street. I think, due to both her presence and her intervention, Tiamaris will lose very few of his citizens to this fight; I cannot be certain."

"And Tiamaris?"

"This is his hoard, as you term it, Private. I do not think he will fall here." He glanced up, as if the struggle in the air was of vastly less relevance than the one on the ground. Kaylin found it easier to watch, possibly because the Dragons were far enough away that she couldn't see the blood, and possibly because even if she could, she knew damn well there was nothing—short of avoiding the random flames—she could do for them.

In spite of the Arkon's words, she didn't have that certainty about Bellusdeo.

"Kaylin."

She closed her eyes. She could still see blood. She could still imagine death.

"We come to our name, or we do not. No one can take our own test of name on our behalf, because the transformation is personal."

"But she's—"

"Yes. What she attempts now is…ambitious. It will either kill her, or she will succeed; she has long been lost to childhood."

"If she dies—"

"Enough, Private. Enough. You cannot comprehend what her survival would mean—both to the Dragon Court and to the race. You therefore cannot comprehend the tragedy of her failure to either. But let me attempt to explain it to you on a more personal level. No matter how much pity you feel for a man, woman, or child, is your pity alone enough to qualify them to work as a Hawk?"

She would have answered, but she'd opened her eyes. What she saw robbed her of words: the runes that had started out so golden were now a pale red. She knew why, and she almost hated them. "Maggaron!"

He knew what she wanted him to do, and shook his head. But mostly? He huddled around Bellusdeo as much as he could, trying to deflect the runes. The runes, Kaylin realized, weren't cutting *him*. Just Bellusdeo. Because it was—if she survived—her name.

The Arkon caught Kaylin by the shoulder; she hadn't even been aware that she'd started to move.

"Chosen," he said, his voice bridging the gap between comfort and command. "None of the wise understand what your marks presage. None. You yourself have little understanding of what they mean or what they can do—but not, as I see, none. What you have done here is what you *could* do. But even the Chosen are bound by natural law and natural rules. In this, you cannot interfere further."

Bellusdeo would die here. She was already injured. She was weakened. This couldn't be the end of the story—it couldn't be. "There should have been *nine* of her," she told the Arkon. His fingers dug in, and she felt the hint of claw. "There's only one—"

"No," he said, shaking her slightly. "There are two." He didn't ask how—or why—Maggaron was with Bellusdeo.

Kaylin opened her mouth—and felt Severn's hand on her other shoulder. "He's right."

She knew it. She hated it. Standing and watching felt too damn much like doing nothing. But, anchored by the Arkon on one side and Severn on the other, she didn't have much choice.

Maggaron held Bellusdeo's life in his hands. Watching his face, it was clear that he held his own in them, as well. The whole of his concern was turned toward her; the shape of the word, the shakiness of its structure, was of far less concern to him than the injuries Bellusdeo was even now sustaining. If all Dragons came to their names this way, it was no bloody wonder they were so cranky so much of the time.

Bellusdeo said something to the Ascendant, because he stiffened, sheltering her—or trying—with the bulk of his shoulders. Her hands were too weak to hold the words she'd dragged in with her, but it didn't matter; they were already enmeshed in the whole. No, that wasn't right. Bellusdeo's word was. Maggaron's, Kaylin could still see as a distinct entity.

He must have seen it, too; he raised his head. Raised it, opened his mouth, shouted something that Kaylin couldn't understand. It was almost—for a moment—as loud as Dragon words; it was, to Kaylin, vastly more significant.

His rune—his simple, elegant rune with its too-straight, thick lines—cracked; the cohesion of the whole shattered. Its parts flew outward, passing through the emerging whole of the other nine, and Kaylin held her breath as she watched. She didn't ask the Arkon or Severn what they could see, but she knew, for just that moment, that they didn't see what she saw.

The lines spread outward, distending and flattening; Kaylin thought, at the speed they were traveling, they would disappear from view. But they shuddered to a halt, and when they did, they hovered above—and below—the forming, nascent name. A foundation and a crown, they pressed inward, holding the shape of the word in much the same way that Maggaron held Bellusdeo. Standing at their center, as if he were integral to their structure, stood the Ascendant. The parts of his scattered word still shed golden light, but they had become shiny and hard, like metal. They began to gleam so brightly it was hard to tell what lay within their bounds; Kaylin was squinting to see.

Severn and the Arkon were not.

She saw the lines of the new word suddenly shudder; she thought they would collapse; they began to fall. They were dark now, distinct; the golden, ethereal quality that had characterized their spoken appearance was gone. More disturbing, they were the color of blood, and had they not retained the shapes of runic elements, she would have mistaken them for exactly that. It was worse than disturbing. She'd seen Red at work for years, huddling on a stool by his tables, handing him the tools he was willing to let her touch with her self-professed Very Clean hands—and she had the stomach for disturbing.

But this?

This now looked like a body might look if it had been skinned alive, and then had most of its trailing bits scattered as far as they could go and still be somehow minimally attached. And alive. Still alive. She dropped instinctively to one knee and she forced herself to keep watching; her eyes were tearing; she was afraid to blink.

Everything she'd seen—everything—about words and runes and marks had been light or shadow; nebulous things. This was visceral. This was—

Oh.

She did look down, then. Not to her own marks, which were now as flat and dark as they always were, but to her hands. She turned them over, examining her palms. She'd helped to deliver dozens of babies, and during those births— always the messy ones, always the difficult ones—there had been blood and water and slimy bits. There'd been fear, too— because sometimes it was just so damn close, the line between life and death so damn thin. There wasn't anything pretty about it at all.

But there *was* something beautiful about it, about the struggle for life, the promise that while death was—for most of the City—inevitable, life continued to offer the fear and hope of its promise.

She began to speak. This time, there was no magic in her words.

"What are you doing?" the Arkon snapped.

She shook her head. "It's just a verse. Like a child's verse. One of the midwives always says it when the birth is difficult."

"It's not Elantran."

"No. It's religious."

"Which would make it pointless."

"Not pointless, no," Kaylin replied. She felt some of the

fear drain out of her. No, not drain, but shift. She looked up again, and this time she was steadier. "Please, let go of me."

"Are you going to try to interfere?"

"No. Not as such."

Severn's hand slid from her shoulder immediately; the Arkon's took a little longer. But she was calmer now; she could wait. When nothing held her back, she walked slowly to where the word in all its visceral glory, hovered. She could touch it now. She could find spaces through which her arms or hands might fit. Why, she wasn't sure—but it didn't matter. It had dwindled in size; Maggaron's protections had not.

She reached out and put her hands on Bellusdeo's forehead, the way she might have had the Dragon been a new mother in her first labor. She brushed matted hair out of the Dragon's widened eyes. She couldn't do more—there wasn't enough space. But she didn't need to. Bellusdeo's eyes met hers; they were a honey-brown—the same color as the eyes of all the corpses in the Tower's morgue.

But they weren't dull or cloudy, and they moved; that was enough.

"You can do this," Kaylin said. She wasn't even certain Bellusdeo would understand what she was saying, but that didn't matter, either; the only thing that did was tone. Hers. She kept her voice as even and soft as she had ever kept it, and she repeated the words over and over again. She didn't have to break for screaming or swearing the way she often did when tending to a woman in labor, and the cadence of her words, if not the meaning, made itself felt.

This close to the Dragon, Kaylin could see the wounds she bore. She wanted to heal them, but as she examined them—at a frustrating distance—she realized that it was the last thing she could try: the wounds themselves were bleeding, but they weren't simple wounds; the parts of the word that were now blood red were tenuously attached to the entry points.

Kaylin couldn't tell if the blood was flowing from the Dragon or to her; at this point, it didn't matter. Bellusdeo, cradled in Maggaron's arms, was struggling; there was no outward sign of that struggle. "You can do this," Kaylin said again, picking up the words and the thought, stroking her forehead as she did.

Bellusdeo's body stiffened suddenly. To Kaylin—not Maggaron—she said distinctly, "I'm scared."

This, too, Kaylin understood. "I know. I know. It's all right to be afraid."

For just a moment longer, the Dragon held herself stiff and taut—and then, of a sudden, she collapsed. It should have frightened Kaylin; it didn't. Before she could so much as check for a pulse, the body began to fade. Maggaron didn't say a word; he held the diminishing weight as carefully and completely as he had held the sword. Kaylin touched his shoulder—or his arm, which is what she could reach—and squeezed. It was a universal gesture of encouragement. She hoped. She felt her arms begin to tingle.

"Watch," she told him.

He was.

The whole of the word was dark and red and wet; it was also warm. The lines peeled away from where they held the Ascendant caged, as if creating a door or a tunnel through which he might escape. When he didn't move, the word did. It extended, at its closest, to an inch from Maggaron's chest. Kaylin could feel its warmth; it was body heat. "Just...watch."

Arms empty, he did.

The word was, as she had said, too complex to memorize, too difficult to speak. But Tiamaris had once told her to look at ancient words for harmony of form, and she knew, looking at this one, that it had achieved that. Everything was now where it should be: everything except Bellusdeo, who had vanished so entirely she might never have been here at all.

Maggaron's eyes were wet and wide; he was silent. His arms were crossed over his chest, as if he was still attempting to hold what was no longer there. But it wasn't over yet. Above their heads, the Dragons were attempting to shred each other's wings, and some of the fallout felt an awful lot like blood. No one, on the other hand, attempted to move. Or speak. It was as if the entire world—or at least the parts of it that were on the ground—was holding its collective breath and had none left with which to make noise.

The flattened golden remnants of the word she had identified as Maggaron's began to bend. They stretched horizontally, expanding above and beneath the massive word until they were so thin they were almost transparent. Kaylin smiled up at the Ascendant as those fine, fine sheets of gold suddenly shifted, wrapping themselves around the word that had finally, fully emerged.

"I don't—I don't understand," he whispered, allowing his arms to drop to his sides, where they trembled visibly.

But Kaylin did.

The gold thickened, tightened, squeezing what had been almost globular into something taller and slimmer; it compressed whatever remained beneath it as it did, refining its shape, its length, adding texture and elongating parts of its form, as if it was a potter working with wet clay. Golden clay.

"Do you recognize the color?" Kaylin asked in the same hushed voice Maggaron had used.

He didn't answer, not even to nod, but his mouth opened on an interrupted word, and stayed there.

It was true: hope could be unkind. You opened yourself up to the worst of wounds because you wanted to believe that something *good* could finally happen. But if you didn't? You missed *this*. This intense and perfect moment in which, while the world was almost literally going to hells all around you, hope and reality blended in a single, perfect note.

The form that emerged now was the large—significantly large—form of a great, golden Dragon, its new wings gleaming, its tail almost disappearing down the street. Its neck was longer and finer than any Dragon neck Kaylin had ever seen— but admittedly, she hadn't been doing a lot of objective observation on those occasions. Its head was higher off the ground than Maggaron's, and its jaws were, at best guess, longer than Kaylin was. Its neck was ridged, its scales were large and perfect, its ears were higher and finer than an angry Leontine's. For a moment it hung, suspended two feet above the mundane ground, and then its wings snapped open, shutting out sky.

It rose on its hind legs and it roared, and even though Kaylin's ears were ringing before the roar died, she was grateful; if it were the last sound she ever heard, she'd still consider herself almost blessed. The noise faded, and the roars that followed were vastly less welcome, if more familiar: three Dragons. Tiamaris, Sanabalis, and the Arkon.

The Outcaste's roar joined theirs, its tenor distinctly different.

But the golden Dragon now swiveled its long neck, turning its head toward Maggaron. Because Kaylin knew a lot of Leontines, she didn't automatically assume a display of fangs was an act of aggression; sometimes, it was a smile. This time, it was almost a purr.

"Maggaron."

He was openmouthed and silent.

"Don't you recognize me?"

When he failed to answer, she pushed him. He fell over. She snickered. It was a much more resonant version of a similar snicker Kaylin had once heard. "Come, Maggaron. You have carried me in safety for years beyond your count; let me carry you. *Come.*"

He levered himself off the ground looking like a much smaller man than eight feet should have allowed.

"Come; we must meet the enemy."

He looked very, very dubious as he attempted to find someplace to sit on her broad and unfortunately spiky back. Kaylin sympathized. She'd ridden on the back of a Dragon before. Maggaron looked as if he'd rather face Shadowstorms. He hesitated.

"Maggaron!"

"Bellusdeo?" he asked in a voice that was so full of fear and hope Kaylin wanted to plug her ears just to give him some privacy.

"Yes. Finally, *yes.*"

"It'd probably help him," Kaylin told the Dragon, "if you let your feet touch the ground before you made him climb up."

She snorted, and flames the color of sunlight raced down streets that had already seen too much fire.

"You remember—you remember everything?" Maggaron finally managed to stutter.

She snorted again. "I do. I remember what you remember. I remember all nine of my lives. I remember the enemy. Come, let us do what we could not do before the cities of the Norannir fell."

He mounted then, finding either his courage or his strength. She bore him up, effortlessly, into the sky's height, her wings so wide they cast a shadow across the entire street in which Kaylin, Severn, and the Arkon were standing.

Kaylin hugged Severn tightly, and then turned to ask the Arkon a question. It would have been a relevant question, too—but the minute she saw his face, it evaporated. His eyes were wide, and they were a gold very similar to the color of Bellusdeo's Dragon form. Kaylin had seen that before—admittedly not very recently—but she had never seen what she saw now: tears. Wide-eyed, lips turned up at the corner in something too tremulous to be called a smile, he let those tears roll unheeded down his cheeks.

Bellusdeo seemed to gain speed as she gained height, at least from the vantage of the ground. Kaylin shaded her eyes just to watch; the golden Dragon was aiming directly for the black one. The fact that Tiamaris also happened to be in the way didn't slow her down at all.

This time, when the Outcaste wheeled in the air, something clipped one wing, and he wobbled in flight, righting himself as he approached ground.

"Severn—"

"Already on it," was the grim reply. The chain began to spin, tracing an arc in the air directly above their heads.

The Arkon roared. Even in his human form, he was loud. The Outcaste saw him; Kaylin was certain of that. But he saw her, as well, and he roared, syllables cresting the sound. She didn't understand the words; it didn't matter. She saw the breadth of his chest expand as he inhaled, and she threw her arms up automatically as he exhaled.

He didn't exhale the fire that seemed to be more common to Dragon breath than air; he exhaled Shadow. The Arkon, however, went the traditional route in response, and his flames were so hot they were hardly red at all. They hit the Shadow-breath that rushed toward ground like smoke with weight, and the Shadow *screamed*. Huge gusts of black, roiling mist became black ash and smoke in an eye-blink.

Some of it escaped the Arkon's fire and continued its downward rush. None of it touched Kaylin; it skittered off the moving, linked wall that rotated above her head. But it landed in the streets, and where it landed, it took root.

Kaylin drew daggers, watching as the Shadows began to coalesce.

But they were coalescing beside a Dragon. If Shadows had any brains, they'd clearly left them in the Dragon's maw. The Arkon didn't have a sword; he didn't need one. Nor, apparently, did he need to be in his Dragon form to use his claws; he certainly didn't need the form to breathe fire. Just incentive. She had no idea what form might have emerged from the Shadows that had managed to survive, because he didn't give them that chance.

Shadow, however, didn't need a cohesive form to speak.

He will kill you for this.

They were talking to Kaylin.

She looked up to where the Outcaste was now fighting on two fronts: a red dragon he had injured and would clearly love to kill, and a golden one. The latter, he evaded, but not easily, and if he had some compunction about harming Bellusdeo, she clearly didn't reciprocate. She did speak—Dragon words—and he responded; his was the louder, clearer voice.

Kaylin had never, ever wanted to learn a language so badly in her life. She turned to the Arkon. "What did she say?"

"She made her displeasure with his existence clear."

"That's it?"

"She made some claims about how she was going to alleviate her displeasure."

"What did he say?"

The Arkon was silent, in part because the Outcaste hadn't finished speaking. Bellusdeo didn't seem intent on giving him the chance, on the other hand; she could move so damn fast she was almost more snake than great-winged creature. Kaylin noted that Tiamaris made no attempt to speak at all; whatever he had to say, he'd already said it.

"Arkon?"

The Arkon's expression slowly lost the radiance of joy and awe that had briefly transformed it; what was left in its wake was an expression meant for graveyards.

He said in very quiet Barrani, "Old friend," and she knew she would never get a translation of what had been said from him.

"Wait, where's Sanabalis?"

"I believe he has landed on the Imperial side of the Ablayne, and is repairing in haste to the Palace."

The Outcaste retreated—and it was a retreat, not a rout. He was strong, that much Kaylin had always understood. Strong enough to withstand two Dragons, and Kaylin privately thought he would have had less difficulty if he'd been intent on injuring both of them.

She was afraid that Bellusdeo would follow him beyond the fief's borders, and it was clearly a fear the Arkon shared—but in the end, she wheeled back to where Tiamaris hovered. Tiamaris himself knew the borders of the fief—even in the air—better than anyone but Tara, and he didn't attempt to leave his own territory.

But he waited until Bellusdeo returned, and followed where she led. She led, of course, straight back to the scorched and scored streets in which she'd left Kaylin. She didn't even have trouble landing, although her expression—all yards of it— implied that the air was most where she wanted to be. Her eyes were red, but the red faded to a dull orange by the time she folded her wings across her back, dislodging her passenger.

She eyed him as he wobbled himself to his feet. "You almost strangled me," she told him, snorting smoke.

"I'm—I'm sorry, Lady—but I—"

She snickered. In a Dragon her size, it sounded all wrong. Maggaron actually reddened, which caused her snicker to deepen. Then she looked down at her very large paws—claws?—and shook her head. Kaylin, who had watched a Dragon transform in close quarters, had enough time to look away before Bellusdeo once again occupied a human-size portion of the street. Without any of the normal, human-size clothing.

This caused the poor Ascendant to redden further and stammer enough that whatever it was he was trying to say couldn't be deciphered. Bellusdeo laughed. Turning to Kaylin, she said, "You see? This is what he's like. He's been like this for centuries now—and it never gets old."

"Lady," he said, looking pained.

"Oh, hush," she replied just before she threw her arms around him. Her eyes were a brilliant, liquid gold. "You did it," she told him as he obligingly bent and lifted her, settling the bulk of her weight on his left shoulder. "You brought me—brought us—home." She glanced up at a sky still occupied by a large, red Dragon. "It seems a bit on the primitive side; it'll take some work."

The Arkon winced, but—to Kaylin's amazement—failed to correct her. This seemed a tad unfair. "Bellusdeo."

She glanced at him from the vantage of the Ascendant's height, and her flawless skin grew momentarily wrinkled around the bridge of her nose. Then her eyes widened, although they remained gold. "Blood of the Ancients—Lannagaros, is that you?" She spoke in slightly accented High Barrani.

Kaylin looked at the Arkon.

The Arkon looked, momentarily, at the ground.

"Lannagaros?" Kaylin asked him.

The Arkon winced. "That is not what I am now called," he told Bellusdeo.

"Oh? What are you now called?"

"The Arkon."

She nearly fell off her seat; her seat caught her. "*You're* the Arkon?"

"That is my title, yes."

"But what happened to—"

"Bellusdeo, I feel this discussion is inappropriate for the venue."

"Oh. How surprising." There was more sarcasm in that voice than Kaylin had ever heard directed *at* the Arkon. She glanced up at the sky again. "Who is that young man, anyway?"

"He is Tiamaris of the Arandel Flight."

Bellusdeo shook her head. "Clearly things have changed since we ran into the Shadowfold. But we're back now. I'm sure it can all be explained." She hesitated and then twisted around on Maggaron's shoulders. "But...all these buildings. Do you keep a lot of humans now?"

Kaylin didn't even bristle.

The Arkon, however, had had enough of this particular conversation, and retreated by bellowing Tiamaris down from his own stretch of sky. It was, of course, in Dragon, and whatever he said was enough to get Tiamaris to land; Tiamaris wasn't notably more flexible than Bellusdeo had been. On the other hand, when he transformed, he made himself some armor.

Bellusdeo, having had enough of mocking her poor Ascendant, now did likewise, and Maggaron put her down.

"You are in the lands of Tiamaris," Tiamaris told her, "and you are both a welcome and honored guest." There might have been a little too much emphasis on the last word; it was hard to tell. "If you would be amenable, we might repair to the Tower."

"The Tower?"

"Yes. It is where your other eight bodies are currently being stored."

She raised a brow, and the teasing smile fell away from her face. "Yes," she told him quietly. "I would be amenable. Perhaps you can tell me what's happened since I last saw this world. Dragons didn't spend all that much time in human cities, here, that I recall."

"This is not entirely a human city," the fieflord replied.

"Oh?"

"It houses many races. The Aerians. The Leontines. The Tha'alani."

"I don't think I know the last one."

"Ah. You will." He offered her an arm and she stared at it. Kaylin had done pretty much the same thing on her visit to the High Halls, and had to stop herself from smiling.

The Arkon, however, did not. He lifted a hand to his brow and massaged it. "Bellusdeo," he said quietly, "much has changed in your absence. There has been war, peace, and war, but those are perhaps not the most significant. While this city is largely populated by mortals, it also houses a number of Barrani Lords."

Her golden brows rose into her hairline.

"The mortals and the Court intermingle from time to time, and certain…forms…are observed. One of them would be the one which is causing you such consternation. For the moment, however, it is not significant."

"Ah. And what is?"

"Your presence here. It will be of significance for all of Dragonkind, whether they wake or sleep." His eyes narrowed.

"And I believe, from your current behavior, that you already suspect this."

Her smile was impish, young, and very, very un-Dragon-like. "Maybe," she said. "Maggaron, come."

He was standing a ways back from Bellusdeo and the two Dragons, his head hanging a little low.

"Honestly, what is it this time?"

"I don't—"

She walked over to him, caught his arm, and almost dragged him off his feet, demonstrating that size and strength in this case didn't match. "I don't have time for your sense of propriety. You're the only person who remembers, and without your intervention, I would never have escaped the enemy. If anyone has a right to be by my side, it's you." She smacked the side of his head, but gently.

He made no further argument, but he did eye both of the Dragons with an expression of pained humility.

Tiamaris led her away, Maggaron in tow, trying at eight feet, or as close as made no difference, to somehow be *smaller* than the two Dragons behind whom he walked. Kaylin turned to Severn, who was quietly tending the burns on one arm. In almost the same tone as Bellusdeo had used, she said, "What are you doing?"

Severn, however, was not Maggaron. He held out his arm, and she took it between both of her palms. In silence, she whispered the marks on her own arms to life, and they glowed gently—and visibly—while she healed the injuries he'd taken. She then looked up to where the Arkon was surprisingly still waiting.

"Arkon?"

"Touch me and I will have your hands removed," he replied.

"It's not that I have anything against your suffering," she

replied, although she stayed clear of his injuries. "But these days, when you're suffering, *I'm* generally suffering, as well. Can I ask a question?"

"Can I prevent it?"

He was in a remarkably good mood, considering the presence of the Outcaste. Good enough that Kaylin took a chance.

"There aren't many other Dragon females around, are there?"

He lifted one brow. "It is not much discussed," he said after a long enough pause she'd almost given up on an answer. "But as it no doubt *will* be, I will tell you. There weren't any, as you have already deduced. There is now one."

Kaylin stared down the street; the lone female Dragon in question was just disappearing around a corner. "And the Outcaste wanted her?"

"She figured prominently in his plans, yes. But as you will also no doubt discover, and in very short time, one doesn't *make* plans that involve someone like Bellusdeo without consulting her first. She was always headstrong."

"What's going to happen to her?" Kaylin asked as she began to walk down the street.

"She will learn about the Empire. I have a few ideas in that general direction," he added with a smile that verged on malicious.

"I mean, in general. In the future."

"Did you not hear me? I said one doesn't make plans for Bellusdeo. If we have hopes, they are unspoken, and they will remain that way. With luck, she will come to understand the whole of our hopes when she understands the situation."

"And if she doesn't?"

"As long as she is alive, Private, *we* have forever."

CHAPTER 23

It should have been over, Kaylin thought as she trudged across the Ablayne—by footbridge—toward her home. She'd taken the time to eat at the Tower, and dearly wished she hadn't, since every single time she'd picked up a utensil of any description—fork, knife, spoon, or glass, which admittedly wasn't a utensil—she'd been offered helpful advice. Tara's. The two Dragon Lords had been notably silent during these helpful rounds of commentary. The food, however, had cooled.

The third Dragon present hadn't bothered with the silence. Because she was a guest, and because she was a Dragon, her constant interruptions—mostly to point out how unnecessary all this so-called etiquette seemed, to her eye—had been both bane and boon. Boon because she could freely say every single word that Kaylin had been thinking; bane because she *did,* absent the cursing, and no one even blinked.

Apparently, Immortal Dragons weren't expected to have the manners that Kaylin was. Even the Ascendant—if that word really applied now—was given a pass; he ate large portions of everything with his bloody fingers. *And* wiped them on the tablecloth. *And* got to burp.

Sanabalis joined them midway through dinner. He was well-dressed, unlike the Arkon, who had resorted to Dragon armor in the absence of his usual librarian robes; while he had, in theory, removed the old ones to preserve them, they hadn't proved immune to fire. On the other hand, about fifteen minutes after Sanabalis's arrival, this was remedied. Kaylin, food practically congealing, was grateful for Sanabalis's presence because it momentarily distracted Tara. Her attention, however, came back.

When it did, Kaylin gritted her teeth and attempted to memorize each and every agonizing detail about the use of a damn fork. Even if she hated it—and she did—she understood that she'd be required to know it. And having Tara's gentle, if pedantic, correction *had* to be better than dealing with Diarmat. Losing teeth was better than dealing with Diarmat.

She surfaced from her lessons—and her cold food, and Tara's concern that the food wasn't to her taste because she'd eaten so little of it, gods having a sense of humor that was black—when she heard the raised voices at the Dragons' end of the table. They were, however, speaking Barrani.

Severn caught her eye before she dumped her knife, fork, and napkin to rise. He shook his head. "Just stick with the dinner," he told her quietly, although his expression had made it perfectly clear.

"I just want to know—"

"They're arguing with Bellusdeo. I'll hazard a guess that you really *don't* want to know."

Tara, however, said, "They're arguing about where she's staying."

Kaylin blinked.

"She has some idea of where she'd like to stay for the next little while, and they don't like it."

A sinking feeling that had very little to do with the excruciating, off-the-cuff dining lessons destroyed what little remained of her appetite. "What do you mean?"

Tara frowned. "I mean—"

"Isn't she staying here?" Kaylin added quickly, hoping to divert a discussion on the literal use of words. For once, she succeeded.

"My Lord offered, but he didn't expect the offer to be accepted," was the Tower's very serious reply.

"Why not?"

"It is his fief. Bellusdeo *can* be a guest here, but…she will be very important to the Empire, or the Emperor."

"You probably can't divide the two," Kaylin pointed out.

"No. Lord Sanabalis has been most clear; the Emperor is grateful for my Lord's offer, but the Emperor considers it unnecessary."

"And that means—"

"It will anger him greatly, yes."

"Fine. I don't see what the problem is. The Palace is a bloody big place; she can probably have whole floors to herself."

Tara nodded again.

"…She doesn't want to stay at the Palace."

"No. I'm not sure why, but she doesn't."

"Didn't she say why?"

"No."

Kaylin gave up on food entirely. "Please don't tell me there's somewhere specific she's decided she'd like to stay."

"Why?"

"Because I have a bad feeling I know where she thinks she's going to stay if she does."

Tara frowned. "She wants to stay with you."

Kaylin dropped her forehead to the dining table. It made a loud thunk, and hurt. Not, on the other hand, as much as the idea of having a guest in her tiny apartment did at the moment. Before Tara could panic—or, worse, ask questions—she lifted her head again. "I live in a one-room apartment. Not a one-bedroom apartment, a *one-room* apartment. Bellusdeo was called the Queen of the bloody Dragons; she's got to be used to better than that."

"She was called—"

"It's emphatic. I know what she was actually called. Or some of it. Look—one room. One small room. No closets. No staff. The place is enough of a mess that *I* find it dangerous to walk across the floor. There's *no security,* and I can bet the Emperor is just going to love that. It's out of the question, Tara."

Tara nodded. "He won't like it."

"I also get mirrored at odd hours of the night and morning. She won't get much in the way of sleep—"

"Dragons don't require sleep."

"*I* require sleep. And *I* won't get much sleep if I know the Emperor is sitting on his throne pissed off at *me* because she's staying at my place."

"I doubt he'll be angry at you, as it won't be your choice."

"You don't know how people in power work. She's not a safe person to be angry at, apparently. He's going to be angry. I'm, in theory, paid by *him,* so guess who that leaves as the target?"

"I doubt the Emperor will show any displeasure at my choice of friends," Bellusdeo said quietly.

Kaylin blinked. The Dragon had joined their conversation from behind, with no warning.

"And before you continue, I *do* understand people in power."

"M-my place is *small,* Bellusdeo. It's cramped. It's messy."

"Then why do you live there?"

"I can't afford anything bigger."

This apparently astonished the Dragon; her eyes rounded. She turned instantly, her slender hands bunched into fists, and stalked back to Tiamaris, Sanabalis, and the Arkon. This was definitively not the result that Kaylin had hoped for. "What is she doing?" Kaylin asked of Tara between clenched teeth.

"She does not feel that you're being accorded enough respect."

Kaylin closed her eyes. Tightly. "Why exactly is she saying that?"

"You're the Chosen. And you're living in...squalor, I think."

"You think?"

"It's not a Barrani word, exactly. The word in Barrani would translate roughly into—"

"Mortal?"

"Yes. But I don't think that's what she meant to say." At any other time, Kaylin would have been proud of the Avatar for making this leap of conversational logic.

"I'm *not* living in squalor." Kaylin stood up and pushed her chair back from the table. It scraped. It scraped loudly. This wasn't enough to cause a pause in the heated conversation at the other end of the table.

"I believe Lord Sanabalis is attempting to convey that to Bellusdeo at the moment."

"He's not succeeding."

"Not in my opinion, no. I believe he is attempting to point out *why* your dwelling is unsuitable."

Because she was contrary, Kaylin found this annoying. It

was one thing for *her* to dump on her own space; it was entirely another for some Court noble to do the same. Dragons grew up in large, unfurnished *caves,* for gods' sake. She walked down to the end of the table that held the annoying conversation. Because she was now there, she could understand every word that was being said.

"No, he's not wrong," she said when Bellusdeo paused for breath. Dragons might not need sleep, but air was helpful. "I live in a small room because that's what I can afford." She longed to slide into Elantran because at the moment, Elantran suited her current mood, and it made information a lot easier to convey. Kaylin couldn't even *remember* the High Barrani word for "job." "Sanabalis, does she understand Elantran?"

"You might ask her that yourself."

"Fine. Bellusdeo, can you understand what I'm saying?"

Bellusdeo listened, thought about it for a few seconds, and then shook her head.

"Well, she's going to have to learn."

"I find it a tedious language; it is even less exact than Barrani," the Arkon helpfully interjected.

"Yes. I'm not saying she has to *speak* it; neither of you usually do. But you both know how. And, more important, you understand it when we lesser mortals are speaking it." She turned back to Bellusdeo. "I'm not unhappy with my living arrangements."

"I see." Bellusdeo folded her arms across her chest in a way that very much implied *she* was. "I will, of course, have to see them for myself."

If Kaylin had been less than happy about the company on her return home, Maggaron was equally unhappy about his lack of the same company, because Bellusdeo—bending slightly to accommodate Kaylin's purported lack of room—had all but ordered him to remain in Tiamaris. She promised to come back and get him should Kaylin's description of her own home be an exaggeration.

Severn had ducked out on them as soon as he crossed the bridge, which Bellusdeo encouraged; this left Kaylin in the company of a Dragon for the long walk home. A walk that didn't normally feel all that long.

"You understand that I don't really require opulence or finery? After all, I was practically born in a cave."

Kaylin laughed. This didn't seem to offend Bellusdeo.

"The cave was preferable to the Shadows," the Dragon added, her voice softening. "I talk a lot, don't I?"

She did. Kaylin decided a curt nod was the safest reply.

"I used to have sisters."

"But they were—"

"We were one, yes. But we weren't. We didn't see the same things, unless we deliberately shared; we didn't experience the same things. Some of us hated foods that the others loved. The dress was Callie's idea."

Callie didn't really sound like much of a Dragon name. Then again, Bellusdeo seemed very much like a person who used diminutives.

"They're gone. Or they're part of me. I don't know which is true. But I don't hear their voices. I can't see the parts of a day I didn't personally experience."

"Not even through Maggaron?"

"Oh, you are observant!" Bellusdeo laughed. In spite of herself and her very real desire for a bit of peace and privacy, Kaylin found herself liking the sound of that laugh. It died when they reached the front doors of the apartment building. "This is really where you live?"

"Every day." She fished a key out of a pocket, which took

time. The door creaked open, and Kaylin held it while Bellusdeo entered. "Up the stairs."

"You really weren't exaggerating."

Kaylin, bent over in a mostly dark room in an attempt to pick up the bits and pieces of stuff on the floor, said nothing. The mirror was flashing, but a quick perusal told her it wasn't an emergency—it was just Marcus and she didn't need to be chewed out in front of a total stranger.

"It's very small. Is it really one room?"

Suppressing the urge to ask her how high she could count, Kaylin grunted a yes.

"Chosen, understand where I spent the better part of centuries living, and you'll understand why I say I don't need much. Here, at least, I can move around. I can lift my arms. I can open the window." She walked across the room, knelt on the bed, and did just that. "There? I couldn't do anything but listen to Maggaron's voice. I couldn't speak to him at all. He had a very, very rough time, but...he survived it. There's something simple about him," she added, but her tone was not unkind. "I think even the Shadow can't corrupt it." Grinning, she added, "I certainly couldn't."

Kaylin didn't know what to make of Bellusdeo. Because she was tired and practical, she said, "The Dragons I know don't eat much normal food. Do you?"

"Define normal."

"It's not moving, it's not breathing, and it probably never was. Bread and cheese. The cheese may be a little bit dry."

"I did eat at the Tower."

"So did I. More or less. I'm going to eat a bit."

"You didn't eat enough?"

"I'd like to eat without the lectures."

Bellusdeo snorted and sat on the bed; she was, no surprise,

heavier than Teela, even if she was shorter. "Why do they lecture you?"

"I'm mortal."

"Are you really?"

Kaylin was silent. Partly because she was chewing, and partly because the question made her uneasy.

"You have a name," the Dragon continued, staring at her in the darkness.

Kaylin glanced at the moon. "Yes," she finally said. "You can see it?"

"No, of course not. But I can sense that it's there. Do you have it because you're Chosen?"

"Indirectly, maybe." She gave up on eating and closed the basket that more or less preserved food. Dusting the crumbs off, she said, "Do you want the bed?"

Since Bellusdeo was more or less on the bed, Kaylin assumed that was her answer, and stumbled across the floor to retrieve blankets. She also pulled the pillow off the bed, because if she was going to take the floor, she deserved some comfort. But as she made space for herself, she remembered the egg under the bed, and set about retrieving it. She hit the slats of the bed's underside at least twice, and cursed liberally.

"What does that mean?" Bellusdeo asked, her voice slightly muffled by mattress.

Kaylin dragged the box out from under the bed and sat up. "You really don't want to know."

"Does that mean you don't know?"

It was Kaylin's turn to snort; she did it with less smoke. "If you use language like that, they're going to know where you learned it. I can't afford that."

"Can't afford?" Bellusdeo's voice was distinctly cooler.

"I serve the Emperor. I get paid to serve the Emperor. I don't serve him directly. I don't know if you're familiar with the concept of policing, but that's what I do." Kaylin began to unwind the wrappings that cushioned the egg, and hopefully kept it warm while she was away. "Because of the marks on my arms and legs, I'm expected to actually meet the Emperor. I've been instructed to take lessons—etiquette lessons—in order to meet him without offending him."

"And he's considered so easily offended that you will face death without these lessons? Does he honestly care how you hold a fork?"

"I haven't had the opportunity to ask. If and when I do meet him, it won't be the first question on the list." She pulled the egg into her lap and curled her arms around it.

"What are you doing?"

There were reasons why Kaylin occasionally valued her privacy. Gritting her teeth, she said, "I'm holding an egg."

"Yes, I can see that. Why?"

"Because I have some hope that one day, if I'm very careful with it, it will hatch."

"May I examine it?"

Kaylin's arms tightened. It was brief, and it was also stupid, but Kaylin had reached the point of stupid-tired.

"Ah. It is yours, then?"

"Humans don't give birth to eggs—" Kaylin stopped speaking, since that's more or less how this egg had come into being. "No."

"I do not believe you understand or interpret the word *yours* correctly in this context."

"I'm mortal. I don't have a hoard."

"No, of course not. But even mortals are possessive."

"I prefer the term *protective*."

"Why?"

"Never mind." She lay down on the slightly warped and creaky floor, and curled around the egg on her side. "I'm not going to be great company tonight. I'm too exhausted. Why don't you get some—"

"Sleep?" Kaylin could hear the Dragon's smile; she couldn't see it.

"Or whatever it is you do when your pet mortals are sleeping."

"Generally, I like to fly. I've been told that flight is off limits, as far as the Emperor is concerned. If you'd like," she added, "you can take the bed."

Kaylin wanted to say yes, but she also didn't want to move. "Sorry," she muttered. "I forgot about the sleeping part when I offered it." Unfortunately, she also forgot about the Elantran part, as well, sliding out of Barrani without thought.

"I am grateful to you, Chosen. I am in your debt. I do not know how much you understand about our kind, but debt is not something we wish to accrue."

It was the last thing Kaylin heard before she slept.

The first thing she heard when morning hit was Bellusdeo's voice. Unfortunately, the second thing she heard was Marcus's. She peeled herself off the floor so quickly she almost knocked the egg flying. She didn't; instead, she picked it up and carried it the few feet to the mirror.

Bellusdeo was standing in front of it, her head tilted to one side; she was staring at a face full of orange-eyed, bristling Leontine. One glance out the window made clear that the morning—or the part in which if she woke quickly she'd make it to the office on time—had passed her by. Part of the reason she hated to have guests at this time of day was the urge to scream, *Why didn't you wake me up?*

It wasn't their responsibility, after all—but it rankled anyway.

In this particular case, it was worse; not only had she not

been woken, but *Bellusdeo* was now chatting with Marcus, and from his expression, he really wasn't appreciating the substitution.

"Bellusdeo," Kaylin hissed from the outer edge of the mirror's view. It was pointless to hope that Marcus couldn't hear her. The Dragon turned her head. Her eyes were a shade of orange that was paler than Marcus's, but not by much.

"Private Neya!"

She cringed her way to where Bellusdeo was standing, in large part because the Dragon occupied most of the mirror's field of view. It was a cheap mirror, relatively speaking, but it was also a popular one *because* it had a limited viewing angle.

"Sergeant Kassan," she said, trying for dignity. Given what she was holding and what she was wearing, it was hard. "This is Bellusdeo."

He growled. "We've established that."

"She's a—a guest of the Dragon Court."

"And the Dragon Court has now moved into your apartment?"

"No, sir."

"Has the Dragon Court changed your schedule?"

"No, sir."

He opened his mouth to bark out another question and then snapped it shut for a few merciful seconds. "What are you holding?"

She glanced down. "An...egg, sir."

"Yes, I can *see* that. What kind of egg?"

"I'm not sure."

"Did it come with your guest?"

"No, sir. I—I picked it up just before the Norannir arrived."

"It's probably rotten, then. Get rid of it, get dressed, and *get your butt into the office.*"

★ ★ ★

Getting dressed took all of two minutes. Packing the egg very carefully back into its nesting crate took ten. Getting Bellusdeo out the door took longer than either. Kaylin had wedged her into some of Kaylin's clothing, and Bellusdeo clearly had ideas about fashion that didn't encompass Kaylin's rather meager wardrobe.

"You didn't eat breakfast."

"Leontines like to remove people's throats when they're pissed off. The Leontine," she added. "Not the people without throats." When Bellusdeo failed to move, Kaylin said, "I need a throat in order to eat. You can stay here if you want; I need to run."

But the Dragon was now staring at the egg that Kaylin had very carefully—if hurriedly—deposited back in its box; she was also frowning. "I didn't care for your Sergeant," she said, not taking her eyes off the egg's shell. "But he didn't seem to care for your egg. Where did you get it?"

"You really need to learn to speak Elantran," Kaylin replied—in Barrani. "It's a long story. Well, if you're mortal. Can we talk about it while we're walking?"

Bellusdeo, even in Kaylin's clothing, turned a lot of heads as they walked the few blocks between home and work. She didn't seem to notice. The merchants along the Ablayne nodded to Kaylin as she passed them; she'd've stopped to introduce the Dragon, but her eye was on the sun's position.

Bellusdeo, however, didn't seem to mind a clipped, fast walk. She didn't seem to notice it, either.

Kaylin climbed the stairs to the Halls' front door. There, she met Clint and Tanner. Clint was grinning. "You're late," he pointed out.

"This," Kaylin said to Bellusdeo, "is Clint. The wingless guy to his left is Tanner. They guard the doors when they're not making fun of me."

"I am pleased to make your acquaintance," Bellusdeo told them.

"This is Bellusdeo. She's a guest of the Dragon Court."

Two Hawks instantly shifted posture. Kaylin snickered.

"Sergeant Kassan is expecting you," Clint told her. "So is Lord Sanabalis."

Getting Bellusdeo from the front doors to the inner office was not a speedy affair. The doors opened into the Aerie, and Bellusdeo's reaction to the Aerie was very similar to Kaylin's. The Dragon's gaze slowly rose to touch the heights, and remained fixed there. The Aerians were drilling, and from the sounds of it, there were new recruits. She watched as they flew, and as they faltered under the weight of unfamiliar armor.

"They're Aerian," Kaylin told her, wishing she'd move, but unable to force the issue. "You didn't see the Aerians before you—"

"No. Where I lived, there weren't any." She was smiling softly. "They're not forbidden flight?"

"No. Only the Dragons."

This caused Bellusdeo to frown. "Why?" The single word was cool. It did, however, take her attention off the heights of the elaborate hall, and Kaylin began to walk, with hope, toward the office.

"I don't know. I'm not the Emperor, and the only way to get an answer to that question would be to ask a Dragon."

"You are clearly acquainted with several."

It was true. "I only know it's illegal for Dragons to transform into their Dragon form within the Empire without the

Emperor's express permission. Tiamaris did it once in the fiefs—which aren't theoretically under Imperial jurisdiction—and he still had to make a complete explanation to the Emperor after the fact."

"He is still alive."

"Yes. The Emperor considered the circumstances extreme enough to justify the transformation. It was not a given," she added, remembering.

"I'm not entirely certain I approve."

Which was, thank the gods, not Kaylin's problem. Kaylin felt, unfairly, that it would be nice to have someone *else* be the problem child for a change. She took a deep breath. "We're coming into the office where I actually have a desk. Sometimes they make me sit at it. The Sergeant is pretty much in command of the office. I like most of my coworkers, and I'd appreciate it if you'd avoid annoying them."

"Why?"

"Because they'll probably make it clear that they *are* annoyed, and at this point, I think the Emperor might disapprove. They don't really deserve to be reduced to ash with no warning."

"You could tell them I'm a Dragon."

"They'd probably think I was making an attempt to be humorous."

"I...will do my best." She hesitated and then said, "Does no one in this City understand the significance of the Chosen?"

"No."

"And you have not—"

"Bellusdeo, *I'm* the Chosen, in theory, and I don't understand the significance, either." She slowed her pace and added, "Maybe I'm being cowardly. Maybe I don't *want* to understand it. I'm trying."

"You have already used the power invested in you."

"Yes. More than once. And I'm fine—with that. But I didn't do it in order to be treated differently. I didn't do it to jump a promotion queue. Not that I'd mind that," she said, because she felt she should be honest. "I did it because at the time it seemed like I either should or could.

"I don't understand what the marks mean. I don't understand why I have them. I know that some of them have disappeared, and some have faded."

"Disappeared?"

Kaylin nodded. "Once, when I told a story to a dead Dragon in the middle of the Arkon's Library. That's not the only time. It was the first."

"And the others?"

"Nothing as clear. The Devourer ate a few of them, though."

Her eyes rounded. "The Devourer."

"Yes."

"I wish you'd mentioned this last night."

"Would you have let me sleep if I had?"

"Of course! After you'd finished explaining it." She was still frowning. "And yesterday?"

"I don't know. I don't have the marks and their placement memorized; since some of them are on my back, I can't. But if I had to guess? I'd say that a comparison of the marks today and the marks before we found you yesterday would show at least one missing."

"Only one?"

"Maggaron's."

"Not the other nine?"

"Maybe. I'll never get to make the comparison if we don't arrive soon."

Because Caitlin's desk was the one closest to the doors—for obvious reasons—Kaylin led Bellusdeo there first. Caitlin had looked up when the two had entered her office. She rose as they approached her desk, and smiled. "You must be Bellusdeo," she said, extending a hand.

"She only speaks Barrani," Kaylin told Caitlin. Caitlin immediately and effortlessly switched languages.

Bellusdeo took her hand. "I am."

"Kaylin doesn't usually bring guests into the office," Caitlin continued. "But I believe you're both expected. Lord Sanabalis has been waiting."

"For how long?" Kaylin asked, trying not to wilt.

"Not more than three hours," was the pleasant reply. No wonder Marcus was in a mood.

"I don't see him."

"He is waiting in the West Room."

"I do not care for your door wards," Bellusdeo said.

Kaylin, who famously disliked them herself, gritted her teeth as door-ward magic shot through her palm, down her arm, and across her spine in one painful, tingling flash. "What don't you like about them?"

"They're not well designed. There's no reason at all why I should have to *touch* them; my approach—or yours—should be more than enough." Although she wasn't that much taller than Kaylin, she could really look down her nose effectively. Kaylin wanted to disagree, but found that she couldn't. She lowered a numb hand as the door slid open.

Sanabalis was seated, as he habitually was, at the head of the table that occupied most of the West Room. There was no candle sitting, unlit, in front of him, which was a distinct improvement.

"Private Neya," he said, inclining his head. His eyes were only a pale orange. "Bellusdeo."

"Lord Sanabalis." She frowned. "Is it possible for us to converse in the language of the Norannir?"

"Not effectively, no."

"Very well." She took a seat.

"You were waiting for me?" Kaylin asked, likewise taking a seat. One farther away from Sanabalis. She suspected that the correct answer was that he'd been waiting for Bellusdeo.

"For three hours, give or take a few minutes." So much for the correct answer. He raised a pale brow. "You are, in theory, still seconded to my service in the fiefs. Given Bellusdeo's presence, and the presence of the Norannir, you may be allowed to return to your normal duties *if* she is willing to intercede on our behalf with the Norannir."

"Intercede in what way?" Bellusdeo asked. It was a perfectly reasonable question.

Sanabalis, however, winced. "It cannot have escaped your attention that you are held in high regard by the Norannir."

"They have not seen me for some time."

"Even so, there must have been paintings, statues, or other artifacts that captured your likeness; they recognized you when an image of you was shown."

Her smile was soft and sweet, and it added years to her face. Not age, but years. "And this presents a problem for your Dragon Court how?"

"The image that was shown to the Norannir was contained in a crystal possessed of other magical properties."

"And?"

"It came, originally, from the Arkon's personal collection. He wants it back."

"And the Norannir are not interested in returning it?"

"They venerate the image; they're not concerned with how that image is conveyed. I understand that they have only myths and legends with which to confront Dragons, as they didn't recognize the Dragon form when they were first exposed to it."

She nodded, her expression grave. "It was the form of our ancient enemy; we did not choose, in the end, to appear as Dragons before the Norannir in order to encourage...caution."

"But they knew what you were."

She nodded.

"And...the ancient enemy?"

"He is not wholly what you—or I—are. He has lived in the heart of the Shadows, and he has been tainted by them. If he is also your enemy, Lord Sanabalis, and you are familiar with his history—"

"The only person who is intimately familiar with his history is the Arkon. He does not speak of it," he added. "Nor will he appreciate the inquiry. He has, at least once, been seen in mortal form—but not by any member of the Dragon Court."

"By whom?"

"The Chosen."

They both fell silent as they considered the ramifications of this statement.

"You may inform the Arkon that I will get his trinket back," Bellusdeo told Sanabalis. "I hardly see that they will need it if I am here in the flesh."

"Thank you." Sanabalis now rose. His chair made a lot more noise. "Private Neya? The Hawklord has requested your presence in the infirmary."

"What—now?"

"Or as soon as possible. He wishes to fully capture the marks on your body as of yesterday's...event, for Records. A copy of the capture will be sent on to the Imperial Palace. I have agreed to this interruption in your schedule. You have enough time remaining to be fully examined before you are required to return to the Palace."

Kaylin tried not to grimace. She knew exactly why a return to the Palace was necessary: she had an etiquette class.

"There is a common mortal phrase," Sanabalis told her as he reached the door.

"Which one?"

"Misery loves company."

She frowned.

The Dragon Lord looked pointedly at Bellusdeo and said, "Private Neya is not the only student Lord Diarmat will have at this evening's lesson."

CHAPTER 24

"The Emperor is only *barely* willing to allow this," Lord Sanabalis said as he examined Bellusdeo's dress. It was a shade of blue that Kaylin found familiar and slightly unsettling because she'd seen it on eight corpses. Bellusdeo, however, had insisted. At the moment, it made Kaylin's arms itch because the color wasn't due to something solid and dependable like an exotic dye; they hadn't the time for it. No, the color was entirely an artifact of magic.

The style of the dress, however, was very much Imperial standard; it was fussy, and it required some help to put on. Kaylin had been relegated to the role of helper, and was clearly not considered competent at the job.

"Barely willing to allow what?" Bellusdeo asked, her voice cool. Her eyes were a shade of amber that was just a trace off its usual gold.

"Your lessons," Sanabalis replied.

"I would be pleased to avoid them entirely," was the Dragon's response.

"You've got that right," Kaylin muttered.

"It is not the lesson itself which is contentious," Sanabalis told Kaylin, his voice sharper; it smoothed out again when he turned to Bellusdeo. "It is the fact that you will have met every member of the Dragon Court before you've been formally introduced to the Emperor."

"Oh?" If possible, Bellusdeo's voice was even chillier.

"That's not true. She hasn't met Emmerian." Seeing the darkening of Sanabalis's eyes, Kaylin hastily added, "Lord Emmerian."

"I fail to see the relevance one way or the other," Bellusdeo told Sanabalis.

Sanabalis said nothing. It took a long time. He finally relented. "The request that you attend these lessons came not from the Emperor, but the Arkon. He seemed to feel you would find them edifying in one manner or another."

"He made the suggestion to the Emperor directly?"

"He made it in the Emperor's presence," was the evasive reply.

"And the Emperor agreed."

"The Emperor made clear that he had some concerns. Nonetheless, the Emperor accepted the Arkon's request. Will you?"

"Have I not already allowed myself to be dressed for the occasion?" was the cool reply. Kaylin wasn't certain if this was a face-saving measure because she wasn't sure what face-saving protocols were required among Dragons with regards to other Dragons; when it came to mortals, Dragons didn't really care all that much.

Kaylin, however, had other concerns. "Sanabalis," she said, voice rising. "The time. The *time*."

Bellusdeo raised a golden brow.

"Lord Diarmat dislikes people who can't be punctual," Kaylin said curtly, by way of explanation.

"Oh?"

"I said *people*. I'm sure Dragons don't count." She headed toward the door. "If you two want to finish your discussion, I'm sure he won't mind. If I stay to listen, he'll bite my head off."

"A moment, Chosen," Bellusdeo said.

Kaylin winced. "Could you call me Private Neya or just Kaylin, instead?" Seeing Bellusdeo's expression, she added, "I mean, in front of Lord Diarmat."

"We shall see," was the noncommittal reply. "Please, lead on. We will follow."

Sanabalis escorted them to the doors with their livid and annoying wards. Framing those doors were the perfect and also annoying Palace Guards. Bellusdeo glanced at both of their chiseled profiles and then said to Kaylin, "Why does everyone equate professionalism with total lack of manners?"

"Lack of manners?"

"Guards like these are all over the Palace halls; not a single one of them has made any attempt to either greet me or respond to my greetings."

"Ah. The men in metal never do; it's not part of their job."

"Their job is to be silent and unapproachable?"

"More or less. You didn't have guards?"

"I frequently had several. They were, however, competent enough that they could both speak and work at the same time."

The Imperial Palace Guard was good; neither of the two so much as blinked. Kaylin knew that the Hawks would have. She glanced at Bellusdeo, who seemed genuinely irritated by their presence, and felt a stab of sympathy and *very* grudging respect for these guards.

Bellusdeo stared at the closed doors. Kaylin, grimacing, lifted her left hand, but Bellusdeo caught it and forced it back down. She glanced at Sanabalis, who lifted a brow in silence.

"Visual identification of the type you've requested," he told her, lifting his hand at her silent command, "is not as secure as touch."

"And your mortals are now so fractious that such security is required?"

"It is not, of course, the mortals that are feared." He frowned as he placed his palm firmly against the two door wards in quick succession. "Or rather, not most of the mortals. Some—as you are no doubt well aware—are quite capable of complex and powerful magics."

"My point still stands."

"It does. Consider, however, the existence—the *peaceful* existence—of the Barrani within the City, several of whom are Arcanists, and none of whom are Imperial mages."

Bellusdeo looked to Kaylin. "What is the difference?"

"An Arcanist is part of the Arcanum. The Arcanum predates the founding of the Empire. For reasons that make no sense at all, it's still allowed to exist; in theory, its members follow the Emperor's Laws, but they owe nothing else to the Emperor. The Imperial Order of Mages are what the name implies: they're beholden to the Emperor, and they pretty much work under his command."

"I...see." She glanced down the perfectly decorated and lit halls, and added, "I suppose the City *is* still standing, so I can't condemn it as entirely unwise."

The doors rolled open.

If Bellusdeo had ever spent time in a normal classroom it didn't show; she didn't even blink at the layout of Diarmat's grand function room. She did not, however, enter the room, leaving Kaylin to cross the threshold on her own. She did, and saw that Lord Diarmat was seated behind his very uncluttered desk, his hands folded on its gleaming surface in a steeple.

He looked up at Kaylin as she entered. Even at this distance, she could see that his eyes were well into orange territory. "You are late, Private."

Kaylin was certain she'd woken screaming from nightmares that had been more fun than this. She opened her mouth to speak and snapped it shut; Diarmat was famous for considering any attempt at making an excuse an additional crime.

He raised a brow at her silence, and then, to her surprise, nodded and rose. "You are not on duty at the moment."

"Sir?"

"You are not to wear your uniform to these classes while they occur outside your duty schedule."

What am I supposed to wear, then? she thought. The answer, which was no answer at all, slowly sunk claws into those thoughts. She had no idea what Diarmat would consider appropriate clothing for civilian classes with a Dragon Lord in off-duty hours. Showing more wisdom than utter panic usually allowed, she said, "Yes, sir."

"Given the hour, I will refrain from sending you home to change. I expect, however, that you will be here—appropriately attired—two days hence."

"What," Bellusdeo asked, "would be considered appropriate attire for these lessons?"

Lord Diarmat looked toward the door, which now contained Bellusdeo in full Imperial Court dress. Her eyes were half closed, but the half that Kaylin could see—obscured by inner membrane—was not that far off Diarmat's orange. The hair on the back of Kaylin's neck began to rise—and not because there was magic in the air.

Sanabalis was standing behind Bellusdeo—in part because she was blocking the doors—in silence. Kaylin couldn't see enough of him from her vantage to see the color of his eyes, but at this point, it didn't matter; of the Dragon Court, Sanabalis was the least temperamental, and any trouble here wasn't going to come from him.

Kaylin cleared her throat, which got her the immediate attention of two annoyed Dragons. "Lord Diarmat," she said, "may I introduce Bellusdeo?" Before he could answer, she turned to Bellusdeo. "Bellusdeo, this is Lord Diarmat of the Imperial Dragon Court."

"So I gathered," Bellusdeo replied. It had never occurred to Kaylin to wonder how the Norannir introduced each other. Regardless, she felt that Bellusdeo's cool reply would still not have qualified as polite.

Lord Diarmat had gathered enough of his temper to say, "My apologies, Bellusdeo. I am currently occupied with a prior responsibility. If I may request that you return at a later time or a later date?"

"You may," was her quiet reply. "Kaylin, come."

Kaylin very much did not want to be the rope with which two Dragons played tug-of-war.

Diarmat's eyes narrowed. "My responsibility," he told Bellusdeo in a much cooler voice, "is the schooling of the Private. She is therefore also occupied."

Sanabalis now cleared his throat. "Lord Diarmat."

"Lord Sanabalis."

"The Emperor has requested that you make room in your teaching schedule for a second student." He waited while the import of the words sunk in; give Diarmat credit, it didn't take long.

"I beg your pardon?" he said in very crisp, very pointed High Barrani.

"I am to be the second student in these lessons of yours," Bellusdeo told him. "The customs of the Emperor's Dragon Court differ greatly—or so I am told—from the customs of the Aerie in which I last lived while in these lands."

There was a much longer pause from Diarmat. Bellusdeo smiled into it, looking very much like Teela in one of those moods, but shorter, and with golden hair. He finally said, "I do not believe that will be possible."

"Oh?"

"What you are required to learn of the etiquette and customs of the Imperial Dragon Court is very much racially dependent. As is what Private Neya is required to learn. Since she is mortal and you are not—"

Bellusdeo lifted a hand and swatted the rest of the sentence away. "I would be very interested in the customs of the Court in either case."

"In your...lands...were mortals accorded the same rights and status as your own people?"

"No."

"Then—"

"But I was familiar with both sets of rules." She smiled briefly and added, "I had some hand in forming them. Your Private would have skirted the boundaries between them," she added.

"I see. Personal favoritism—"

"Not for that reason, although I will state clearly and unequivocally that I am both fond of the Private and in her debt." Bellusdeo finally said, "May I enter?"

Lord Diarmat nodded curtly, and Bellusdeo stepped across the doorjamb and into the room, where her skirts trailed across the surface of the dark carpet. She came to stand beside Kaylin. "She is Chosen," she told Lord Diarmat curtly. "And in my lands, the Chosen were accorded a great deal of respect."

"She is mortal," he countered. "And the respect she is accorded is a respect she will earn, to her benefit or detriment. How you choose to treat her is of little relevance to either the Imperial Court or these classes, as your respect does not determine or define *either*. I will attempt not to belabor the obvious," he added. "But *these* lands are currently habitable. Your lands, if I am not mistaken, are not."

"Through no fault of her own," Kaylin said.

Lord Diarmat chose, for the first time, to utterly ignore her impertinence. He had fixed Bellusdeo with a look more appropriate to a late Private than a Dragon Queen, and he clearly did not intend to break it for something trivial.

"You are not mistaken," Bellusdeo finally replied. Her eyes were a darker shade of orange, but they hadn't shaded to red. "However, if your Emperor had kept his Flight in check, the Outcaste from *your* Court would never have been free to wage his war against the outlands. If I have failed my people, your part in that failure is large."

Kaylin looked to Sanabalis for support; Sanabalis, however, was watching Diarmat.

Diarmat roared.

Kaylin—who was not, and would never be, Imperial Palace Guard material—flinched and took a step back. Sanabalis had entered the room, and he placed one hand on her shoulder.

"Cover your ears," he told her curtly—and loudly. She took it as permission and did exactly that as Bellusdeo replied. Her roar was as loud as Diarmat's, and it lasted longer, broken by syllables in the same way storms are broken by thunder and lightning.

Sanabalis dragged Kaylin to the door and pulled her out of the room. He then spoke one very loud word at the doors, and they slammed shut.

★ ★ ★

When the ringing in her ears had subsided enough that she could hear relatively normal speech, Sanabalis said, "They will converse for some small time yet."

She could hear them "conversing," as he called it. But it was far more muffled than it should have been, given their proximity. "The doors are—"

"Yes. They are magicked. They are not heavily enough magicked, apparently, for the intensity of the conversation now occurring. If it helps, I did tell the Arkon that I thought this singularly unwise."

"What are they saying?"

"They are exchanging insults; they have not yet descended to the level of challenge."

"Will they?"

"We will have to hope not. Lord Diarmat, of the Court, is the least likely to bend to Bellusdeo's whim. Her importance to the race will not sway him one way or the other, and he will be far less amused by her general behavior than the Arkon."

The Arkon hadn't seemed entirely amused by it, but Kaylin didn't point this out.

"They are both, at base, correct in their accusations, which *will* help her. It will help you in future if you can convince her—by whatever means necessary—that your status in her lands is entirely irrelevant here."

"Tried that."

"Try harder."

"Easy for you to say. In case it escaped your notice, *she's* a Dragon."

"Believe that at this point," he said, wincing at whatever it was Diarmat had just roared, "I am unlikely to forget that fact."

Kaylin nodded as the roaring continued. After a few frustrating minutes in which she cursed her lack of linguistic knowledge, she said, "There's a bright side to this."

"Please enlighten me, as I am having minor difficulty seeing it for myself."

"Whatever she's shouting at Diarmat now is something she's far less likely to shout at the Emperor when they finally meet."

He started to speak, stopped, and then laughed. The laughter was loud enough to hint at a roar. When it subsided, his eyes were a lambent gold. "You still have the capacity to surprise me, Kaylin. Yes, you are correct. She will rage at Diarmat; Diarmat will rage back. There will be relatively little bloodshed because she can afford to offend Diarmat."

"And the Emperor?"

He was silent for a moment, considering the question. When he answered, he was more sober. "I cannot predict what the outcome would be. She *is* important, and I believe she is fully aware of her import. But the Emperor is the Emperor; no Dragon who was unwilling to accept his rule or his Law is now awake—or alive. We have lived that way for centuries, and it is clear that we can continue to do so for centuries yet, regardless of whether or not there are hatchlings."

"She isn't an idiot," Kaylin told him, trying to speak quietly. The guards were still outside the door, and could no doubt hear every word—without reacting to any of them. "She preserved her people for as long as she could—and she gave up almost everything she was to continue to do so. They're here because she fought so long."

He nodded, his fingers straightening the tapering edges of his beard. "It is easy to forget that fact," he finally said, "when confronted with her general behavior; she is not possessed of an obvious gravitas." He cringed.

"What did she just say?"

"Lord Diarmat made clear that her value—in his view—is high, but it is not paramount."

"That wasn't Diarmat just now."

"No. Bellusdeo replied that it is due to the abject failure of the Flights to protect the Matriarchs that she is so incredibly valuable to the Emperor."

"Those Flights would be yours?"

"Yes."

"You're *sure* they're not going to descend to challenges?"

"I am certain Diarmat will not. Dragons very, very seldom fight each other in their mortal guises." And the Emperor wasn't likely to grant permission—or absolution—for this particular fight. "Have you eaten?"

Kaylin stared at him.

"Given the tenor of the conversation, it is unlikely to end within the next half hour. I would dismiss you, but if it does end and you are absent, Lord Diarmat is unlikely to be forgiving."

She glanced at the guards. "No," she told him. "I haven't eaten much."

"I will arrange for food; join me in my rooms."

"Bellusdeo," Sanabalis said, "does present a bit of a difficult situation for the Dragon Court. In particular for Lord Diarmat, the staunchest traditionalist."

"He trains humans as guards; he doesn't eat them. How traditional can he be?"

Sanabalis coughed politely. "He holds the Emperor in the highest respect or he would not now be a member of the Court. It is his fear—and it is not entirely unjustified—that Bellusdeo will not likewise hold the Emperor in the same esteem."

Kaylin begrudged conceding any points to Diarmat, and was silent.

Sanabalis watched her eat for a few moments, his fingers still tracing the lines of his beard.

"Was it the Arkon's idea to delay her introduction to the Emperor?"

"Yes. The Emperor is anxious to meet with her, but understands the Arkon's concerns."

"Are they a lot different from your concerns about his meeting me?"

"As you surmise, they are not—although the results of a disastrous introduction are unlikely to result in *her* death." He steepled fingers under his chin. "She has spoken very little about her past, and her past may be of consequence to her present and her future."

Kaylin, who had a Hawk's intuition in a pinch, suddenly didn't like where this was going.

"She appears to be, in some ways, very similar to you, Private Neya. She is both irreverent, short-tempered, and quick to speak her mind. She is clearly accustomed to privation, but just as clearly accustomed to the accoutrements of power; she expects her opinions to be respected."

Kaylin raised a hand; Sanabalis raised a brow. "I'm not accustomed to power," she pointed out.

He glanced pointedly at her arms. "You can save a life that is beyond any other aid at the touch of a hand and your whim."

"But—"

"Power takes and wears many guises; not all of them are obvious or public." He rose and headed toward the window; the streets were silver-gray under night-lights, as were the Halls of Law beyond the glass. "Records," he said in quiet Barrani.

The windows stopped showing the outside world as they gradually lost their transparency. "Bellusdeo."

She appeared across the central panes of the threefold window, larger than life. To her left, she also appeared—but in Dragon form, an almost brilliant, glowing gold. To her right, in shadow, the obsidian form of the Outcaste emerged. Kaylin sucked in one sharp breath and held it.

"You played a part in her survival. The Arkon witnessed. What he witnessed, he did not choose to convey to our Records, and that is unusual."

"The Emperor didn't demand it?"

"No. Were it necessary—and in the future it might be—he would have. Understand, Kaylin, that power necessitates the choosing of one's battles, no matter what rank one has attained." The images at his back, he turned. "Will she join the Court?"

"She's a Dragon; does she have any choice?"

"According to the Arkon, she must be given that choice. He feels confident that in the end, she will make it."

"Then why are you asking me?"

"Because she is young, Private."

"She's older than Tiamaris, at the very least. If what she said is true, she was born when the Arkon was young—"

"She was. But she has lived a half-life; if events of yesterday are as we understand them, she can only *now* be considered adult. She had a name, according to the Arkon; it was *not* a name meant for Dragons, but in some fashion it sustained her. Do you understand how, or why?"

"No."

"No more does the Arkon or the Court. It is…troubling."

"You're afraid of what it's done to her."

He raised a brow. "And yet you were considered a poor student. Yes, Private. We are."

"Sanabalis—what do you expect *me* to do about it?"

"I? I expect nothing. But what you did do allowed her to return to us—as an adult, as a Dragon. She is attached to you, possibly because of your intervention. She is—in the end—not unlike you. You can be ordered to certain action; so, in spite of her reservations, can she. But you cannot be ordered to *any* action; you cannot be controlled by *any* whim. You privilege your own opinions over the opinions of those who are older and, in theory, more experienced, sometimes to your benefit and sometimes to your detriment.

"But you surprise us, Private. If we are not always in agreement about your methods or your presentation, we at least find your goals acceptable. We are not entirely certain what Bellusdeo's goals are, and in Bellusdeo's case—"

"She's significant enough that it's important?"

His eyes narrowed, but his inner membranes lowered. He turned back to the windows that had become, for a moment, mirrors. "She is a Dragon," he finally said.

Kaylin, used to this, was not offended. She stopped to think about this, because had Diarmat said it, she would have been. "I think," she told him, pushing the momentary discomfort away, "you can trust her."

"And in spite of our many reservations about you, Private, your opinion in this case is of some value." His hands slid together behind his back. "I do not believe she intends to leave your abode in the near future."

Grimacing, Kaylin said, "And if you can't stop her from screaming at Diarmat, you probably can't make her move."

"The Emperor is willing to grant you a living allowance that would give you both more room and possibly more privacy. I am not entirely certain that the privacy is necessary."

"That's because you're not living with someone under your armpit!"

The images vanished; the night sky and the Halls of Law returned.

"He expects, however, that you will monitor the situation. Should things become dangerous, you are expected to make a report."

"To?"

"Me."

She nodded. Her impulse—to tell the Emperor to shove his living allowance—clashed with her desire for at least a room of her own as a retreat. "Can I get back to you about the living allowance?"

"Of course. It is now on the table; it will not be withdrawn."

"What happens when she decides to move out? If I move someplace bigger I won't be able to afford it without—"

Sanabalis lifted a hand. "The Emperor would be pleased to buy a suitable location. He would be pleased to cede one of the main freeholds within Elantra to you, personally. Before you refuse, think about it."

"I'll try. I don't want to live in the Emperor's space. I want it to be—"

"Yours? You are renting space now that could easily vanish because in the end, you don't own it; how is it different?"

"I don't care if I piss off a landlord. I'll have to care if the landlord is the Emperor."

"Fair enough. I believe," he added, "that the hostilities have ceased for the moment."

As far as actual lessons went, it was painless—for Kaylin. The discussion to which she was thankfully not a party had taken most of the time allotted for the class itself; Lord Diarmat therefore summoned Kaylin into the room for a quarter of an hour, to listen to a lecture about the Dragon Court.

In his fifteen minutes, he reiterated the known laws governing Dragon form within the Empire. He made it clear in six different ways that flight, requiring as it did the Draconic form, was also illegal; that the speaking of native Dragon was "highly discouraged" in areas that were not the Imperial Palace; that mortals were neither the equivalent of cattle—which Kaylin assumed meant food—nor pets. Nor were they to be enslaved or otherwise compelled by magical power or greater force to act against their will.

Kaylin was, of course, familiar with most of this, but was *also* aware that it was highly theoretical. Laws of this nature had to be enforceable, and as far as she could tell, the *only* people who could enforce it with any chance of survival were the other Dragons. The Halls of Law certainly couldn't do more than ask—politely.

This would have been true of Barrani crimes, as well, albeit to a slightly lesser extent—but the Hawks had a dozen Barrani, and if Barrani were suspected of crimes, it was those Hawks that were sent to deal with them.

Tiamaris had served—briefly—as a Hawk, but Kaylin doubted he could have been deployed against a rogue Bellusdeo even when he hadn't been the lord of a fief.

"How, then," Bellusdeo asked, her voice chilly, her eyes burning, "does one become a member of the Dragon Court?"

"Before your arrival? By being a Dragon. We swear allegiance to the Emperor."

"And if we do not choose to do so?"

"Sleep," he replied. "Or death."

She was silent for a beat, and then said, "Does he hold your names?"

Kaylin almost forgot to breathe. It was a question she would never have dared to ask—if it had even occurred to her to ask it.

Lord Diarmat was annoyed—but it was hard to tell if it was because of the question; he always looked annoyed. Granted, his eyes were a dark shade of orange, but they'd been that way since he'd allowed her to return to the classroom. "No," he told her curtly. "We are not his slaves and we are not his possessions."

"But the Empire is his hoard."

"Yes."

"And everything in the Empire is therefore part of his hoard."

"In a broad sense, yes. He is not a fool, Bellusdeo; his use of law in this case is subtle."

She nodded. "And if I choose not to take this oath of allegiance?"

"You will not be accorded either the rights or the privileges due a member of the Imperial Court."

"Nor will I have the responsibilities."

"Indeed."

"Will I be considered a citizen of the Empire if I elect not to join the Court?"

"Yes."

"And if I choose not to remain in the Empire?"

"You will be a visitor or a guest, Bellusdeo, but you will still be required to follow all of the Emperor's Laws while you live within the boundaries of the Empire."

"Very well." Bellusdeo rose.

"The next class will be two days hence."

"I look forward to it."

EPILOGUE

Sanabalis was waiting for them in the hall; he escorted Bellus-deo back to the rooms she had used for changing, and returned her clothing—which was mostly Kaylin's old clothing—to her. He did, however, also tell her to keep the dress.

Bellusdeo was silent throughout most of this, which was awkward; she took the dress—which was now a serviceable and very pretty emerald hue—and bundled it up as if it were an old blanket. Sanabalis, however, took this silence in stride. He escorted both Hawk and Dragon toward the front doors, and since this took time, he once again offered Bellusdeo what he knew she wouldn't accept: rooms within the Palace itself.

"You will remain with the Private?" he asked when she demurred.

"If that is acceptable to the Private, yes." The answer was subdued and quiet. Her eyes were no longer an incendiary orange, but they weren't gold, either; they looked like flat-tened, scarred brass.

"Of course it is," Kaylin said, meaning it. Meaning it and knowing she'd probably regret it bitterly in the morning.

Sanabalis offered them the use of a carriage. Bellusdeo preferred, she said, to walk. Since walking was half of what Kaylin did during a normal day, she had no complaints, and since she didn't really like the insides of a carriage—although admittedly, if she had to be *in* one, Imperial Carriages were always the best—she was happy to lead Bellusdeo back to the one-room apartment she called home.

The moons weren't full, but they were still bright; the Ablayne was loud.

"Bellusdeo—"

"I'm sorry," the Dragon said softly, staring at the Ablayne as it moved slowly across either bank.

"For what?"

"Everything, Chosen." She began to walk along the banks of the Ablayne itself, and Kaylin joined her. The banks of the river could occasionally house criminals—usually petty drug dealers with delusions of future survival—but she had no doubt at all that Bellusdeo was perfectly capable of dispatching them. "I am grateful not to be dead," she finally said.

Kaylin saw where she was walking: toward a bridge. It was the bridge that led to Tiamaris. "But?"

"It is so crowded here. It is crowded, it smells strange, the people speak a language I don't understand. I haven't lived in my home for *so* long, I thought—" She broke off, crouched, and slid the hand that wasn't holding a rumpled bundle of silk into the water.

"Nothing is ever home right away," Kaylin told her quietly, meaning it. "Come on. Let's go to Tiamaris."

Bellusdeo hesitated, although it was she who had led them, meandering, toward the bridge. "The Outcaste," she said when she finally rose.

Kaylin stiffened but waited.

"He gave me both form and name. He made me almost adult."

"He murdered twelve children when I was twelve in order to enslave me." Kaylin was surprised at the bitter anger that slipped out with the words. "And he broke my arm the second time we met. I don't like him," she added.

"I don't believe he cares for you, either," the Dragon replied with a smile. "But I—" She fell silent again.

Kaylin couldn't guess at what she wanted to say, and didn't try. For once, she was content to walk and wait. And they did walk, although they didn't walk quickly. "There are Ferals here," she told Bellusdeo when they'd cleared the bridge.

"Ferals?"

"They come from the Shadows, but only at night. I don't think they're going to cause you much trouble."

"No, not much." She fell silent again as they walked the streets. In the glow of moonlight, without the lamps that defined most of the rest of the nighttime city, the struts and beams of buildings that were slowly being reconstructed looked skeletal, and to Kaylin, beautiful. "I don't think I was ever meant to leave the Shadows."

"But you did."

"Yes. Because of my Ascendant. I escaped. Do you understand what the Outcaste wanted of me?"

"No. I can guess."

"Can you?"

"Children."

"Yes. That. Children. Hatchlings. Nameless hatchlings," she added softly. "When I…was lost…there were others. Females, among my kin, are always rare. But I was not the *only* one."

"What did he want them *for*?"

"It was never discussed. But what he made of me, he might

have made of hatchlings: half-named, shadowed, never quite independent." She glanced at Kaylin. "We do not feel, about our young, the way you do, the way I saw you care for that egg. It is not in us."

"Then you—"

"It was not for the sake of the hatchlings—all theoretical—that I loathed and despised what he desired. He wanted to *own* me. He wanted to name me because he could then own me. I have escaped that fate," she said again. "And yet, I am now here. In an Empire, not an Aerie. In a world without Mothers. I have no sisters. I have no city and no lands of my own; I have no Ascendants, and no way to create them.

"I have no crown, and I have no throne; I have no windows into other worlds and no way of touching the knowledge I once touched while the world crumbled around me."

"You have Maggaron," Kaylin said quietly, remembering, with clarity, the night she had run into the fief of Barren. She had lost her home. She had lost her family. She had lost everything she had ever known about her life.

"Yes," was the soft reply. "I do. But can he stand against an Emperor?"

Kaylin's brows rose into her hairline. "I don't think that's going to be necessary."

"No? What do you think the Emperor wants of me?"

"...Children."

"Yes. Children. How far do you think I will fly—if I fly at all—as the only Dragon alive who can bear eggs?"

"I—Bellusdeo, I've never met the Emperor. I honestly can't say."

"You're being deliberately evasive."

She was. She turned down Avatar Road, familiar even in the nightscape, pausing only to listen for the baying of Ferals.

If they were there at all, they were too distant. "How did you meet the Norannir?"

"How?"

Kaylin nodded.

"An odd question. I met the Norannir when I first emerged from the Shadowfold, Chosen. They were…a strange people to me at the time. Not Barrani, not human, not Leontine. They were tall, and loud, but they were not then as you see them now. They lived in cities much like yours; they were learned and patient. They taught me to speak their tongue. I could not teach them to speak mine, and although Barrani is a language I understood, I did not speak it often. Not then.

"There were no Dragons in the Norannir lands, save those that traveled through the storm."

"How did you come to rule them, then?"

"There were no Immortals in Norannir lands, either. If you mean did I conquer, did I subjugate? The answer is both yes and no. If they were not then what they are now, they were *always* capable of war. They merely fought among themselves with no clear victor to unite them."

"You became that victor."

Bellusdeo inclined her head.

"Why?"

"Because the people who rescued me—if indeed that is the correct word—and taught me gave me both a home and hope that someday I might return to my Aerie. They opened the doors of the greatest library I have ever seen for my use. They did not deny me what they might have, had they been less generous. When they were attacked, I joined in the defense of their lands—because their lands had become my home."

"And they became your people."

Bellusdeo was silent for half a block. "Yes," she finally said.

"My people." She glanced at Kaylin and then asked, "How did the Emperor become your Emperor?"

"He's a Dragon?"

"That is hardly an answer."

"I'm not exactly sure. I mean, I know how he became *my* Emperor, personally; I crossed the bridge over the Ablayne. But I don't know how he became *our* Emperor. In part, it was because of the war with the Barrani—the three wars? Four? But I'm not sure how mortals fit in with that. Probably by dying a lot."

"It is the only thing that gives me hope."

"Hope?"

"The Outcaste would have been Emperor, could he; he could not rule as your Emperor does. You, Chosen—you serve your Emperor's whim and his will, but you serve it as if it were your own. You make choices and decisions in the spur of the moment without his knowledge or his permission. You have your laws, and you serve a force created to enforce and uphold those laws—laws created, in the end, by a Dragon. You are Chosen, but you remain in obscurity in the life of your choice; you do not use the power you've been granted at his whim.

"I am sure that if the Outcaste ruled, there would be no such freedom. I am certain that if he ruled the Empire, there would be far fewer mortals living in it in the end; he would feed them to the Shadows."

"They're not the same—"

"No, I know. But what I fear is what I fear. I do not want—not yet—what the Dragons want of me. I can't."

"Ever?"

"I will not say I will never want it; never is a very long time." She glanced at the moons in silence. "I do not want to meet your Emperor."

"Neither do I."

Bellusdeo raised a brow, and then smiled and shook her head. "I will meet him, of course. I will meet him, and regardless of what I see when I do, I will accept that he is your Emperor. I will not endanger myself and I will not embarrass you."

"You don't have to, trust me. There's nothing you could do to embarrass me that I couldn't do faster—or better."

Bellusdeo laughed. It was, for a moment, the only sound in the quiet of the fief's night, and it was warmer and deeper than the lingering night chill. When her laughter faded, she glanced at Kaylin. "I was not like this before. I thought that the Shadows had not touched me." She lowered her head a moment.

Kaylin understood this, as well. "It seems so unfair," she finally said.

"Life is unfair. Which part of it pains you?"

"We suffer, and it breaks something. When we win free— by gaining our name, by crossing a bloody bridge—we still live in a cage of scars. If life were fair, we would never have suffered what we suffered at all; having suffered it and survived, we're still reacting to things that don't exist anymore."

"But they did."

"Yes. I hate that they still define me." Voice lower, she said to Bellusdeo, "I want that to change. I don't know *how* to change it. But I'm willing to spend the rest of my life trying." Shaking her head, she forced herself to smile; it was surprisingly easy. There was something about Bellusdeo that she liked. "Home is a strange thing."

"What do you mean?"

"We lose it, and we think it's gone forever. That's how I felt the first time I lost mine. It took me years to understand that I could find—and make—another. I couldn't do it on my own,

though; I don't think—for me—home exists in isolation." Her
smile deepened as she shook her head. "Come on."

The Dragon frowned. "Where are we going? The Tower
is just over there."

"Not to the Tower," Kaylin replied. "We're just passing by
it so you can pick up Maggaron if you want to see him."

Bellusdeo confirmed at least one suspicion that Kaylin held:
Maggaron came bounding out of the Tower almost before the
doors had fully opened. Kaylin sincerely hoped his very heavy
feet weren't actually trodding on the carrots that had been
planted in places where most rich people planted grass; Morse
would spit him, even given the difference in their height and
weight, because Maggaron would fight *cleanly*. Morse fought
to win, always.

Bellusdeo laughed at the expression on his face as he approached, and even given what the moons' light did to the
color of his face, Kaylin could tell that he was blushing. "What
Kaylin said was deplorably, absolutely true: she lives in a single
room. I don't think you could walk through the door without
bending."

"Have you come to stay in the fief, Lady?"

"I think, for the moment, you must call me by name. And
no, not yet."

"The Dragons—"

"I have only met one more," she replied.

Maggaron stilled.

"...And I have no desire to lose you in a pointless fight, so,
please, do not even think it. How was your day?"

"It was long," he replied, extending his hands. Bellusdeo
could see much better in the dark than Kaylin could.

"They had you digging?"

"Yes, Lady."

"Maggaron—"

"I will call you by your name in the presence of strangers. The Avatar felt that I was restless, and she asked me to aid her in her garden."

"I...see."

"I did not mind. There is much work to do in the lands Lord Tiamaris rules." He hesitated and then said, "Could you not dwell here until you have made your decision?"

Kaylin frowned. "Maggaron—you learned to speak Barrani?"

"Pardon?"

"He is speaking the tongue of the People," Bellusdeo told her.

"But—but I understand what he's saying."

"Do you hear it as Barrani?"

Kaylin nodded.

"You held his name, Chosen. You touched what he was."

"He doesn't *have* a name anymore."

"Perhaps not. Perhaps," Bellusdeo said softly, "he is part of mine. I cannot tell; I feel him as part of me now. But it is not surprising that you understand him."

"Where are you going, Lady?"

"I am not certain. At the moment, I am following the Chosen."

Maggaron hesitated, and then said, "She is walking behind you."

"Time-honored tradition," Kaylin told him. "Following from in front." She paused; in the distance she could hear the howl of Ferals. "This way," she told her companions.

She led them down streets she knew well by daylight; night changed them, but not enough to make them foreign. She hadn't often walked in Barren at night; she hadn't walked in

Nightshade at night much, either. Maggaron was unarmed, but Bellusdeo, by her very nature, was not; Kaylin wasn't worried. The streets, however, were empty. If Tiamaris—with Morse—was on patrol, he patrolled at a distance; she could neither see nor hear him. She did watch, hoping to catch a glimpse of a Dragon on the wing.

She had to settle for a Dragon bound by gravity, instead.

Maggaron didn't talk much; Bellusdeo, in his presence, talked more, but not a lot. She spoke Norannir for the most part; Kaylin knew this because Bellusdeo's Norannir was beyond her. It sounded familiar, but its syllables didn't coalesce into something that had any recognizable meaning. Kaylin almost felt that they should. But she didn't begrudge Bellusdeo the use of a familiar language—it's what she would have wanted had she been in the Dragon's position. It also gave Bellusdeo some small amount of privacy. The open, empty streets gave her the rest; in the fiefs, only the drunk or the suicidal wandered at night. Kaylin felt neither drunk nor suicidal.

But the streets of Tiamaris—Tiamaris, not Barren—had changed. The farther away from the Ablayne they traveled, the less empty the streets became. In twos and fours, like large looming shadows, the Norannir began to appear. They didn't exactly move silently; they spoke and they sort of clanged as they walked. She even recognized the walk; they were patrolling.

Looking at her sleeves, Kaylin sighed and undid the cuffs; she rolled them both up to her elbows, exposing the marks. She wasn't even surprised to see that they were glowing faintly. She approached a group of four patrolling Norannir; they turned toward her, falling silent as they shifted their grips on their weapons. She didn't exactly hold her hands up, but she exposed her arms as she walked.

They didn't relax; they did straighten up, and they did lower their weapons. They also spoke. She couldn't understand much of what they were saying, so they repeated themselves slowly. Which, of course, didn't help.

Kaylin turned to see that Bellusdeo and Maggaron were exactly where she'd left them. Maggaron began to walk down the street, but Bellusdeo hung back. As if, Kaylin thought, she was afraid. No, not afraid—nervous. Maggaron was not; he approached the Norannir, who frowned. They didn't immediately recognize him, and at this point, they probably recognized most of the other refugees.

But he introduced himself by name—not title—and asked if they might be taken to speak with the Elders. The men on patrol asked a few curt questions, none of which Kaylin understood, but most of which she could guess, before they conferred among themselves.

"Are we here too late?" Kaylin asked him. "Do you think they're sleeping?" She could think of about a hundred things that were wiser—and more fun to do—than waking Mejrah.

Maggaron frowned. "At night? No. The Elders will not sleep at night, not here. Not so close to the border. The Shadows are strongest in the darkness, and if the power of the Elders or the drums is needed, it is now."

"Bellusdeo?"

The Dragon was standing alone, to one side of the street, as if she hoped to melt into the very narrow space between buildings. She stiffened as Kaylin called her name a second time.

So did the Norannir. Their eyes widened, and they looked once again at Kaylin's glowing marks. They began to speak in hushed and hurried words, and then they turned to Maggaron, their words colliding as they all asked him questions at once. She recognized one word clearly: *Bellusdeo.*

Maggaron said, "Yes." Just that. But he turned and he held out a hand.

Bellusdeo might as well have grown roots. "Chosen," she said in Barrani, "I—I'm not ready. I'm not ready for this."

Kaylin walked toward her. "Yes, you are."

"I'm not. I'm no longer their Queen. I'm no longer what I was. I have no lands, and I have little power. What can I possibly offer them?" She held out her empty palms.

It was the right question to ask Kaylin Neya. Kaylin smiled and shook her head. "Sometimes," she told the Dragon, taking her by the hand, "you also get to ask what *they* can offer *you*."

"They are doing everything that I would ask of them if I were among them. They patrol the streets and they guard the border."

"How do you know?"

"Tara told me. Before dinner. They have a Lord; they don't *need* a Queen."

Kaylin tugged gently at her hand, and an obviously reluctant Bellusdeo came with her. "They're just as lost as you are," Kaylin told her as they walked—slowly—down the street. "They've had a few more days—a week at most—to adjust, but they've lost their home, their world, and everything they knew except each other and the Shadow."

"Yes, but they're pledged to Tiamaris. I can't—not with his hoard—"

"You're not taking anything away from him. You're still going to come back to my place after you talk to Mejrah."

One of the four almost frozen men turned and ran down the street. Kaylin stifled the urge to tell him not to run off alone, mostly because he wouldn't have understood a word she shouted even if she tried. Bellusdeo didn't appear to notice. As she approached the men who were now staring at her, she let go of Kaylin's hand and drew herself to her full height. It wasn't impressive, when compared to the height of the standing Norannir—but at the same time, it was.

She spoke three words, and the men—whose eyes were almost as golden as hers—slowly dropped to their knees, holding their weapons vertical against the cracked cobblestones. Maggaron came to stand to Bellusdeo's left in silence.

She spoke; they listened.

When she finished, one of the men lifted his head; his cheeks were wet. "Bellusdeo," he said, and repeated it as if it were a prayer.

She nodded, her expression grave. When she spoke again, they rose almost as one man. One of the men fell in behind Maggaron to her left; the other two stood to her right.

"Chosen, join me."

Kaylin hesitated, and Bellusdeo smiled; there was both warmth and edge to it. "If I have to go at your insistence, this is your penance."

They walked down the streets of the fief. The moons were high, and the occasional howl of a Feral sounded in the distance as if it were music. The Norannir, Maggaron included, didn't speak a word; they walked, for the moment, as if they were Palace Guards.

Kaylin watched as the tents of the Norannir came into view. A fire burned at the crossroads around which the tents had been erected; the street that they were walking down continued past fire and tents into the darkness at the heart of the fiefs. Norannir stood guard just beyond the burning wood, and those on watch didn't turn as Bellusdeo approached. They were, however, the only ones who didn't.

Mejrah stood in dark robes, the fire at her back casting a flickering shadow; to her right and left, the older men she often called. They were both armed; Mejrah, for once, wasn't.

She couldn't be; both of her hands were cupped beneath a very familiar crystal. It was the Arkon's memory crystal, and it was active: standing just above it, pale and translucent, was the image of Bellusdeo taken from Severn's memories of seven corpses.

The image was ghostly—ethereal but exact. The three Norannir guards who had escorted them down the length of the street stopped walking; Bellusdeo and Maggaron did not. Kaylin hesitated, feeling very much like a fifth wheel—a curious fifth wheel.

"Chosen," Bellusdeo said in a voice that didn't tremble at all.

Kaylin joined her, and this time Bellusdeo caught, and held, her hand. Maggaron began to kneel, but she caught his hand, as well, denying him the shelter of obeisance.

Mejrah's eyes were a brilliant gold; they matched Bellusdeo's as the old woman gazed down at her. She knelt and placed the crystal at Bellusdeo's feet, and this, Bellusdeo allowed—she had only two hands, after all.

Kaylin's marks began to glow; they were warm, not uncomfortable, and the light they shed was golden. As the Norannir began to speak, she knew why: she could understand them.

"Bellusdeo," Mejrah said in a rough voice. She frowned and glanced up; the Elders to either side shifted from formal bows to knees at her unspoken command. "You return to us."

"Yes, Elder."

"And you bring the Ascendant."

"Yes. I come at the side of the Chosen to the lands of my birth."

A whisper went up in a circle around Bellusdeo. Standing almost between the tenting, lingering like children who are afraid to get too close in case they catch too much attention, stood a dozen armed and armored Norannir; a third of them were women.

Mejrah's eyes closed a moment; her wrinkled face was wet. She opened her eyes and she smiled at Bellusdeo. "Your lands, Lady?"

Bellusdeo shook her head. "I was not Queen here, in my youth, nor am I Queen now. There is a King, and he is a great King. For centuries now he has kept the Shadows—and the enemy—at bay. Your Lord—"

"Lady, no—"

"Your Lord, Mejrah. You gave him your word, and my people have never sworn false oaths."

Mejrah looked stricken, but bowed her head; when she lifted it again, all that remained was the grim determination that characterized most of the Norannir Kaylin had seen in the fief.

"Your Lord, Tiamaris, is liege to this King. Serve him well, and you will build a home that no Shadows will taint or destroy."

"And you, Lady? Have you returned to us?"

Bellusdeo was silent. She clutched Kaylin's hand tightly for just a moment; if it had been any longer, Kaylin's bones would have snapped. She managed to say nothing. "Do you remember my history?"

Mejrah nodded slowly.

"When I first met the Elders, it was much like this. I came before them accompanied by only my sisters and my guards. I had the clothing on my back, no more.

"They fed me, Mejrah. They offered me shelter. They understood that I had wandered very, very far from my home. I was...a child. I was a child, and the People gave me a place in which I might grow into adulthood. You were never in my debt." She slowly released the hands of both Maggaron and

Kaylin. "You are not in my debt now. The People survive because of your choices, your decisions; they survive because you knew that to cling to home and the artifacts of history would be death, in the end.

"I did not guide you here. I did not counsel you. I did not walk the long and empty road. You need not kneel to me."

"You are—"

"I am Bellusdeo, yes." She glanced at the image of herself. "And in these lands, that is *all* that I am. I have no throne, I have no lands. The home I built in the lands of the People is lost, and the world into which I was born is so much changed, I do not recognize it."

Mejrah rose. Without looking down, she touched the shoulders of the men on her right and left, and they rose, as well. They were so much taller than either Kaylin or Bellusdeo.

"Lady," Mejrah said. "You gave us the Ascendants. You taught our Elders. You created our drums and you schooled us in the use of the words that might drive back the Shadows for a little while."

"Yes. But I taught, Elder. I taught the People. It was the People who became those Ascendants; the People who used those drums; the People who sang those words. Were it not for the strength of the People, no lesson, no gift, would have sufficed.

"Do you understand?" she asked softly.

Kaylin didn't, but waited. So did Mejrah.

"You are here," Bellusdeo finally said.

"These are not our—"

"Are they not? You have proven your worth to Dragons, Elder. Do you doubt it? Your men patrol the streets and your men face the Shadows who manage to slip beyond the borders. You retreated from the war; you did not flee it. And I? I am come to your home, as I did to the home of your ancient ancestors, with nothing but the clothes I wear. I have no sisters but the Chosen and no guards but the Ascendant."

Before Mejrah could stop her, Bellusdeo knelt. She looked inordinately tiny surrounded by the Norannir. Tiny, Kaylin thought, the way diamonds were tiny.

Mejrah reached out and caught the Dragon's slender hands, lifting her to her feet. "Come, then," she said, voice breaking. "We offer food, Bellusdeo, and fire, to you, your sister, and your guard. We do not have what the Ancients had, but if—" Her voice broke again, and she struggled to master it. "But what we have, we offer." Bending, reaching down, she wrapped Bellusdeo in her arms and lifted her; nor did Bellusdeo attempt to evade her.

"And maybe, when I am dead, and my children, and my children's children, and theirs, as well, you will hold all our stories and our memories and you will build your home from them—as you once did."

★ ★ ★ ★ ★

What will happen next?
Find out in
CAST IN PERIL

Acknowledgments

Thanks, as always, go to my household: my parents, my husband, my sons; John and Kristen; my Australian alpha reader. They've perfected the art of ignoring my ability to disappear while standing in place.

Thanks, as well, to Chris Szego, for being a very encouraging sounding board.

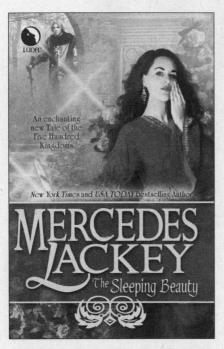